**EVERYONE
KATIE**

FOUR-TIME AMAZON BEST BOOK

"I love Ruggle's characters. They're sharply drawn, and vividly alive. I'm happy when they find each other. These are wonderful escapist books."
— **Charlaine Harris**, #1 *New York Times* bestselling author

"Gripping suspense, unique heroines, sexy heroes."
— **Christine Feehan**, #1 *New York Times* bestselling author

"Sexy and suspenseful. I couldn't turn the pages fast enough."
— **Julie Ann Walker**, *New York Times* and *USA Today* bestselling author, for *Hold Your Breath*

"Chills and thrills and a sexy, slow-burning romance from a terrific new voice."
— **D. D. Ayres**, author of the K-9 Rescue series, for *Hold Your Breath*

"Katie Ruggle, you amaze me! What a perfectly clever plot, with smoking-hot characters and an arresting environment that begs to be the scene of the crime."
— *It's About the Book* for *Hold Your Breath*

"This series just keeps getting better! For outstanding romantic suspense, strong characters, and a fabulous plot that keeps thickening, read Katie Ruggle...and prepare to get burned by an amazing story."

—*Romance Junkies* for *Fan the Flames*

"I cannot read these books fast enough. Waiting for the next book to see what happens is going to be pure torture."

—*Fresh Fiction* for *Gone Too Deep*

"As this series draws to a close, the most fascinating of the heroines is introduced. Her story is both heartbreaking and uplifting at the same time. She's a sympathetic sweetheart who carries the reader along on her journey to emotional healing."

—*RT Book Reviews*, 4 Stars for *In Safe Hands*

"I have a feeling that this is just the beginning to another great series by Katie Ruggle."

—*Fresh Fiction* for *Run to Ground*

"Realistic characters who are fragile and heroic in equal measure mix with just the right amount of humor and tension to create a delicious cocktail."

—*Publishers Weekly* STARRED Review for *On the Chase*

"An exciting read, complete with an ending that hints of more to come."

—*Booklist* for *Survive the Night*

ALSO BY KATIE RUGGLE

ROCKY MOUNTAIN COWBOY *Christmas*

KATIE RUGGLE

sourcebooks
casablanca

Published by Sourcebooks Casablanca, an imprint of Sourcebooks, Inc.
P.O. Box 4410, Naperville, Illinois 60567-4410
(630) 961-3900
Fax: (630) 961-2168
sourcebooks.com

Printed and bound in the United States of America.
OPM 10 9 8 7 6 5 4 3 2 1

To my amazing editors, Mary Altman and Rachel Gilmer.
Without you, my plots wouldn't make any sense and
there wouldn't be nearly enough explosions. I'm so
lucky to have you both as my book copilots.

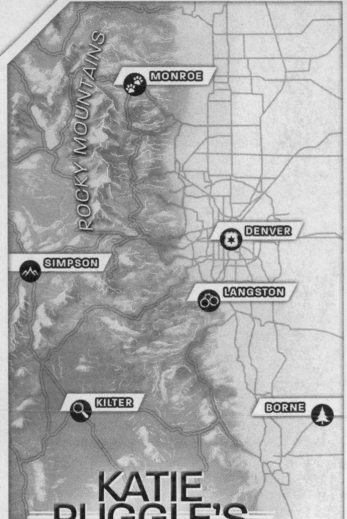

KATIE
RUGGLE'S
ROCKIES

CHAPTER 1

STEVE SPRINGFIELD HAD BEEN A BORNE FIREFIGHTER FOR less than five minutes when the missing-person call came in.

"Grab some of the spare gear and let's go," the chief told him. "Search and Rescue will meet us there."

Steve was moving toward the equipment room before the chief even finished speaking. As he yanked on his borrowed bunker gear, a trickle of adrenaline warmed his blood. This was what he lived for. It'd been too long since he'd headed to a scene without a sense of dread weighing him down. The past couple of years had held too many tragedies and betrayals.

Borne would be different. He'd be able to go back to helping people, rather than cleaning up after it was too late.

Pushing away memories of his past two towns, Steve jammed his feet into a pair of boots and headed for the rescue. Swinging up into the passenger side of the cab, he turned to the chief, who was firing up the engine. The radio lit up as various people called in, giving their ETAs, and Steve grimaced slightly. He had a lot of names to learn. Starting over for the second time in less than two years wasn't much fun.

"Who's lost?" he asked. He'd deal with this call and

then worry about the rest. Someone was missing, and that took priority.

"Camille Brandt, our local eccentric artist," the chief said, easing the rescue out of the station and into the swirling snow.

"Camille? She still lives in Borne?" Steve was surprised. He'd figured that the dreamy, shy girl he remembered would've escaped the small Colorado town as soon as possible to live in New York or California or some artists' paradise. As much as Steve loved his childhood home, Borne wasn't kind to those who marched to their own beat.

The chief gave him a quick sideways glance before refocusing on the road. Although the snow wasn't too treacherous yet, a strong north wind had picked up, tossing the inch of powder around and messing with visibility. "You knew her growing up?"

"Yeah." That didn't feel like the complete truth, though, so he added, "Sort of. She was three years younger than me, but I saw her around. Borne High School's pretty small."

The chief gave a laugh. "True."

"You didn't go there, did you?" As Steve asked the question, he looked out the window, noting what had changed and what had stayed the same since his last visit home. A few houses had been painted, and what used to be a taco shop now sold coffee. Other than that, it was still the Borne he'd always known.

"Nope." The chief turned onto a side street, careful not to bump a car parked at the curb. "Moved here fifteen years ago." A wry expression crossed his face. "Still a newcomer, according to most people."

Steve gave an amused grunt. That was Borne, all right. "Who reported Camille missing?"

"Mrs. Lin, Camille's neighbor," the chief said as he rolled up to the curb in front of Camille's grandma's house. *No*, Steve mentally corrected himself, *Camille's house*. The older woman had died a decade or so ago.

Reaching for his door handle, Steve said, "Hopefully, she's just at a friend's house, safe and warm."

The chief snorted as he opened his door. "Friend's house? I thought you said you knew Camille."

Before Steve could ask what he meant by that, the chief slammed the door shut. Climbing out of the cab, Steve ducked his chin into the collar of the borrowed bunker coat as the wind spat a handful of sharp snow pellets against his exposed neck. If Camille really was in need of rescue, they had to find her soon. It'd be dark in a couple of hours, and the weather would only get worse.

Jogging across the street, Steve caught up with the chief on Mrs. Lin's doorstep just seconds before she opened the door.

"Well, come in, come in," she fussed, stepping back so they could both enter. "You're letting the heat out."

Steve closed the door behind them, but Mrs. Lin didn't look any happier. Then again, he'd never seen her look happy about much of anything.

"Steve Springfield?" she asked, and he gave her a nod of greeting. "Does this mean you're finally back for good then? 'Bout time you stopped traipsing around the world and came home. Your poor parents will finally be able to relax and enjoy their retirement."

Steve set his molars to keep from telling Mrs. Lin that

rather than "traipsing around the world," he'd only been a few hours' drive up into the mountains, that his "poor" parents were happily basking in the New Mexico sun, and that none of that was really her business anyway.

The chief must've guessed some of what Steve wanted to say, because he cleared his throat and flicked an amused glance at him. "Mrs. Lin, what time did you see Camille leave?"

"Like I already told the dispatcher, it was at ten forty-eight yesterday morning. I know that because I was on the elliptical downstairs, watching out the front window. I always go a full sixty minutes, from ten to eleven, and the display showed forty-eight minutes. Camille walked outside—without locking her door, even though I keep telling her she's going to be brutally murdered if she's not careful—and went into the woods across the street."

"You haven't seen her return?" the chief asked, scribbling in his small flip notebook.

"She hasn't gotten back yet." Mrs. Lin's tone was certain. "She's been gone for a day and a half. Her car hasn't moved. I even checked the snow for footprints by the garage and on the front walk. She's still out there, probably freezing to death, unless she's been kidnapped to be sold into sex slavery."

Steve blinked. "Doubt there's much of a risk of that around here."

"You've been gone for years," Mrs. Lin scolded. "Things have changed in Borne. It's not the sleepy little town you left."

"It's still pretty sleepy," the chief said as he wrote.

"There's been a huge jump in crime." Mrs. Lin folded her arms over her narrow chest and glared.

The chief didn't seem to feel her laser-like stare burning holes in his downturned head. "Not really," he said.

"There *is* crime, Chief Rodriguez." Mrs. Lin's voice was frosty. "What about the felon who took Misty Lincoln's lawn furniture?"

"That was her ex-husband." The chief finally looked up from his notes. "And I believe he'd been awarded it in the divorce." Mrs. Lin huffed, but he spoke again before she could start rattling off any other local crimes. "Do you know where Camille was headed?"

Although she held her glare for a few moments, Mrs. Lin finally let it go. "Probably to find all sorts of trash for her…things." Mrs. Lin gestured vaguely in the direction of Camille's house.

Her…things? Steve opened his mouth to ask for clarification when the chief flipped his notebook closed. "Did you try calling her?"

"Of course. It goes to her voicemail—her *full* voicemail, so I couldn't even leave a message."

The chief moved to open the door. "Give the dispatcher a call if you spot her or if she calls you back."

Mrs. Lin gave them a tight nod as they left her house and walked toward Camille's. Steve kept an eye out for any footprints, but he had to concur with Mrs. Lin on that. The only things he spotted were some blurry indentations leading away from the house. He assumed they were from when Camille had left. Her elderly car was parked on the street, covered by a light blanket of fresh snow.

"I'm still not sure why you're so certain she's not with a friend," Steve said as he climbed the front steps and pounded on her door. There was just the silence of an empty house on the other side.

"Camille's not really the drop-in-on-friends sort," the chief said absently, peering into a window. "The few times I've seen her out in public have been at odd hours, times when she didn't think many other people would be out and about, I'm assuming. She's not exactly the town hermit—that's your brother Joe—but she's pretty close to earning the top spot."

Knocking one final time, Steve considered that. It didn't seem to fit the Camille he remembered. Sure, she was shy, but she'd been sweet, too, and pretty enough to stick in his head, even though she'd been three grades below him. When he thought of a hermit, he pictured someone cranky and sour. Camille Brandt had either changed a lot since high school, or the chief was exaggerating.

As they knocked on the side door that led into her workshop, Nate's pickup pulled up behind the rescue. His brother climbed out, and Steve waved him over. He noticed Nate's slight limp as he hurried to join them and felt a twinge of concern that he kept to himself, knowing his brother wouldn't appreciate the fussing. Nate had twisted his ankle while turning horses out into the pasture a few days earlier, and he'd refused to have it checked out. Ryan, another of Steve's brothers, climbed out of the passenger side of the truck and followed Nate. Even though Ryan wasn't officially a member of Search and Rescue or the fire department, Steve wasn't surprised to see him. Ryan always loved being where the action was.

"Camille's missing?" Nate asked as he reached them, zipping his coat a little higher. Steve couldn't blame him. The wind was vicious today.

"According to Mrs. Lin, she headed into the woods

yesterday morning and hasn't returned," the chief summarized, waving toward the trees across the street. More vehicles arrived, and deputies, firefighters, and Search and Rescue members joined their growing huddle. As he hunched against the stinging assault of snow and wind, Steve eyed the trees, antsy to start searching.

The chief handed the scene over to a woman from Search and Rescue that Steve didn't recognize. She introduced herself as Sasha and quickly divided everyone into teams. Steve, the chief, Ryan, and Nate were together.

"Betsy will be here in about ten minutes with her tracking dog," Sasha said in a loud, clear voice that managed to carry over the wind. "I don't want to wait for them to arrive before we start searching, though... not with dusk approaching and the temperature dropping like it is."

Steve was glad for that. He was antsy enough with the delay as it was. Every search reminded him of when his two girls had been lost in the mountains, and the memory of those horrifying hours still hit him like a punch to the gut at times like these. The idea of someone—especially shy, sweet Camille—being caught in the frozen night, alone and afraid, made his stomach churn with worry. He needed to get out there and start searching for her. With the temperature dropping and the wind picking up, each minute could be critical.

The teams spread out and started making their way through the trees, calling for Camille. Their voices were quickly snatched away, dulled by the thick forest and the now-roaring wind. The trees creaked ominously, threatening to drop thick branches on their heads, and Steve moved a bit more quickly.

The sun was slipping toward the mountain peaks, and the light cast strange shadows. Steve's pulse kept leaping every time he caught a glimpse of a promising shape, and disappointment caught him after each false alarm. The searchers spread out, the space between the chief, Steve, and his brothers gradually increasing until the only sounds were the crunch of snow beneath his boots and his voice calling for Camille in the gathering dusk.

He held an image of her face in his mind from when they'd both been teenagers. She'd been so delicate-looking. It was hard to imagine her surviving a few hours in the snowy wilderness, much less a whole night. A fresh sense of urgency pushed him to move faster.

"Camille!" he called, raising his voice so it would carry over the wailing wind. He paused to listen, but there was no response—at least none that he could hear. Steve pressed on, tromping around trees and through snowy brush that threatened to trip him. Evergreen branches scraped against the heavy fabric of his borrowed bunker gear, showering him with their layer of snow. He drew a breath to yell for Camille again, but a distant yelp made him whip his head around as he realized the muted cry of pain had come from Nate. Steve turned and hurried through the trees to his brother's side. "You okay?"

"Fine." He didn't sound fine, and his face was drawn with pain. "Just took a bad step."

"Do you need to head back?" Steve asked, watching closely as Nate lowered his foot to the ground. As soon as he put weight on it, he grimaced but waved Steve off.

The chief joined them. "Everything okay?"

"His ankle's bothering him," Steve said. "I'll help him back to the staging area."

"No, he's *fine* and going to continue searching," Nate gritted out, limping away.

"What's up?" Ryan called through the trees. "Something wrong?"

"We're good!" Steve called back, even as he exchanged a concerned look with the chief. He knew there was no point in fighting Nate on this. His brother was stubborn and took his search-and-rescue duties too seriously to give up without a fight—something that, in this case, would waste precious time.

So instead, they spread out again and continued to search. Although Steve knew that Nate was doing his best to push through, he'd slowed considerably, and Steve was torn between hurrying to find Camille as soon as possible and refusing to leave his obviously hurting brother behind. The tree branches clacked and groaned, snow whipping into Steve's face and shoving his shouts for Camille right back down his throat. The light was quickly fading, the thickening storm clouds and heavy evergreen branches around the searchers blocking most of the remaining sunlight.

Reaching to turn on his headlamp, Steve gave an annoyed grunt when his fingers only found his helmet. That was the problem with starting over at a new fire department, especially as a volunteer. Until he'd proven that he was there to stay, he was stuck wearing left-over equipment that definitely wasn't set up the way he liked it. He patted the pocket of his bunker coat and was relieved to feel the heavy cylinder of a flashlight. At least he wouldn't be stumbling blindly around the woods once the last of the light disappeared.

"Camille!" he yelled, his voice rough from repeatedly

calling for her. His mind was busy running through all sorts of possibilities—what if she'd fallen off a ledge or had a seizure or encountered a bear or stepped in a ground squirrel's hole and broken her ankle? If something had happened, how many hours had she been stuck in the freezing temperature, possibly unconscious?

He moved more quickly, and Nate dropped even farther behind. Steve couldn't let that affect his speed, though. The priority was to find Camille. Nate was upright and moving. Despite his injured ankle, he was fine.

Camille might not be.

The trees thinned, and Steve shoved aside an evergreen branch as he stepped into a clearing. With the sun setting, it took him a moment to recognize where he was—the old scrapyard. The spot was familiar, a favorite place to search for treasure as kids, but it was also slightly menacing in the dim light. The scrapyard had grown as more and more people dumped junk cars and other metal trash, the piles mounded even higher with a solid layer of snow. It had been an exciting, almost magical place when he'd been a kid, but now he saw it through a parent's eyes, and there was danger everywhere. All of the worst-case scenarios he'd thought up while searching came back to him in a rush.

"Camille!" he bellowed, jogging through the snow, feeling his boot catch on uneven footing. So many parts and pieces were buried under sheets of white, just waiting to trip him up and send him flying. Considering the condition of the metal he could see, whatever he landed on would be sure to give him some mutant, vaccination-resistant strain of tetanus, too.

The wind roared, sending a piece of rusted sheeting

flying end over end until it struck the remaining back half of an old Chevy van with a clatter. Glancing behind him, Steve saw Nate emerge from the trees, and a new urgency hit him. They needed to find Camille before Nate hurt himself even worse trying to stubbornly navigate the uneven terrain.

"Stay there!" he shouted, but Nate slogged through the snow, either not hearing or ignoring him. Knowing his brother and how he'd disregard his own pain if someone else was in trouble, Steve figured it was the latter. Biting back a growl of worried frustration, he moved even faster through the piles. "Camille!"

There! Had there been movement over by the ancient washing machine off to his left? He headed toward it but was forced to slow as he picked his way between an old piece of farm machinery and the remains of a bed frame. "Camille! It's Steve Springfield! Yell if you can hear me!"

A head suddenly popped up above the pile right next to him, seeming to appear from nowhere. "*Steve*-freaking-*Springfield*?"

Startled, Steve lurched sideways and barely avoided tripping over the junk surrounding him. He peered at the small figure, his eyebrows flying up as he took in her safety goggles and Elmer Fudd hat. "Camille?"

"Yes?" She drew the word out tentatively, and Steve felt a rush of relief—and the slight annoyance that followed on the heels of worry. It was a familiar sensation, since his kids were too smart and adventurous for their own good.

"Are you hurt?" he asked, focusing on the parts of her that he could see. Between her heavy layers of clothes and the junk hiding her bottom half from view, it wasn't much. "Do you need help?"

"No?" Again, she said the word slowly with an upward incline at the end.

"Good. A lot of people have been worried about you."

"They have? Why?" She stared at him, her brown eyes wide behind the clear plastic of the safety goggles. Blond wisps of hair had escaped the hat and curled around her face. Eyeing her rosy cheeks and full pink lips that were parted slightly in confusion, Steve was transported back to high school, where he'd surreptitiously eyed her in the hall, feeling guilty for his interest in a freshman but unable to keep his eyes off her. Even then, there'd been something about the shy loner. They'd only talked a few times, but she'd had a way of looking at him that made him feel like he could move mountains. If she'd been closer to his age, he would've been tempted to ask her out.

"Mrs. Lin called and said you left yesterday morning and never returned," he explained. "Did you spend the night out here?"

Her eyes rounded, and her pink cheeks darkened even more. "What? No! I went home last night and came back out this morning. Why'd she call you?" she asked on a squeak.

"Not me specifically," Steve said. "She called dispatch. I'm here because Fire and the county deputies respond to all search-and-rescue calls."

All the color left her cheeks, and Steve's smile slipped away. "Search and rescue?" Her voice was barely audible above the wind. "Looking for me? Everyone's here trying to search and rescue *me*? Are they all coming here? I'm not lost or hurt or anything. I don't need to be searched and rescued!" Looking more and more horrified, she ended on what could only be described as a wail.

"It's okay." Steve took a step closer, trying to soothe her. "Most searches are false alarms. We're used to that."

"*I'm* not used to it!" His reassurances didn't seem to be having much of an effect. "I'm not used to it in any way. Oh, geez Louise, everyone's been searching for me. They're all going to be running over here, aren't they?" The wind settled for a few seconds, and a dog's excited barking could clearly be heard. Camille winced at the sound. "Dogs? Dogs are leading people toward me? I'm not lost! I'm right here, where I usually am. There was just so much to pick up yesterday and today, since I need extra pieces for the Christmas orders, and it took me a little longer than I'd planned, but I didn't think there'd be search and rescuers and *dogs* and cops and Steve-freaking-Springfield…"

"Hey, now. Take a breath." Hiding his amused bafflement over how she kept adding *freaking* to his name, he kept his voice gentle but firm enough to cut through Camille's building panic. "Things will be fine. Everyone will be relieved to see that you're safe. The medics will check you over, and then we'll all go home."

"Medics? Plural? As in more than one? They'll check me out in front of everyone, while people watch?" She seemed to alternately pale and flush, as if torn between horror and embarrassment. "No. No, no. That's not good. I'm fine. I don't need checking out. All my parts are where they should be, and I even wore my warmest hat, so my ears aren't even cold. I'm *fine*." She took a step back, her boot bumping against a sled piled with pieces of metal scrap. Steve wondered what she needed the parts for. There didn't seem to be any rhyme or reason to the items she'd collected.

Shaking off his distraction, he focused on the panicked woman in front of him. If he didn't do something, she was going to bolt, and then things would get messy—and even more embarrassing for her as the well-intentioned rescuers gave chase. Steve really didn't want that to happen. For whatever reason, he had an overwhelming urge to make things better for Camille. He just wasn't sure how.

"Springfield!" the chief called, circling a scrap pile some distance away. "Did you find her?"

"Oh no." Camille's eyes grew wider and wider as the chief approached. "Here they come. All the people and medics and questions and *staring…*"

"Don't worry," Steve said, and Camille whipped her head around to look at him, wild-eyed. "I'll fix this."

He just needed to find the right… *There!*

"Oof!" Steve fake-yelled as he jammed his foot between the piece of farm machinery and the old bed frame he'd just skirted. He pinwheeled his arms dramatically for effect.

"What's wrong?" The chief jogged up to them, his face furrowed with concern. "Is Camille hurt?"

Steve straightened with exaggerated care. "Camille's fine. Mrs. Lin had it wrong. Camille went home last night." He gestured toward his foot. "I'm the one that's in need of a rescue. Give me a hand out?"

As he had hoped, the chief's attention instantly turned to his predicament. After examining the metal surrounding Steve's boot, he asked, "How'd you even manage to do this, Springfield?"

Pulling out his portable radio, the chief sighed heavily enough to be heard over the wind. "We found Camille in the scrapyard. She's fine, but the new guy got himself stuck."

Steve felt a twinge of annoyance at the amused condescension in the chief's tone, but then he glanced at Camille, who was looking just slightly less like she wanted the earth to swallow her. The mocking that was sure to follow this incident was worth it if his supposed clumsiness took some attention off her.

Ryan hurried toward them, took the scene in at a glance, and started laughing. "Oh, how the mighty firefighter has fallen."

Steve glowered at his brother. Of course Ryan took pleasure in his predicament. He'd always been the most competitive of all the Springfield brothers.

"Hey, Camille." Ryan turned his attention to the petrified woman, who gave him a dorky wave that made Steve smile. Her awkwardness was still incredibly endearing. "You okay?"

"Fine. I'm good. Nothing wrong here." She shifted back another step as if she was worried that Ryan would insist on checking her over, and Steve let out a grunt of pretend pain.

"A little help?" Steve asked Ryan, trying to pull his brother's attention away from Camille before she bolted.

"Nah," Ryan teased. "I'd rather help Camille. She's much prettier than you are."

Camille turned bright red and made a slight choking

sound. Annoyed, Steve grabbed a handful of snow and tossed it at his brother.

"Hey!" Ryan brushed off his coat. "Careful there. You don't want to start a snow war. I'm not the one who's stuck."

The rest of the Search and Rescue members, firefighters, and cops trickled in, including Betsy and her tracking dog—a shaggy, excited mixed breed of unknown parentage.

"Camille, there you are. You need to get checked out." Nate started determinedly in her direction, but Steve reached out and snagged a handful of his brother's coat before he could pass. Knowing Nate's predilection for rescuing damsels in distress, he'd make a big fuss over her, and she very clearly did not want the attention.

"Hang on, Nate. I need you to pull back on this piece here."

"But…" Nate turned back toward Camille, who scooted farther away from them.

"Nope. She's fine. I'm the one who needs help right now." He wasn't a big fan of being the center of attention, either, but he was willing to make the sacrifice. After all, sometimes saving people didn't involve anything as dramatic as burning buildings. "Are you going to leave your favorite brother trapped?"

Although Nate gave him a suspicious look, he bent and yanked at the metal frame. Ryan watched in amusement, clearly unwilling to help. Well, no surprise there. At least he was distracted by the show.

Steve scanned the growing crowd of first responders and spotted the Search and Rescue scene commander. "Sasha," he called, hooking the toe of his boot a little more firmly under the piece of metal it was wedged against. "Camille's fine, and Nate, Ryan, and the chief can help me with this. No reason for everyone else to stand around getting cold."

Sasha studied the awkward-looking Camille and then Steve for a long moment before giving him the slightest wink. "Agreed. Okay, everyone! Head back to staging, and don't forget to check out with Boris. If you do forget, we'll be searching the woods for *you*, and no one wants to do that again!"

"Shouldn't someone do a medical check on Camille?" Nate asked as everyone else started heading back toward the trees. Steve wished his foot was free so he could kick his brother with it.

"She declined medical attention," Steve said quickly, and Camille looked confused for just a moment before she started nodding.

"Yes. I declined that. I do decline it. It has been declined."

Steve coughed to hide a laugh, settling for a smile that instantly gentled the moment their eyes met. "Why don't you walk back with Sasha? I bet she'd be willing to let Mrs. Lin know that you're safely home."

Sasha grimaced. "Sure, stick me with Mrs. Lin duty. I'll get you back for this, Steve Springfield. C'mon, Camille."

Meeting Steve's gaze, a flushed Camille mouthed *thank you* before following Sasha back into the woods. Steve felt a warmth in his belly as he watched her walk away, towing her collection of found items on the sled behind her. Ryan gave him a long, calculating look before turning and hurrying after them, and Steve swallowed a groan. He'd made his interest in Camille—as innocent as it was—too obvious, and now his brother's competitive spirit had kicked in. When they were younger, Steve hadn't been able to look twice at a girl without Ryan trying to elbow in.

The trio was swallowed by the darkening woods, and Steve looked away. There wasn't anything he could do about that now.

When he glanced down, he saw Nate eyeing him with a knowing look. "Found a new way to be the hero, huh?" he asked in a low voice. Apparently, there was no fooling *this* brother.

A string of muttered curses brought Steve's attention back to the chief. "This isn't budging," he said. "I'm going to have to call someone to grab the tools from the rescue and haul them in here."

"Hold on," Steve said when the chief reached for his radio. "I felt it give. Nate, pull back just like that…" He contorted his face as he pulled out his foot, trying to make it look like a huge effort and not something that he could have easily done for the past ten minutes or so. "There! I'm free. Good work, team."

From the chief's suspicious scowl, he knew something was up, but he didn't challenge Steve's miraculous rescue. "Fine. Let's head back. It's only going to get colder."

Steve fell in behind the chief, careful not to move so quickly that Nate couldn't keep up—and being even more careful not to let on that he was doing anything of the sort. Now that everyone else was gone, an eerie quiet spread over the snow-covered mounds. The wind whipped against his skin, and Steve tucked his chin into the collar of his coat, thinking about Camille and how glad he was that she hadn't been trapped in the icy dark all night. Even as the trees groaned and creaked around him, he smiled slightly, holding the picture of her in those goggles and that earflap hat in his mind.

He barely knew her, but for some strange reason, the thought of Camille Brandt, all grown up, was keeping him warm.

Why did this keep happening to her?

Camille flattened herself against the toilet paper display, resisting the urge to thump her head against the rolls. There was a reason she only came to the Borne Market early on Sunday mornings, and that was because she didn't want to be forced into awkward conversations with any of her neighbors. It helped that sixteen-year-old Kacey Betts worked the checkout on Sunday, and her focus stayed glued on her cell phone the entire time. Camille could slip in, buy what she needed, and slip right back out without having to make polite chitchat with anyone. Today, however, she and Kacey weren't alone.

Steve-freaking-Springfield was there.

The last time she'd seen him, he'd sweetly helped her escape her "rescue." She still hadn't forgiven Mrs. Lin for sending everyone and their brother on a search for her. The whole situation had been mortifying, and that was with Steve's help. If he hadn't been there, it could've been so much worse. Camille's stomach churned and her cheeks flushed at the thought of all that attention—and the potential additional humiliation.

Now, though, she was in a whole new pickle.

Why, today of all days, did Steve have to need groceries? Why did she have to have the urge for peanut-butter blossoms? She glanced at the bag of chocolate stars in her hands and sighed. If she'd just eaten a spoonful of peanut butter and called it good, she wouldn't be in this mess.

Come on, Camille, she scolded herself, *grow up already*. Just because Steve was here didn't mean they couldn't have a normal conversation. It wouldn't be awkward unless she made it that way. Sure, she might have had a huge crush on him as a teenager, and his gallant actions at the scrapyard might have revived that crush to its full, painful glory, but she was a mature adult, capable of casual social interactions.

Camille winced a little at the mental lie. *Okay, maybe not*. New plan: she was going to sneak past his aisle and get to the checkout without him even noticing that she was in the store. Resolved, she peeked around the corner of the display and saw that he was focused on the products in front of him. Refusing to let her gaze linger on his rugged profile or broad shoulders, she forced herself to concentrate on her goal—escape.

Now!

She shot forward, but her knee caught the edge of the display, knocking down a column of toilet paper. Time seemed to slow as the rolls tumbled down, hitting the floor in a series of dull thuds.

She scrambled to pick up the packages, her heart thumping fast in her chest, still hoping that she could pull off her escape. The horrible awkwardness could still be avoided if she hurried. Maybe he hadn't heard her. The falling rolls hadn't been that loud. Not like cans of peanuts or unpopped popcorn or…a cylinder of ball bearings or—

"Camille?"

She stopped abruptly, keeping a death grip on the toilet paper. That wonderful voice was just a shade deeper than she remembered from high school, but the thrill that rushed up her spine at the sound of it was all too familiar. Turning her head, she met Steve's eyes before dropping her gaze to her armful of Charmin. She replaced the last of the fallen rolls, feeling her hairline prickle with sweat as her thoughts twisted into useless tangles.

Why, *why* was she always embarrassing herself in front of this man?

"Camille. How are you?" His voice was certain now, and as friendly and calm as it always seemed to be. The Springfield brothers had all been sought-after in high school—even snarly Joe'd had a fan club—but Steve had always been Camille's favorite. No matter how popular he'd been or how handsome he'd gotten or how many girls had been crushing on him, he'd always stayed so steady and kind.

Now he was waiting for her to speak, though, and she needed to focus on the conversation. "Fine." *Good. Great.* She'd managed an answer, and it'd actually made sense.

"No issues after your time out in the cold?"

"No." He didn't respond right away, looking expectantly at her instead. She knew that meant she was supposed to add to her one-word answer, and she scrambled to think of something, anything she could say. "I was wearing clothes." *Ugh.* That didn't sound right at all. "I mean, there was no chance I'd get frostbitten since

I had multiple layers on, plus my boots are waterproof. That's important… Keeping dry, I mean. Since, you know, wet is cold." Her voice trailed off at the end as she resisted the urge to wince. Why was it that she could put words together in her head, but they always came out all wrong?

"True." He sounded amused, and now she couldn't keep from grimacing. Of course he was amused. She was being ridiculous. "I'm glad you're okay."

"How about you?" *That's good*, she praised herself. *Turn the attention back on him. He'll talk, and you can just nod and stay quiet and everything will be okay.* "Is your foot all right?"

His smile widened, one corner tucked in wryly. "Yeah. It was always fine. I just thought you might want everyone's focus on someone else."

She knew it. His dramatic fuss had been so unlike the Steve Springfield she'd sort of known in high school. It had been so obvious to Camille that he'd been faking that she'd been surprised when Nate, Ryan, and the chief had fallen for it. "I did. Thank you." There. That was normal-ish. "I owe you one. I mean, it'd be hard to duplicate that situation with our roles reversed, but if you ever need to be saved, then I'm your man. Well, I'm your *wo*man. Not that I'm your woman in *that* way, of course." Closing her mouth so firmly her teeth clicked together, she swallowed a groan. Why did she never stop at normal-ish?

Steve was silent. When she managed to get up the nerve to peek at his face, he didn't look amused or offended or even baffled. Instead, he seemed…thoughtful. "Actually, I could use your help right now."

Taken off guard, she blinked. "My...help? Now? Here? At the grocery store?"

His mouth pulled down in a grimace as he waved a hand at the products lining the shelves. Dragging her gaze off him, Camille actually noticed what he'd been examining so intently.

"You need my help with...feminine hygiene products?" She wasn't sure why she'd used the technical term, but it was such an odd situation. Steve had reappeared out of the blue after sixteen years. He'd saved her from what could've been a horribly humiliating event in the woods, and he was now standing in front of the tampon display. She was just happy she was capable of talking at all.

"If you don't mind." He gave her a slight smile, not wide enough to create the charming creases in his cheeks she so vividly remembered. "This is an area I... Well, I don't really know what I'm doing."

"Okay." She cautiously moved closer, drawn by him as she'd always been, even as a gawky fourteen-year-old. "What kind of help do you need? Is this for your wife?" She remembered when she'd heard about his marriage, just two years after he'd left town after graduating from high school. Even though she and Steve had only exchanged a handful of words, Camille had still felt a painful twist in her chest at the news.

"No." He focused on the boxes as he tipped his head from side to side, the motion drawing Camille's attention to the way the rounded muscles of his shoulder angled to meet his neck. In his time away, Steve had not slacked off in the working-out department. "She died eight years ago."

"Oh." Jerking her attention off his body, she stared at the familiar line of boxes, not knowing the right response, as usual. "I'm so sorry."

He accepted her words with a tight nod.

Camille mentally scrambled to think of something to say. What could possibly follow "My wife's dead"? Camille hadn't known her, so she couldn't say something like "She was a wonderful woman," since she had no idea what his wife had been like. She didn't even know her name. Anything unrelated to his wife's death, on the other hand, felt so silly and blasé, as if she was blowing off what had happened to him as something small and casual and not the hugely devastating event it surely had been.

"So." He cleared his throat. "This is for my daughter."

"Right." Of course Steve was the wonderful kind of dad who went to the store to get tampons for his kid. Camille was not surprised at all—impressed and even more smitten, but not surprised. "What does she usually use?"

He rubbed his neck—it was like he was *trying* to get her to focus on his excess of muscles—and twisted his shoulders in an uncomfortable shrug. "She doesn't...not yet. I know it's coming, though. Zoe's almost twelve, and she's living in a houseful of guys, except for her little sister, Maya, and I want her to have"—he waved at the tampon display—"whatever she needs on hand when the time comes. It's been hard enough for her to grow up without her mom. The only thing I can do is to hopefully make things a little easier for her."

With a frustrated grunt, he turned to face Camille. "Unless this is just going to make it worse? Should

I bring her here and let her pick out what she'll need instead?" Before she could answer, he groaned and scrubbed a hand over his face. "I've been a parent for fourteen years, and it didn't used to be this hard. Now that they're growing up, it feels like all the rules are changing, and I don't know what I'm doing anymore."

Camille's mind went blank. She was horrible at thinking of the right words in the moment—at three the next morning while lying sleepless in bed, sure, but in the moment, never. As the silence stretched, Steve's shoulders began to sag, and he looked so defeated that Camille couldn't stand it.

"My grandma raised me," she blurted out, horrified at the words that were leaving her mouth. Was she really going to tell Steve-freaking-Springfield this story, of all stories? What was she doing? Despite the impending humiliation, though, she kept talking while focusing on a box of panty liners. If she met Steve's warm hazel eyes, she knew she'd stumble over her words and it'd all come out sounding even worse. "I've always been shy, so I didn't have many friends." *Or any.*

"When I got my period, I was eleven. I panicked. My grandma was long past having to use any of this, so there wasn't anything in the house. Since I didn't know what to expect, I didn't know if tissues would be enough, so I used one of Grandma's dish towels, emptied my piggy bank, and came here."

She grimaced at the memory and at the fact that she was actually sharing this traumatizing story with anyone, much less Steve. Freaking. Springfield. "It wasn't an early Sunday morning like this, though. It was Saturday afternoon, packed with everyone doing their weekly grocery shopping, including the prettiest and meanest girl in sixth grade, Hayden Larchmont."

Her cheeks burned as red as they had two decades ago. "There I was, Grandma's embroidered dish towel stuffed in my underwear, feeling like everyone could take one look at me and just *know*, lurking in the candy aisle as I waited for Hayden's family to leave so I could grab what I needed and run. Finally, this lane was clear, and I hurried over—and I stood right here, in this very spot, staring at all this helplessly. I had no idea what to buy. Hayden and her mom came around the corner, and she stared at me standing in front of the tampon display and started to giggle, like she knew about the dish towel and *everything*, and I realized that soon everyone at school would know every humiliating detail, too. I was so flustered and embarrassed that I just grabbed a box at random and ran."

Now that the story was out, her word vomit spewed all over poor Steve, she had no choice but to leave before she melted into a puddle of liquid humiliation. She plucked two types of tampons and a box of pads from the shelf and piled them into Steve's arms. "Here. She can start with these. It might take some time for her to find out what works best for her, but one of these should get her through the first period."

Steeling herself, she turned and met Steve's wide eyes. His mouth was open slightly, but he didn't say anything.

"And for the record, I think you are a very good dad." Turning, she marched to the checkout counter, not looking back at him, even when he called out a thank-you. As Kacey rang up her chocolate stars, Camille stared at the debit card reader, trying very hard not to think about what she'd just done.

I told Steve Springfield the story of my first period.

There was no other option. Camille was going to have to move.

———————————

"How many times do I need to say this?" Steve frowned at his two girls. "No more blowing things up—especially not in the house."

"But, Dad..." Maya gave him the sweet smile that worked a little too well when it came to getting out of trouble. "It was only a tiny explosion. Just a little *pop*."

"I didn't mean for it to blow up." Zoe frowned at the blackened parts in her hands as if she could read what had gone wrong from the bits that remained. "It wasn't an *intentional* explosion. I'm not sure what happened... Maybe a leak in the fuel line?"

"That shouldn't cause an explosion. A fire, maybe, but..." His eyes narrowed. "No. You aren't distracting me this time. Both of you know the rules. No working on combustible, explosive, or otherwise dangerous projects without an adult present. You"—he pointed at Maya—"are on stall-cleaning duty every day until Christmas." Ignoring her groan, he turned to Zoe. "You are cleaning out the shop. Once that's done, you're helping your sister with the barn chores." Although she grimaced, she accepted the punishment absently, and he knew her mind was still on the cause of the explosion. "No more working on this engine unless I'm directly supervising—or Joe, if I'm not available."

"What? No!" That had gotten her full attention. "Uncle Joe isn't around this close to Christmas. He's better at hiding from the customers than Micah is, and Micah's, like, *invisible* this time of year. I'll never get to work on my engine." Her big brown eyes, so painfully reminiscent of her mother's, widened as she pleaded with him.

"Fine." He knew he was too big a softy when it came to his children, but he couldn't help it. They were good kids—just a little too smart and creative for their own good sometimes. When they were little, it'd been easy to know the right thing to do, but parenting grew harder and harder the older his children got. Now, he often felt as if he were trying to put together one of Zoe's engines without a manual—and with a good chance that everything would blow up in his face. "No working on your engine unless it's in the shop and one of your uncles is supervising or I'm there."

"Or Will or Micah?" Zoe added hopefully.

Steve snorted a laugh. "You know more about mechanics than either of your brothers, so no. Besides, they just encourage chaos." He turned his stern glance on Maya. "As does your sister, so she doesn't count as supervision, either."

Maya grinned. "This wasn't even close to making it into Zoe's top ten."

Closing his eyes, Steve groaned. "Go ride your ponies. At least they don't blow up."

"You should make a mechanical horse," Maya said as the two girls headed for the door, stopping to pull on boots and coats. "No, a whole mechanical cavalry! That would be a-*maz*-ing."

"That'd take a lot of raw materials," Zoe said, although her thoughtful tone told Steve that she was considering the idea. He squeezed his eyes closed, making a mental note to tell his brothers to let him know if any large pieces of machinery suddenly disappeared.

"Before you create a robot army," Steve suggested dryly, "why don't you focus on designing a solar stock-tank heater for the back horse pasture."

Zoe's face lit up with excitement at the idea of a new project, and he looked at his two girls, marveling that they'd be teenagers soon. That reminded him of what he'd picked up at the store earlier that morning, and he frowned uncomfortably. There was no sense in putting it off. Camille had said she'd gotten her period when she was eleven, and Zoe would be twelve in a month. She could get it at any time, and Maya probably wouldn't be far behind.

"Girls." They must've caught a different note in his voice, because they immediately turned toward him. "I got something for you at the store."

They both lit up, and he tried to wave away their anticipation.

"It's nothing exciting." He felt his neck heat and mentally scolded himself as he rubbed it. This was basic biology, and the girls needed to know that it wasn't anything to be embarrassed about. He wanted them to ask questions and tell him what they needed. He hated the thought of them going through the unnecessary humiliation and discomfort that Camille had experienced.

"What'd you get us?" They'd moved closer. His long pause must've intrigued them; he had their full attention.

"You're getting older." He cleared his throat, reaching

for the grocery bag. He'd tossed it on the kitchen table when he'd gotten home just in time to witness Zoe's explosion. "I wanted you to have these when the time came. I'll put them in the bathroom closet. There are instructions, and you can ask me questions if you have any." He remembered how he couldn't even pick out the right products without Camille's help. "If I don't know the answer, we'll…Google it or something."

Opening the bag, he held it out to show the girls what was inside. They both peered into the bag, and Zoe's eyes went wide. She jerked back, as if she could catch something from the contents, and her face flushed brick-red.

Maya looked puzzled. "What are they?" she asked.

Without answering, Zoe turned and hurried toward the door. Steve took a deep breath, trying to think of the best way to answer. Before he could say anything, Zoe called, "C'mon, Maya."

"But what are they?" she asked, moving obediently toward her sister.

"Tampons," Zoe whispered, yanking open the door.

"Oh!" The confusion cleared from Maya's young face. "For when we get our periods!"

Steve didn't think it was possible for Zoe's face to get any redder, but somehow it happened. She seemed so embarrassed by just the sight of the bag's contents that Steve knew his vague plan for having a father-daughters open discussion about puberty was not going to happen anytime soon. Zoe couldn't run away fast enough.

"We'll talk about it later," she said to Maya under her breath, before basically shoving her sister through the door and following her outside.

Steve's gaze stayed on the door after it closed behind the girls, a creeping sense of failure enveloping him. How had he managed to fumble that so badly? It seemed to be happening a lot lately, especially with Zoe and Micah. Until recently, he'd always taken pride in being a competent dad, but now he seemed to be missing more pitches than he was hitting. He wondered if once she was an adult, Zoe would tell the story of when she was eleven and her dad completely humiliated her by buying her tampons. He silently cursed, wishing for the thousandth time that Karen had lived and was part of their children's lives. She would've known what to do. Unlike Steve, she wouldn't be failing their kids.

The door swung open, jerking him out of his mournful thoughts, and Zoe stuck her head back inside. Her cheeks were still red, and she didn't meet his gaze.

"Thanks for getting those, Dad. Love you."

She quickly disappeared again, shutting the door behind her. After a few shocked seconds, Steve smiled. Maybe Camille had been right. Maybe he was doing okay after all.

CHAPTER 2

"AM I TURNING INTO A CLICHÉ?" CAMILLE ASKED.

Lucy paused her grooming long enough to give Camille a scornful look before returning to licking her tail. It served her right, Camille supposed, for trying to hold an existential conversation with a cat. She didn't need to hear the answer anyway. She already knew she was hurtling right through her quirky-cat-lady phase and heading much too quickly toward full-blown hermit-ville. The problem was that she didn't know how to change course—or even if she wanted to. Change of any sort, especially the kind that involved interacting with people, was terrifying.

With an impatient huff, Camille grabbed a peanut-butter blossom and plopped down on one of the wooden kitchen chairs. This useless self-reflection was all Steve Springfield's fault. She'd been perfectly happy living in Borne, finishing up another year alone, only talking to people online or if she couldn't avoid them when running errands. More than once, she'd been tempted to move to Denver or Colorado Springs, figuring that people might be more inclined to ignore her in a big city than in tiny Borne, where everyone knew everyone.

This was her town, though. She'd lived in the same house since she was six and her mom had died of an overdose. Camille's grandma had driven to Southern California to pick up her skinny, bewildered self, and they'd lived together in the little house on Pickett Lane until her grandma had passed away when Camille was nineteen. The only time Camille had gone away was for a miserable, anxiety-ridden semester in Boulder as a college freshman. After returning to Borne for winter break, Camille had noticed her grandma had lost weight—and most of her hair. When she admitted that she was being treated for cancer, Camille had switched over to online courses and moved back into her childhood home. In six months, her grandma was gone.

"It's weird, isn't it?" Camille asked Lucy, despite the cat's complete disinterest in the conversation. "A thirty-two-year-old woman sleeping in the same bedroom as when she was six? I know I've taken down the unicorn poster and put away the stuffed animals...*most* of the stuffed animals," she corrected herself, since it seemed silly to fudge the truth while talking to her cat. "Still, I should be living in a trendy Denver loft or a suburban fixer-upper or a farmhouse with my husband and six kids by now, right?"

That made her think of Steve again. He and his brothers owned a Christmas tree ranch east of town, and she could picture him sitting around a big country kitchen with his beautiful children—since there was no way his kids could be anything but gorgeous—and his handsome brothers. The mental picture Camille conjured up was so Norman Rockwell perfect that it made her heart hurt, desperate for something she'd never even thought she wanted.

A chime from her laptop brought her out of her daydream, and she shook off the lingering wistfulness.

Unrealistic thoughts of Steve wouldn't pay the bills. Pulling up the new email, she entered the order on her spreadsheet. It was another ranch sign, designed to hang above a front gate, and the customer needed it before Christmas. That was doable—it wasn't like she had anywhere else to go—but first she'd need to finish her other orders.

Scolding herself for wasting time by letting her mind wander to fanciful places, she hurried out to her workshop. It had been the garage, but her grandma had parked her twenty-year-old Buick outside and had the space renovated once Camille had gotten into metal- and woodworking.

"Watercolors are fine inside," her grandma had said, "but anything requiring a power saw or a blowtorch stays out in the shop."

With a shiver, Camille pulled on a sweatshirt hanging on a hook by the door. Although the shop was heated, she kept it a good twenty degrees cooler than the house. Once she started working, she didn't notice the chill, but the first ten minutes could be uncomfortable.

Moving to her workbench, she allowed herself a small, pleased smile as she looked over her work in progress: a weather vane she was making from scrap metal and found parts. That was another reason she couldn't leave Borne for a big city. Right now, she was surrounded by ranchers, most of whom were happy to let her pick through their scrap piles of old machinery and fencing and broken tools. She paid them for what they considered junk, and everyone was happy.

She quickly wrapped her curly blond hair into a messy bun and grabbed her welding helmet and gloves. Once she attached the wind cup assembly, she could move on to her favorite part—cutting the running horse out of the ancient truck hood she'd picked up just for this project.

A heavy knock on the outside door brought Camille's head up, and she pulled off her gloves and helmet, frowning. She wasn't expecting any visitors, and she tended not to answer the door if someone didn't call or text ahead of time. In fact, she didn't like answering the door even when they *did* give her advance warning. For all her complaining to Lucy and her daydreams of some ideal dream life with Steve and his perfect Von Trapp children, she generally was happiest when people left her alone to do her art and bake sweet things and cuddle her cat.

Silently placing her helmet and gloves on her workbench next to the pieces of the vane, she tiptoed across the concrete floor, careful not to make any noise to give away her presence. She held her breath as she peered through the peephole in the door, specially installed for situations like this. Unless it was a neighbor with a tray of Christmas cookies, Camille was fully prepared to quietly hide in her shop until whomever it was gave up and went away. Not for the first time, she was grateful that her workshop didn't have any windows.

It wasn't a neighbor bearing cookies. Instead, Ryan Springfield stood there, his hands jammed in his coat pockets and an impatient look on his face. Of the four Springfield brothers, Camille found him to be the least appealing, although she knew the women of Borne would disagree with her about that. Technically, he was the most classically handsome, and he was the most confident in his charm, but he'd always left

Camille cold—not that he or any of his brothers had ever expressed much interest. She made a face, debating whether to open the door. Ryan was a big talker, and she just wanted to work on her weather vane in peace.

"Camille!" he called, leaning forward to bang on the door again, making her jump back as the loud thuds echoed through the workshop. "I have that barn wood you wanted!"

Her frown turned into a grimace. She needed that wood for five separate orders, all of which had to be sent by Christmas. If she didn't answer the door, she'd have to get the wood by going out to the ranch, where she might run into Steve. Even just the thought of seeing him again made her wilt from humiliation. Why had she thought it'd be a good idea to tell him the story of her first period? *Why?*

Still peering through the peephole, she came to the reluctant conclusion that she had to answer the door and talk to Ryan. As he started to walk back toward his truck, she yanked open the door.

"Ryan, hi!" She feigned breathlessness so he'd think she'd had to run to the door. "Sorry it took me so long. I tend to play my music too loudly." It wasn't a lie… not really. She stepped back, giving him room to enter.

He looked a little startled by her uncharacteristic volubility but quickly recovered his normal smooth smile as he stepped inside and closed the door behind him. "Camille." His gaze flicked over her so quickly that she almost missed it. "Good to see you."

"You, too." Now that her fake rush to the door was over, she felt her usual awkwardness settle over her, and she scrambled for something polite to say. Steve, still hanging out uninvited in the forefront of her mind, was the only topic she could think of, and she seized on it eagerly. "So...Steve's home for a visit. That must be...nice."

Camille thought that Ryan stiffened slightly, but then he smiled so easily that she was pretty sure she'd imagined his reaction. "It's not just a visit." He leaned back against the door, looking like he was settling in for a long chat, and Camille wished she'd gone with her gut and hidden until he'd left. "He and the kids are staying. Guess mountain living got too dangerous for him."

"I don't blame him." Even though Borne was tucked at the base of the foothills, close to the mountains, they felt like a far-off world to Camille. She liked safe activities like dancing and swimming and yoga. Sports like snowboarding and mountain biking that involved high speeds and steep hills and possible death just didn't appeal to her. Plus, there were avalanches and rockslides and bears and strange mountain people—not that she could say anything about strange mountain people, being an odd hermit type herself. She was only a few babbled conversations away from the townspeople crowning her the local weirdo.

She realized that Ryan had been talking while her mind wandered, and she refocused on what he was saying.

"...as soon as the fire department in Monroe hired his replacement, he joined his kids on the ranch. They're great kids. You should stop out and meet them. I'll give you a great deal on a tree." His smile pulled up higher on one side than the other, giving him a sort of sly charm. That look had always made Camille feel like he was secretly mocking her, and she mentally chided herself. That was just how Ryan looked. She was a grown woman, and she needed to quit letting high school insecurities creep into her brain.

"Um...sure." Clearing her throat, she decided it was past time to bring this little chat to a halt. "So, the barn wood...?"

"Yeah. I think you're going to like it. We finally took down that old shed before it fell. The wood has got to be a hundred and twenty years old, but it's in great shape."

Camille hit the button to open the overhead door. "Go ahead and back your truck inside, and I'll take a look." She tried to hide the thrill that had gone through her at his description, not wanting him to see how excited she was in case he jacked the price up. Reclaimed barn wood was crazy popular at the moment. Everything she made from it—signs, furniture, decorative paintings—sold as soon as she listed the items on her website. Maybe it had been worth answering the door after all.

Once he backed his pickup into the shop, she closed the overhead door and went to check out the wood stacked in the truck bed. It was in even better shape than she'd hoped. "How much?" She tried to keep her voice casual.

He was silent for several moments, long enough for her to stop examining the wood and look over at him. She wasn't sure how to read his expression, and that made her a little uncomfortable. It had seemed like a pretty straightforward question that required a simple answer, but apparently Ryan was in a mood to complicate things.

"Tell you what," he finally said. "Do you still make those little metal animals?"

"Sure." She glanced at the shelves holding her smaller pieces, pretty sure that she'd sold the last one—a whimsical scrap-metal beagle—the previous week. The animal sculptures were almost as popular as the barn-wood items. "I don't think I have any available right now, but I can make some if you want."

"I'd like to sell some at the ranch shop," he said. "We sell wreaths and pine boughs now, but I think those animals of yours would fly off the shelves. Could you do some angels or maybe some nativity pieces?"

"Definitely the angels." Her tone grew thoughtful as she considered the question. It sparked an avalanche of ideas, and she smiled, excited at the possibilities. "I'll try some different nativity arrangements, too. Maybe some horses... You use draft horses on the ranch, don't you?"

"We do." His eyes lit up at the suggestion, and his usual smirk transformed into an honest grin, one that made Camille like him more. "That's a great idea. The customers love the horses. Some people drive an hour or more to get a tree from us just because they love the feel of the ranch. Your animal sculptures have that same warm, nostalgic thing going."

"I'll make a variety for you to try." Her mind was working at a hundred miles an hour now, and she really wanted Ryan to leave so she could sketch out some of her ideas before she lost them. "Back to the wood...how much per foot?"

"How about you give us a discount on the wholesale cost of the metal sculptures, and I'll do the same on the wood?"

"Sounds good."

They worked out specifics quickly. From Ryan's

smug smile as he unloaded his truck, it was a better deal than he'd expected, but she wasn't bothered by that. She'd gotten a good deal on the wood, and he'd agreed to pay a fair wholesale price for the metal pieces, so Camille was satisfied—or she would be if he'd just leave. She wanted to get the conversation over with so she could immerse herself in her brainstorming.

Unfortunately, it didn't look like that was going to happen anytime soon. He was leaning against his truck, telling her a story about a hunting trip he'd just returned from, and Camille was having a hard time continuing to pretend to care about what he was saying. Her fingers twitched with impatience, and she shifted her weight from foot to foot, yet still he talked on.

Why is he still talking? She was getting almost desperate. This was exactly why she dodged people at the post office and only went to the grocery store when she knew almost no one else would be there. Her skin felt tight and itchy, as if her soul was going to burst out and run away if Ryan didn't shut up and leave her alone in the next five seconds. *Four…three…two…one…*

"Okay!" she interrupted, the word bursting from her as her patience came to an abrupt end. "Nice to see you. I'd better get started on those metal pieces for your store."

He stopped midsentence, his mouth still slightly ajar, and she didn't wait for him to respond. Hurrying across the shop, she hit the button for the overhead door and turned back to Ryan. Although she attempted to smile, she was pretty sure it was more of a grimace.

"Thank you for delivering the wood," she said, knowing that her belated attempt at graciousness wasn't going to smooth over her earlier rudeness, but she didn't really care that much. If it had been anyone else, she might have worried about hurting their feelings, but Ryan had enough confidence to absorb the blow to his pride. When he didn't immediately move toward the driver's side of his pickup, she briefly considered hiring a shop bouncer. "I don't want to keep you from your work. This must be a really busy time for you, since Christmas will be here in a few weeks."

Finally, he pushed away from the truck. "Right. I'll see you when you have some pieces for the ranch store, then?"

"Yes!" She was so relieved he was finally leaving that she smiled at him much more widely than the moment deserved. He paused, looking thoughtful. She made a *keep moving* motion with her hands, and he finally climbed into the driver's seat, although he shot her a smirk first. Camille didn't even attempt to interpret his look. He could make whatever faces he wanted, as long as he *left*.

When the engine turned over and he started pulling out of the shop, she waved, her thoughts already back on the nativity scene she'd mentally sketched out already, her mind ticking through her scrap inventory, trying to pick out pieces that would work.

The truck stopped, and the passenger window rolled down.

"Have you eaten yet?" Ryan asked.

She stared at him, the majority of her brain still focused on metalwork. "Yet? You mean today?" It was a stupid question. She realized that as soon as it was out, but it was Ryan's fault for throwing out such a non sequitur.

His smirk was back. "Actually, I was talking about

lunch. We could go to Birdie's to celebrate our new partnership. My treat. Sound good?"

No, it sounds awful. Camille barely caught herself before she blurted out the words. They were too rude, even for Ryan, who apparently was never, ever going to leave her workshop. "I've eaten already. Besides, I have a pile of orders to do before Christmas, plus these new pieces, so…um. No." It sounded so stark that she added a limp "Thank you."

His smirk faded, his mouth drawing into a tight line that she actually preferred to his usual smile. At least it showed how he was really feeling. "Another time, then." The window slid closed, and the truck began rolling again.

As soon as the pickup trailer hitch cleared the opening, Camille pushed the button to close the overhead door. When the bottom met the ground and the door's motor went silent, she let out a long breath. The workshop was hers again. She took a moment to appreciate the wonderful solitude before she hurried over to her workbench and grabbed a sketch pad. The weather vane was going to have to wait until she'd gotten some of these ideas out of her head and down on paper.

Ryan's aggressively flirty behavior niggled at her thoughts for only a second before she dismissed him and focused on the nativity scene taking shape on the paper. He was finally gone, and she'd know better the next time someone knocked.

There'd be no answering the door; she'd just hide until they left.

I didn't think this through. Camille tapped her gloved fingers nervously on the steering wheel as she drove up the curving driveway toward the Springfield ranch. She cursed herself for not considering the fact that, once the metal sculptures had been planned out and welded and finished, they somehow had to get to the ranch shop. Since she was pretty sure Ryan wouldn't ever come by her house again after the way she'd shoved him out the door, there was only one option left.

She'd boxed up the pieces, loaded them into her car—the same old Buick that her grandma had driven—and made the trek out to the Springfield Christmas Tree Ranch. Despite her nerves, she had to admit that the surroundings were beautiful. The drive was festooned with garland and lights and red bows, and a pristine blanket of snow covered the gently rolling pastures that made up the front of the property. The rows of cultivated evergreens provided a dark-green backdrop to the shop and the main house, and the mountains in the distance were both hazy and huge.

The whole place seemed almost too perfect to be real, like something out of a cheesy Christmas movie. There was even a snow sculpture of a horse in the front yard. As Camille parked in the almost-full lot, she craned her neck to take in the surprisingly fine detail on the snow horse. She wondered whose work it was, since it was several steps up from the traditional three-ball snowman.

Refocusing on the store in front of her, Camille blew out a breath as she pulled the key from the ignition. The shop was cute, a miniature version of the Victorian house behind it. The engine of the car ticked as it cooled, reminding her that the seconds were passing, and nothing would be accomplished if she stayed out here like a chicken—except that she'd get very cold.

"Let's do this," she muttered to the box of metal sculptures. The words didn't really motivate her, but a minivan trundling up the driveway toward the store did, reminding her that the longer she waited, the more people would see her sitting out in the cold. With her luck, it'd be one of the chattier Borne residents. They'd try to talk to her, and she'd either go silent or start babbling, depending on how her brain wanted to embarrass her today, and then she'd have to pretend she was waiting for someone to explain why she was sitting like a lump in her car outside the gift shop. Then whomever she'd gotten stuck talking to would know she was lying, since everyone in town was painfully aware that she was the friendless almost-hermit.

The nightmare scenario played out a little too realistically in her mind. Hurrying to get out of the car, she circled to the other side to grab the box. It still took a mental pep talk to get her feet to carry her to the entrance, and she shifted the heavy box to her hip to open the door.

It swung open, and she braced herself for the sight of Steve, but he wasn't there, only wreaths and decorations and people she didn't recognize. Warm air filled with the smell of pine and cedar and cinnamon surrounded her as she used her hip to bump the door closed. Moving toward the register, she took a better look around, but she still didn't see a single acquaintance. *Thank God*.

It wasn't until her shoulders dropped that she realized how tightly she'd been holding herself. Now that she knew the only people in the store were strangers, she relaxed, and her anxiety about coming to the ranch seemed almost silly.

At the checkout, she set the box on the floor next to the counter. The person working the register looked to be in his early or midteens, with short, black hair and eyes almost as dark, mile-long lashes, and brown skin. He cocked his head slightly to the left and smiled at her, his nose wrinkling just a bit in a way that was achingly familiar.

"You're one of Steve's kids," she said without thinking, wondering if Steve's wife had been Native American. The boy hadn't gotten Steve's light-brown hair or his hazel eyes, although he looked like he'd be as tall as his dad once he finished growing.

The teen blinked, his welcoming expression changing to a look of surprise. "How'd you know?"

"Your mannerisms are identical," she said, nodding at the hand that was rubbing the back of his neck. "Your coloring's different, but your smile and the way you move are all Steve."

"He's not my bio-dad," the boy blurted, looking almost guilty, as if she'd accused him of being an imposter.

Camille gave a small shrug. "Matching DNA or not, you're still a mini Steve—well, not that mini." He was half a foot taller than she was. "I could've picked you out as Steve's from a crowd of blond kids."

"Thanks." He looked pleased even as red darkened his cheekbones. "I'm Will. You know my dad, then?"

"Uh…" She took a moment to hunt for the right descriptor. It didn't seem right to claim that they were friends, but calling him an acquaintance seemed wrong, too. Her pause made curiosity light Will's eyes, and she hurried to speak before he misinterpreted things. "I grew up in Borne with him. I'm three years younger though, so he didn't notice me much."

Will sucked in his cheeks, looking as if he was holding back a smile, yet again reminding Camille of Steve. "You noticed him, though?"

"Sure." She tried to play it off in a casual sort of way, as if she hadn't had such a monster crush. From the way Will's grin widened, she didn't think she'd managed. With a mental shrug, she gave up trying to sound blasé. "How could I not? He was my favorite of the Springfield brothers."

"Really?" Will leaned toward her, clearly fascinated by the potential for old stories about his father. "From what Dad says, Uncle Ryan and Uncle Nate were the popular ones." His attention moved to a woman holding a tree stand who was hovering behind Camille, and he turned his charismatic, Steve-like smile on her. "Don't leave yet," he said in an aside to Camille. "I want to hear about teen Dad."

With a nod, she stepped out of the way so Will could ring the woman up. This visit to the ranch was going much more smoothly—and more enjoyably—than Camille had expected. Will was easy to talk to, sharing Steve's sweetness and good-heartedness but not his reserve. With that infectious smile and his striking features, Camille knew Will had to be even more popular than any of the previous generation of Springfield guys. Their easy rapport made her wonder what would've happened if she'd drummed up the courage to talk to Steve in high school. Once she'd gotten past his quiet stoicism, would he have been just as comfortable to be around as his son was now?

"Camille." Ryan's voice made her stiffen. She turned to see him making his way through the small store. His cheeks were red from the cold, and he seemed a little out of breath as he approached the counter. "I thought that was your car. There aren't many others like it around here…or anywhere nowadays."

"Hey, Ryan. Yeah, that's Bess. My car, I mean. I, um, named her Bess. Bess the Boat, actually, but I shortened it to just…Bess." Feeling awkward about their last encounter, she gave him a small wave she knew was ultra-dorky, even before Will dissolved in a fit of teen-boy giggles that was equal parts annoying and adorable. She shot him a quelling glance, which didn't seem to cow him at all. In fact, he leaned on the counter as if getting comfortable to watch the show. The customer was clearly finished checking out, but she didn't leave. Instead, she also turned to watch. In a town as small as Borne, you had to learn to make your own entertainment…which was part of why Camille kept so much to herself.

This trip to the ranch was quickly taking a nosedive.

"Would you like to see what I made?" she blurted, not even giving Ryan a chance to respond before bending down and pulling out one of the smaller boxes. The only way to get through this with the least amount of humiliation was to keep the interaction as short as possible. No more chitchat with Steve's kid, or his brother, or anyone else with the last name of Springfield. Just get the business taken care of and then leave her sculptures and this little piece of Christmas paradise behind.

Placing the box on the counter, she untied the twine holding it closed and opened the flap.

"Nice presentation," Ryan said, and Camille gave him a small, pleased smile. It'd taken some experimenting before she'd settled on her current packaging, and she was proud of it.

"Thank you." She picked the cloth drawstring bag containing the sculpture out of its nest of colorful shredded paper. "This keeps bits of the packing material from sticking to the metal." She slid the piece out and set it on the counter. It was her favorite—an abstract of Mary and Joseph, their bodies curving as they leaned over the baby in the manger. To her, protectiveness and love were obvious in every line of the sculpture.

A little anxious about the Springfields' reactions, she immediately bent to retrieve another box, trying to ignore the heavy silence.

"How much is that?" The woman was the first to speak. "I want to buy it."

"Give us fifteen minutes," Ryan said in what was obviously his jovial customer-handling tone. "We'll need to prepare these for sale first, but I promise that you'll have first dibs if you decide you want to purchase it." When the woman nodded grudgingly, he turned his smile up a notch. "Have you picked out your tree yet?"

"My husband's doing that now." The woman craned her neck, as if trying to see what else was in the box, and Camille ducked her head to hide a smile. The woman's enthusiasm was good for her ego, especially since neither Ryan nor Will had commented on the first piece yet. As much as she tried to tell herself that not everyone would like her art, it was still painful to expose her sculptures to potential criticism.

"There they are," Ryan said as he turned to look out the window. When Camille followed his gaze, she saw Nate Springfield and another man she didn't know tying a blue spruce to the top of one of the cars. "Looks like he picked a good one." He paused, his forehead wrinkling with obvious concern. "Hmm."

"What?" the woman asked, looking from the view outside to Ryan and back again. "What's wrong?"

"Oh, nothing." He didn't sound convincing. "I just have a different method of securing the tree. It'll be fine, though."

The woman's eyes grew wide with alarm. "I'd better go supervise."

She rushed toward the door, and Ryan turned back to Camille with a self-satisfied grin. "That'll give us a few minutes. Will, grab the price tags, would you? Camille, this is incredible, and it's obviously in a higher price bracket than the animals. How much?"

She blinked, taken off guard by the question. She'd been so involved in the process of making them that she hadn't considered the price, but Ryan was right. The nativity pieces were larger, more intricate, and had taken almost twice as long as the whimsical animals he had initially asked for. To give herself time to think, she unboxed the other five sculptures—two more nativity scenes, a horse, an angel, and a lamb—and placed them on the counter.

"Whoa," Will said, lightly running his finger over the back of the metal draft mare that was touching her nose to her foal. "Wait until Micah sees this. He's going to flip."

"Micah?" Camille repeated, trying to place the name.

"My brother. He made the snow horse outside."

"He did that? It's beautiful," Camille said. "How old is he?"

"Thirteen."

Her eyebrows rose in surprise. "Impressive."

"Yeah." Will grinned, obviously proud of his brother. "His drawings are even better."

The other customers had noticed the pieces and were drawing closer, and the threesome outside had finished tying the tree to the car roof and were headed toward the shop door. Their moment of semiprivacy was coming to an end. The tiny hairs on the back of Camille's neck stood on end at the thought of being trapped in the little store. Quickly averaging her work hours and material costs in her head, Camille said, keeping her voice low, "I'll need double what we agreed on for the animals."

"Done." Ryan didn't hesitate. Grabbing a piece of paper, he scribbled some numbers and handed the list to Will. "Here are the retail prices. Make a tag for each of them, and set them up in the window display. Just ring them up under miscellaneous until I get them entered in the inventory system. I'm betting we sell half of them in the first ten minutes." He turned to Camille. "C'mon. I'll write you a check in the office."

Once they were out of the store, Ryan slowed and fell into step next to her. The cleared pathway was wide enough to walk shoulder to shoulder, although Camille still felt a little awkward when their coat sleeves brushed. Nate was leading a gray draft horse away from the lot, and he stopped, waiting for them to catch up.

"Hey, Ry," Nate said. He looked surprised when he saw her. "Camille? How are you? Have you recovered from the other day?"

"Hi, Nate." She gave him her dorky wave, which seemed to be becoming a bad new habit. "Um. Yeah. I mean, there wasn't much to recover from. I wasn't really out that long. There were, you know, layers." Nate looked puzzled, and she clamped her mouth shut. If she kept trying to explain, she'd just get more and more confusing.

"That's good, then." He walked with them, the giant horse ambling quietly on his other side. Even though Nate was a tall guy, his head topped the mare's withers by only an inch or two. Although he wasn't as traditionally handsome as Ryan, he had a rugged, wholesome look, reminding Camille of an actor in an old-school cowboy movie. He'd always been athletic, playing football and baseball in high school and spending a couple of years after he graduated roping on the rodeo circuit. According to Mrs. Lin, he'd given up what was looking to be a promising career to help save his parent's struggling ranch. "Where've you been hiding? Up until the other day, it'd been years since I'd run into you."

Since the answer was that she'd been *literally* hiding in her workshop, Camille was stuck on how to answer without sounding like a sad little hermit. "I've been around. Busy. With making things. Metal things...sculptures, actually. There are some in the gift store, in fact. That's why I came here today, to drop them off. Normally, I don't leave the workshop much in December, except to sleep, of course, and eat and sometimes go to the grocery store or the gas station or…" She cleared her throat, knowing she needed to stop talking or she'd only make it worse.

Neither man filled the following pause, though, and the silence grew until it was thick and heavy, weighing on her chest and making it so she couldn't breathe. Not even the horse made a sound except for the quiet plod of her dinner-plate-sized hooves. The tension built with every step until Camille couldn't take the silent awkwardness for even one second longer. She had to say *something*. "What's with the horse?"

"Buttercup?" Nate tugged affectionately at her long forelock. "She's on duty." At Camille's curious look, he continued. "We use the horses to bring the trees to the lot. The customers pick the one they want, we cut it down, and then Miss Buttercup here pulls it to their car. It's not the most efficient way, but the customers love it." He rubbed under the strap of the mare's halter, and she twisted her head, pushing into his hand as if he'd found an itchy spot.

"I can see why," Camille said, pleased by the easy turn in the conversation. Despite the cold, she found that she was relaxing slightly, the beauty of the ranch easing her nerves. Behind the well-kept barn and outbuildings, neat rows of evergreens created dark-green stripes on the snowy ground, making the place look like a handmade quilt. The entire ranch seemed to radiate old-fashioned Christmas spirit. It was beautiful and charming and somehow soothing, as if none of life's usual worries existed at the Springfield ranch. No wonder people drove for hours to get their trees here.

"Besides," Ryan chimed in, "it gives the horses

something to do while we're tied up with selling trees and manning the shop."

"What do they do the other ten months of the year?" Besides the Christmas trees and the store, Camille realized that she didn't know what else the Springfield brothers did. She assumed they raised cattle like their neighbors, but she didn't see any sign of livestock in the pastures except for horses. After Steve had moved away, Camille's interest in the Springfield family had sharply declined.

"They skid logs for us." Nate was the one who answered, not sounding at all offended that she knew so little about her almost-neighbors.

"Horse logging?" Her doubt was obvious in her voice, but she couldn't help it. Even though the ranch felt like a trip back in time, using horses to skid logs seemed ridiculously old-fashioned. "Isn't that...well, really slow?"

Nate laughed. "Nah. It's making a comeback as people get more interested in sustainable forest management. Logging with horses leaves behind a lot less damage, and it means I get to work with my best girl."

"Buttercup?" Camille asked, charmed, even as Ryan snorted.

"Of course." Nate rubbed the mare's forehead, and she half closed her dark, liquid eyes in bliss. "I'm going to see if she wants some water before we head back to the store. Good to see you, Camille."

"You, too," she said, meaning it.

He and the horse headed for the barn door as Ryan led Camille toward the next building. They entered a good-sized office with four desks, one in each corner, blocking off the space to make wall-less cubicles. A long conference table sat in the center of the space. It was basic but looked tidy, and the room was blessedly warm. Her fingers prickled with pins and needles, half-frozen after just the short walk from the store. She tucked them in her coat pockets, vowing to bring her warm gloves the next time she came—if she got up the courage to come a second time. Maybe she could pay Mrs. Lin to drive the next batch out to the ranch...although that meant she'd have to deal with Mrs. Lin, so it probably wasn't worth it.

Pulling out one of the conference table chairs, Ryan said, "Have a seat."

Although she sat in the proffered chair, she wondered why he was having her get comfortable. How long could writing a check take? One minute? Two?

Rather than pulling out a checkbook, however, Ryan leaned his hip against one of the desks and crossed his arms over his chest in a showy gesture. She remembered that he'd always done that a lot, even back in high school, and she wondered if it was to make the muscles in his arms and chest stand out. If so, his ploy wasn't very successful, since his winter jacket hid any extra bulging. The thought made her want to laugh, but she managed to swallow it in time.

"So, what do you think?" he asked, and for a brief, illogical moment, she worried that he'd read her thoughts.

"What do I think about what?"

"The ranch." He waved a hand around, as if indicating all the buildings and land around them. "I know you've just seen a limited amount of it, but you were looking cold, so I thought we could warm up in here before we finished the tour."

"Tour?" *Please just write the check and let me go.* "Oh. Um… Maybe we could put that off until spring?" Her hands were still uncomfortably prickly. Besides, even though she was interested in seeing the barn and the other horses, it seemed like it'd take more time than she cared to spend alone with Ryan.

His smile drooped a bit before returning. "You're right. It's too cold to be dragging you around the unheated outbuildings. How about we move this tour to my house? My place is on the west side of the property, just a couple minutes from here. We could warm up, have some lunch."

She blinked at the unexpected offer. What was up with Ryan's new obsession with trying to feed her? Even though she wasn't the most cosmopolitan of people, she was savvy enough to know not to accept an invitation to go with some guy she didn't really know to his isolated house, especially if she was already having that itchy feeling that something was off. "Sorry, but I should get home. Christmas orders, you know, and a cat. I mean, I have a cat, a hungry cat that needs to be fed, so…I should go."

His smile dipped again and didn't recover this time. "Sure. I get it. Let me write you that check, and you can head home to…feed your cat."

Although her cheeks burned at how inane she must've sounded, relief rushed through her. She wanted to laugh at herself, at how panicked she'd gotten. Ryan's interest felt awkward, and his constant come-ons made it easier to run back to the safe haven of her workshop.

Too bad she couldn't have Steve's teenage son Will as her one-and-only Springfield ranch contact. She'd been able to talk to him without descending into her usual babble. Well, there might have been a little babble, but definitely not as much as when she had to talk to another adult. Maybe she could make that a condition of selling her sculptures at the store.

Pulling a key ring out of his pocket, Ryan unlocked one of the desk drawers and extracted a checkbook. They were both quiet as he wrote out the check, the scratch of his pen against the paper the only sound in the room. As Camille waited, nerves steadily climbing, she decided that electronic payment would be a second stipulation for future orders. Too bad Will didn't look old enough to drive, or he could've picked up the sculptures from her workshop.

"Here you go." Ryan's voice interrupted her wandering thoughts, and she jumped to her feet, eager to leave. As she took the check, Ryan's pocket buzzed. "Excuse me for a moment." Pulling out his phone, he read something on the screen and gave a grunt of annoyance. "Joe left his keys in the store and needs me to grab them for him. I'll be right back."

She followed him to the door, unwilling to give up the opportunity to escape. "That's okay. I should be going anyway."

"No, please stay here. We still need to talk about the next order."

"Can't we talk about that some other time?" she asked with more than a little desperation. She'd already talked to more people in one day than she usually did in a week. The very little bit of social butterfly-ness in her had been used up, and she needed some workshop time to recharge. A month or so should do it.

"Sure." Why didn't she trust his instantaneous smile? "I'll come by your place tomorrow. Should we say about seven? We can go out to dinner. If you don't like any of the places in town, we could drive to that new place in Ebba. It's only an hour or so away, and I've heard good things about the food."

That's why she couldn't trust his smile. "Okay, I'll wait here until you get back."

He actually looked disappointed by that, making Camille wonder if he really *had* been asking her to dinner, rather than just trying to terrify her into waiting while he retrieved Joe's keys.

"Why can't Joe get his own keys?" She knew she sounded sulky, but she didn't care. It'd been a long day already, and it wasn't even noon.

"Because he's a cranky hermit, and everyone enables him." Ryan rolled his eyes. "Everyone including me, because if I don't do this, he'll text me every two minutes until I give in. He only goes into the store when no one's there. If there's a customer within a mile of the place, he goes phantom on us and finds something that has to be done at one of the far corners of the property." He paused. "Anyway, this'll take me two minutes. Don't go anywhere, and I'll be right back."

With a silent sigh, Camille settled back in her recently abandoned chair, thinking that she could sympathize with Joe, the cranky, customer-avoiding hermit. His easy avoidance of any and all strangers was pretty much her life goal. Maybe she needed a ranch. Her house and workshop had limited places for her to hide.

On a ranch, no one would be able to find her unless she wanted them to.

A loud *bang* shook the floor, and Camille jumped to her feet, jolted out of her thoughts. She searched for the source, for whatever had fallen or exploded, but nothing in the office looked out of place. The sound had come from behind the door set in the back of the office, and Camille eyed it, trying to decide whether she should investigate or just stay where she was.

It seemed rude to just wander around someone else's property investigating strange noises, but wasn't it her duty to check out a possible accident? The sound had been really loud, almost like an explosion, and someone could've been hurt. What if they were waiting for help right now, and Camille was the only one who was close enough to get to them in time?

Curiosity and a bone-deep sense of responsibility drove her to hurry across the office. She carefully pulled open the door slightly. Something was burning, judging by the hint of acrid smoke, but it wasn't enough to warn her to evacuate the building. She opened the door wider, revealing an expansive, well-outfitted shop—and a pre-teen girl who looked both grease-spattered and guilty as she stood over a table covered with what appeared to be pieces of a disassembled engine, extraneous parts that Camille didn't recognize mixed in with the others.

"You okay?" she asked tentatively, taking a few more steps into the shop once she saw that nothing was actually on fire.

"Yeah." The girl sighed as she wiped half-heartedly at her face with her flannel shirtsleeve. Camille didn't mention that her efforts only smeared the grease spots, turning the black freckles into streaks. "I just hope my dad wasn't around to hear that." She eyed Camille with tentative optimism. "Do you know if he's back from the fire station yet? I'm hoping not, because I can probably convince my uncles to keep their mouths shut about this." She waved her arms, the gesture encompassing the entirety of the shop.

"Which one is your dad?" Camille asked, even though she was fairly certain that this girl was another one of Steve's. Her light-brown hair, tied in a messy knot on the back of her head, matched his, although her eyes were a deep, dark brown, rather than Steve's light, greenish hazel. Her firm, stubborn chin was his, as well.

"Steve," the girl said.

"That's what I thought." Camille studied her, seeing more and more similarities between father and daughter, from the shape of their eyes to the angle of their cheekbones to the way their wide mouths gave them an amused, kind look, even when they weren't smiling. "You look like him."

"Really?" She sounded surprised. "He always says I look like my mom, but sometimes I wonder if he just says that to be nice. She died when I was three, so I can't really remember her, and it's hard to tell with pictures and even videos, you know? People look different in real life."

"I know what you mean." Intrigued by the odd collection of engine parts, Camille moved closer to examine them as she spoke. Although she tended to see mechanical pieces as potential sculptures, she had a basic working knowledge of engines, and, for the life of her, she couldn't figure out how all of these parts would fit together. "My mom died when I was six, so I'm sure my memories aren't the most accurate, but the photos I have of her don't match the pictures I have of her in my mind."

"How'd she die?"

Camille studied an intake manifold. After a close-up view of the collection of parts, she still had no idea what they were going to be used for. It would be a crazy, Frankenstein-esque motor if all the pieces were put together to form one engine. "She overdosed." The words came out absently, most of her attention focused on the metal parts in front of her. As soon as she heard her own words, though, she jerked up her head and met the girl's gaze. "Sorry! That probably wasn't a good thing to tell a kid."

With a snort, the girl waved off her apology. "I'm almost twelve. I know about overdoses. My mom had ovarian cancer."

"I'm sorry." Camille studied her. This candid exchange of dead-mother stories was new to her. Normally, the conversation ended with awkward abruptness as soon as her mom was mentioned, so this unabashed curiosity was actually refreshing. This was the second almost-comfortable conversation she'd had at the ranch, and both had been with Steve's kids. Maybe she should make it a personal rule not to interact with anyone over eighteen. It would dramatically cut down on awkward interactions. "I'm Camille."

"Zoe."

They studied each other for several moments until Camille couldn't hold back her curiosity any longer. "What the heck are you hoping to make here?"

When Zoe smiled, the corners of her mouth slowly curling up like the ends of a long bow, Camille couldn't help but grin back. "A personal hovercraft, eventually."

"Like the ones people make out of plywood and leaf blowers?"

Zoe shook her head, her nose crinkling in distaste. "Smaller than that, and less boring. Mine will have more range and power, and it'll fit through doorways and in tighter spaces."

Raising her eyebrows, Camille asked, "Like a flying broomstick?"

Instead of laughing, Zoe seriously considered the comparison. "Sort of, but more comfortable. Like a flying luge."

"That sounds fun. I'd ride in one of those." Camille studied the components again and then gave Zoe a sideways look, not sure if she should mention the obvious or not. In the end, she couldn't hold back. "Isn't a traditional internal combustion engine—even just a 500cc one—going to be too heavy for that small a craft?"

"Of course." Zoe's patient tone was just a hair away from patronizing, and Camille ducked her head to hide a smile. "The hovercraft—well, flying luge—is my end goal. What I'm trying to do right now is put together a combination of an ATV and a trail wheelchair so my friend Wyatt can use it when he visits me out here. Right now, he has to stay in the store or on the plowed, paved paths, and what fun is that? A wheelchair that lets him hike and climb stairs and cut through the pastures will work until I build the hovercraft. Once Wyatt has that, he'll be able to go anywhere."

Camille absently fingered a spark plug as she

considered Zoe's plan. "You're thinking a gas engine for the off-road wheelchair, then?"

That sweet, curling smile appeared again. "Hybrid, so Wyatt doesn't get stuck in the middle of nowhere by Uncle Joe's cabin. I've been experimenting with different fuels, too." She gestured toward a stripped-down push lawn mower. The only pieces left of it were the frame and the motor, both of which looked like they'd been pushed over a cliff, straight into a bonfire. "That's what you heard earlier."

Alarm bells went off in Camille's head. "Um, you're mixing different chemicals?"

"It's okay. Normally, they don't explode like that."

"Explode like what?"

Steve's deep voice made them both spin around to see him entering the workshop through the office door. He was frowning sternly at Zoe, who immediately dropped her head to stare at her steel-toed work boots. His severe gaze moved to Camille, who felt both inexplicably guilty and enormously drawn to him. Neither feeling was comfortable, but she still couldn't manage to look away.

"Camille." Surprise lightened his frown. "What are you doing here?"

Her mind instantly blanked. It was ridiculous, really, her inability to function around Steve. She should've grown out of this nonsense a long time ago, but apparently he still had the ability to reduce her to a timid fourteen-year-old. Sure, she wasn't that great at dealing with other adults, but most of her interactions with the other townspeople were just awkward. When she was around Steve, she was filled with a mix of bubbling excitement and anticipation, but there was also the overwhelming knowledge that she was Camille Brandt, Borne's resident oddball, which meant that she was going to say something inappropriate or overly personal or completely bizarre.

It didn't matter much when most people thought she was irredeemably weird, but it hurt to think of Steve seeing her that way. The only way she could think to prevent that was to stay completely silent when she was around him. Sure, he might *think* she was strange, but she didn't have to confirm it.

Zoe looked at her curiously, jarring Camille out of her mental paralysis and making her realize that the silence was stretching awkwardly. She had to say something. "Um…the sculptures. My metalwork, I mean. In the shop, they are." Great, now she was talking like Yoda. Clearing her throat, she arranged the words in her head before trying again. "I dropped off some metal sculptures at the shop. Ryan had me wait in the office so he could bring Joe his keys, and then I heard a—"

Catching Zoe's anxious glance, Camille quickly switched words. "I heard a sound in here and was curious. I met Zoe, and we were talking engines and personal transports when you arrived." To her relief, she managed to stop talking before the words *flying luge* made it out of her mouth. It sounded weird enough in context without her babbling it to Steve because his strong jaw was making her light-headed.

He made a *hmm* sound before turning to his daughter. "Where's your adult?"

Camille cleared her throat. "I'm officially one. An adult, I mean."

Steve glanced at her, and his mouth softened slightly

before he firmed it again, giving her the impression that he was having a tough time holding his stern expression. "We can't have you blown up. You're not covered under our insurance."

Camille blinked. "You're insured for explosions?"

"It seemed like a smart financial move." He gave her the slightest of winks before returning his attention to his daughter. "Before Camille came in here, when you were working on your engine and there was a sound that might or might not have been an explosion, what adult was with you?"

"No one?" Zoe risked a glance at her father's stony expression before rushing out the rest of her explanation. "Uncle Ryan was in here with me before, but then he saw something out the window that made him run out really fast, and I tried waiting for him to come back, but he was taking forever, so I worked on something, but it wasn't technically *this* engine." She gestured toward the parts on the table, very obviously not looking toward the blown-out lawn mower remains.

"What was it then? Technically?"

Her voice came out very quietly. "Fuel experimentation?"

"Fuel experimentation." Steve briefly closed his eyes and rubbed the back of his neck. When he reopened them, all the earlier restrained humor seemed to have disappeared. "Zoe. What are we going to do about this? You can't keep this up. I've seen too many people burned or worse…" He clamped his lips together, cutting off that line of thought. After a long pause, he spoke again. "You're grounded from the workshop for a week. No working with fuel or mechanical parts or anything even slightly combustible, got it?"

"But..." Her protest sounded half-hearted, and Camille had a feeling that Zoe knew she was getting off lightly.

"No. You can do research on the computer, you can sketch ideas, you can read small-engine repair manuals, but that's it." He looked suddenly tired. "I just want a week where I don't have to worry about you or the ranch exploding. Give me that, please?"

"Okay, Dad." Zoe's voice was resigned. With a last, longing look at the parts arranged on the worktable, she headed for the door.

"Bye, Zoe," Camille called after her, receiving a wave and a small smile in reply.

The door closed behind the girl, and silence settled over the shop, making Camille itchy. This was the first time she'd been alone in a nonpublic space with Steve, and it was very different from her high-school daydreams. Sending him a quick, nervous glance, she saw he was still staring at the door his daughter had gone through, his expression sad.

"Are you okay?" Camille asked tentatively, feeling like she was intruding on his private thoughts.

Letting out a sigh, he turned toward her. She wasn't surprised he was rubbing the back of his neck again. This seemed like a situation that would call for it. "Not really. Never thought parenting would mean feeling guilty for stopping your kid from blowing herself up."

"My grandma got off lightly," she said, studying the blackened lawn mower engine Zoe had been experimenting on. "She was just afraid I'd burn the house down."

He stared at her, his preoccupied expression replaced with one of startled fascination. "That's getting off lightly?"

"Sure. Less shrapnel that way."

A laugh boomed out of him. She remembered how rare a sound it had been back when they were growing up, and how utterly contagious. Camille realized that she was smiling just from hearing it, even all these years later. "Right," he said. "Not sure if that's better or not."

She shrugged, pleased at being the cause of his amusement—and not in a mortifying way for once, thank God. It was getting easier to talk to Steve. His calm, easy acceptance allowed her to relax, knowing that she could talk freely without him thinking she was strange. "Maybe you could help her build it."

"I try to help—well, supervise—as much as I can. So do my brothers, now that we've moved back here. This time of year, though, everyone's busy, and when there's a fire call, I have to go. Zoe tries to be patient, but when she gets an idea..."

Camille understood the driving force that inspiration could be. She couldn't count the number of times she'd rushed out to the workshop at two in the morning when some new project popped into her head. Studying Steve, she tried to think of something helpful to say, but she couldn't think of any possible solution, although she could feel for both Zoe, the inspired creator, and her beleaguered single father. Still, she didn't want this conversation to end. Not yet. "Were you a firefighter when you lived in the mountains?"

"Yeah." He smiled slightly, obviously proud of his job. "Here I'm a volunteer, since there aren't any paid openings. It actually works better for now, with the kids still adjusting to the new place and all the work there is to do around the ranch."

"So…" Pushing away the too-tempting memory of Steve in bunker gear, she tried to fish for another one of those wonderful laughs. "*You'll* be the one showing up when I finally manage to burn down my workshop, then?"

Before he could respond, the door to the office swung open with enough force to bang the knob against the wall. Camille jumped, and Steve turned to face the sound, stepping in front of her as he did so. She felt a warm, melting sensation in her belly at the protective move. It reminded her of what had happened when she was a freshman in high school and he was a senior, and again just a few days ago. There weren't many people who'd protected her in her life, but Steve seemed to be making a habit of it.

"Ryan," Steve said, making his brother's name into both a reprimand and a greeting, even as he relaxed.

"Camille. There you are," Ryan said, sounding relieved at first. As his gaze moved back and forth between her and his brother, he began to frown. "Hey, Steve. What're you two doing in here? I've been looking all over the ranch for you, Camille. Thought you were going to wait for me in the office."

She shrugged a little, not liking his proprietary tone. Just because he'd twisted her arm until she said she'd stay didn't mean she was a skid steer he could park and return to at his leisure. "I was talking to Zoe, and then Steve found us."

"Zoe." He clapped a hand over his eyes. "I left her waiting in here, didn't I?"

"She went ahead without you," Steve said coolly, although there wasn't any accusation in his voice.

Camille figured he knew his daughter would find a way to work around his supervision rules, even with the most dedicated uncles.

"Sorry. I'll talk to her." His hand dropped back to his side. "Did she blow anything up?" Steve nodded wordlessly toward the blackened lawn mower, and Ryan moved closer to get a better look. "Nice. How'd she do that?"

"She's experimenting with mixing fuels," Camille said.

Although Steve winced, Ryan looked impressed. "Smart. I told you to have dumb kids. They're easier." He moved over to where Camille and Steve were standing and maneuvered to stand between them. He gave his brother's shoulder a teasing shove, and Camille surreptitiously shifted a little to the side, away from Ryan. For some reason, standing close enough to Steve to smell his distinctive scent—peppermint and evergreen and a tiny bit of horse—didn't bother her, but she needed a bit more of a personal bubble with Ryan.

"How do you know?" Steve asked. "The only kids you're around are mine, and they're all smart."

Ryan waved off his brother's objection. "Everyone knows dumb kids are easier." Not waiting for a response, he turned to Camille, shifting closer and eating up the space between them again. "Ready for lunch?"

"Lunch?" Steve repeated before Camille could think of the best way to politely decline. Ryan had been aggravatingly persistent during the past few encounters, and she was running out of excuses. All she could think of was telling him she needed to feed her cat again, and that was only half a step up from telling him she needed to wash her hair. Maybe she'd have to be blunt to the point of rudeness with Ryan, though. Her stomach twisted at the thought. She hated confrontation and hurting people's feelings, and she had an uneasy feeling that she'd have to do both before Ryan would give up the idea of…whatever it was he wanted to do with her.

"I'm taking Camille to my cabin for lunch," Ryan explained, confirming Camille's suspicions that it would take one of Zoe's explosions to break through the hard shell of his ego and get him to accept that she wasn't interested. She wondered what had caused his sudden fascination. They'd lived in the same town for years, and he'd never looked at her twice before.

She gathered all her gumption and straightened her shoulders. "Sorry. I don't have time. Thank you for the offer, but I need to go now. Bye." Before he could argue, she marched toward the office door. "Bye, Steve." She didn't let herself slow or look back, knowing Ryan would pounce on any slight sign of hesitation.

"Wait!" By the sound of his voice, Ryan was following her, and she sped up to a fast walk. "I thought we were going to talk about the next set of sculptures."

"Just text me which ones sold, and I'll make more of the popular ones." Slipping through the office door, she quickly pulled it shut behind her. Once the two men couldn't see her anymore, she bolted outside and down the path to the gift-shop lot. She didn't dare relax until she was in her car.

As she backed out carefully, she heard the faint sound of sleigh bells and stepped on the brake. Looking around, trying to spot the source of the unusual sound, she spotted Nate leading Buttercup toward the lot, dragging a small sled with an evergreen tree tied to it behind her. A smiling couple walked on the other side of Buttercup, and two small, well-bundled-up children straddled her. Camille had to laugh at the way their little legs stuck straight out to the sides as they rode on her broad back.

It was such a perfect Christmas-card moment. Growing up, Camille's grandma had put up an artificial, two-foot-tall tree every year. After she died, Camille hadn't bothered with a tree, being too busy with Christmas orders. Besides, seeing her grandma's tree—as small and fake as it was—hurt too much. The holidays were painful and lonely enough. She didn't need any reminders of when she'd had someone who loved her.

Seeing this family, so happy and excited, made a tiny, hollow part of her ache. Those kids would never forget this visit to the ranch, and it would most likely become both a joyful memory and a yearly tradition. Camille rubbed her chest absently, watching until they arrived at the edge of the lot and Nate reached up to help the kids slide off Buttercup's back.

Shaking off her distraction, Camille let the Buick roll forward down the driveway. *Silly*, she told herself. Why was she feeling nostalgic for something she'd never experienced? There was something about the ranch that brought her emotions, usually so neatly tucked away deep inside her, to the surface. It was aggravating and uncomfortable, and she decided to do her best to stay in her workshop where she belonged.

Despite her resolution, she let her gaze stray to the rearview mirror—wanting to catch a final glimpse of that happy holiday scene—and did her best not to think of all the things she would never get to have.

CHAPTER 3

"WHAT ARE YOU DOING?" RYAN DEMANDED ONCE CAMILLE
had escaped from the workshop.

Steve's eyebrows pulled together in confusion at his
brother's confrontational tone. "What?"

"Quit trying to poach." Ryan stalked closer, looking
honestly annoyed, which made Steve even more baffled.

"Poach? What are you talking about?"

"Camille. I call dibs, so back off."

Oh. He'd hoped that he'd misread Ryan's intentions,
but it looked like they were back to that same old one-
upmanship. At least there were no more football games
or athletic scholarships left to get *Nate's* competitive
spirit flaring. "I hate to break it to you, Ry, but you can't
call dibs on a person. Besides, Camille's not interested.
She pretty much ran out of here." He left out the part
about her slamming the door in Ryan's face, not wanting
to kick his brother while he was down. It was refreshing,
though, to see there was at least one woman immune to
Ryan's charm, especially since that woman was Camille
Brandt, who seemed to have grown from a sweet, shy,
awkward teen into a sweet, shy, gorgeous adult.

She wasn't *just* beautiful, though. She had a way of
listening carefully before saying exactly what someone
needed to hear. They'd talked three times since he'd

returned to Borne, and each time, he'd left feeling more optimistic and hopeful than he'd felt in a while. Shaking off his thoughts, he realized that his brother was glaring at him.

"That's just how she is," Ryan said. "She's shy and easily overwhelmed by male attention."

Steve had to bite his cheek to keep from snorting. Sure, Camille was timid, but that just made her flat refusal to have lunch with Ryan more obvious. There was absolutely no sign that she was interested in him. "Okay, Ry." Feeling a little bad for his clueless, rejected brother, he reached out to give Ryan's arm a gentle pat. "I'm going to relieve Will so he can take a break."

"You don't believe me, but you'll see," Ryan called after him as Steve headed for the door. "You're not going to win this one. She'll be mine by Christmas."

There was no point arguing *once again* that women weren't prizes to be won. Steve just raised his hand in a wave. As he followed the path to the store, he shook his head. He was going to enjoy watching Camille give Ryan his first-ever smackdown. As much as he loved his brother, Ryan had it coming.

"Dad!"

Steve stopped and turned to see Maya running up to him. "Hey, Maya."

She caught his hand in both of hers, making him smile as she always did. "How do you feel about riding?"

"Now?" When she nodded, bouncing on her toes until it became a whole-body movement, he motioned toward the shop. "Will needs a break. How about you work in the store with me for a half hour, and then we'll go for a ride."

"Okay." Still holding on to his hand, she fell in next to him as they walked toward the gift shop.

"Have you seen Micah since breakfast?" he asked when the snow horse caught his eye.

"Nope. It's Saturday, though. There're too many customers around, so he's probably hiding out with Uncle Joe."

Steve made a sound of agreement, even as an old worry flared to life. Lately, he'd been a little preoccupied with Zoe's experiments, but he was also concerned about Micah. Thirteen was very young to turn into a hermit, but Micah seemed to be pretty far down that road already. Steve wondered if the two moves in two years had traumatized the kids. There hadn't been much of a choice in the matter, though. Both places they'd lived before—Simpson and then Monroe—had become too dangerous to raise his family there. He'd felt trapped between keeping his kids safe and keeping them happy, and he'd chosen the first. It wasn't that he regretted his choice now, but he wished his kids still felt like they could talk to him as they used to.

"Are you happy here?" he asked Maya abruptly.

Tilting her head in thought, she didn't look put off by the out-of-the-blue question. "Yes. I miss my friends from Simpson sometimes, and the firefighters who used to babysit us, but this is the best place we've lived. I like having all my uncles around."

"Me, too." Until he moved back to the ranch, he hadn't realized how alone he'd felt, especially in Monroe. As newcomers, they hadn't had the same type of support system as they'd had in Simpson, where they'd lived for more than a decade. Although his brothers drove him crazy sometimes, they were family, and they loved the kids. It was good being home. "I'm glad you like it here. I know moving so much has been hard."

"A little, but it wasn't like we had a choice, not if we wanted to be safe." For a moment, she sounded like she was a forty-year-old speaking out of her ten-year-old mouth, and Steve gave her a sideways glance. She quickly reverted to her usual self. "I mean, Monroe pretty much blew up. A lot worse than Zoe's explosions, even."

As he held the gift shop door open for her, Steve felt the urge to laugh and cringe at the same time. She wasn't wrong.

The store was crowded with shoppers, and Steve nodded politely to them as he followed Maya to the register.

"Hey, Dad, Maya, check out Camille's metal art in the window," Will called as he rang up a wreath a man was buying. "Three sold already, but I took pictures of all of them first."

"Who's Camille?" Maya asked as she obediently headed toward the display.

"An artist who knew Dad and the uncles when they were kids," Will answered. "She said she has stories, but Uncle Ryan dragged her out of here before she could tell me any."

Stories? Steve thought as he followed Maya to the deep shelf in front of the bay window. Will's interest in Camille's work made Steve even more curious. Although Will enjoyed working in the store, it was mainly because he liked talking to people and getting paid for it. Normally, he was fairly uninterested in the store's contents, so for him to comment on Camille's sculptures was unusual. Will's theory was that one ornament or wreath or figurine was no different from the next. Steve wanted to see the artwork for another reason, too. After his most recent encounters with Camille, he found he was more than a little interested in the way her mind worked.

As soon as he saw the sculptures, Steve smiled. They were completely different from what he'd imagined, but absolutely perfect. Camille's personality radiated from both of the two remaining pieces: a mare and foal, and an angel. He recognized some of the parts from their original forms—delicate-looking gears and a piece of quarter-inch copper pipe and a small gasket—but she'd combined them in a way that was beautiful and expressive.

"Whoa," Maya breathed, reaching out to touch the edge of the angel's wing. "I *like* these. She took everything that's supposed to be plain and ugly and made it pretty."

Steve crouched down to get a closer look at the mare and foal, amazed at the delicacy of a piece made out of metal scrap. "They're pretty incredible, aren't they? I wonder if Micah's seen these yet."

"He's going to love the horses," Maya said, echoing Steve's thoughts. He picked up the sculpture without even bothering to look at the price tag, knowing that the cost wouldn't make a difference. He wanted the piece and knew that he'd kick himself if he didn't grab it before someone else did. The idea of having something so beautiful—especially since it had come from Camille's imagination and artistic hands—made him feel warm inside.

"Should we get this one?" Steve asked Maya, even though he'd already decided the horses were his. She enthusiastically nodded. Giving the angel a final awed touch, Maya bounced toward the register where Will was waiting.

"We're getting the horses!" she called out to him, and Will grinned.

"Good." Taking the piece from Steve, he slipped it into a cloth bag and placed it in a box well lined with shredded paper. "That was my favorite, and Micah's going to go nuts over it."

"That's what I said, too!" Maya bent closer to the patterned bag that encased the sculpture. "Are those robots printed on there?"

Steve leaned in, and sure enough, the fabric was covered in cartoon robots. A wide grin stretched his cheeks. That detail seemed so perfectly Camille.

"Yep." Will was the one who answered.

"Nice." Maya gave the bag an impressed look before Will closed the box. "I call dibs on the robot bag after we take the horses out of the box."

Steve didn't want to fight his daughter for the bag, but he was getting more and more intrigued by the artist herself. He wished Ryan wasn't playing his usual game. He didn't want to fight over Camille as though she were a bone and they were two hungry dogs. She deserved more than that—much more.

"Take a break," Steve said when Will finished tying up the box with twine twisted together with green ribbon.

"Great. I'm *staaarving*." He drew out the last word dramatically, and Maya giggled. Even Steve smiled a little, feeling slightly more effervescent than usual. He tried to pretend that he didn't know why that was and handed the newly packed box to Will.

"Mind taking this to the house?" he asked. "Micah can open it tonight, since he hasn't seen it yet. I bet Zoe will be impressed, too."

"Either impressed, or she'll think it's a major waste of perfectly good engine parts," Will said, holding the box under his left arm as he scribbled the hours he'd worked that morning onto his tally sheet with his right hand. It was their low-tech version of clocking out.

"You done for the day, then?" Steve asked. "Who's working this afternoon?" He hoped he didn't get roped into it. Not only did he and Maya have a ride planned, but he was only good in the store for about half an hour before all his customer-service skills dramatically declined. Besides, his ribbon curls were sadly subpar.

"Zoe. She wants to earn some money for Christmas presents."

"Not alone she's not."

"Uncle Nate said he'll do paperwork in the office, in case she needs backup." Will nodded toward the closet-sized room at the back of the store that barely fit a desk and chair.

"On a Saturday afternoon? It's our busiest time. She'll be swamped. What about Ryan?"

"He'll be on tree and Buttercup duty." There was an amused note in Will's voice. Everyone knew that Ryan's least favorite job was following customers around as they picked the perfect tree. Steve sighed, not even asking about Joe or Micah. There was no way either of those two would come into the store while it was open.

"Maya, I'm sorry, but we're going to need to put off our ride until tomorrow morning after church."

Although she looked disappointed, she didn't argue. "That's okay."

Putting an arm around her shoulders, he squeezed her against his side. "Thank you, Maya."

She leaned in to him for a moment before skipping away to reorganize the messy pine-bough display. Turning back to Will, Steve asked, "What are you planning for this afternoon?"

"Homework." He laughed at Steve's startled expression. "That was the deal, remember? If I want to go with Connor's family to the Avalanche game in Denver tomorrow, I need to have everything ready for Monday before I leave."

"Right." Steve gave himself a mental shake. Now that the kids were getting older, their schedules were getting busier. Between keeping up with their activities, working at the ranch, and starting with the Borne fire department, he struggled to stay on top of everything. "Good. Go ahead then."

As he watched Will head for the door, calling out a goodbye to his sister, who waved pine boughs at him in response, Steve wondered how he'd managed to raise such gregarious, cheerful children. He'd always been serious and introverted—like Micah was—and he kept waiting for Will to suffer from teenage angst, but at almost fifteen, Will continued to be blissfully sunny. Steve hadn't expected his kids to turn out so brilliant and talented and...well, complicated, either. Rearing them had become something of a minefield as he tried to encourage them while dodging hurt feelings and sudden mood changes and—with Zoe—literal explosions.

"Do you have any more of these?" an elderly woman asked, holding up Camille's metal angel. "I want to get these for my daughters, but I only see the one."

"That's the last one, but the artist will be making more." The reminder that Camille would be coming out to the ranch with another delivery brightened his mood. His impatience to see her again surprised him. It had been a long time since he'd been this interested in a woman, and the realization both excited and concerned him. He wouldn't be the only one affected if things didn't work out. The kids had already experienced too much loss in their lives, and he didn't want to set them up for more.

"When will they be coming in?" the woman asked, pulling him out of his thoughts.

"Soon, hopefully." Despite the Ryan issue, Steve really did hope Camille would return soon. The last thing he needed was another complication in his life, but his heart wasn't listening to reason. He was already much too eager to see her again.

CHAPTER 4

CAMILLE GLARED AT THE PARTIALLY FINISHED PIECE ON HER workbench. "I hate to tell you this, but you are hideous."

The metal horse stared back…well, with one eye, at least. The other, a repurposed bolt, wandered off in the other direction. It was just one of the things wrong about her latest attempt at sculpting—one of very, very many things. Its head was cocked in a way more reminiscent of a terrier than a draft horse, and its body twisted awkwardly to the side. She couldn't even look at what was supposed to be the two children on its back. They looked like vicious elves from a twisted fairy tale, riding a lopsided beast.

The piece was the furthest thing she could imagine from the idyllic scene she had in her mind. Ever since she'd watched Buttercup carrying the two adorable kids through the snow, dragging a tree behind her, Camille had wanted to recreate that feeling of Christmassy goodness and wonder. This, though, was just scary and awful and monstrous and…no. *Nope. Nope. Nope.*

"I need a break."

She charged out of the workshop and burst through the door, startling Lucy into bolting from the kitchen.

"Sorry, LuLu," she called after the cat, knowing that Lucy was headed to her favorite hiding spot—the top shelf of the bookcase in Camille's bedroom. Guilt eased her frustration, and she felt more mopey than angry by the time she plopped down on the couch with a container of peanut-butter blossoms in her lap. "I really shouldn't be eating you for lunch." She glanced at the clock and blinked, shocked at how much time she'd wasted. "Or dinner, I guess."

After regarding the cookie in her hand thoughtfully for a moment, she took a bite and shrugged. Once she was finished with Christmas orders, she'd have time to do things like cook nutritious meals and grocery shop for more ingredients than a single bag of chocolate stars. She glanced around the kitchen and winced, mentally adding housecleaning to her post-Christmas to-do list.

A knock on the front door made her freeze, cookie halfway to her mouth. Her first instinct was to go perfectly still, like a deer faced with a hunter. Her next thought was to hide, but she knew it was too late. The couch—and Camille—was in the direct line of sight of anyone standing at the front door, and she could see Mrs. Lin peering through the window. Camille had already been spotted. Hiding was useless at this point. Swallowing a groan, she returned the cookie to the container and pushed to her feet. As she headed for the door, giving Mrs. Lin a wave and a forced smile, she vowed to stay in the kitchen next time, where she could hide from any well-meaning neighbors all day, if she had to.

"Mrs. Lin," she said, opening the door. "Hi."

"Camille. I brought an assortment of cookies." Mrs. Lin stepped forward, using the tin of cookies in her hands like a battering ram, forcing Camille to step back before she got knocked over. A moment later, when Mrs. Lin was inside the house, looking around disapprovingly, Camille wished she'd held her ground.

"That was...nice of you," she said lamely, closing the door. As much as she wished that Mrs. Lin would hand over the cookies and leave, she knew from bitter experience that wouldn't be the case.

"Didn't your grandmother teach you how to run a vacuum?" Mrs. Lin asked, *tsk*ing as she took in the state of the room.

"Yes, she did," Camille said on a sigh. "This is my busy season, though, so I get a little...behind." She swiped at the dust that had gathered on her stained-glass lamp. The clean streak left by her fingers just made the rest of the lampshade look dirtier.

"Busy season? People buy those things you make for Christmas? For gifts?" From her tone, it was obvious that Mrs. Lin couldn't imagine who hated their friends and family enough to do that.

"They do, actually." *Be nice to the elderly lady*, she reminded herself. Mrs. Lin and her grandma had been the very definition of frenemies. After her grandma's death, Mrs. Lin had seemed lost, losing her sharp wit and even sharper tongue. It was just in the past few years that Mrs. Lin had seemed to rally, starting up a competitive rivalry with Mrs. Murphy, the owner of Borne Market. Camille still felt a sense of relief along with her irritation at Mrs. Lin's trademark feistiness, since she'd been worried the woman would never recover.

Mrs. Lin *tsk*ed again. It was one of her favorite sounds, Camille had discovered, along with loud, martyred sighs. "People throw their money away on the craziest things. Did you know they have spas for dogs now? Spas." She shook her head. "For dogs."

"I suppose that's good for my business," Camille said, trying to joke. Working on the hell beast of a sculpture looked wonderful now, compared to a long chat with Mrs. Lin, who gave her a sharp look as she handed Camille her coat.

"You're going to start a dog spa? Oh, no. That's not happening. The zoning is all wrong. Who wants to live next to all that barking? You're starting one of those dog spas over my dead body, missy!"

"No," Camille said faintly. "I meant my art business…" When Mrs. Lin's glare didn't lighten, Camille let it go. "Would you like some tea?"

"I don't know. Is the kitchen as much of a mess as this room?"

Yes, Camille thought but figured it was wiser to keep her mouth shut. Besides, Mrs. Lin was marching toward the kitchen, so she'd soon see for herself anyway.

"Oh my heavens, this is terrible!"

With another deep sigh, Camille hung Mrs. Lin's coat in the hall closet, debating whether it would be smart to hide in there with it. She decided to be brave and join Mrs. Lin in the kitchen, where she was huffing and puffing so much that Camille wanted to make a *Three Little Pigs* joke.

"Your grandmother must be rolling over in her grave when she looks down from heaven and sees what you've done to her house." Despite her complaints, Mrs. Lin settled at the table, not protesting when Camille filled the kettle with water to make tea. Apparently, the kitchen was not enough of a disaster to make Mrs. Lin want to leave. As she retrieved two teacups, Camille made a mental note to work on that. Perhaps if it was *really* messy, Mrs. Lin would run screaming and never visit again. Camille ducked her head to hide her smile at that thought.

"How's Xavier?" she asked, knowing that mentioning Mrs. Lin's grandson was her best chance of turning the conversation away from ways that Camille was a disappointment to her departed grandma.

"He's excellent and made the varsity basketball team this year, but I'm not here to talk about him."

"You're not?" Camille asked, handing Mrs. Lin a cup of tea. She was curious in spite of herself, unable to remember a time when mentioning Xavier didn't bring an hour-long recitation of his accomplishments.

"Of course not." She took a sip of tea as Camille waited to hear what was more urgent than Mrs. Lin's grandson. "Where did you put those cookies I brought for you?"

Camille went to retrieve both Mrs. Lin's tin and the peanut-butter blossoms from the living room, hurrying to stuff in her mouth the remains of the cookie she'd been eating when Mrs. Lin arrived. Chewing quickly, she slowly made her way back into the kitchen, swallowing the evidence before she returned to place both containers on the table in front of Mrs. Lin. From the suspicious glance the woman sent her, Camille wondered if she knew about the half-eaten cookie anyway. Mrs. Lin always seemed to know everything.

"What I wanted to discuss with you," the older woman said after selecting a cookie, "are the bad habits I'm seeing you fall into."

Camille's hand stopped in midair, hovering over the cookies. *Bad habits?* The only bad habits she could think of were eating too much sugar and hiding—or trying to hide, in Mrs. Lin's case—from visitors. Neither seemed worthy of an intervention. Even if it did have something to do with her love for sweets, she defiantly picked up a cookie anyway. She was well aware that tiny Mrs. Lin could put away a whole tin of them, and she wanted to snag a mini pecan pie before they were gone.

"Bad habits?" Camille asked before shoving the entire thing into her mouth. Mrs. Lin's bitterness was in no way reflected in her baking, and Camille felt like she should get at least *one* good thing out of this sure-to-be-unpleasant visit.

Mrs. Lin pinned her with a sharp gaze over her teacup. "Don't play innocent with me, missy."

"Sorry, Mrs. Lin." Camille took another mini pecan pie. "I have no idea what bad habits you're talking about. These tiny pies are excellent, by the way."

"Don't eat too many. That shirt is awfully tight as it is."

Glancing down at her front, Camille saw that her mostly unbuttoned flannel overshirt was gaping open, showing the one beneath. "It's long underwear," she said, not too concerned by Mrs. Lin's critique. After all, the only people who'd see it were the two of them. "It's supposed to be tight."

Mrs. Lin let out a small huff that managed to convey all her disdain in one wordless sound. "Well, your revealing attire is not helping with your situation."

"My situation?" She reached for a third mini pie, but Mrs. Lin slapped her hand away, so Camille settled back to drink her tea. She was starting to feel a little queasy from all the sugar anyway.

"Don't think I haven't noticed all the men hanging out around here lately."

Camille blinked. That was not what she'd expected Mrs. Lin to say. Not at all. "I'm sorry... What?"

"All of your men." Mrs. Lin raised her voice and enunciated each word carefully.

"I heard you the first time." Camille wondered if this was a sign that her elderly neighbor was suffering from dementia. There hadn't been any other indications, though. "I'm just confused. What men are you talking about?"

"Gladys Murphy said you'd deny it." She *tsk*ed yet again, and Camille resisted the urge to throw a cookie. This was one of the most frustrating conversations she'd ever had with Mrs. Lin, and that was saying a lot. "As Dr. Beacon always says on his show, the first step toward getting better is admitting you have a problem."

"A...man problem?" Dementia was seeming more and more likely. "And since when are you and Mrs. Murphy agreeing on anything?"

"Since you've turned your grandmother's lovely home into a brothel."

"A brothel? I'm not only having sex with a bunch of imaginary men, but I'm charging for it, too?" The total ridiculousness of the conversation hit her, and she fought the urge to laugh. "I promise you, Mrs. Lin, that this house has more in common with a convent than it does a brothel." *Unfortunately*.

"Don't lie to me, missy." Mrs. Lin shook a piece of

shortbread at Camille before taking an angry bite. There was a stiff silence until she finished chewing. "I've seen these men with my own eyes."

"That's impossible, because there are no men."

Delicately brushing the crumbs off her fingers, Mrs. Lin reached into her handbag and pulled out her phone and a pair of reading glasses. "I have photographic evidence," she said, setting the glasses on her nose and tapping at the screen.

Getting up, Camille moved around the table to look at the phone over Mrs. Lin's shoulder. "Let's see this parade of men, then." She was honestly interested in seeing the photos.

"Here's one," Mrs. Lin said triumphantly, thrusting the phone toward Camille's face. Pulling back a little so she didn't get smacked in the nose, Camille peered at the screen. The picture was indeed a man, standing by her workshop door.

"That's Ryan Springfield," she said, taking her seat again, feeling a little disappointed in the anticlimax. For a second, Camille had almost thought that Mrs. Lin would have evidence proving that Camille's life was just a touch more fascinating than it actually was. Ryan Springfield's visit, however, was not the least bit interesting. "He sold me some barn wood."

"Is that what you're calling it?" Mrs. Lin said archly, her eyes on her phone as she flipped through pictures.

"Is that what I'm calling him selling me barn wood?" Camille was confused again.

Instead of answering, Mrs. Lin thrust the phone toward her, screen out. "You invited him in."

Camille glanced at the picture of Ryan stepping into

the shop, and she thought how strange it was that her neighbor had been taking pictures of this banal meeting. If Camille had known at the time that she and Ryan were being photographed, it might've made the whole affair more interesting. After considering that for a moment, she gave a small shake of her head. All knowing would've done was make her more self-conscious.

She realized that while she'd been silently lost in her thoughts, Mrs. Lin had been waiting for an answer. "Well?"

"Well, what?" Sitting back in her chair, Camille took a sip, making a face when she realized her tea was lukewarm. "Should I have made him stand in the open doorway while we talked? My workshop's heated. That would've been a waste of energy."

With another one of her expressive huffs, Mrs. Lin began swiping through the pictures on her phone again. "You're being intentionally obtuse. It wouldn't have taken thirty-seven minutes for Ryan Springfield to sell you some barn wood. That's a ridiculous excuse, anyway. What would you even *do* with barn wood? You barely have a yard, much less room for a barn."

Camille couldn't decide which completely insane point to argue first. "You timed us? Why?"

Peering at her over the top of her reading glasses, Mrs. Lin said, "Well, someone needs to pay attention to what shenanigans go on in this neighborhood. I promised your grandmother that I'd watch out for you after she was gone, and she would not have approved of this at all." She waved her phone at Camille as if exhibiting evidence. "What about *this* man?"

This time, Camille didn't bother to get up and move

behind Mrs. Lin to see the picture. Instead, she just leaned forward and squinted at the screen. As soon as she recognized the subject of the photo, she sat back to sip her now-cold tea. "That's the mailman."

"We don't have a mail*man*," Mrs. Lin said in a *gotcha* tone. "The very female Gloria Hunn delivers our mail."

The urge to laugh built up inside Camille again. "Gloria has to have an occasional day off. He's got to be her temporary replacement." By the way Mrs. Lin's mouth puckered, Camille got the impression that she didn't like that very reasonable explanation, and an amused snort escaped. "He's in uniform! Did you think I got a stripper-gram?"

From the judgmental look Mrs. Lin gave her, it seemed that a stripper-gram was more likely to her than a postal worker needing a vacation. "Well, you do seem to…enjoy a man in uniform," Ms. Lin said, holding out her phone again.

Camille leaned across the table. "What is that? It's too dark to see anything."

"Come closer," Mrs. Lin demanded. Repressing the urge to roll her eyes, Camille took up her earlier position behind her neighbor and peered at the phone. The picture had obviously been taken at night, but now she could make out the shape of a person standing by her front door. The brightest parts of the photo were what appeared to be reflective strips on the heavy coat.

"Who is that?" Camille asked, reaching to zoom in.

"A fireman, judging by what he's wearing," Mrs. Lin said. "Yet another man, standing on your porch."

Although she racked her brain, Camille couldn't recall anyone coming to her front door after dark, especially not a firefighter. She definitely would've remembered that. "When did you take this?"

"Just a few days ago." Mrs. Lin sounded triumphant that she'd managed to finally catch Camille's attention.

"Huh." For the last month, she'd been working in her shop until late, so maybe she'd missed the knock. Why would a fireman show up on her porch, though? Her brain immediately went to Steve Springfield, but she dismissed that option as wishful thinking. "Who is it?"

"There wasn't enough light to make out his face," Mrs. Lin said, disappointed. "With that bulky coat on, he could be any one of the Borne firefighters—except for Rose Marie Mackenzie, of course." She tilted her phone to get a better look at the photo. "She's just an itty-bitty thing. Stubborn as all get-out, though. I always said she only wanted to become a firefighter because someone told her she couldn't."

"Or she just wanted to be a firefighter, so she did that, despite what anyone else said," Camille said absently, her eyes still on the photo. "You're right, though. That's not Rose Marie." There was something eerie about the figure, the hulking form silhouetted against the familiar shape of her front door. It was dark enough that everything except the distinctive reflective strips was in shadow, making the figure look menacing. Camille repressed a shiver. "Maybe someone stopped by to sell tickets to their annual fund-raising dinner." That had to be what it was…right?

"Ten months before the event?" Mrs. Lin responded doubtfully. "Don't try to spin this, missy. Dr. Beacon always says—"

"—admitting I have a man problem is the first step.

Right." She knew she was going to get scolded for not taking Mrs. Lin seriously enough, but her attention was still focused on the photo. She wasn't sure why it bothered her so much. As she'd told Mrs. Lin, he'd probably been fund-raising or checking to make sure she had batteries in her smoke alarms or to let her know about a meth lab in the area or *something* innocuous—well, as innocuous as a meth lab could be. For whatever reason, though, she couldn't tear her eyes away from that dark picture.

"Don't be flippant." Mrs. Lin's reprimand sounded half-hearted, and Camille wondered if her neighbor had felt the same shiver going down her spine.

"Did I answer the door?" Camille asked, knowing that she hadn't, but needing to ask. After all, Mrs. Lin had a picture of some random firefighter standing on her porch at night. Maybe she also had a photo on that phone of Camille opening the door to him.

"No." Mrs. Lin sounded disappointed, but Camille was hugely relieved. She'd started doubting reality for a moment. "Not that time."

"Not that time?" The words jerked Camille out of her contemplation of the dark, eerie picture. "There was no other time." Mrs. Lin raised one overplucked eyebrow, and Camille amended her statement. "Fine, I let Ryan in, but that was an energy-saving issue, and absolutely nothing scandalous happened." When Mrs. Lin just pursed her lips again, Camille returned to her seat and rebelliously grabbed a sugar cookie from the tin. "Was that it? Any other men?"

Mrs. Lin brushed at invisible crumbs. "Not that I took pictures of," she finally admitted.

"So, a substitute mailman, a barn-wood salesman,

and a mysterious and kind of creepy firefighter, two of which I never saw or invited in." And one she'd never, ever date, no matter what he seemed to think.

"You might twist things around with your excuses," Mrs. Lin said, "and I might not have any definitive evidence yet, but mark my words...I'll get those pictures eventually. Then you can try to explain away your behavior, but everyone will know the truth." She smiled slightly—a small, satisfied grin. "Just wait. I asked my daughter-in-law for night-vision binoculars for Christmas. She's still desperate to suck up to me after the potato salad incident, so you know she's getting the most expensive, high-tech binoculars that she can find." Mrs. Lin gave an evil, cackling laugh worthy of the most heinous super-villain, and Camille held back a nervous chuckle.

"If I turn this place into a brothel," she said, "I promise that I will pose for any and all pictures you want to take with your phone or your night-vision binoculars."

Mrs. Lin sat back, crossing her ankles delicately, and Camille noticed that only a few scattered crumbs were left in the cookie tins. She'd sat through an entire crazy conversation with Mrs. Lin and didn't even have any leftover cookies to show for it.

"That does not sound like something I would wish to see," Mrs. Lin said.

Camille sputtered. "You just said—"

"The binoculars will be purely for research purposes. I need to keep an eye on this neighborhood. It's gone downhill ever since the Murphys moved in." Before Camille could address the many things that were wrong with her neighbor's statements—with her entire *visit*—Mrs. Lin gave her a thin, triumphant smile. "My tea has gone cold."

Swallowing a resigned sigh, Camille stood to make more tea.

You'd better appreciate how nice I'm being to your friend, Grandma, she thought as she filled the kettle with water. *I've only had about three homicidal thoughts the entire time.*

"Do you have any more cookies? You've eaten all of the ones I brought."

Okay, four homicidal thoughts.

CHAPTER 5

HE WAITED IN THE DEEP SHADOWS OF THE TREES, THE HOWL-ing wind and creaking branches covering the sound of his breathing as his eyes fixed on the neighbor's bedroom window. At exactly ten, just like every night, Mrs. Lin left her perch and went to bed. Still, he waited. After the window stayed quiet and dark for another half hour, he finally moved, crossing the road and cautiously approaching Camille's house.

The wind whipped at him, plastering his bunker coat against his body and making his eyes water from the cold. He blinked away the moisture, his eyes fixed on the one window—the kitchen, he knew from previous visits—that was illuminated. Even though he was sure she was in her workshop, he still approached the window cautiously, staying in the shadows next to the house and avoiding where the light drew golden rectangles on the snow.

Creeping closer, he eased alongside the window, his heart thumping from the surge of adrenaline. He peeked into her kitchen, relaxing slightly when he saw it was empty except for her cat sitting by the workshop door. Although he'd known she'd still be working, he felt a lurch of disappointment. It was always such a thrill when she was in the house where he could watch her.

The cat stared in his direction, its yellow eyes

narrowing as its ears flattened. He shifted back so the darkness would hide him, not wanting the cat to make noise that would draw Camille's attention. Still, the cat's focus on the window didn't waver as its back arched and its mouth opened in a silent hiss.

He tensed, ready to disappear back into the shadows of the trees, but the workshop door stayed closed. Whatever sound the cat was making wasn't loud enough to draw Camille into the kitchen. Some of his readiness trickled away as he settled in to wait.

Sooner or later, Camille would emerge from her workshop. When she did, he'd be there.

"I'm calling it." Camille picked up the horse sculpture and eyed the two demon riders. "You are officially beyond saving and will always be a monstrosity that no one else should ever be subjected to. Time of death..." She glanced at the clock and winced. "Oof. Two twenty-three. It's past time for bed."

Plunking the sculpture down, she turned off her music and flipped off the light above the workbench. Her spine popped as she stood and stretched out the kinks that came from bending over a piece for way too long. She made a face, thinking of those lost work hours.

"Let it go," she told herself, her voice echoing in the space. "It's a good lesson: Never try to do any work after an hour with Mrs. Lin. The unfurled rage is too obvious." Grabbing the failed horse, she started to toss it into her scrap bin, to be taken apart and the parts reused, but then she hesitated, taking another look at the piece.

There was something about it that made it so awful it was almost…endearing? No, she was just so tired that she was getting punchy. Despite those logical thoughts, she carefully placed the horse and its riders back on the bench, deciding to give it another look in the morning.

"Later in the morning," she said, giving the clock another glance. She needed to find her bed immediately, or she was going to be a wreck when she brought the latest batch of metal sculptures out to the ranch.

She snorted, the sound loud in the silence. Who was she kidding? No matter how much sleep she did or didn't get, she'd be a wreck going out to the ranch. The thought of seeing Steve made her stomach churn with a mixture of anticipation, excitement, and nerves, which she just made worse by thinking of all the possibilities of what might happen if she did see him. There were so many ways she could embarrass herself in his presence, and she was pretty sure her imagination had run through every humiliating scenario at least twice.

"Stop," she told herself firmly as she turned off the overhead lights and let herself into the kitchen. "Everything seems scarier in the wee hours. It'll be fine." If she let herself daydream about possible future encounters with Steve, she'd just get worked up and she'd never sleep.

A meow pulled her out of her circling, anxiety-producing thoughts, and she glanced down to see Lucy doing figure eights around her ankles. "Hey, LuLu. Did I forget to feed you tonight?"

A plaintive mew answered in the affirmative, although Camille wasn't too concerned. After all, Lucy had four meals a day, so waiting an extra few hours for her bedtime snack wouldn't hurt her, no matter how much Lucy thought it would. After she fed the cat, Camille headed upstairs, debating whether she was too tired to shower. As she moved to turn on the bedroom light, she hesitated, remembering Mrs. Lin's photos. Her neighbor might not have her night-vision binoculars yet, but she surely had the regular kind.

Camille could picture her neighbor cozily snuggled into a comfortable chair by the window, using binoculars to peer through the cracks between the closed blinds into her bedroom. With a groan, she left the light off, making a mental note to buy heavy curtains for every window that faced Mrs. Lin's house.

"It isn't like I have much of a life to spy on," she grumbled, using the faint moonlight to make her way across the room. The effort was only partially successful, since she banged her leg painfully on the edge of her cast-iron footboard. As she dug in her dresser drawers, trying to find pajamas by feel, she heard a slight rustling on the other side of the room.

She froze, just as the noise stopped. After a good half-minute of holding her breath, she heard the light pattering sound start up again. Trying to stay quiet, Camille slid the dresser drawer closed, pajamas gripped in her hand, and tiptoed across the room. The ancient wood floor betrayed her, creaking loudly, and she went still.

It took longer this time for the sound to start up again. When it did, it was in the other corner of the room, close to the floor. Camille had a sneaking suspicion that she knew what it was, and she moved toward the door, fumbling for the light switch. She flicked it on, not caring if Mrs. Lin saw her. If she was going to stalk a mouse, she needed to be able to see, even if that meant she'd be Mrs. Lin's entertainment for the night.

Camille stared at the corner where she'd last heard the noise, but there was nothing there now. As she waited for the rodent to either show itself or make some sound, Lucy padded into the room.

"You've been slacking on the job, LuLu," Camille said, but the cat ignored her and jumped on the bed. "You're just lucky I'm a lenient boss, or I'd write you up for this." Curling up into a ball, Lucy closed her eyes, apparently not concerned about their small, furry, probably pestilence-carrying roommates. After a few minutes when the mouse didn't bother to reappear, Camille headed for the bathroom.

This is why I should be living in a condo in LoDo Denver, rather than a hundred-year-old house in Borne, she thought as she turned on the shower, stripping as she waited for her ancient water heater to deliver. *No mice, new appliances, no nosy Mrs. Lin as a neighbor...* It sounded heavenly.

No workshop, no Springfield ranch, no more Steve... That didn't sound as fun. Despite the anxiety that flared to life at even the thought of an encounter with Steve Springfield, the idea of not running into him during her visit the next day made her feel flat and let down.

She shook her head. "You're a mess, Camille Brandt...worse than that atrocious horse sculpture." After a moment, she made a face. "No, nothing else is that big of a mess."

Sick of obsessing about Steve, she stepped into the shower, even though the water hadn't fully warmed yet. She flinched as the chilly spray hit her, but she figured it was for the best. Ever since she'd encountered Steve in the grocery store, she'd been in fairly constant need of a cold shower.

After her shower, she dried off and put on the pajamas before wrapping her wet hair in a towel. As she padded toward her bedroom, a light scratching sound made her huff an exasperated breath.

"It's like the mice know that Lucy's lazy and I'm too softhearted to set traps." Maybe she'd get some humane traps and release the mice she caught in the scrapyard. There were plenty of good hiding spots for a mouse there.

In her room, she paused, listening. The *scritch*ing sound came again, but it wasn't coming from her bedroom. Frowning, she followed the faint noise downstairs. At the bottom of the stairs, she reached for the light switch and then paused. It wasn't just the thought of Mrs. Lin peering in through the windows that made her leave the living room in darkness. *Anyone* could be watching. The memory of Mrs. Lin's picture, that menacing figure standing on her porch, ran through her mind, and she felt goose bumps lift on her arms.

The sound came again, making her jump. She laughed at herself for being so easily scared, but even her huff of amusement came out shaky. Trying to force away her nervousness, she crossed the living room, ignoring the shadows that pooled around her furniture, creating dark hiding places for all sorts of bogeymen.

"Stop it," she muttered, pausing again to listen. The noise was close. She moved toward the window, reaching for the string to open the blinds. Her hand trembled on the cord, and she tried to mock her fear, but it didn't help. She still didn't want to look out into the dark night.

Gritting her teeth, she gave the cord a sharp pull. A pale shape appeared right in front of her, flashing across the glass when she jerked back in fear. Her heart pounded loudly in her ears, and her breath froze in her chest as she forced herself closer to the window. It wasn't until she peered into the empty darkness outside that she realized that she'd been startled by her own reflection in the glass.

Giving a nervous huff of a laugh, she leaned closer, trying to see outside. A part of her wished that she'd just assumed the sound had been a mouse. If she'd done that, she'd already be in bed, not scaring herself silly for no reason.

The scratching sound came again, and she saw the evergreen branch that was brushing against the window. All the air inside her came rushing out in one long exhale.

"Stupid," she said, feeling almost light-headed with relief. "Scared by a tree branch."

She started closing the blinds again, but then paused when she saw an odd smudge on the outside of the glass. Curious, she tugged the blinds back open just in time to see the last of the smudge disappear.

"That's weird." Leaning in, Camille peered more closely at the spot where the smudge had been, but nothing was there. Her breath fogged the glass, making it harder to see, and she gave up trying to figure out what the magically disappearing mark had been. Her imagination was apparently working overtime tonight.

As she moved away from the glass, the condensation from her breath quickly evaporated. She froze, staring at the spot. That was exactly what the smudge—on the *outside* of the window—had looked like. As the image of someone standing outside her window, so close that their breath fogged the glass, ran through her mind, she jerked on the string, abruptly closing the blinds.

"You're just freaking yourself out," she said firmly. "It was from your breath on the inside of the glass. There's no random monster outside breathing on your windows. Go to bed."

Despite how much she knew her practical side was right, she still had a hard time falling asleep that night.

"Camille!"

Steve's shout made her turn around, clutching her box of sculptures to her chest. It really wasn't fair. She'd braced herself for seeing him, for possibly running into him in the store or in the tree lot, but this… How was she supposed to keep herself together when he was like *this*?

He was riding a leggy bay gelding through the snow with the easy grace of someone who'd been tossed up onto a horse before he could walk. His face was flushed from the cold, and he had a wide, welcoming smile that made Camille a little dazed. He just looked so happy and rugged and *warm*, and her stomach was doing a loopy little flip at the sight of him.

"Hi! You're Camille? You knew my dad when you were kids? Will said you're going to tell us *stories* about him."

The barrage of questions yanked Camille's attention away from the vision that was Steve and onto his riding companion, a girl who looked to be about ten. She was mounted on the fuzziest, cutest gray pony that Camille had ever seen. Trotting alongside the pair was a large, shaggy mixed-breed dog, his tongue hanging out and snow balled in his fur all the way up to his belly. Behind him was a...goat?

"Yes, I'm Camille. Are you riding with a goat?"

"That's Maybelle." Despite her darker hair and more pointed features, the girl clearly shared genes with Steve and Zoe. "She thinks she's a dog, so she likes to go on walks with us."

As if giving a demonstration, Maybelle bounced over to the shaggy dog and bumped into him, clearly trying to get him to play. The dog, however, was too busy sniffing at Camille's boots to do more than give the goat an absent wave of his tail in response.

Shifting the box to her hip, Camille offered her hand to the dog and then scratched his neck. He leaned in to her and groaned in appreciation.

"Let me get that," Steve said, dismounting with relaxed ease—impressive, since his horse's back was almost taller than she was. As he led his horse across the lot, she noticed something.

"You ride English?" she asked. That didn't really fit the Colorado cowboy image she always had of the Springfield men. The girl appeared to be sitting in a jumping saddle as well.

Steve gave a half shrug as he patted his horse's neck. "I go back and forth. Freddy here goes better in English tack."

"He used to only ride Western," the girl said, hopping off her pony. "I wanted to learn how to jump, but the other kids I used to ride with made fun of me, since they all rode Western, so I told my dad I was thinking about quitting. He told me he'd start taking lessons with me if I stuck with it. When my dad started riding English, all the other kids shut up about it, because no one would dare to make fun of him." She grinned at Camille. "Since he's really big."

Camille glanced at Steve—who appeared just a little more flushed now than he had a minute earlier—and then back at his daughter. "I think you have a very kind dad."

"Yeah, I like him," the girl said, making Camille laugh.

"Can you please take Freddy back to the barn with you?" Steve asked. He was definitely redder than could be attributed to just the cold air.

"Sure." The girl hopped back onto her pony, and Steve handed her Freddy's reins before taking Camille's box. Although it was nice not to be holding the heavy weight, Camille missed having it as a barrier. She felt a little exposed without it. "You can't leave until I get back to the store, though," the girl said to Camille. "I have lots of questions for you."

Leaving Camille wondering what sort of questions she had and if she should be worried about the upcoming interrogation, the girl turned her pony toward the barn, Freddy walking politely next to them. The goat and dog took off ahead, running toward the barn.

"That was Maya," Steve said, bringing her attention back to him.

"She's not shy," Camille said. "I wish I'd been more like that at…ten?"

"Yeah, she's ten, and you're right… There's not a shy bone in her body." He held the box in one arm and waved her ahead of him toward the gift-shop entrance with the other. As she walked in front of him toward the door, Camille felt a flash of self-consciousness, knowing that he was watching her. The thought made her move a bit stiffly, and she was grateful for the bulky winter coat that helped to hide her awkwardness.

The problem, she decided, was that Steve had been occupying her thoughts too much. It made her feel like everything she said and each gesture she made might give away that she was a tiny bit obsessed with him, and she had no idea how he felt about her. His poker face was too unreadable for her peace of mind.

She opened the door, and he caught it over her head, holding it for her.

Things like that, she thought, *are making it worse*. He'd always been polite, with ingrained gentlemanly manners. She was worried that she was seeing more in those simple acts than he intended. The problem was that she didn't know how to discover if he was interested in her as more than just a childhood acquaintance turned art vendor. Ryan was obvious to the point of aggravation, but at least Camille knew where she stood with him. She didn't *like* where they stood, but there was no room for misinterpretation, unlike with his brother.

For just a moment, she wished they were back in junior high, when the whole thing could've been settled by a simple passing of notes, but then she immediately retracted her wish. The negatives of junior high had been much more numerous than the positives for her. She liked being an adult much better than being a teenager. There was no way she'd ever want to go back to that misery.

"Hey, Camille!" Will greeted her, his face lighting up with a smile.

"Hi, Will." Relieved to be pulled from her rather depressing thoughts, she moved to the register, noticing with relief that the shop was fairly empty, with just a small family browsing. She'd hoped that Sunday morning would be quieter than Saturday. "You're working again?"

"I had last Sunday off to go to an Avs game, so I wanted to get more hours in before Christmas. I'm saving for a car."

"A car?" She eyed him more closely. Although she wasn't the best at guessing kids' ages, she didn't think he looked sixteen. "Already?"

"I'll be able to get my license in one year, three months, and three weeks," he said, and she tried not to smile. "Zoe and Dad said they'd help me fix a car up, so we can work on it here until I turn sixteen. I can already legally drive on the ranch property."

"What are you thinking about getting?"

His face brightened even more, but before he could tell her, a couple of kids ran over to the register with some candy canes, so he turned to help them.

"What'd you bring us this time?" Steve asked, setting the box carefully on the floor between the front counter and Camille's feet. As he straightened, she expected him to take a step back and put some distance between them, but instead he stayed close enough for her to smell his distinctive scent of peppermint and horse and clean outdoors.

"Uh…I brought some pieces of…um, animals? Just different sculptures of…things?" Her thoughts were completely taken up by his nearness and the way he tipped his head down toward her. As close as he was, it felt like he surrounded her, enveloping her in a bubble of safety and warmth. Her mind blanked, and she was unable to think of a single piece that she'd worked so hard on over the past week. Scrambling for words, she settled for saying, "I'll show you."

Crouching, she tugged open the folded-over cardboard flaps and pulled out a smaller box containing one of the angels Ryan had requested. She looked up, meaning to hand the piece to Steve, but she realized that he'd squatted down next to her. When she raised her head, their faces were just inches apart.

Camille froze. This close, she could see the greenish-brown of his irises and the way his pupils dilated as she stared. Her gaze dropped lower, taking in the fullness of his lower lip, the way his mouth had dropped open the slightest bit, and how his flannel-covered chest beneath his unzipped coat expanded with each breath—faster than she expected. As Camille moved her gaze back to his, she realized that she was breathing just as quickly, her heart pounding hard, as if she'd run all the way from her house to the ranch.

"Let's see the new stuff!" Will's cheerful voice broke through her daze, and she stood abruptly, moving so quickly that she lost her balance. Reaching out, she caught Steve's shoulder, holding on to it as she steadied. When she realized that she'd just grabbed him, she could feel her face warm, and she knew she was most likely turning bright red. He straightened up more slowly, his gaze never leaving hers, and there was the smallest hint of a teasing grin on his face.

She busied herself with taking the angel from the packaging. By the time she set it gently on the counter, she'd regained most of her self-possession and was scolding herself for getting so giddy over such a silly thing. She needed to get ahold of her scattered emotions, throw a bucket of water on the smoldering fire Steve had just lit inside her belly, show them the new pieces, and get the heck off the ranch before she did something stupid.

"This is for the special order," she said, clearing her throat when the words came out huskier than she'd planned.

"Yeah, I took that one," Steve said, pulling out the rest of the smaller boxes and stacking them on the counter for Camille to unpack. Although he sounded perfectly normal, his gaze seemed a bit warmer than usual, making her wonder if the moment maybe *hadn't* been as one-sided as she'd first thought. "Iris Peebles bought the first one, too. They're Christmas gifts for her daughters."

One by one, Camille unwrapped each of the seven pieces, until they were all standing on the counter. Steve and Will examined each carefully, and Camille waited for their verdicts, trying to hide her anxiety. It was always nerve-racking when people viewed her work, but she realized that she was especially on edge when Steve was the one about to give his opinion. As much as she tried to tell herself that it was just one person's viewpoint and that it didn't matter, deep down it really *did* matter to her. It mattered a lot, and she was a little worried about why that was.

"These are incredible," Steve said, not looking away

from the sculpture he was examining closely—a simple abstract of Mary holding baby Jesus. "How you take old bits of metal and make them so beautiful is beyond me."

Relieved warmth flooded through her, and the words she'd been holding back escaped in a rush. "Thank you. I added a candleholder to the back of that one, so the flame would give a sort of halo effect, but I worried that it might be too gimmicky. What do you think?"

He eyed the bracket for the candle before turning the piece around. "I don't think that's gimmicky at all. People will love it."

"This one's my favorite," Will said, holding up a longhorn steer with a string of multicolored lights tangled around his stocky metal body.

"Oh!" That reminded her. She dug through the steer's box and pulled out a battery. "This goes in the spot underneath." Will flipped over the sculpture and inserted the battery. The lights immediately started to glow. "I'm starting to add electrical elements to some of the pieces."

Steve cleared his throat. "Electrical elements? You're being careful, I hope."

"Of course." She waved off his concern. "I'm not doing any wiring. The lights and the connection to the battery are pretty simple, self-contained elements. I promise that nothing I do could electrocute me." She paused and then added, "I'm much more likely to injure myself while welding than by messing with electricity."

"That's not reassuring." Steve's voice had a slight growl to it that Camille found oddly attractive.

Something devilish pushed her to goad him, just a little. Putting on a thoughtful expression, she pressed a finger to her lips as if contemplating a developing idea. It also worked to hold back the smile that wanted to sneak out. "Now that I think about it, fire's really more my element than electricity. Maybe my pieces need more pyrotechnics. I could make a nativity scene that sets off tiny fireworks when the fuse is lit."

"Yes!" Maya joined them in time to catch the last of her teasing suggestion. Glancing around, Camille noticed that the customers had left, so she and Steve's family were the only ones currently in the store. "Do *that*."

"No," Steve said. "Please don't do that. The last thing we need around here is more pyrotechnics."

Camille pretended to ignore him and looked at Maya, giving her a subtle wink. "I could do a whole Fourth of July series. Maybe I could ask Zoe how to maximize the dramatic effect of my explosions."

When Maya started to giggle, Steve's expression relaxed. "Very funny."

"Ooh!" Maya spotted the steer. "You added lights! I like that one the best."

"That's because you like flashy things." The voice was young but had a rough, scratchy edge to it. When Camille turned toward the newcomer, she blinked in surprise. It was like traveling back in time to when she was nine and Steve was thirteen. The kid standing behind Maya, his gaze running over each sculpture, looked just like a young Steve…only crankier. He had to be Micah, the artist. Camille marveled for a moment that Steve had raised these four kids by himself since his wife's death. The idea of being solely responsible for four children was terrifying to Camille. Sometimes, just knowing that it was up to her to keep her cat alive and happy was overwhelming.

"Yeah, I do," Maya responded, not sounding at all offended. "I'd probably like the exploding one the best, if Camille made it."

"Well, I hope she's *not* going to make anything involving explosions, fire, or pyrotechnics," Steve grumbled. "It's exciting enough around here."

As if on cue, Zoe came into the store and headed straight for the counter, her face lighting up when she saw Camille and the new batch of sculptures. "You brought more! I love our horse, but I only saw the pictures Will took of the rest of the ones you dropped off last week. They all sold in one day."

"You made a Maybelle!" Maya had finally torn her gaze off the lit-up steer to look at the other pieces.

Camille picked a bit of fuzz off the goat's metal ear, still a little shocked and hugely pleased that Steve had kept one of her sculptures. "I didn't realize I was at the time, but you're right. It looks just like Maybelle, doesn't it? I thought people might want more animals for their nativity sets, but I made them ranch animals to fit…" She swept a hand out, indicating the shop and the whole ranch.

"No more horses?" Micah asked, sounding disappointed. His frown hadn't lightened since he'd come into the shop, and Camille was starting to think that was just his usual expression.

"There was, but it didn't turn out how I'd hoped."

Micah looked away from the angel he was examining to eye her closely. "What was wrong with it?"

"It was supposed to be Buttercup, but she ended up looking like a beast from he…ck." She changed mid-word, not sure if she was supposed to say *hell* around kids. Was it an official swear word? Steve's children seemed so well-behaved that she was a little worried her bad habits would wear off on them if she was around too much. "The two kids riding her look like evil, possibly flesh-eating elves."

"Flesh-eating elves?" As she repeated Camille's words, Maya's eyes widened with glee, and Camille shot a guilty glance toward Steve. Instead of appearing disapproving of her bad influence, though, Steve looked amused.

"Was it really that bad?" Micah asked skeptically in his rusty-sounding voice.

Camille met his gaze. "Worse. Words cannot describe how awful it is."

He regarded her with a hint of suspicion. "Didn't that bother you? Making something bad?"

"Of course." She gave a small shrug. "That's life as an artist, though. Not everything is meant to be seen by others. I'll have lots more failures. I just have to appreciate when something does turn out okay." She realized that all four kids and Steve were listening to her intently, and she cleared her throat, a little thrown by their attention. "You're an artist, right?"

His face reddened as he ducked his head, suddenly looking more like a kid and less like a serious, angry adult. "I draw and paint, but I'm not really an artist."

"You did the snow sculpture outside, right?" she asked.

He gave her a quick glance before dropping his gaze to the counter again. "Yeah."

"It's wonderful and so detailed. It looks like the horse is going to come to life and gallop across the yard."

Micah looked pleased for a fraction of a second before his expression dropped into its usual grim lines. "You can come over to the house and see some of my drawings."

Startled by the invitation, Camille didn't respond immediately, and he started to turn away. "Oh, I'd love to, if we're done…?" She trailed off, her voice rising in question as she looked over at Steve. Last time, Ryan had dragged her to the office for the check, but she had a feeling that he'd been extending her visit, so she wasn't sure what the actual requirements were. So far, this product drop-off had been much more enjoyable than last week's. If she could be promised just to hang out with Steve and his surprisingly charming children, without having to elbow her way through customers she didn't know or fend off Ryan's heavy-handed come-ons, she'd be willing to visit the Springfield ranch every day.

Steve was focused on Micah, looking pleased and a little surprised. He turned toward Camille with a broader smile than she'd been prepared for, and her head began to spin. "Go ahead," he said. "I'll bring your check to the house." He glanced at the clock. "It's almost lunchtime. Why don't you stay and eat with us?"

"Oh, I…" Her mind went blank. When Ryan had asked her out, she'd just wanted to run in the other direction, but the idea of eating with Steve and his kids was surprisingly appealing.

"You should have lunch with us," Zoe said, and Maya nodded encouragingly, bouncing on her toes in excitement. "It's Micah's turn to cook, and he's really good. So is Uncle Nate. If Will was cooking, on the other hand…" She pretended to gag.

"Hey!" Will protested, making Zoe and Maya laugh.

An unsmiling Micah said, "You should stay." Camille noticed that Steve gave his son another surprised glance before refocusing on her. Despite her worries that she was seeing interest in Steve that wasn't actually there, she was almost certain that he wanted her to have lunch with them. In fact, everyone was staring at her with varying degrees of hope.

"Okay," she said faintly, feeling a bit overwhelmed.

"Good." Steve smiled at her again, and his honestly pleased expression made her insides warm. Turning to Will, he said, "I'll help you price these. Nate should be in here soon to watch the store while we have lunch."

"I hope he hurries up," Will said with put-on grumpiness that quickly dissolved into a grin. "I'm starving."

"You're always starving," Maya teased before she grabbed Camille's hand and towed her toward the door. "Your superpower is the ability to eat your way out of trouble." She squeezed Camille's fingers.

Surprised but touched by the girl's easy, affectionate gesture, Camille gave Steve and Will a little wave over her shoulder as Zoe asked her sister, "How would that work, anyway? I mean, the only way he could eat his way out of trouble would be if there was a volcano that spewed pudding rather than lava."

"It'd help if someone dropped enormous pancakes on Will's lair, too." Maya dropped Camille's hand and turned around so she could face the others while walking backward toward the main house.

"Maybe the supervillain is made out of food," Micah suggested. Even now, his expression was completely serious, which made the whole thing even funnier.

Tipping her head to the side in thought, Camille asked, "Aren't we all made out of food? Not that we'd especially want to chow down on other people, but we're food for something."

"Like sharks." Maya took the turn in conversation gracefully. "Or bears."

"So, what if Super Will could eat through anything?" Zoe suggested. "Like, it didn't have to be food at all. That's his superpower, that he could eat metal and wood and plastic and not die."

"I like it," Camille said. Their conversation was so similar to one she'd have in her head—or with Lucy— that she had to smile. Who knew her nerdy soul mates would be Steve Springfield's kids? "That'd be an excellent superpower. No one would be able to hold him, since he could eat through handcuffs and prison bars."

"How long would it take him, though?" Micah's frown was still in place, but it looked more thoughtful now. "Would it be instant, like the cartoon Tasmanian Devil, or more like how long it takes a mouse to chew its way through the grain-room wall in the barn?"

"Instant might be too much," Zoe said as they climbed the front steps. Right now, the wide porch was barren and snow frosted the railing, but Camille could picture how homey and perfect it would look in the summer, scattered with comfortable wicker chairs and a swing. "If he can eat through *anything* in a second, then how would anyone stop him? He'd have too much power."

"He could be stopped," Maya argued, opening the door. A rush of warm air flowed out, filled with a spicy food smell that made Camille remember she hadn't eaten yet, except for a small chocolate Santa early that morning after she'd given up on sleep. With thoughts of mysterious noises, she'd had a restless night and had woken up for good before the sun was even thinking of rising. "Someone could pull his teeth out."

"Or wire his jaw shut," Micah suggested as they all piled into the entryway. Camille looked around with interest as she pulled off her coat and hung it on one of the wooden hooks that lined the wall. Shoes and boots of various sizes were tucked under a bench that ran along the wall, and she placed her own boots in an open spot in the row. It was such a small thing, adding her footwear to theirs, but it still made her chest warm. The conversation with the kids, the little line of shoes—they made her feel like she was part of their family, even for just a short while. All her life, she'd never really fit in anywhere outside her workshop, but this family had made a place for her.

"If his teeth and jaw are strong enough to eat through metal or concrete, it'd be really hard to pull out his teeth or keep his mouth closed," Zoe argued, leading the way into a huge open kitchen.

"Speaking of eating things, something smells really good," Camille said as she glanced over at Micah, who scowled and ducked his head. Despite his frown, he seemed more bashful than angry. "What'd you make?"

"Tacos." He moved over to the stove to check the contents of a pan, and Camille fought a smile. His grumbles and grumpy manner reminded her a little of his uncle Joe. As he turned away from the stove, she quickly glanced around the kitchen so he wouldn't guess that she'd been amused by him.

Although the room's layout seemed old-fashioned— with the traditional window over the sink and room for a long table rather than any sort of a center island or breakfast bar—the ceramic tile floor looked like it'd recently been installed, and the colors of the walls were modern and obviously freshly painted. The appliances appeared to be newer, too.

"Did you redecorate recently?" Camille asked.

"Grandma and Grandpa had it done as our early Christmas present, right after we moved in." Maya grabbed Camille's hand again, this time towing her through an archway into the living room. "I'm glad. It was kind of dark and creepy in here before that. Come see the rest of the house."

"It wasn't that bad," Zoe said, following them. Micah took up the rear silently. "Everything was just…old. This is much better now, though."

The living room was large and homey, with more of an emphasis on comfort than fashion. Camille noticed her mare and foal sculpture on one of the shelves next to the flat-screen TV and felt a glow of pride. Having that little piece of her here made her feel as if she was part of their cozy home, almost one of the family.

"Dad's office is in there," Maya waved toward a doorway before heading up the stairs. "He hardly ever uses it, though. Most of the time he's outside or in the shop or on fire calls. When he has paperwork stuff, he does it at the kitchen table while we do our homework."

Camille could easily picture the homey scene of the whole family gathered around the table in the evening, and that warm glow reignited in her chest. *Careful*, she warned herself. *This is just for lunch, and then life will return to normal*. The problem was that she wasn't sure she wanted it to. She'd always been perfectly content with her peaceful, solitary existence, with her art and her cat and plenty of precious alone time. This was just a case of the grass being greener, especially since she was already caught up in the whole nostalgic, Christmas-wonderland feel of the ranch.

And, as much as she hated to admit it, she was even more caught up in Steve.

CHAPTER 6

"This is my room," Maya said.

"Mine, too." Zoe slipped past them to bounce on the lower bunk bed. The room wasn't huge, but it was cute and tidy, with lots of books lining the shelves.

Camille walked over to the closest desk. Drawings of mechanical things were held down by metal parts and a stack of equipment manuals. "I bet this is yours, Zoe."

"Yeah." Zoe gave a slightly sheepish smile and a half shrug, as if she was bracing for teasing. Camille remembered the feeling of having interests that none of the other girls at school shared, and she hated that Zoe was caught in the same position.

"Are you back to working on the flying luge, or are you sticking with the all-terrain wheelchair?" she asked, not sure of the best way to reassure Zoe that being passionate and brilliant and different were *good* things.

"I can't decide," Zoe said with a groan, falling back on the bed dramatically. "While I was grounded from the shop this week, I did a bunch of research, and I'm moving away from the idea of a hovercraft and more toward a jet pack."

Camille studied the top drawing on Zoe's desk as she considered that. "That seems like a good idea. The size of a jet pack would fit what you need it to do better than a hovercraft. If you want your friend to use it inside, though, you're going to have to be careful about the kind of emissions it produces."

"That's true." Sitting up again, Zoe got the look that Camille was starting to recognize as her thinking expression. "My research also changed my mind about the all-terrain wheelchair." When Camille gave her an interested eyebrow lift, she continued. "I've been too stuck on the idea of a chair with a motor. If I want something that can handle stairs and go over rough ground, I need something that moves like people or animals do—on legs, rather than wheels."

"Like a robot?" Micah asked from where he was leaning against the doorframe.

"Yes and no." Zoe bounced a little on the mattress, her whole face alight. "I don't need the processing power of a robot, just the ability to move. It'd be more like a robot suit, or robot stilts, even."

"So, two prosthetic legs connected to a body brace?" Camille asked, trying to picture Zoe's idea in her head.

"Maybe? I don't know. I'm just starting to research what's out there, and I really want to make something soon, so Wyatt can visit the ranch." Zoe grimaced. "If he has to wait until I build him a jet pack or robot legs, it could be *years*."

"Can I try out the jet pack when you make it?" Maya asked, her eyes huge with anticipation.

"Sure, but only after the prototypes stop blowing up."

Camille couldn't hold back an amused snort. "How do you know the prototypes will blow up?"

"Everything blows up at first," Zoe said matter-of-factly. "I just need to get through that phase without freaking out Dad too much."

Even as she laughed, Camille had to wince at that. "And without losing any fingers."

"Well, yeah. That'd be good, too." Zoe blew off that restriction as if it wasn't of any consequence, and Camille felt her laughter rise again at the girl's matter-of-fact tone. Swallowing her amusement, she moved to examine Maya's desk as a distraction.

The younger girl's workspace was more varied, with drawings mixed with what looked to be handwritten stories and some homemade jewelry, but Camille quickly spotted a common theme: horses. On the wall behind the desk, Maya had pinned up pictures of her and her pony at shows and on trail rides and just playing around—including one of her pony wearing a Santa hat. A rainbow row of ribbons underlined the pictures.

"What's your pony's name?" Camille asked, noting that it was the same adorable gray in all the photos.

"Quibble, but I call him Q."

"I like that name." She bent to get a close look at the pictures. "He looks like a sweetheart."

Zoe burst into laughter as Micah gave an amused huff.

"He *is* sweet." Maya defended her pony. "Usually. Just…occasionally naughty."

With a scoffing sound, Zoe said, "He's naughty about ninety percent of the time."

"Not that much!" It was obvious that Maya was trying to hold on to her offended expression but was having a hard time not laughing along with her siblings. "And when he's good, he's really, really good."

Camille scratched her nose to hide her own smile. "But when he *isn't*...?"

"He's really naughty," Maya admitted. Micah burst out with a laugh, the first Camille had heard from him.

"What's so funny?" Steve's voice brought Camille's attention to the doorway, where he was standing behind Micah. His mouth was already curling up at the corners, as if he was prepared to laugh along. She was suddenly struck once again by how attractive Steve was. Before he'd returned to Borne, Camille had figured she'd exaggerated his handsomeness in her memory, but the real-life Steve was even better. When she'd known him in high school, he'd had the boyish good looks of a teenager. Somehow, he'd managed to improve with age. His rugged, square features were softened by the kindness in his eyes, making him seem strong without being harsh, and his muscled, powerful body made her feel uncomfortably warm. When he met her gaze and held it, she realized she was staring and quickly turned her head. Just those few moments of eye contact made her heart flutter.

Camille, the little voice of reason in her head warned. *You're in so much trouble.*

"We were telling Camille how naughty Q is," Zoe said, giggling.

Grimacing, Steve said, "He's a...challenging ride."

"He's good sometimes!" Maya argued plaintively, and he gave her a smile.

"Even when he's not being his best, you ride him very well," Steve said, and Camille was impressed by his diplomacy. "Let's go downstairs and eat."

"But I haven't shown Camille my drawings yet," Micah protested.

"After lunch," Steve said, turning his son around by the shoulders and pointing him toward the stairs. "Will and I need to eat so we can get back to work. Nate's all by himself in the store right now, and things start getting busy by one on Sundays."

Maya and Zoe followed Micah out of the room, and then it was Camille's turn to slip past Steve as he stood sentry in the doorway. Although there was enough room that she didn't brush against him, her heart still beat quicker as she got near enough to catch a whiff of his intoxicating scent. Steve waited until she'd passed to fall in behind her, resting one of his broad hands lightly on the small of her back.

The unexpected touch almost made her jump, but she managed to stay calm—externally, at least. Inside, she was enjoying every moment his warm, strong palm pressed lightly against her spine. His hand was so big that his fingers nearly touched her side. Although she was short, she wasn't waiflike in any way. Even with her plentiful curves, though, she felt tiny and fragile when he was near. Her growing need to have him close was both addictive and a little frightening.

"Good tacos, Micah!" Will said with his mouth full as they entered the kitchen.

"Manners," Steve said sternly, only then dropping his hand from Camille's back. She noticed that Will eyed the movement, but he didn't look at all bothered by the fact that his dad had just been touching a woman. If anything, he seemed pleased.

This time, Will swallowed his mouthful of food

before speaking. "Sorry. Good tacos, Micah. Sorry I didn't wait, but Uncle Nate's on tree sales *and* watching the shop until one of us gets back to help him."

His brother gave an abrupt dip of his chin as he headed to pull foil-wrapped tortillas out of the oven. Camille took a turn washing her hands in the bathroom off the kitchen before rejoining them.

"Can I help?" she asked as Micah transferred food into serving dishes and the girls started pulling shredded lettuce, cheese, and other taco toppings from the fridge.

"I think we're set." Steve looked up from pouring water into glasses. As he passed behind Micah, he gently squeezed the boy's shoulder. "Looks good, Son."

Maya pulled out a chair. "Sit here, Camille." Her excitement made Camille smile, even though she felt a little unworthy of such enthusiasm. She settled into the chair Maya offered, only realizing when everyone else took their seats that she was right next to Steve. He was so broad across the shoulders that his arm was within brushing distance of hers, and a warm buzzing started in her belly. Maya was on her other side, grinning at her as though Camille's presence at lunch was the greatest thing that had ever happened. Camille was rather baffled by their enthusiastic welcome, since she didn't think she was interesting or amusing enough to deserve their eager, focused attention. With a mental shrug, she decided to just accept and enjoy it. They'd figure out soon enough that she was quirky, odd, and not really all that fascinating.

As they filled their plates, passing the dishes around the table, the kids filled Will in on his superpower. Camille wondered if she would've turned out differently if she'd grown up with such a big, noisy family. Over the chatter, the sound of the front door opening and closing again caught her attention, but she couldn't see into the entryway from her seat. She hoped it wasn't Ryan and then immediately felt a little ashamed of the thought. He was just so persistent that he made her feel uneasy and guilty, and then resentful that he'd made her feel uneasy and guilty, and then even guiltier that she felt resentful. Everything seemed so much more comfortable and relaxed when it was just Steve and the kids, even with the way Steve seemed to set off sparklers in her chest every time his muscular arm brushed lightly against hers.

When Joe walked in, she felt her shoulders drop slightly in relief. It wasn't Ryan after all. Joe, however, didn't look as thrilled with her presence as she felt about his. As soon as he spotted her, he stopped abruptly in the doorway and scowled. Instead of being offended, Camille found it hard not to smile. His expressions were so close to Micah's.

"Who're you?" he barked.

Before she could answer, Micah spoke. "This is Camille. The horse artist. She's having lunch with us."

Joe's grumpy expression changed to one of surprise as he looked at Micah, and Steve let out a cough that sounded suspiciously like a strangled laugh. Without another word, Joe got a plate and glass from the cupboard and took the empty chair next to Zoe.

"Where's Ryan?" Camille asked as Joe started to fill his plate. She wanted to be prepared if he was going to join them. "Is he off the ranch today?"

"Disappointed?" Steve's tone had an uncharacteristic edge, and she glanced at him in surprise.

"Ah…" She floundered a little as she tried to think of a truthful, yet tactful answer. When enough seconds ticked by that things were becoming awkward, she tossed the idea of being polite and just blurted out, "Not really. I just noticed he's gone, since we're all here except for him—and Nate, but he's by himself in the store—so I wanted a little warning…uh, not a warning, since that sounds kind of rude, so just curiosity, maybe? Mild, very mild curiosity, though." As she trailed off, she kicked herself for reverting to babble when she'd been doing so well with the Springfields, even talking in whole coherent sentences. She wished she hadn't brought Ryan up in the first place.

"Oh." Steve grimaced slightly, looking abashed. "He's in Ebba, at the ranch-supply store." When he went silent, no one spoke for a solid minute, and Camille realized that all of his kids were eyeing him with the same surprise she'd felt. Joe, on the other hand, was focused on his food.

"Okay," she said, more to break the silence than anything. The kids were now exchanging looks that she couldn't interpret, but they were making her a little antsy. She mentally hunted for a topic, any topic that would make everyone stop being weird. Finally, an idea popped into her head. "Will!" When his eyes widened as if she'd startled him, she realized she might have said that a little too enthusiastically. She was just so relieved to have thought of something to say. "What kind of car are you thinking about getting?"

He immediately lit up. "I'm not set on anything for sure, since I don't want to pass up something good just because it doesn't match what's in my head, you know?"

"That's smart," she said, grateful for the easy transition. The kids made normal conversation so easy. She wished it were as simple with other adults. "What are you hoping for, though?"

"Wellll…" He drew out the word while flicking a teasing look at Zoe. "There was a red Ford Mustang that we went to look at in Denver, but *somebody* told me that I couldn't get it."

Zoe groaned dramatically. "It was a 2006, Will. A 2006! I told you how many problems the Mustang had that year, but if you want to have to deal with the engine stalling or the spark plugs breaking off when you try to remove them, then—"

"Okay, okay!" Will interrupted her, laughing. "That's why I bow to Zoe on all car-buying decisions."

"You were lucky to have someone along who knows her stuff," Camille said. "Even if she did destroy your dream of owning a Mustang."

"Nightmare, more like," Zoe grumbled, although she couldn't hide her pleasure at the compliment.

"Yeah, he is lucky," Steve said with obvious pride, and Zoe beamed at him.

Will's phone beeped several times in a row, and he pulled it out.

"William." Steve's eyebrows drew together, and Camille's stomach clenched in reflexive pleasure. She wondered what was wrong with her that she thought his stern look made him even more attractive. "No phones at the table."

"Sorry, Dad, but it's Uncle Nate." Standing up, Will took his empty plate over to the sink. "Things got busy early. He has a bunch of customers wanting to get trees, and he can't leave the store. I can tell he's freaking out, 'cause he sent about five texts, and the last couple don't make any sense."

"All right, then. I'll follow you in just a minute," Steve said. Will gave him a nod and the rest of the table a quick wave before heading into the entryway. Steve gave Joe a wry look. "Don't suppose you want to take some customers out to get trees?"

"No." Joe blinked quickly. "I…uh…I need to fix the Chevy. It's been running a little rough." He seemed so relieved to have thought up an excuse that Camille had to hold back a snicker.

Steve had obviously been expecting Joe to wiggle out of the job, since he just grimaced slightly as he stood. His expression sweetened when he looked down at Camille, and she couldn't stop herself from beaming back at him. "I'm glad you had lunch with us," he said simply. It was another long moment before he tore his gaze away from hers, and she discovered that just that extra bit of eye contact had her breathing a little too quickly.

"Thank you for inviting me," she said, grasping for an easy platitude to tide her over until she could organize her thoughts into sentences that made sense. She didn't want Steve to know how easily he could set her head spinning. Even though she suspected he was interested, she couldn't tell for sure. She mentally cursed both her own inexperience and the fact that people didn't just blurt out their feelings. It would make social interactions so much easier if she didn't have to figure out every subtle cue. She turned her gaze away from Steve with some effort and focused on Micah. "The tacos were great. Thank you for cooking."

He responded with a grunt and a slight dip of his chin, but his face reddened enough for Camille to know that he was flustered by her appreciation.

"Micah," Steve said, a touch of gentle reprimand in his voice.

"You're welcome." Micah's words were almost inaudible, just a low grumble as he stared at his plate. Steve moved around the table, giving all three of his remaining children a kiss on the head and a gentle shoulder squeeze in farewell.

"Dad, can I work with Uncle Joe on the Chevy?" Zoe asked, and then beamed when he nodded. Joe gave her a sideways smile that made him look a thousand times more approachable than usual.

"Help Micah and Maya with kitchen cleanup first," Steve said. "If you're ready to go, Camille, I can walk you to your car."

As appealing as that sounded, she had a promise to keep first. "Micah said he'd show me his drawings. I'd like to see them." A pleased expression flashed across Micah's face, and he immediately pushed back his chair and stood up.

Steve gave her an approving nod. "Mind stopping by the shop before you go?" He rubbed at the back of his neck, and she wondered what was making him uneasy. The thought occurred to her that *she* might make him nervous, just as he made her, but she quickly dismissed it. He was always so stalwart and steady. There was no way that she, Camille Brandt, socially awkward semi-hermit, could throw Steve Springfield off-balance.

"Sure."

"Good." He hesitated a second too long, and she

wondered again if he was as confident as he always appeared to be. "I'll...see you later, then."

Maya started giggling, drawing Camille's attention away from Steve. All three kids appeared amused, even Micah. Steve gave Maya a look that was probably supposed to be stern, but the effect was ruined by a slightly sheepish smile that tugged on the corners of his mouth.

"Behave," he grumbled, heading for the entryway. With a shake of his head, Joe followed. As soon as the kids heard the front door close behind them, all three started laughing.

"What's so funny?" Camille asked, puzzled. The sound of their amusement was contagious, and she found herself smiling, even though she still didn't know what was going on.

"Dad," Zoe said, although it wasn't really an answer. "You, too, a little bit, but mostly Dad."

"Me? What'd I do?" she asked, but the kids just waved her off as they got control of their giggles.

"C'mon," Micah said, his face settling into its usual serious lines as he headed into the living room.

When she realized she wasn't getting an answer out of Zoe or Maya, Camille gave up on trying to understand and followed Micah upstairs to his room.

"You and Will share?" she asked, noticing that the setup—two beds and two desks—was similar to the girls' room. Micah gave an absent nod as he dug through a stack of notebooks and loose paper piled on his desk. "How do you like that? I'm an only child, so the only time I shared a room was for one semester at college, and that was horrific." When Micah paused his search to give her a surprised look, she waved a hand, dismissing her words.

"I'm sure that was only because my roommate wasn't the most...considerate or hygienic of people, so don't take that as me saying that no one should go to college. Plus, I was really homesick the whole time, and my grandma wasn't doing well, so..." She cleared her throat. "Anyway, I'm just curious how you like sharing with your brother."

"It's fine," Micah said after a pause, as if checking to see if she was done babbling. She squashed the urge to make a face at herself. It was a little unsettling to realize that all four of Steve's children were often more mature than she was. "Sometimes he bugs me, but most of the time he's nice. He's pretty much always happy, and he doesn't like to start fights."

Camille pulled out Will's desk chair and sat. "That's good. He does seem really easygoing. It must be nice to have your brother and sisters around, especially after moving. You can take your friends with you."

"Usually, yeah." He pulled a sketchbook from the stack and leafed through it. "It'd be nice to be alone once in a while, though. Here." The drawings must've passed muster, because he thrust the sketchbook at her.

"Thanks." Accepting it, she flipped it open to a drawing of a log cabin in the mountains. As she slowly paged through, she grew more and more impressed. Stopping on a drawing of Steve in his bunker gear, looking soot-stained and weary but satisfied, she resisted the urge to trace the pencil lines of his face. "Wow. Micah, you're so talented. You really capture the feeling of a moment." Turning the sketchbook page out so he could see which one she was looking at, she added, "This is like a scene from the end of a battle. I can tell he's exhausted, but the fire's out, so the drawing has this sense of weary triumph. Has your dad seen this?"

"Yeah." Micah's face was bright red, and he couldn't seem to stand still, shifting from one foot to the other. Camille had a good idea of how he was feeling. Whenever someone looked at her work, she was torn between bashful pleasure at their praise and the need to rip it out of their hands and hide it from any possibly critical eyes. "He liked it. He keeps offering to have my stuff framed and hang it up downstairs, but I don't know…" Shrugging, he glowered at his socked feet. "I don't want everybody to see it."

"It's scary, isn't it? Both times when I brought a new batch of pieces for the store, my stomach was a twisted-up mess." She finally flipped the page and laughed at a sketch of Maya's pony, a roguish expression in his eye, trotting along in full tack but without a rider. "This is right after he dumped Maya, isn't it?"

Moving next to her so he could see the sketchbook too, Micah gave an amused huff. "It was Zoey, but yeah. We all had to ride Q when we were first learning. He taught us how to stay on."

"I'll bet," Camille said dryly, flipping to another sketch, this one a woman that Camille didn't know, although she looked a bit familiar. She glanced at Micah, intending to ask, but his expression, combined with how the set of his mouth resembled the woman in the sketch, told her who this was. "Your mom?"

"Yeah." Tearing his gaze away from the drawing, he studied his feet again. "I did that off a photo, since my memory's getting…" He waved a hand, as if to dismiss his words, but it only gave them greater weight. "She's getting blurry around the edges."

Camille studied the picture. "She was beautiful. Is this Will?" She pointed to the chubby baby his mom was holding in her lap.

"Yeah."

She smiled. "He was cute…all that dark hair." As she looked at the woman's features, she grew curious. Although it was a pencil sketch, it was obvious that the kids' mom had light-colored hair and eyes. "Was Will adopted, then?" she asked and immediately realized the question was probably rude. "If that's too nosy, you don't need to answer. Sorry."

"It's fine," Micah said. "Everyone in Simpson— where we used to live—knew. It's just because we're new here that people gossip about why Will's browner than the rest of us, but they never ask."

"That's because most people aren't as rude as I am," Camille said dryly.

Micah gave her a quick smile before returning to a more serious expression. "Will's dad was a soldier in Iraq. He died before Will was even born, and then Mom and Dad got married when Will was just a baby."

"Ah." Camille was itching to ask so many questions, but she managed to keep her mouth shut. It really wasn't any of her business, and there was something shady about trying to get the details out of a thirteen-year-old. She refocused on the drawing. "Was your mom blond?"

"More of a light red." He grabbed a framed photo off the bookshelf and brought it over to her. "This is the picture I used to draw from. I'm going to do a painting someday, but I'm not good enough yet. All I do is wreck my drawings."

"Have you tried pastels?" Camille suggested. "That'd let you play with color, but they feel more like sketching to me, so you might like those more than paint."

"Not really. Aren't they just crayons for adults?"

She snorted a laugh. "Sort of, but they're less waxy." Leaning over so she could see the picture, she made an admiring sound. "Micah, you did a great job capturing her. Her smile is perfect...so kind. It makes me wish I could've known her."

"Thanks," he said, the word a bit stiff with discomfort but still obviously sincere. "Her nose is off, though, and I don't know how to fix it. Right here... See?"

"Hmm..." Camille looked back and forth between the drawing and the photo. "I think the problem is that there's really no line here between her nose and her cheek." She pointed at the spot on the framed picture and then the matching spot on his sketch. "But you added one here. I think it's a case of your mind telling you what should be there versus what your eyes are actually seeing."

His forehead wrinkling in concentration, Micah looked back and forth between the two pictures. "You're right." He took the sketchbook off her lap and hurried over to his desk. "I'm going to fix that right now."

Happy that she'd been able to help, Camille stood up. "I'm going to give your sisters a hand in cleaning up from lunch. Your drawings are wonderful, Micah. They're technically very good, but they're also very evocative."

He looked up from his sketch, frowning. "What does that mean?"

"Evocative?" When he nodded, she said, "It means that I feel strong emotions when I look at them. That's good. It's what art is supposed to do."

Although he flushed a little, he held her gaze. "Your sculptures make me feel things. When I look at the horse Dad got for us, it makes me remember what it was like when my mom was alive, safe and..." His voice trailed off as he dropped his gaze to the paper in front of him.

"Thank you," Camille said softly, touched. "That's the best compliment I've ever gotten. I'm glad the horse stayed here with you, since it gives you that."

Micah kept his head down, his attention fixed on the sketch, although he didn't move to draw anything.

"Thank you for showing me your drawings." She cleared her throat, still a little emotional. "I'll see you later, okay?"

"Bye." The word was more of a grunt, and Camille bit back a smile that was shaky around the edges. His surly, Joe-like exterior hid an emotional, creative soul, and she felt lucky she'd gotten a glimpse of the real Micah. She slipped out of his room, closing the door silently behind her.

When she reached the kitchen, everything was clean and put away, and Maya and Zoe had already left the house. Even with everyone except her and Micah gone, the house still felt warmly welcoming, as if the Springfields' personalities had already left a mark on the place, as if their laughter and squabbles and chatter had soaked into the walls, bringing the house to life. It was hard to leave, especially when she thought about spending the rest of the day in the quiet solitude of her workshop. She loved her house, but even when her grandma was alive, it had never felt as much like a home as this place already did. Shaking herself out of her reverie, she pulled on her boots and coat and let herself back out into the chilly outdoors.

As she started toward the store, Camille heard the jangle of sleigh bells and saw Steve jogging toward her, a draft horse that wasn't Buttercup trotting next to him. She stopped, struck yet again by his rugged beauty and the picture-perfect scene of his strong form next to the huge chestnut horse, their breath turning to steam in the clear, cold air. Even the sunny day seemed to exist just to be a perfect backdrop for Steve in this moment.

"Hey," he said, not even breathing hard after his jog. "Glad I caught you before we had to head out to get another tree."

The horse lowered his head to her shoulder and breathed puffs of warm air onto her neck, making her giggle. "Who's this?"

"Harry. He's green, and we need to work on him respecting people's boundaries, but he means well."

"Oh, I don't mind him breathing on me." She rubbed the horse's cheek as he lipped at her collar. "He's very handsome." *But not as handsome as Steve*, a wicked voice whispered. She firmly ignored it, knowing that she couldn't focus on thoughts like that if she wanted to be able to have a conversation without blushing.

"He knows it, too. He's like Ryan that way."

When Camille let out a surprised laugh, Steve winced, rubbing his neck with the hand not holding Harry's lead rope. "Sorry. That was rude."

"Maybe," she said, still amused, as Harry nosed at her pockets, probably checking for treats. "But it was also true."

"Hey," he said to Harry, giving the lead rope a sharp tug so that the horse backed up a few steps. "Quit trying to mug her for carrots." He shot her a quick glance, looking uncharacteristically uncertain. "So...you and Ryan really aren't...?"

"Aren't what?" she asked, confused by the half of a question. As soon as she said it, though, she realized what he'd meant. "Oh! No. We're not doing anything. I mean, he's asked, a bunch of times, actually, which surprised me, since he'd pretty much looked right through me until you found me at the scrapyard—not that I was lost, of course—and he walked back with me and Sasha. Anyway, whenever he tries to drag me somewhere for lunch, I run away or tell him I can't because I need to feed my cat."

Steve gave his rare, booming laugh. "You turned him down because you needed to *feed your cat*? No wonder he's so touchy when it comes to you."

"He's touchy about me? Why? I don't think he's all that interested." Not really interested, the way she was in Steve. "I know he's been persistent about trying to get me to go out with him—well, for the last few weeks, at least—but I figured he asks out everyone he runs into, and most people don't reject his offers, so I'm just a challenge."

"It's true he's not used to being turned down."

She shrugged. "He'll need to get used to it with me. I'm just not interested."

"Good to know." Steve's gaze seemed several

degrees warmer than usual, and Camille found prickles of sweat beading under her coat as she tried to puzzle out his meaning. Why was it good to know that she wasn't interested in his brother? The way he was eyeing her made her almost think that Steve was actually attracted to her.

Her breath caught at the thought, but she immediately doubted herself. Beautiful, kind, and strong Steve Springfield had to have just as beautiful, kind, and strong women falling at his feet on a regular basis. Why would he be interested in an almost-hermit who answered almost every question with a nervous monologue? Despite all that, she knew she wasn't imagining the heat in his eyes when he looked at her.

Suddenly tired of not knowing what was going on in his mind, she blurted out, "Why is it good to know?"

He shifted closer, nudging Harry back when the horse took the opportunity to try to nibble on Camille's coat again. With Steve this close, she could smell his evergreen and peppermint scent. His coat was unzipped slightly, showing his insulated flannel shirt underneath, and the urge to press her face against that soft-looking fabric was so strong that her breath caught. She jerked her gaze back to his. There was no missing the heat in his eyes now, especially as he tipped his head down so their faces were even closer. Her heart thrummed in her chest at his nearness, making it almost impossible for her to hear his words. "I wanted to ask y—"

"Steve!" Nate's yell drifted from the store lot, cutting Steve off midword and smashing the perfect, crystalized moment between them. Closing his eyes for a moment, he let out a hard breath that stirred the strands of hair on her forehead before he turned toward his brother.

"What?" he called back, his voice a little growly.

Blinking as reality returned with a rush of cold air, Camille shifted back a step, needing some distance from Steve to get her thoughts working again. Even as she tried to tell herself that she'd imagined that moment, that he'd been about to ask her a normal, not-at-all-sexy question, she couldn't keep the butterflies from tumbling around in her belly. *Stop*, she told them firmly. She should know better than to think that he'd be interested in her, and she needed to knock it off before she ended up embarrassed and hurt.

Despite the internal lecture, she still wanted to throw a pinecone at Nate's head. Why did he have to shout right when Steve was getting to the interesting part? Now she was going to die of curiosity if she didn't find out what he'd been about to tell her. She liked Nate well enough, but right now she wished he'd fall in a hole.

"You're up!" Nate gestured toward a family clustered together by the edge of the lot. Even at a shout, Nate's words sounded testy, and Camille felt a rush of annoyance. Couldn't he have helped the family? Even as she thought it, she knew she was being unreasonable. This was why she shouldn't indulge in daydreams about unobtainable firefighting ranchers. It stole all of her good sense.

Steve gave Nate a wave of acknowledgment before turning back to Camille.

"Duty calls," he said with a slight, rueful grimace. His gaze lingered on her face for a charged second before he sighed and turned Harry around, being careful the horse's oversized rump didn't knock into her. As he started leading the gelding away, Steve glanced over his shoulder at her. "We'll talk soon."

With that completely unsatisfying ending to their conversation, he jogged back toward the family waiting in the lot. Realizing that she was staring after him like a lovestruck idiot, Camille forced her feet to move. She followed more slowly, watching as he greeted the parents and their three kids, tying Harry's lead rope to the hitching post. As he put on the horse's harness, he explained each step to the customers, letting the kids touch each piece with curious hands. When the smallest child toddled too close to one of Harry's oversized hooves, Steve swept him up with the ease of long practice before handing him off to the boy's dad.

Camille loved how he worked around the horse and the kids, calm and easy, but with a careful firmness that showed he wouldn't put up with any nonsense. Although she wished they'd been able to finish their conversation, she enjoyed being able to stare at Steve to her heart's content without him noticing. He stroked Harry's thick, fuzzy neck absently as he listened to one of the kids, and she was transfixed by the movement of his hand, so firm yet gentle. As stupid as it was, she couldn't keep her mind from dwelling on how that hand would feel against her skin.

As if he'd heard her thoughts, he looked straight at her, the corners of his mouth tucked in as if he were holding back a smile. Heat rushed to her cheeks, and she knew she had to be bright red. If he hadn't guessed the direction of her thoughts before, her vivid blush had to be giving her away now.

Completely flustered, she lifted her hand in an awkward wave. His smile stretched more widely, and Camille lost what little ability she had to act normally. It was time to retreat. Turning away from the tempting man in front of her, she hurried the rest of the way to her car, not allowing her gaze to stray in his direction. Once she got into the old Buick, she closed her eyes and shook her head at herself. Why couldn't she have even a smidgen of game? Why had she given Steve that goofy wave?

Carefully backing out, she ran through their brief encounter in her mind. What had he been about to say before Nate interrupted? From the way he'd prefaced the question, it had felt as if it was going to be important. She huffed out a breath. Between thinking about this, her spying neighbor, the creepy night noises, and the industrious mice who shared her home, she'd never be able to sleep that night.

CHAPTER 7

THE NIGHT WAS UNUSUALLY STILL, WHICH MADE HIM uneasy. Every squeak of snow beneath his boots, every heavy breath—even the low thud of his heartbeat—seemed too loud. With every second that ticked by, he expected Camille to pop her head outside or Mrs. Lin to look out the window or—even worse—emergency sirens to head in his direction, letting him know that someone had spotted him skulking around. Despite his fears, the night remained silent...too silent.

He waited in the trees for over an hour longer than usual. Common sense told him to go home, to come back when the wind was noisily whipping the snow around, hiding any sounds or movements he made. He couldn't do it, though. He couldn't leave, not when there was a chance that something might happen. If he missed it, all those nights of waiting and watching would've been for nothing.

Carefully, quietly, he slipped across the road toward Camille's house.

It was still dark when Steve woke. Years of predawn rising had trained his body not to need an alarm, although they had destroyed any chance he might have of sleeping in, now that his kids were old enough to allow that. Pushing back the covers, he shivered as the air chilled his sleep-warmed skin. His parents had very generously remodeled the old ranch house when Steve had first spoken with them about moving his family back to Borne, but the place was still over a hundred years old. No matter what kind of new flooring or paint it received, the house was going to be drafty.

As he made the bed in the dim moonlight, the undented pillow on the right side caught his notice. It'd been over eight years since he'd last shared his bed, and he still hadn't gotten out of the habit of staying to his side while he slept. For some reason, that untouched pillow sent a wave of loneliness through him, worse than anything he'd felt in years. He'd never needed someone by his side more. After Karen had died, he'd been devastated by grief and secretly terrified. She'd been such a good mother, and he hadn't known how their family was going to survive without her. Somehow, they'd managed, and he'd become accustomed to being a single parent. Although he'd never call it easy, he'd always felt like he was doing a good job rearing his children on his own.

Now that the kids were getting older, things weren't so simple. All four were incredibly smart and amazing and so good it made his heart squeeze just thinking about them. But parenting was more complicated now, especially with Micah and Zoe. They were both so brilliant and at the same time so sensitive, and he knew that the wrong words from him could easily crush them. It was hard to find the right thing to say, though. He'd always thought of himself as a pretty straightforward, uncomplicated guy, and things that wouldn't have fazed him as a child sent Micah—and sometimes Zoe—into an emotional tailspin. He'd never felt so out of his depth.

He tried. Even when conversations were awkward and painfully uncomfortable, he still attempted to push through, but sometimes trying wasn't enough. If he said the wrong thing, they'd shut down and go silent, and he'd know he'd screwed up, but not be sure how to fix things. They weren't like a piece of equipment that came with replacement parts and an instruction manual.

Sometimes he felt like he needed a translator to communicate with his two middle children. Karen would've been that. She'd felt things just as deeply as Zoe and Micah did, so she would've helped Steve understand the best way to parent them…maybe. He realized that he was having a hard time imagining what Karen would've been like if she'd lived, or how she would've parented their kids as preteens and teenagers. They'd all changed so much over the past years, and she would've, too, he was sure. It hit him suddenly that he'd been without Karen longer than they'd been together, and at some point, the crushing grief had softened to a lingering ache, a hollow spot in his chest where she used to be.

Shaking himself out of his thoughts, he gave the quilt covering his bed a sharp tug to straighten it and then turned away. He dressed in the mostly dark room, putting off the moment that his eyes had to become accustomed to the harsh artificial light.

When he'd finished getting ready, he walked quietly down the hallway, glancing in the girls' room to see them both sound asleep. He tapped lightly on the boys' door.

"I'm up," Will said in a semi-alert mumble, making Steve smile a little as he quietly descended the stairs. He scribbled a note on the whiteboard on the fridge, letting the other three know where he and Will would be, and filled a water bottle at the sink. As he drank, his gaze settled on the chair where Camille had sat the day before, and his smile threatened to return. He liked having her there at his family's table. Ever since he'd seen her in the scrapyard, Camille had fascinated him. She fit with his children, like a puzzle piece snapping into place so effortlessly that he was a little envious. He wondered if she thought he was bland and dull in comparison to their vividly inventive minds that were so like hers, and he wished that Nate hadn't interrupted the previous day before Steve could finish talking to her.

"Ready?" Will asked quietly as he entered the kitchen, pulling Steve out of his thoughts.

"Drink some water first," he said, filling another bottle and handing it to Will before topping off his own. They pulled on their boots and coats in silence, donning their hats before adding their headlamps. Will unhooked their snowshoes from the wall and handed Steve's to him, although they waited to strap them on until they reached the foot of the porch stairs. This had been their routine since before they'd moved away from Simpson, and their movements came automatically for both of them.

"Long route or short today?" Steve asked.

"Long." Will reached toward the star-speckled sky, stretching. "I sat in the store too much this weekend."

They turned right, heading for the north edge of the property, picking up a slow jog to get their muscles warmed up and to accustom their brains to the different motion required to run in snowshoes. Snow-blanketed pastures stretched to their left, while the tidy rows of evergreens created lines of dark shadows to their right. The entire ranch seemed to be sleeping. Even the wind was quiet, leaving just the brush of their clothing and the soft thuds of their snowshoes to break the early-morning silence. "Want to switch to tree duty next weekend, get a break from the store?" Now that they were out of the house and wouldn't wake the sleepers, Steve spoke at a normal volume. There weren't many bears out at this time of year, but there was no harm in making enough noise to scare off any wildlife.

"Sure." Will's jacket rustled as he shrugged. "I don't mind the store, though, and Uncle Nate hates getting stuck in there. He'd rather be outside with the horses."

"Wouldn't we all?" Steve asked, making Will huff out a laugh. "Any plans for next weekend?"

"Not...yet." There was a slight hesitation that made Steve look at his son sharply. He stayed quiet, knowing Will would tell him. "There's someone I sort of...well, want to get to know better."

"Hmm." Steve tried to keep his voice noncommittal even as he groaned inside. He'd known this was coming, though. Will would be fifteen in April, and he'd always been a popular, good-natured kid. "How are you thinking about going about that?"

"I know the rules, Dad," Will said, back to sounding like his usual self. Steve figured he was lucky to be going through this with Will first, since his older son's straightforward and easygoing attitude would hopefully let him coast relatively drama-free through puberty. He had a feeling that Micah would have a harder time. "No dating one-on-one until I'm sixteen. We can do group things, though, right?"

"Yes, as long as I okay each group *and* each event." After Will made an agreeing grunt, Steve asked, "What are you thinking about doing this weekend?"

"I don't know." Will sounded a little defeated. They reached the fence and followed it to the trees. The scent of pine and cedar surrounded them, and Steve inhaled. Even when he'd lived in the mountains, the smell had always made him think of the ranch. Although he'd loved Simpson and hadn't minded living in Monroe, something inside him had clicked into place when he'd returned to Borne and the ranch where he'd grown up. He'd just been thinking of a place where his kids would be safe when he'd decided to move back here, but he hadn't realized how much he'd needed to return to the ranch.

"Want to have some friends come here? You could take them on a ride and then have a bonfire. Ryan wants to burn the junk wood that's left from the old barn…the stuff he can't reuse or sell to Camille." He was a little proud of himself for not hesitating over her name. For some reason, he found himself stumbling over his words around her.

"Maybe." Will's tone turned teasing. "Speaking of Camille…"

Steve stayed silent, glad that the darkness covered his expression. Apparently, he hadn't sounded as unaffected as he'd hoped.

After a moment or two, Will spoke again. "What's going on between you two? It's obvious you're into each other."

It was obvious? "Will…" he said.

"C'mon, Dad. I told you about Taylor." Steve winced at the touch of hurt in Will's voice. It seemed so wrong to be discussing his love life—well, his *potential* love life—with his fourteen-year-old son, but it wasn't right to keep his kids shut out of it, either, since it would affect them, too. He'd always tried hard to be honest with everyone, especially his children, but he'd never had to deal with this situation before. On the rare times after Karen's death that he'd dated someone, things had never gotten serious. He didn't want to introduce a woman into his kids' lives when he knew she would be transitional. They'd suffered enough when their mom died; they didn't need more loss.

"Dad."

"There's not much to share." It was true, but his chest squeezed with disappointment at hearing the words out loud, forcing him to add, "Yet."

"Yet?" Will jumped on that gleefully, as Steve knew he would. "Are you going to ask her out?"

Steve adjusted his hat and the headlamp as a prickle of sweat made his forehead itch. "If I did, how would you feel about it?"

"I approve," Will said immediately and enthusiastically, making Steve laugh. He loved this kid. "So would Zoe and Maya. Micah might be upset, though."

"Why?" Steve frowned, disappointment hitting him again. He'd thought that his younger son and Camille had bonded over their art. At dinner the night before, Micah had been positively effusive about how she'd helped him fix one of his drawings.

"I think Micah's halfway in love with her himself," Will said teasingly, and Steve reached over and gave his son's shoulder a reproving push, shoving him off-balance. With a laughing yelp, Will recovered, racing forward so that he was several strides ahead. Allowing his stride to stretch, Steve quickly caught up to Will, and he realized that if he'd had a mirror handy, he'd see a big, dopey grin on his face.

They ran in silence for a few minutes, and Steve felt a rush of anticipation. Talking about it with Will had made the idea of dating Camille more real—actually possible, rather than just a daydream.

"If you like her, Dad," Will said, sounding completely serious, "you should ask her out. She's nice, and she obviously likes you."

"What if it doesn't work out?" Steve asked, the question escaping before he could stop it. "If you kids get attached, and then she's gone… I don't want any of you to get hurt."

"I don't want you to get hurt either, Dad." His voice was so kind that Steve was struck again by what a great person Will had turned out to be. "But we—all of us—want you to be happy. Sometimes, you just gotta take the risk." His tone lightened, changing to teasing. "Can't believe I have to tell this to a guy who runs into burning buildings."

With a playful growl that masked the ache in his chest, Steve chased his laughing son.

Camille groaned at the knock on her workshop door.

She'd been working pretty much nonstop since five that morning, and she'd managed to get the last of the website orders finished and packaged. It was still almost two weeks before the twenty-fifth, but past years had been so frantic at the last minute that she'd moved up the arrive-by-Christmas deadline this year. Now she was glad, since it gave her the opportunity to concentrate on her new wholesale client. To her chagrin, her face warmed just thinking about Springfield Ranch.

It'd only been two days since she'd last been there and had lunch with the family, but she'd already thought about them—well, okay, mostly Steve—way too much for her peace of mind. She couldn't seem to control how her daydreams wandered to him as she worked. The more she was around him, the more she fell for him. She knew Steve had flaws, but they only seemed to add to his appeal.

The knock came again, yanking her back to the present, and she turned off her music.

"Stupid," she growled at herself as soon as the workshop went silent. That had been a rookie mistake. Now whoever was out there would know she was here and that she'd heard them knocking. Resigned to talking to her visitor, she stood up, and her muscles protested having been locked in one position for so many hours.

As she reached the door, she peered through the peephole. "Oh good!" Yanking the door open, she actually smiled at the person standing on her porch.

"Why're you so cheerful?" Barry, the package-delivery guy, grumbled.

"Because you're here to pick up the last of the holiday orders, and then I won't have to look at them or think about them anymore." Despite his usual crankiness, she couldn't stop grinning. Not only was he taking the final boxes, but he never wanted to chat. If all visitors were as reluctant to linger as Barry, she'd answer her door more often.

"Well?" he demanded, as if proving her unspoken point. "Get them, then. I don't have all day. You're not the only one sending a bunch of useless crap out today. Busiest season of the year, so let's go!"

While he was grumbling, she'd shifted the hand truck holding the stack of boxes over into the doorway. It had only taken a few seconds, but he still sighed audibly.

"Finally." He scanned each of the labels and then stacked them onto his own dolly before wheeling them toward his truck.

"Happy holidays!" she called after him, and he lifted a hand without looking back. For a second, she thought he might be about to give her a rude gesture, but he kept it at a wave.

"Christmas miracle right there," she said under her breath as she closed the door. She wondered if Mrs. Lin had watched the exchange and was right now getting photos of Barry on her phone. Her neighbor probably thought that Barry was another stripper-gram, complete with a tear-away delivery man costume.

Shaking off the rather disturbing image, Camille turned back toward her workbench and saw Lucy sitting primly next to her latest project. "Hey, LuLu," she crooned, walking over to stroke the cat. "Have I been neglecting you?" With a small meow, Lucy arched her back into Camille's hand, and she felt a flash of guilt. Lucy rarely used the cat door Camille had installed in the door between the house and the workshop, since the cat didn't care for the chillier temperature of the shop. If she was venturing into what she considered the Arctic, then Lucy must really be feeling lonely.

"Should we get some lunch inside?" Camille asked, lifting Lucy off the bench and cuddling her. To her surprise, the cat allowed it. Normally, she hated snuggles and would grumble just like Barry until she was back on her own four feet. "I've been a terrible cat mom, haven't I?" She carried Lucy back into the kitchen. As soon as they were through the door, Lucy twisted free and darted through the cat door into the workshop again.

"Huh." Apparently, Lucy wanted to hang out in the workshop today. Camille figured that she wouldn't mind the company, although she'd have to put the cat inside when she used her blowtorch. Camille tended to get lost in her work, and she didn't want her cat to investigate and get burned by stray sparks.

But now that Barry had pulled her out of her work fog, she realized that she was, indeed, hungry—really hungry, in fact. A glance at the clock told her why. It was almost four in the afternoon. Peering into the depths of the fridge, she sighed.

"Why are you so disappointed," she mumbled to herself, giving up on finding anything in the empty appliance and heading to the pantry. There had to be something in there that she could eat. "If you don't go to the store, then your fridge stays empty." She hated grocery shopping during the busier times of day, especially in the weeks before Christmas. There were so many people. The worst part was that she was acquainted with most of them, but not really friendly with anyone, so conversations were always stilted and uncomfortable.

She didn't know why others couldn't just keep their heads down and go about their shopping, but no one seemed to have the same grocery-store etiquette as she did, so she suffered through multiple awkward exchanges in each aisle. At the end of that misery, when she couldn't take it anymore and left with one-tenth the number of items she'd planned to get when she'd entered the store, Camille still had to face Mrs. Murphy, who was nosy and abrasive enough to make Mrs. Lin seem like a sweet, unobtrusive angel.

As a result, her pantry was pathetically bare. "Nice prepper you'd make." It wasn't like she had an excuse for not having any unperishable food, either. That, she could just order online. She poked through the few cans. "What did I think I was going to make with bamboo shoots? Stir fry, maybe?" That actually sounded good, but she was lacking every other ingredient she needed. She realized that she was going to have to either suck it up and go to the grocery store or, alternatively, suck it up and go to Birdie's.

After mentally reviewing the potential horrors a grocery store visit would entail, she settled on the diner as the slightly better option. Although Birdie's didn't take orders over the phone or online, they would box up her food so she could take it home to eat, and she could get enough to last her several days. That way, she could put off visiting the Borne Market a little longer. Even better, it'd give her time to finish the Springfield ranch order, and then she could possibly finagle another lunch invitation. Micah's tacos had been really good, and she felt comfortable with Steve's kids. With Steve himself, she didn't feel anything as bland as *comfortable*. He *did* make her feel nervous and excited and hopeful and buzzing with anticipation.

Now she was thinking about Steve again. Closing the pantry door with a firm click, she headed toward the front closet to get her coat. She needed food, and then she could go back to work. The sooner she finished the order, the sooner she could visit the ranch. She snorted a small laugh. How quickly she'd changed from dreading a trip to the ranch to avidly looking forward to it.

It wasn't until she was outside Birdie's that she realized she wasn't really fit for public viewing. Her sweatpants had a small hole burned in one thigh and a paint stain on the other knee. At least her coat covered most of an even more disreputable hoodie. She tugged on her stocking hat, hoping it would hide the fact that it'd been several days since she'd last washed her hair... or brushed it, actually.

"Quit being silly," she said under her breath as she opened the door to the diner. "You're not going to see anyone you care to impress anyw—Oh. Hey, Ryan." Her gaze flicked over his shoulder, looking for Steve. A mix of anxiety and anticipation swirled through her at the thought that he might be at the diner with his brother. Sure, she was a hot mess at the moment, but she couldn't help wanting to see him. When she didn't spot Steve, a mixture of disappointment and relief filled her, with the former heavily outweighing the latter.

"Camille. Good to see you." Ryan's wide smile made her feel a bit guilty for her preoccupation. "I'm just about to get some early dinner. Come sit with me." He reached for her elbow, as if to escort her across the small seating area, and she automatically stepped back out of reach. This time, her glance over his shoulder took in all the other people in the diner. Yes, they were watching avidly, just as she'd expected. Her sigh was deep but silent. If she'd known that she'd become the entertainment to go with the diner's early-bird special, she would've taken her chances with the grocery store.

"No, thank you." She realized that Ryan was watching her, his smile fading. "I'm just going to get some food to go. This being my busy time of year and all."

Making an obvious effort to erase his frown, Ryan scolded, "You need to take time to eat." He reached toward her arm again, and Camille retreated another step. With all her daydreams about Steve, having Ryan be his usual aggressively flirty self with her was especially unappealing. Now her back was literally against the wall, and she knew she needed to be an adult and deal with the situation.

"Ryan…" Taking a deep breath, she glanced at their hushed audience. The two servers had shifted closer and were unabashedly eavesdropping. It was hard enough to have this conversation without a good portion of the Borne population listening in. There was nothing to be done about it, though. If she put off the conversation or allowed Ryan to drag her over to one of the booths, it was only going to complicate things. What was developing—or what she hoped was developing—between her and Steve felt very fragile at the moment, and she didn't want to do anything that might ruin it before it could become something wonderful.

The thought of Steve gave her courage. She lowered her voice, knowing it wouldn't do much good. "Ryan, I'm not the most socially…aware person. Because of that, I'm not sure if you're just being friendly, or if you're flirting because that's what you do with everyone, or if you're really interested in me, but I just want to make it clear that I don't want to be anything except friends with you." When he just stared at her, she figured she should make things very, very clear, since she was being all brave and up-front for the moment, and she knew it probably wouldn't last, and she'd go back to trying to wiggle out of uncomfortable social situations by being as nonconfrontational as possible. "*Platonic* friends. And, you know, business associates, since I really like being able to sell some of my pieces at your ranch, and I think that's been a good deal for you, too. I hope it has been, at least."

The silent seconds ticked by, and she was pretty sure that no one in the diner even breathed as Ryan's face gradually hardened. She braced herself for his reaction, hoping it didn't involve yelling or swearing.

To her surprise—and relief—his usual smile returned. It was a bit stiff around the edges, but it was there, which meant that Ryan was going to follow the regular social rules and not scream at her in Birdie's in front of everyone. "Sure. Of course. I've only thought of us as friends, so I'm sorry if I misled you into thinking I wanted it to be…more."

A huge breath of relief escaped, and she reached out to pat his arm but thought better of it before her hand made contact. She was so glad that Ryan was going to be civil that she didn't even argue with him about his implication that *she* pursued *him*. If he was going to stop asking her out, then it was worth allowing him this sop to his pride. "Good. Thank you. Great. Okay. Now that

that's settled, I'm going to just…go. Lots of work to do, with Christmas and everything."

"Didn't you want to order some food?" Ellen, one of the servers, called out as Camille shoved open the door.

"No, thanks! Not really hungry!" She was much more desperate to escape. The thought of sitting at the counter, waiting interminable minutes for her food to be ready while the other customers gossiped about her, killed any desire she had for food. She'd brave the Borne Market, since most of the town was obviously eating at Birdie's and had already witnessed her painfully uncomfortable chat.

Despite the awful awkwardness of it all, she felt like a huge weight had been lifted off of her. She hadn't realized how much she'd dreaded Ryan's repeated come-ons until she'd put a stop to them. Even though she knew running into him in town and at the ranch wouldn't be all that pleasant, at least for a while, it would still be much better than it had been.

Taking a deep breath, she let it out and smiled, picking up her pace. After what had happened at the diner, going to the grocery store would be a breeze.

CHAPTER 8

By the time she'd reached Borne Market, some of her ebullient cheer had faded, but Camille forced herself through the doors anyway. Unless she wanted to eat scrap metal, barn wood, or cat food, she had to do this.

Grabbing a cart, she speed-walked toward the produce aisle, avoiding any eye contact. It didn't help.

"Camille Brandt!" Mrs. Murphy called from where she stood next to her register. "I haven't seen you in ages. Come over here and talk to me."

Quickly debating and abandoning the idea of feigning sudden acute deafness, Camille turned and headed toward the checkout, telling herself that the upcoming conversation couldn't be any worse than the encounter she'd just had with Ryan, and she'd managed to survive that.

"How are you?" Mrs. Murphy asked with heavy sympathy and a whole lot of avid curiosity.

Blinking in surprise, Camille tried to figure out why Mrs. Murphy was using that tone. "Um…fine. Busy with all the Christmas orders, so I should probably…" She gestured toward the aisles, knowing that it was likely a useless escape attempt.

She was right. "June Lin and I were just talking about you." *Tsk*ing, Mrs. Murphy shook her head with sadness belied by the gleam in her eyes. "She said she sat you down and talked to you about your little *problem*."

Here we go. With great effort, Camille resisted rolling her eyes. "I don't have a problem, Mrs. Murphy. Mrs. Lin is just a little too good at noticing when I have visitors, that's all."

"That's what I told June. She needs to butt out of your sex life. You should have fun while you're young. At least you have company now. It's better than you spending all your time alone like you did after your dear grandma died."

Don Nally rolled his cart toward Mrs. Murphy's checkout lane, and Camille eyed him, hoping he'd distract the cashier long enough for her to slip away. "I'm not…" She trailed off, not even knowing where to start correcting all of Mrs. Murphy's false assumptions.

"I just have to ask one thing," Mrs. Murphy said, and Camille braced herself. Don, her potential savior, was no help, listening avidly as he very slowly emptied his cart onto the belt, one item at a time. Camille frowned at him as Mrs. Murphy continued, "Barry? Really? He's so…unpleasant."

"Already? How'd you even know about him? That *just* happened." Seeing Mrs. Murphy and Don light up with glee at the admission that wasn't really an admission, Camille shook her head. "Not that *anything* happened with Barry, except that he picked up my packages. He didn't even come inside!" Taking a deep breath, she tried to smother some of her indignation. For two people who professed not to be able to stand each other, Mrs. Lin and Mrs. Murphy had an awfully efficient system of gossip. Forcing a smile, Camille mentally reminded herself that

Mrs. Murphy was an elderly lady, and as infuriating as her insinuations were, they weren't actually harmful. "Good to see you, Mrs. Murphy," she lied. "You have a customer, so I'll just go get my shopping done."

"Don't stop talking on my account," Don said, but Camille was already moving. How had she thought that grocery shopping was going to be better than her abbreviated trip to the diner?

She sped through the aisles, keeping her gaze focused firmly on the items on the shelves. As she reached the dairy corner, her last stop before checking out, she'd managed to evade attempted conversations with no fewer than five different people, and she was feeling almost triumphant as she grabbed a half gallon of milk out of the cooler.

"Camille!" The instinctive cringe at the sound of her name was quickly followed by relief when she recognized the voice. Turning, she saw Maya rushing toward her, and she just managed to move the milk carton out of the way before the girl squeezed her around the waist. Giving her a semi-awkward, one-armed return hug, Camille felt a bubble of hope rise in her as she looked over Maya's shoulder. This time, she wasn't disappointed. Steve was headed her way, looking as rugged and handsome as always, pushing a half-full grocery cart.

"Hey, Maya." Camille couldn't take her eyes off him. How anyone could look so good in the awful fluorescent lighting of the Borne Market was beyond her. The thought reminded her of her own rather rumpled appearance, and she resisted the urge to smooth the hair tumbling over her coat in messy curls. "Hi, Steve. Doing some shopping?" The second the question was out, she wanted to suck it right back in. What else would they be doing at the grocery store?

Kindly, neither of them pointed out the stupidity of her question. "Yeah. I had choir practice after school," Maya said. "I'm doing a solo at our winter concert next week."

"Congratulations," Camille said, finally able to rip her gaze from Steve so she could focus on Maya. "You must be a really good singer."

"I'm okay." Maya shrugged, ducking her head a little as she peeked up at Camille. "I wouldn't say I'm *spectacular*, though."

"I would." Steve stopped his cart next to Camille's and leaned on the handle.

"That's because you're my dad," Maya said, although she couldn't hide her delighted smile. "You *have* to say that. It's, like, in the dad rule book."

"Your choir director didn't *have* to offer you a solo, though," Camille said. "I bet your dad's saying that because it's true, not just out of fatherly obligation."

"Do you want to come to the concert?" Maya asked, and Camille shot Steve a quick look. When he nodded his agreement to the invitation, she turned back to Maya.

"I'd love to hear you sing." The thought of packing into an auditorium with a bunch of Borne parents didn't thrill her, but she figured she could hover near the back for a quick escape after Maya finished her solo. She wouldn't mind sitting with the Springfields, either, despite the crowd. "When is it?"

"A week from tomorrow," Steve said. "We can pick you up beforehand."

"Yes!" Maya agreed enthusiastically before Camille

could respond. "That way, you can go out for dessert with us. That's what we always do after concerts."

"Uh…okay." Despite her hesitation, she couldn't stop the smile that spread over her face. Was that a date? Had she just been invited on a date by Steve Springfield? Okay, it'd officially been his daughter who asked, and it was a family date, but Camille didn't care. It still felt amazing and exhilarating and like the start of some new, wonderful thing.

"Camille!" Deanna Lin called out as she pushed her cart toward their small huddle in the corner. Camille groaned, and Maya giggled, leaning against her arm.

"Sorry," Camille grumbled quietly to Steve. She didn't want to be a bad influence on his daughter, but Deanna was a chatterbox—*and* she was Mrs. Lin's daughter-in-law, which meant that it was going to be hard to escape the upcoming conversation.

"I completely agree," Steve muttered back, and Camille had to bite the inside of her cheek to keep from grinning.

"Oh!" Deanna eyed the three of them with a smile. "Don't you look like the sweetest little family?" Her expression turned puzzled. "I thought June said that you and Ryan were dating?"

Even though Steve's exasperated look was directed at Deanna, Camille still felt an urgent need to at least try to set the record straight…again. "There's not anything between me and Ryan. He just sold me some barn wood."

Leaning closer, Deanna lowered her voice to a carrying whisper. "So you didn't just have a huge lovers' quarrel at Birdie's?"

"What? No. No quarrel, and Ryan and I are definitely not lovers, so no. Not a lovers' quarrel or anything even close to that." More words of denial wanted to spill out, but Camille managed to hold them back as she glanced down at Maya, who was watching with avid attention. "We talked for a minute, that's all. Ryan flirts with everyone without meaning anything by it. Maybe that's what your informant saw." Her tone became a little bitter on the last few words, but Deanna was unintentionally ruining the toasty warm feeling Steve and Maya had caused. With them, for just those few moments, she'd felt like a normal person, someone who could possibly fit into their family. Now they were watching as she reverted back to the town weirdo.

Although Deanna was good-natured and obviously not intending to cause distress, Camille desperately wanted the conversation to be over so she could slink out of the store and return to the safety of her workshop.

"Informant?" Deanna blanched, looking confused by the snap to Camille's words. "You make it sound like I have a whole team of spies reporting back to me."

Despite her irritation, Camille couldn't help but laugh. "That actually sounds like something Mrs. Lin— June—would do. Aren't you getting her night-vision binoculars for Christmas?"

Deanna's smile tentatively returned. "It does sound like her. How'd you know about the binoculars?"

"She let me know that she's going to be keeping better watch over any goings-on at my house." Camille grimaced. "I wish someone interesting would move into the old Smith place across the street so that she'd have someone else to obsess about." Remembering that she was talking to Mrs. Lin's almost-as-gossipy daughter-in-law and that everything she said would likely get back to her—and that Maya was listening to everything with wide eyes—Camille closed her mouth.

"Oh, I don't know." Deanna's gaze flickered toward Steve, a small smile quirking up the corners of her mouth. "Your life seems plenty interesting to me."

In her periphery, Camille saw Steve glance at her, and she inwardly cringed. Why hadn't she just sucked it up and eaten that solitary can of bamboo shoots for dinner? She would've been hungry, but at least she would've been spared this humiliating conversation.

"I should go." Suddenly, Camille couldn't stand there another second. "My milk's getting warm." She gave Maya, who was still leaning against her, a quick side hug as a goodbye and pushed her cart forward before Deanna could say anything else.

As she passed Steve, he caught her cart handle, stopping her. She hesitated to look up at him, worried that she'd see doubt in his face, that he'd join the ranks of Borne gossipers who thought she was strange and antisocial. She stiffened her spine. Even if she was strange and antisocial, it wasn't his or anyone else's business. Emboldened by her rush of indignation, she looked up and met his gaze.

His eyes weren't judging her, though. Instead, he looked warm and affectionate and even sympathetic, and Camille was caught, unable to look away. She vaguely heard Deanna saying something, but she didn't really care what it was, not while Steve was looking at her in that unexpectedly lovely way.

"Will you be coming out to the ranch soon?" he asked, his voice quiet and so intimate that goose bumps spread over her skin.

"Yes. Tomorrow, probably." She couldn't have told him no at that moment if her life depended on it. Besides, she couldn't wait to get out to the ranch. Except for when she was in her workshop, everything else in her life seemed so hard and uncomfortable, like a pair of shoes that didn't really fit. With Steve and his kids, though, she felt as if she clicked effortlessly into place, as if they'd made a spot in their family just for her. The thought immediately made an alarm sound in the cautious corner of her brain. She was just getting to know the Springfields. If she continued thinking like that, she knew she'd end up getting hurt. Somehow, though, with Steve looking at her with that sweet yet intense way, it was hard to stay coolly pragmatic about what could be.

"Come for dinner," Maya said, sounding excited. "It's my night to cook, so Dad's helping me make pizza."

Camille glanced at her, happy to see that Deanna must've left while she was focused on Steve. "By 'make pizza,' do you mean sliding a frozen one in the oven? Or putting sauce and cheese on half an English muffin?"

Steve laughed softly as Maya answered. "Neither. We actually make the crust and roll it out and throw it in the air and everything."

"Non-frozen, homemade, hand-thrown pizza? How can I refuse?" It was only after she'd accepted that she remembered to check with Steve, since accepting an offer from one of his very generous children seemed a little too close to inviting herself to dinner. "If that's okay?" she asked him.

Steve came amusingly close to rolling his eyes. "Of course. We love having you." They beamed at each other, and Camille forgot where she was again for a moment, until he tipped his head toward her cart. "You should probably go before your milk gets any warmer."

"Oh!" She gave an embarrassed half shrug and lowered her voice. "I just said that so I could get away from Deanna. Some of the gossip she and Mrs. Lin come up with is just crazy. I mean, Mrs. Monroe thinks I have a thing going with *Barry*? Really? They couldn't have made up a better booty buddy for me than him?"

Steve's laugh boomed out, and Camille smiled as she watched him. His face was totally transformed by happiness, and it was even more beautiful than usual. "I agree," he said. "You deserve so much more than Barry."

His words made her float as she pushed her cart away from them.

"Dad?" Maya's high, clear voice reached her ears clearly. "What's a booty buddy?"

Heat flooded Camille's face as she rushed toward the checkout at the front of the store. Despite her embarrassment, the warm residue of Steve's words remained with her. Even Mrs. Murphy's risqué stories about her life before she'd married Mr. Murphy couldn't dim her happiness. Camille paid, scooped up her groceries, and walked out the door, giving thanks that Mrs. Murphy couldn't follow her.

When she reached her house, she scurried toward the workshop door before Mrs. Lin could catch her. Camille knew that Mrs. Murphy had definitely found a moment between customers to text Mrs. Lin everything that'd happened at the grocery store. She was pretty sure that Mrs. Lin would be lying in wait for her to get home so she could either lecture her some more about her man-hoarding ways or try to pry more details out of Camille so that she'd have more information to lord over Mrs. Murphy at their next gossip club meeting or whatever they did when they got together.

Darting through the door, Camille quickly shut it behind her, letting out a huge breath of relief. Lucy jumped down from the edge of the scrap-metal bin where she'd been perched next to the rejected horse sculpture. It hadn't quite made it into the bin, but Camille had managed to perch it on the edge, mainly to free up more room on her workbench.

Making her way across the shop, Camille held the kitchen door open for Lucy to walk through. Although she knew perfectly well how to use the cat flap, Lucy preferred to have Camille hold the entire door open for her, like the reigning queen that she was.

"I bought you some treats," Camille said, kicking off her boots before setting the bags on the table. She started sorting through her groceries, surprised that she'd actually gotten a good amount of food. Since most of her shopping had been done with her chin to her chest and her eyes on the floor, she'd half expected to bring home fifty cans of lima beans and a double bunch of parsley, but she'd managed to pick out actual meal-worthy food.

As if lured by the mention of treats, Lucy padded over and sat at Camille's feet.

"Aren't you the sweetest," Camille cooed, crouching down so that she could pet the cat. "Such a pretty kit... Ah!" Lucy opened her mouth and let a baby mouse drop to land on Camille's socked foot. Lurching back, she lost her balance and toppled onto her butt as the mouse fell to the floor. Apparently, it was not as dead as

Camille had assumed, since it got to its feet and darted toward the fridge.

"Lucy!" Camille yelled, scrambling to grab the mouse before it made it underneath the appliance. Once it was under the refrigerator, she knew it would be nearly impossible to get it out, and then there'd be a mouse loose in her house—or, rather, *another* mouse loose in her house. "What are you doing? You're a cat! You don't catch and release mice! You eat them or drop corpses at my feet or ignore their existence. I don't care what you do, as long as you don't bring them into the kitchen and let them run free!"

The last word was more of a grunt as she lunged toward the mouse. Knowing she'd be too slow to catch it, she tried to put her body between it and the fridge. It worked somewhat, sending the mouse scuttling in a different direction.

"Oh no." Camille grabbed for it again, but missed by several feet as the mouse darted into the space between the counter and the stove. She glared at where it had disappeared and then turned to her cat, who was sitting on the floor, cleaning her chest and looking quite proud of herself. "Lucy…" she muttered, but she knew it wouldn't do any good to lecture her. Pushing herself to her feet, Camille allowed herself a few muttered curse words that did, in fact, make her feel better.

"At least I have food," she consoled herself, trying not to think about how hard it would be to sleep tonight knowing that yet another mouse was sharing her home. The sight of a frozen pizza reminded her of her conversation with Steve and Maya, and that did help. By the time she started the oven—after first loudly warning the mouse to stay away from the stove—the memory of their encounter had her smiling again.

There was something about Steve Springfield. Just the thought of him made her happy.

CHAPTER 9

IT WAS LATE, AND CAMILLE KNEW SHE SHOULD GO TO BED, but her mind wouldn't turn off. One of Micah's drawings had given her an idea for a piece—an intricate design that had the potential to be vastly difficult and very possibly heartbreaking. Past experience told her that she'd lie in bed, sleepless, until she at least got her idea sketched out on paper, so she headed for the workshop.

The shelves looked empty, since she'd finished all of the pieces for the ranch. Too excited about seeing Steve and the kids the next day to sit around, she'd packed up everything and even put the box in her car so she was ready for her trip tomorrow.

"Silly. You're not even going there until evening," she scolded herself as she shuffled through the notebooks stacked on the shelf beneath her workbench, trying to find one with blank paper remaining. "What're you going to do all day tomorrow except fuss around trying on different outfits and—Oh no." She froze in the middle of lifting a half-filled pad. What was she going to wear?

"Stop." She said the word firmly, setting the sketch-book down with a sharp slap. "You'll wear casual, normal clothes like you did the last two times you went to the ranch. It's pizza at his house with his kids. You're not going to a ball."

Despite her lecture, she knew the only chance she had of not obsessing about which jeans made her butt look the best was to lose herself in a new project. Grabbing a pencil, she started sketching, letting the piece take its initial shape on the page. As she drew, she grew more and more excited about it, and she knew that it was going to be amazing if she managed to pull it off. She already had a feeling that this was going to be Steve's Christmas present, rather than just another piece for the store.

By the time her eyes started blurring from exhaustion, she had ten pages of sketches, with lists to the side of metal parts and pieces of scrap she had on hand that she might be able to use. Tapping the screen of her tablet, she woke it up and started scrolling through old photos. "Two horses or three?" she muttered, flipping back and forth between the pictures. She was leaning toward three, liking the wild, almost out-of-control feel that the galloping horses had when they were three abreast.

Yawning, she pushed the tablet and sketchbook to the back of her workbench and laid her head on her folded arms. *I'll just rest my eyes for a minute, and then I'll drag my tired butt up to bed.* Despite the rough surface under her arms and the hard seat of the stool, she felt her eyelids sinking shut.

A shriek startled her awake.

Her eyes popped open, but what she saw didn't make sense to her sleep-clouded mind, as if a thick haze covered the familiar landscape. The shrill blast came again, cutting through her mental fog, screaming at her that something was very wrong. She straightened so abruptly that she almost fell backward as her brain fumbled to figure out where she was. It was hot, and there was a strange red cast to the light. The repetitive high-pitched squeal and a roaring, crackling sound drowned out the music.

She'd fallen asleep in her workshop. But the once-familiar space was blurred now, alien. Nothing around her seemed to make sense. It was loud and smoky, and the light was all wrong, too bright one second and too dark the next. Stumbling to her feet, her disorientation cleared in a snap.

Her workshop was on fire.

As soon as the realization struck, her lungs felt as if they were being squeezed in a clamp. Her gaze darted around, taking in the flames licking at the walls and ceiling, their bright light muted by the thick fog of black smoke filling the air. The acrid smell burned her nose and throat, scraping its way into her lungs. Her eyes watered, and she started coughing. The force of the hacking made her bend double, and suddenly the smoke was thinner, allowing her to gasp in a few breaths. It reminded her that air was clearer closer to the floor, and she dropped to her hands and knees.

Get out! her mind screamed, and she started crawling toward where she knew the door to be. Even down so low, the smoke still stung her eyes. As she tried to blink them clear, one of her shelves collapsed in a line of flame, crashing to the floor. Burning shrapnel flew in all directions, and she curled forward instinctively, trying to protect her face and front.

Embers stung her arms where they landed, quickly burning small holes through her clothing to sear bare skin. She smacked at the spots where pieces had landed as she tried to suck air into lungs that wouldn't stop coughing. Another floating fleck of debris hit her cheek, and she quickly batted it away. It reminded her of the sparks her welding torch gave off when she used it on metal, and she scooted back to the bench. Reaching up, she fumbled along her workbench until her fingers touched her welding helmet. Grabbing it, she yanked it on and then felt for her gloves. She knocked a pad of paper to the side before she stood briefly so she could see the top of the workbench.

Even that short time spent standing made her lungs seize up, and she hurried to grab her gloves and return to the floor. After covering her hands, she shuffled forward, trying very hard not to look at the flames surrounding her. The shrieks of the fire alarm made it hard to think, but she clung to the only important thought right now: she needed to get out.

The smoke had thickened. Even with the mask protecting her eyes, it was hard to see. The leaping flames seemed to surround her, and she didn't know if she was crawling in the right direction. It almost felt as if the room was spinning around her, an exit-less trap of fire and smoke. Only the concrete floor beneath her palms and knees was safe, and even that was growing dangerously warm.

The alarm suddenly went silent. The sudden cessation of high-pitched shrieks made Camille freeze in place. Tipping up her chin, she stared at the flames blanketing the ceiling. The fire roared unabated, but the alarm had quit, and she knew that was a bad sign. Although the absence of the piercing squeals was a relief, it also terrified her. The fire had won over the alarm, and she was next if she didn't manage to get to the door.

The helmet's mask limited her peripheral vision, and she tried to ignore the roaring of the flames and the walls of heat on all sides, focusing just on crawling forward. The stacked pile of barn wood blocked her way, and she felt a pang of sadness that this lumber had lasted over a hundred years, only to be incinerated in her workshop.

She moved to go around it, but a loud cracking sound made her freeze. With a *whoosh* of displaced hot air fanning her arm, a large, flaming chunk of the ceiling hit the floor next to her with a crash. Jumping at the close impact, she shoved away from the fiery wreckage, rolling in the only direction that was left to her.

For a moment, she lay still, futilely gasping for oxygen, the close call making her heart pound so loudly that it blocked out the roar of the flames around her. Her head was spinning from adrenaline and smoke inhalation, but she forced herself back onto her hands and knees. She couldn't let herself lie there. If she didn't get out soon, she'd be burned alive. Slowly shuffling forward, she continued crawling around the bonfire of barn wood. She was completely turned around now, and reaching the door seemed like an impossible feat. A sob burned its way up her throat, and she clenched her teeth to hold it back.

Think. Despite her dizziness, that firm, commanding voice was still clear in her head. This was her workshop, her space. She knew it better than she knew the house she'd grown up in. She wasn't about to get lost in her own shop, fire or no fire. If she was going left around the pile of wood, then she needed to follow a diagonal line, and she'd hit the door.

Ignoring the confusion of the flames and the heavy grayness of the thick blanket of smoke, she crawled, the heat from the floor searing her knees. She couldn't let the pain and her paralyzing fear overwhelm her, or the fire would win. She pressed forward, knee and hand, other knee and hand. It felt endless, this slog across the floor of her workshop, her sanctuary.

If she'd been able to get any air in her lungs, she might have laughed at that. Nice sanctuary it had turned out to be.

There was something lighter ahead of her, a rectangular shape that was slightly less gray than the surrounding area. She shuffled closer on her hands and knees and realized what it was with a rush of relief so intense that tears came to her eyes.

She'd found the door.

Blinking away the blurriness, she scrambled forward, moving faster now. Rising onto her knees, she was grabbing the handle with her gloved hand when a crash behind her made her duck and turn to look. Her display shelf had collapsed, leaving just flaming, charred remains, but her attention quickly moved past the wreckage. Fresh flames licked up the wall—the one connecting the workshop with the kitchen.

Lucy!

She started crawling toward the interior door before she realized what she was doing and stopped, forcing her mind to work, for logic to override panic. Rather than trying to make it through the fire-engulfed workshop, she needed to get out and go around to the front door. If the fire had started in the garage, it would take a few minutes to make its way into the house…she hoped.

Forcing herself to turn back, Camille fumbled with the knob in her gloved hand and yanked the door open. As the cold air rushed in, the flames around her billowed up with a deafening roar, and she automatically ducked, her arms flying up to protect her head. She dove out of the opening, scrambling to her feet and running for the front door. Her breath was loud under her helmet, and the mask had gone foggy, either from condensation or soot, but she couldn't slow down long enough to try to wipe it clear. She needed to get Lucy out of the house before she burned with it—or they both did.

Taking the four porch steps in one leap, she reached for the storm door handle. Just as her gloved fingers were about to close around it, hard arms wrapped across her middle and yanked her back.

Shock stole her voice for a brief second, allowing the person behind her to drag her several steps away from the house before she started struggling. "Lucy!" she shouted, but her voice was drowned out by sirens and truck engines she hadn't even noticed until that moment. "I need to get Lucy!"

She shoved at the iron bands locked around her waist, twisting her body from side to side in frantic attempts to free herself, but she couldn't get away, couldn't stop them from pulling her farther and farther back from her burning house, away from any chance she had to save Lucy.

"Stop!" she cried out, a sob harshly burning her throat, her eyes locked on the black smoke curling out of the eaves, the windows glowing red. "Lucy's in there!"

"Camille!" It was Steve's voice. "Listen to me. You can't go in there. You'll die, and so will Lucy. I'll go

get her. I have the gear, so I can go in that house." As
he continued to talk in his calm but firm way, his words
started making sense and she began to still. This time,
her sob was one of overwhelming relief. Steve was here.
He'd save Lucy. It'd be okay. They'd both be okay.

Turning, she fumbled with her welding helmet, and
he helped her pull it off. The sirens had ceased, but
the flashing red and white lights still lit up her yard in
pulses. The only sounds were the fire-truck engines,
people shouting commands, and Steve's calm, steady
reassurances. She concentrated on his words until even
the fire became a muted roar in the background.

"You with me?" he asked gently. A face shield and
breathing equipment masked his features, and bunker
gear added bulk to his already sturdy frame, but his
voice reminded her that he was here. He would make
everything okay.

"Yes." Her voice shook and rasped, raw from the
smoke. "Please get Lucy out."

"I will." There wasn't any hesitation, and Camille
believed every word. "Who's Lucy?"

"My cat."

Another firefighter Camille recognized as Rose
Marie Mackenzie ran toward them with a medical bag,
but Steve didn't look away from Camille. "Is there a
place she likes to hide when she's scared?"

"My bedroom. S-second floor." She tripped over her
words, tears welling in her eyes at the thought of how
scared Lucy must be. "Top shelf of the bookcase."

"I'll get her." There it was again, that sure, steady
assurance that made Camille believe that he could do
anything.

"Thank you." Her heart ached with gratitude. "Be careful."

"I will." He turned the simple phrase into a promise. "Stay with Mackenzie here, and don't try to go back in that house, okay?"

"I won't." She tried to put as much resolve into her words as was in his, wanting him to believe her so he wouldn't have to worry.

She must have succeeded, because he tipped his head in a nod and left her with the other firefighter. Mackenzie wrapped a blanket around her shoulders and tried to lead her away, but Camille didn't want to move.

"Just a few steps over there," the firefighter said, her voice soothing, though not as reassuring as Steve's had been. "That way, you can sit down and still see everything that's happening."

By the time she was seated on the back of the fire rescue truck with an oxygen mask on and Mackenzie checking her blood pressure and blood oxygen levels, Steve was entering her front door. Light caught the reflective stripes on his bunker coat, and the sight reminded her of the photo Mrs. Lin had taken on her phone. The dark image seemed even more foreboding now, as if it had been a prediction of this terrible night.

Then Steve stepped inside, and all her anxiety focused on him, on the fact that he'd just gone into her burning house to save her cat. She thought of his kids, of how they'd be orphaned if Steve never made it out. Terror and guilt churned together in her stomach as all the horrible possibilities ran through her head. Why hadn't Lucy been her first thought once she'd realized the workshop was on fire? She should've gone into the house, rather than just thinking about her escape. "It should've been me," she said softly, her eyes locked on the open front door of her house.

Despite the oxygen mask, Mackenzie managed to hear her words. "No, it shouldn't've." Her tone was upbeat but firm. "He has the training and the equipment, and you barely managed to get yourself out. He's done this hundreds of times. It's his favorite thing, saving kittens. He's great at it, too."

The matter-of-fact way she spoke made Camille's tightly wound muscles relax the slightest bit. She remembered the way Steve had said he'd be careful and that he'd get Lucy out. It'd been a firm promise, and she needed to trust him to keep his word. "That's a dangerous hobby. Aren't you worried, watching him walk in there like that—or when *you* walk into a fire?"

"Sure." Mackenzie unwrapped the blood pressure cuff from Camille's arm. "It's always there, at least a little, on every call. It keeps me careful. I can't let it take over, though. Panic never helps anyone. We just have to trust in our training and our partners to keep us safe."

As true as that was, Camille couldn't keep from staring at the house, willing Steve to walk out unharmed. The red glow seemed to be brightening in the lower-level windows, and Camille flinched at the sound of breaking glass. "Did something explode?" Her heart felt like it was going to beat out of her chest.

"No." Mackenzie sounded just as calm as she had before, and Camille took comfort in that. "The glass just got too hot."

Her gaze raked the windows and doors for any sign

of Steve, but there was nothing. "Shouldn't he be out by now?"

"It hasn't been very long," Mackenzie reassured her. "It just feels that way." After a pause, she nudged Camille with her elbow. "Look over there." She pointed at a trio of firefighters carrying a tall ladder toward the house.

"What are they doing?"

"Opening a back door."

As Camille watched, they set the ladder against the house, next to her bedroom window. Two of the firefighters stayed at the bottom, supporting the ladder, while the other quickly scaled it. By the time he reached the top, the window had opened and a helmeted head poked out.

"Steve," she murmured, relief pouring through her at the sight of him, alive and upright and apparently unhurt. As he climbed out of the window, assisted by the fireman already on the ladder, her heart dropped again. He wasn't holding a cat. "He doesn't have Lucy."

Gently rubbing Camille's back, Mackenzie said, "I'm sorry."

The simple words made Camille realize that it was true—Lucy was gone. Steve hadn't been able to find her. Grief hit her hard, making her rock forward as she clutched her arms around herself. She'd had Lucy for over eight years, since the cat was an ill-tempered stray who'd started sleeping on Camille's porch one winter.

Now Lucy was gone. Camille was completely and utterly alone in the world.

As ravaged as she felt on the inside, her eyes stayed dry. It hurt too much to cry. For the first time that night, she wondered what had caused the fire. Had she made a mistake, left something burning, missed a smoldering spark? Had she done this—killed her cat and destroyed her grandma's house, her home?

Steve strode over to her, and she braced herself to hear him say it, to tell her that he hadn't been able to keep his promise, that Lucy would never curl into the bend of her knees at night or drop a live mouse on her toes again.

He pulled off his helmet as he approached, and unzipped his jacket partway. His expression was his usual implacable one, but she knew it had to be hard for him to admit that he'd failed, and Camille added his pain to her growing pile of guilt so she could agonize over it later, when the numbness she was feeling now started to wear off.

Completely empty of words, she silently watched him approach. She wanted to tell him that it wasn't his fault and that she was grateful—hugely grateful—that he'd attempted to save Lucy, but she couldn't manage to say a thing. Instead, she watched blankly as he reached into his jacket. He stopped in front of her and withdrew his hand, extracting a small bundle. The harsh area lights the firefighters had set up illuminated a ball of calico fluff. Camille blinked, her brain trying to process what she was seeing, and it wasn't until she heard Lucy's deeply unhappy growl that the truth sank in.

Steve had saved Lucy after all.

Sucking in a harsh breath and ignoring the protest of her sore throat, she stared at Steve's smile and then back at her cat—her beautiful, angry, totally alive cat. Even with the evidence in front of her, she found it hard to believe. Steve and Lucy began to blur as tears filled her eyes and ran unchecked down her cheeks.

"You found her?" Her voice came out hoarse and breathless, the last word catching on a sob.

Steve held out the squirming, spitting cat. "She was just where you'd said she'd be."

Taking Lucy into her arms, she hugged the cat to her, not caring that Lucy's claws were digging through her clothes and pricking her skin. She welcomed the pain, actually. It was what convinced her that Lucy was really and truly alive.

"You saved the cat!" Mackenzie cheered, and Steve gave her an offended look.

"Of course I saved the cat. I *always* save the cat."

Camille gave a soggy laugh. "Thank you. Sorry I doubted you. I just..." The tears started again, clogging her voice. "When we d-didn't see her at first..." She couldn't say it. It was too fresh and painful, even with Lucy now safely in her arms.

"Sorry for scaring you." Steve crouched down so they were face-to-face. "I needed my hands free for the ladder."

She shook her head. "No, you don't need to apologize. You're wonderful. You saved Lucy. I—" *I love you* almost slipped out, but she caught it in time. "Thank you, Steve. Thank you for Lucy...and for not letting me go back inside to die."

"I'll always keep you safe." In the charged silence that followed his quiet declaration, he dropped his eyes for a moment. When he raised them again, his gaze was cautious. "That's part of my job description, after all. Keeping everyone safe...people *and* cats."

There was tension in his voice and in the way he rushed out his words that Camille didn't understand. On a good day, she wasn't that great at subtext, and this definitely was not a good day. She was stripped raw inside and incapable of saying anything except the truth.

"It's not just the job," she told him honestly, holding his gaze. "It's you. You're an honest-to-God hero, Steve Springfield."

He went still, his eyes heating as they focused on hers. "Camille…" He moved closer, his expression intent.

It was Camille's turn to freeze. The way he leaned in, his gaze locked with hers, that intense stare that made her belly squeeze with anticipation, made her breath catch. He looked like he wanted to kiss her. The butterflies in her stomach looped and swirled, and Camille tightened her grip on the cat in her arms. Now? Steve was going to kiss her *now*, when she was sooty and snotty and still hiccuping with sobs? He shifted even closer, until their faces were only inches apart, and Camille's eyelids fluttered shut.

Her heart was full to bursting with emotions for Steve, pushing aside all of her other worries. If he was going to kiss her, she was surprisingly okay with that.

"Springfield, I need you on the engine. There's an issue with one of the pumps."

Chief Rodriguez's shout made Camille's eyes pop open. Steve was still close enough that the air from his sigh brushed her lips. Looking discomfited, he stood up.

"Sorry, Chief." He gave his head a small shake, as if reorienting himself. "I'm on it." Turning back to Camille, he gave her an intense look that only lasted a second but made her heart squeeze with the weight of his gaze. "Glad you're okay, Camille." Before she could pull herself out of her flustered daze to reply, he'd already jogged off toward the engine's malfunctioning pump.

"You okay?" Mackenzie asked. Camille realized that the woman had been focusing on the contents of her medic bag while Steve and Camille had been caught up in each other, and she gave Mackenzie a small, appreciative smile for her discretion. "The EMTs should be here in less than a minute."

"I'm wonderful." Camille gave the firefighter a tired smile, all the stress and horror and adrenaline of the night hitting her at once.

Mackenzie gave her a careful once-over. "Okay, then I'm going to jump in and give one of the others a break. Just let the chief—he's the one in the white helmet who keeps shouting orders at people—know if you start feeling dizzy or cold or not right in any way, okay?"

"Got it. I'm fine." It was the truth, now that Steve and Lucy were safe. "Go ahead."

As Mackenzie headed to relieve one of the other firefighters, Camille held Lucy tightly. Now that she had her cat in her arms, she was able to look at the house and really notice the damage. She wasn't a trained firefighter, but Camille still knew that the house wouldn't be able to be saved. Even if they magically managed to put out the fire in the next few moments, there'd only be a blackened shell left.

Her tears came again, quietly this time, rolling down her cheeks one by one as she silently grieved for the house she grew up in. Her grandma had been so proud of that place and the care she'd taken to furnish and decorate it. Even after she'd died, Camille hadn't had the heart to change much of anything. She wanted to keep everything the way it was so she could be reminded of her grandma. Now all that was gone. Her home, her workshop, her tools, every last keepsake and possession.

Gone.

Even more practical things, like her driver's license and her bank card, would need to be replaced. Where was she going to stay? She couldn't even drive somewhere and stay in a hotel, since she didn't have an ID or a way to pay or even the keys to her car—although at least the Buick was still intact and parked safely at the curb. Her grief and exhaustion merged, leaving her feeling empty and completely hopeless.

"Camille!" a male voice shouted. She turned her head to see Nate rushing toward her, his expression tight with worry. "Are you okay?"

"I'm fine," she said automatically, pushing back all of her tumbling thoughts. "What are you doing here?" For some reason, the thought of all of Search and Rescue descending on her again made her want to hide.

"I was going home after a search-and-rescue call and heard the dispatcher give your address. What happened? What started the fire?"

"There you are!" Ryan jogged toward them, his gaze running over Camille's bundled figure. "I came as soon as I heard about the fire. Are you hurt?"

"She's okay," Nate answered before she could.

Ryan reached her, opening his arms as if he was about to pull her into a hug.

"You might not want to do that," she warned, drawing back. She tipped her chin toward the cat in her arms. Although Lucy had stopped growling, Camille was positive that the cat would not appreciate being smashed between two bodies. "My cat's a little upset right now."

"Understandable." He eyed her like Mackenzie and Nate had, as if checking for any burns. "Were you hurt at all? I'm so glad you managed to get out." He glanced at the bonfire of her house and then back at her. "When I heard the dispatcher give your address for a fire call, I had to make sure you were all right."

"The dispatcher?" Camille felt like her mind had slowed down to half speed. What Ryan was saying didn't make any sense. "Where'd you hear the dispatcher?"

He hesitated for a beat. "The radio was on in Steve's · bedroom."

"Oh." His answer reminded her of another question. "Who's staying with the kids if you're here?"

"Joe. I waited until he arrived before I left the ranch." His hand moved toward her face, but she flinched back, oversensitive from everything that had happened. "Sorry. You have some black streaks. Is that soot?"

One of her shoulders came up in a half shrug. She didn't really care about her appearance.

"Were you inside when the house was burning?" Nate sounded so worried for her, but Camille couldn't seem to scrape up any emotions at all. It was as if she'd felt so much and so strongly that she'd hollowed herself out and couldn't feel anything anymore—at least for a while.

"In the workshop." The smell and the brightness and the heat of the fire came back at her in a rush, and she barely stopped herself from flinching back. "I got out, but Steve had to go in and get Lucy."

"Lucy?" Ryan asked.

She tipped her head toward the cat in her arms again. "My cat."

"Steve saved your cat?"

"Yes." Her chest ached at the memory of those awful minutes before Steve had emerged from the burning house and placed Lucy in her arms. "I'll never be able to repay him for that. It was the bravest thing I've ever seen."

Nate made a sound that Camille assumed was agreement. "He's a brave guy, our Steve."

She just nodded, not sure even where to start thanking Steve for everything he'd done in the past hour—from saving her life to saving Lucy's. What thanks could possibly be enough for that?

"If you're sure you're okay, I'm going to see if they need any help," Nate added, his eyes glued to the buzzing hive of activity. He gave her shoulder a gentle squeeze before hurrying away. Camille watched him go, numbly observing the way he melded into the work the firefighters were busy doing. She couldn't help but think that if Nate had been here, he would've braved the heat to try to save Lucy as well. The Springfield boys were pretty amazing. Her gaze moved to find Steve, and she couldn't help but give a tiny, shaky smile when she saw him striding toward her.

"Where are you going to stay?" Ryan asked, dropping a proprietary hand on her shoulder as Steve rejoined their small group.

Okay, so maybe three of the four Springfield boys are amazing.

Camille shifted to shrug Ryan off, tears beginning to roll down her cheeks again at the question. "I-I'm not sure." Her voice sounded small and choked, but she was too overwhelmed to care about maintaining a brave face. "I… Um, I don't have an ID or a debit card or anything really. Maybe I can trade you a sculpture for a few nights in your barn? It is the season for sleeping in stables, after all. All the famous people do it."

Her joking fell flat, and Ryan didn't even crack a smile. "You're coming home with me."

"No." Mrs. Lin walked over, her coat covering most of her pajamas and robe. "She's staying with me. Her grandmother would haunt me for the rest of my days if I didn't take her in."

The thought of staying with Mrs. Lin was almost as horrifying as sharing Ryan's cabin. The thought made Camille's chest tighten with anxiety. She had to sleep somewhere, though, at least for the night. Maybe tomorrow she could go to the hotel in Ebba—if they'd let her stay without an intact credit card. "I…" she started, having no idea how she was going to finish her sentence, much less find a bed for the night.

"She'll be staying with me." The stern edge to Steve's words was as sharp as an ax blade, but she didn't even feel the cut as she smiled at him wholeheartedly. For the third time that night, he was saving her. Staying with Steve and his kids would be wonderful, she knew. She already felt like she fit with them, and now she'd be living with them. That, however, presented another dilemma.

"Where? The kids already share, and the bedrooms are full." Ryan's objections echoed Camille's thoughts.

Before Steve could respond, she said, "I'm happy to sleep on the couch. Besides, it won't be more than a couple of days, just until I can get my ID and credit cards replaced."

"She'll be staying with me," Mrs. Lin insisted.

"No," Camille said baldly. She knew it wasn't polite, but she couldn't live with Mrs. Lin, not even for a few days. One of them would end up murdered for sure. "I'm staying with Steve. Don't argue with me about this. I'm not going to back down. My cat and I nearly died, and I'm right on the edge of losing it completely, so please, just accept that I'm going home with Steve." Mrs. Lin looked so stunned that Camille felt a tiny spark of sympathy and offered a sop for her neighbor's pride. "I would appreciate it if you could watch the property for me, though, and keep it safe."

Mrs. Lin looked at the remains of Camille's house suspiciously. The fire had burned surprisingly fast, and there wasn't much left except the home's blackened skeleton and an ashy heap. "From what?"

"Looters," Camille blurted out, and she noticed that Steve had to look away, his mouth tightening in the way it did when he was trying to hold back a smile. "I read about it on…uh, the internet. There's a gang that scans the fire stations' radios and goes from site to site, picking through the wreckage. They could come anytime, and you need to be on guard. I don't want thieves to get anything that's left of Grandma's stuff." Mrs. Lin was softening, but Camille could tell she wasn't there yet. "And the car. I don't have keys for it right now, so I'll need to leave it here, and a fire-scavenging gang like that would strip Grandma's car in minutes."

"Fine." To Camille's relief, Mrs. Lin went with the made-up story. "I'll watch out for that gang."

"Thank you, Mrs. Lin."

"In exchange, you're going to tell me the truth about all those men."

Camille was speechless, her mouth hanging open as she tried to come up with a retort. After a half second of silence, Ryan and Steve both asked the same question at the same time.

"What men?"

CHAPTER 10

THE FLAMES WERE EVERYWHERE, RED RIMMED IN BLACK, surrounding her on all sides, boxing her into a flickering coffin made of fire. Get out! *her mind was screaming, but her body wouldn't move. All she could do was lie on her back as the inferno raged around her, getting closer and closer to her vulnerable skin. Frantically, she looked around, trying to find the door, but there was no exit. Even if she could've forced her limbs to move, there was nowhere to go.*

She was trapped.

There! A dark figure moved toward her, and her heart jumped with hope as she recognized the shape of a fire helmet. Steve was here. He'd save her. She tried to shout, to let him know she needed help, to show him where she was, but all that escaped was an almost-silent gasp.*

Despite her inability to call to him, the figure drew closer, and Camille let out a sob of relief when the details of his bunker gear became clearer. The firefighter strode through the smoke and flames, seemingly heedless of the fire that licked at his pants and coat. The reflective stripes lit up red from the surrounding flames, but his face stayed in shadow. Rather than radiating safety, the approaching figure seemed menacing.

Fear and dread filled Camille, extinguishing her

brief flash of hope. She struggled to move, needing to escape—not from the flames, but from the person bearing down on her. She'd hoped for a rescuer, but everything inside her was screaming to get away from the menacing figure inexorably closing in on her.

She was too late.

Unable to move anything below her neck, she lay frozen, her breath coming in terrified pants, as the dark shape loomed over her, silhouetted by the roaring flames. As the figure bent closer, gloved hands reaching out, Camille squeezed her eyes closed and choked on a scream that couldn't escape, waiting for the first bite of pain.

Camille's whole body jerked, waking her up. She lay still for a moment, her eyes closed, reorienting herself, trying to figure out what was real and what had been just a terrifying dream.

The light was wrong.

There was too much of it, and it turned the insides of her eyelids red, not letting her sink back into sleep. As she blinked them open, she took in the unfamiliar room, and everything came back in a rush—the fire, Steve saving Lucy and then offering them both a place to stay. Oh, but the house and all her things…

She sat up abruptly, cutting off that line of thought before she could tumble into a deep lake of grief. The quick movement disturbed Lucy, who'd been curled against her hip. The cat gave an annoyed grumble before closing her eyes again. Glancing at the clock sitting on the nightstand, Camille saw it was almost noon, which explained why everything was so bright.

The sun-drenched room was such a far cry from the burned wreck she imagined her own bedroom was now that her stomach pitched. All her fear and sadness threatened to seep into her thoughts again, and she firmly pushed them back, swallowing down her nausea. "I'm alive," she said, and the words sounded loud in the quiet room. "Lucy's alive. Steve's alive. That's all that matters."

Knowing that she needed to move, to distract herself from her lingering thoughts, she slid out of bed, looking around the room—Steve's bedroom. He'd had to finish the "mopping up," as he'd called it, so Ryan had dropped her off. Steve had texted Joe, so he knew the basic details of her situation, and he'd shown her to Steve's room.

When she'd protested, saying that she'd take the couch, Joe had scowled and said gruffly, "Steve'll take the pullout in the den. He wants you in here." Since Camille found cranky Joe a little intimidating, she didn't argue with him. She did feel bad about pushing Steve out of his room, though.

It was a really nice room, too. The kids' rooms were bigger—there were two people in each of those, after all—but Camille liked Steve's the best, and not just because it had an en-suite bathroom. The bed was large, with a simple headboard, and it took up a great deal of the space. There was a large window on the south wall, which was the source of all the sunlight that had woken her, and the east had another with a window seat. The best part was that the top portion of that window was made of stained glass. She could just imagine how the rising sun would splash the room with bright colors.

Despite the light pouring through the windows, the room was chilly. She shivered, hugging herself. After showering, she hadn't wanted to put any of her smoky, dirty clothes back on, so she'd borrowed a T-shirt and some exercise shorts from Steve's dresser. They hung off her, so loose that the shorts threatened to fall off her hips, reminding her that the clothes she'd been wearing the previous night were the only ones she had left.

The creeping grief started to sneak back in, and Camille once again shoved it back. "They can be washed," she said firmly. "Maybe one of the kids has something that will tide me over for a few hours."

She used the bathroom, making a face at the sharp smell of acrid smoke coming from her pile of abandoned clothes. She borrowed Steve's hairbrush and scrubbed her teeth with a little toothpaste on her finger, adding a toothbrush and floss to the mental list of things she needed to buy. First, though, she needed to talk to her bank and get a new card, or she wouldn't be able to buy anything—or even withdraw any cash without ID.

She realized that she needed to start writing things down. Otherwise, she'd keep running through her mental list, and that would just make her sadder and more frantic. Gathering up her smoky clothes, she left Steve's bedroom to search for a washing machine.

The house was so quiet it seemed empty, and she found herself tiptoeing down the stairs, feeling like an interloper. Even though Steve had invited her, she still felt strange to be alone in a house that wasn't hers, especially while she was wearing his clothes. It wasn't all bad, though—even though it was obviously clean, his

T-shirt still smelled like Steve. The bedding had as well, and being able to bury her face in a pillow bearing his scent had allowed her to drift off into fitful sleep.

The door to Steve's study was closed, and Camille figured he was still sleeping. She hadn't heard him return from the fire the night before, so she wasn't sure what time he'd gotten back. She hadn't climbed into bed until after 4:00 a.m., so he'd probably been dumping water on the remains of her house until close to dawn. The mental image of Steve and the other firefighters working on the blackened, ruined shell of her house popped into her mind, and she stopped in the middle of the living room and squeezed her eyes closed.

That only made it worse, so she opened them again to find Steve standing in the now-open doorway of his study, looking rumpled and sleepy and incredibly tempting. "Oh! I mean, good morning."

The greeting struck her as wrong—it wasn't a good morning, not when her house had just burned down—and she grimaced.

"'Morning." Glancing at his watch, he amended that. "Afternoon now."

She clutched her smoky bundle tighter against her chest, feeling awkward and vulnerable in her oversized clothes—*his* clothes. "Did I wake you?"

"No." His gaze flicked down to her bare legs before snapping back up to meet her eyes, his face reddening. "I'm just bad at sleeping during the day, even after staying up most of the night on a call or when one of the kids is sick." He rubbed a hand over the lower part of his face, which was covered in rough stubble that made him even more attractive than his usual clean-shaven look. Camille hadn't thought it was possible for him to be hotter; obviously, she'd been wrong.

Dragging her gaze off the sexy, scruffy shadow that covered his jaw, she glanced down at the bundle of clothes in her arms. "Would you…" Her voice came out raspy, and she cleared her throat before continuing. "Do you mind if I wash these things? I was hoping to get the smoke smell out of them."

"Go ahead. The laundry room is off the kitchen. It's the door next to the bathroom."

"Thanks." It was a chicken move, she knew, but she took advantage of the out that doing laundry offered. If she continued talking to mussed, sleepy-eyed, just-rolled-out-of-bed Steve much longer, she knew she'd end up saying something embarrassing—or just standing there and staring at him, which would be just as bad. It was better to run while she had the ability to pull herself away from temptation.

In the archway leading to the kitchen, she stopped. She couldn't leave without at least trying to express her gratitude for everything he'd done for her in the past twelve hours. "Thank you," she said, looking over her shoulder to catch him staring at her—her butt, to be exact.

He jerked his head up, quickly shifting his gaze to meet hers, but it was too late for him to pretend it didn't happen. His eyes were lit with heat. "What?"

In all the years she'd known him, Camille never seen him so off-balance, and it made her like him even more. "Thank you," she repeated, unable to keep a smile off her face. Steve Springfield had been checking her out. She'd honestly never expected that to happen. "Thank you for everything you did last night, and for letting me stay here…and giving up your bed. You didn't have to do that."

"You're welcome." He was obviously working very hard to keep his gaze from wandering, and her pulse began to flutter. "I wouldn't have felt right knowing you were down here on the pullout."

"Is it awful?" The ever-present guilt floated up again. "Didn't you sleep well?"

He waved a hand, as if brushing off her worries. "It's fine. I've had that couch for years and know exactly how to avoid the uncomfortable spots."

"Well, thank you again for letting me sleep here. Your bed was very comfortable."

His eyes narrowed slightly, heat flaring in them again, and she shifted her weight, both delighted and a little flustered by his reaction. Despite her borrowed, ill-fitting, very unflattering outfit, he was obviously interested, and her body was responding with corresponding arousal. "Good." His voice was deep, even gritty.

Her arms squeezed her clothes against her convulsively. "Um. So. These are all smoky and sooty and really pretty gross, but they're my only clothes left in the world now, so I'd better go put these in…" Her nerve broke, and she darted into the kitchen. By the time she'd found the laundry room and was putting her clothes in the washer, she was already regretting not staying and seeing where her strange conversation with Steve would've led. It had seemed so *intimate*, talking to him after they'd both just woken up, with her in his house, in his bed, in his clothes…

Her cheeks felt like they were on fire. Blowing out a long breath, she added detergent and started the washer.

She needed to stop thinking about it, or she wouldn't be able to look at him, much less have a normal conversation. It was stupid to focus so many of her thoughts on him right now, anyway. Her house had burned down. There were a lot of critical things she needed to do, and they did not include mooning over Steve. Determined to act like a normal person for once, she stepped out into the kitchen.

Steve was standing at the counter, his back to her. Despite her resolution, she had to admire the way his strong form filled out his T-shirt and jeans…especially the jeans.

"Coffee?" he asked, pulling a filled mug from the Keurig and holding it out to her.

"No, thank you. I'm not a big coffee fan." At times like these, when any normal person would have used coffee as a comfort and a brace, she wished she did drink it. "Could I have paper and a pen?"

After placing the coffee on the table, he rummaged in a drawer and pulled out a notepad. After a few more moments of digging, he offered it to her, along with a pencil, a sparkly blue marker, a black Sharpie, and a broken piece of chalk. "Will one of these work? Otherwise, I should have a pen in the study."

For some reason, the motley assortment of writing utensils made her smile. It reminded her of how varied—and delightful—his kids were. She selected the blue marker. "This is perfect."

She sat down at the table and immediately started making her list, writing down the essentials that had been spinning in her head since the fire. Settling into the chair across from her, Steve quietly sipped his coffee.

When she finally began running out of things to put down, she'd covered a full page and part of a second in sparkly blue words. The length of the list made her sag in her chair. It seemed enormously impossible, especially without a vehicle or a phone or any form of ID or access to her money or even a coat—

"Here." As if he'd read her mind, Steve slid his cell phone toward her. "Call your insurance company first. When you're ready to go, I'll bring you into town. You can borrow a coat from me. It'll be too big." For a moment, his gaze darted down to her—well, his—T-shirt. "But it'll keep you warm. We'll go to the bank, and then we'll drive to the Target in Ebba. You can get clothes, toiletries, and pet supplies there. There's a DMV, too, so we can find out how to go about getting a copy of your license. Once we get back, you can use my laptop to order a copy of your birth certificate and do whatever you need to do as far as notifying your customers goes." Gently taking the marker out of her hand, he made a mark by the first ten or so items on her list. "If you promise not to tell anyone, we'll get Zoe to hot-wire your Buick so we can drive it to the dealership and get a new key made. That way, you won't have to have it towed."

She could only stare at him, so grateful she felt shaky and close to tears.

"If you're up for it, we'll stop by Jackie's office. She's the fire marshal. You can give your statement, and she has some helpful information about what to do after a fire. You'll get through this, Camille. It won't be much fun, but we'll all be here, doing whatever we can to help."

Setting down the marker, he picked up his coffee

again, as calm and steady as if he hadn't just taken her upside-down world and turned it right side up again. She was trying to focus on what she needed to do in the next few minutes or hours so that she could ignore the enormity of what had happened—how her home, her haven, had been completely destroyed. Everything had seemed so hopeless and overwhelming and impossible until Steve lined up the first steps for her.

She blinked back tears and took quavering breath after quavering breath, trying to think of the words that would express how grateful she was and how wonderful *he* was. When she could finally speak, what came out was not what she'd planned. "Zoe knows how to hot-wire a car?"

He grinned at her from behind his coffee cup, looking so mischievous and adorable that she fell in love with him a little. "It's a handy talent."

"Yeah, it is." She looked down at her list again. Although it was still painfully long, it wasn't nearly as overwhelming anymore. Even the items that Steve hadn't checked off seemed much more possible now. Looking up at him, she said simply, "Thank you."

He tipped his chin down in acknowledgment, falling silent as she turned back to her list. She made notes on the items he'd mentioned and added a few more things that she'd missed the first time. Now that the list didn't feel as hopeless, it felt good to be doing something constructive.

A short time later, Camille looked up again. "There. Now I feel like I have a rough—really rough—plan for getting my life back together."

"Good." Steve had finished his coffee and was sitting back in his chair, stroking Lucy, who was curled on his lap. The sight of her reminded Camille of how close she'd come to losing her cat, and her eyes grew blurry yet again.

Blinking rapidly, she managed to keep the tears from falling. There was too much to do for her to collapse now. "Thank you again for saving her."

He dipped his head in a nod. She figured he was probably tired of her thanking him, but that was just too bad, since she had a feeling she'd be doing it a lot more in the coming days and weeks. Besides, he deserved every thank-you—and so much more.

"What…" She paused, not wanting to ask since she really didn't want to know the answer. It was important for her to find out, though, so she took a deep breath and tried again. "What's left of the house? Anything?"

He paused before he answered, and Camille's stomach tightened with anxiety. "Not much. We pulled a few things out that you'll need to take a look at, see if you want to salvage anything…especially your metalwork. The house itself, though… It's gone." He held her gaze as he spoke, not cringing away from sharing the bad news.

Camille, however, did flinch. She'd thought she'd accepted that the house had been reduced to blackened scrap and ashes, but it still hurt to hear it said so bluntly. There must've been a little bubble of hope tucked way down deep that her home, her grandma's home, could be fixed. "Okay." The word quivered, and she straightened in her chair, determined not to break down over something she'd already known. The second question, however, was even more difficult to ask. "D-do you know…" Her mouth felt uncomfortably dry, and she swallowed hard. Steve's sympathetic gaze was about three seconds away from making her cry, so she just blurted out the rest of it. "What caused the fire?"

As the question hung in the air, Camille felt her muscles tighten more and more with every second that ticked by. She knew that Steve wasn't trying to torture her. He just wanted to choose the right words. Still, the waiting was almost intolerable when she was about to find out if it was all her fault.

"The fire marshal's just started investigating," he said, and that didn't help at all.

"There's a theory already, though, isn't there?" She tried to hide that her breaths were coming in quick, shallow gasps, but Steve's concerned gaze showed that he was aware of how emotionally fragile and on edge she felt.

"She's a stickler about not running her mouth before she's thoroughly investigated and has solid conclusions," Steve said, and Camille resisted the urge to protest. She didn't know how long a fire investigation usually took, but her nerves wouldn't be able to withstand waiting days, weeks, or even months for an answer. "Just between us, though, her initial impression is that it was an issue with the wiring."

"What kind of issue?"

He raised his free hand in a slight shrug. "When fires start in an older house like that, it's commonly because the knob-and-tube wiring gets compromised."

"Compromised?" she asked.

"Usually by rodents."

"Oh." Her mind immediately went to the mice. Even though they could've been the reason her house burned down, she hoped that they'd managed to escape. "There were mice. Lucy didn't seem to have much interest in catching them." She thought of the one that her cat had dropped on her foot. It had seemed so long ago, even though it'd only been a couple of days. "Well, killing them, at least."

Smiling a little, he looked down at the cat. "We all have different strengths and interests, don't we, Lucy?"

She purred, seemingly not at all bothered by their new homeless state. Camille felt a little lighter, but she wanted to know for sure that Steve wasn't protecting her feelings.

"It couldn't have been something I did?" she asked. "A stray spark from the torch or forgetting to unplug something or…" Her brain ran over everything she'd done that night before falling asleep, but she'd been so tired and so much had happened since then that she couldn't remember doing anything that could end up being a fire hazard. She'd been sketching, for Pete's sake. That seemed like the safest thing she could do in her workshop. "I don't know. Maybe an equipment short or something?"

"No." The bald answer made Camille's muscles go limp with relief. The vague guilt she'd been feeling since the night before drained out of her as he continued. "We do know for sure that the fire started inside the north wall of the workshop. It wasn't anywhere close to your workbench."

She mentally ran over everything that had been close to the north wall. All she'd had on that side of the workshop was a set of shelves holding wood and metal that had been too big or too fragile to be tossed in her scrap bin. Nothing had even been plugged into any of the outlets on the north wall.

Another wave of relief coursed through her. "Good." The word seemed so small for the huge weight that had been lifted off her. "Stupid mice, though."

Steve huffed a quiet laugh as he continued to stroke Lucy. "I'm surprised she's willing to get near me," he said, his hand continuing its regular movement, stroking Lucy's back over and over. Camille found it mesmerizing. "She wasn't that thrilled with me last night."

"She's forgiving." Camille made a wry grimace. "When she first showed up at my house, she had pretty much every medical issue known to vets. The number of pills I've forced down this cat's throat... She still lets me love on her, though. Well, if she's in the mood."

He chuckled, rubbing under Lucy's chin, and the cat closed her eyes in bliss, purring loudly.

I don't blame you one bit, Lucy girl, Camille thought. If Steve had been rubbing her, she was pretty certain she'd be purring, too. Just the thought made her cheeks heat, and she quickly ducked her head, pretending to add to her notes until she could get her reaction under control. *It's the fire*. That was the reason her emotions were jumping around all over the place—from grief to hopelessness to gratitude to lust.

As much as she enjoyed staying with Steve, she hadn't even begun to process the loss of her house. It had been the only safe shelter she'd ever known, her sanctuary since her grandma had brought her there as a child. Now, that was gone, and she felt raw and naked and utterly vulnerable. All the physical mementos of her grandma and even her mom were gone, and it felt as if she was truly alone in the world. No family, no house, no workshop...just memories.

Clearing her throat, Camille stood abruptly. "My clothes are probably ready to go into the dryer."

After gently placing Lucy on the floor, Steve got up as well. "There's a plastic bin in the shop that would work for a litter box, at least to tide Lucy over until we get back. I'll go grab it. Figured we'd have lunch while your clothes are drying." He gave her a quick up-and-down. Instead of being offensive, his almost bashful manner made the gesture seem sweet. "You can't go outside like that. Your legs would freeze."

Now that her spinning thoughts had been mapped out with Steve's help, her stomach had settled down enough for her to realize she was actually really hungry. "That sounds good."

Giving her legs a final, quick glance, he went into the entryway. As she turned toward the laundry, she heard him talking. His words were quiet, so she didn't think he was directing them toward her. Curious if someone else was there, especially since she hadn't heard the door, she moved to the entryway.

Steve was the only one there. His back was to her as he pulled on his boots, stomping his feet into them almost angrily. "Get yourself together," he muttered. As Camille realized that he was talking to himself—*lecturing* himself, more accurately—she started to smile. It was something she always did, and seeing strong, calm, and confident Steve exhibit the same quirk made her feel like less of a dork. "You're not a sixteen-year-old kid. Quit talking about her legs. Quit *looking* at her legs. She's going to think she's living with a creeper."

Covering her mouth with her hand to keep her laughter from bursting out, Camille tiptoed backward into the kitchen. It wasn't until she was in the laundry room with the door closed that she let her giggles escape. Underneath her amusement was a tickled sense of pride. She'd never thought about her legs much or considered them one of her outstanding features. Her hair and her full lips were her favorites, and the rest she thought to be fairly average. Steve, however, had apparently been entranced by them. She'd spent so much time getting distracted by how good-looking Steve was that it was nice to know it wasn't a totally one-sided admiration after all.

Once her clothes were in the dryer and her pleased laughter had settled, she returned to the kitchen and headed for the fridge. One thing she'd decided while making the list was that she was going to do her best to pull her weight at the ranch, whether that meant cooking or cleaning or barn chores or even working at the store.

She cringed at the thought of the last one. Crowds of demanding customers weren't her favorite thing, but she'd deal with them if Steve requested it.

By the time he returned from the shop, she'd fed Lucy some leftover chicken and had two cheese sandwiches in a skillet on the stove.

"That'll be perfect," she said, seeing that he'd half filled the plastic bin with fine wood shavings. "Thank you. Lucy thanks you, too." The cat was, in fact, rubbing around Steve's ankles.

"I put some stall bedding in there," he said, tucking the bin into an out-of-the-way corner of the kitchen before washing his hands. His cheeks were ruddy from the cold, and Camille felt much better admiring how great he looked all wind-tossed now that she knew he had similar thoughts about her. "Think that'll work? I thought about using chicken grit for cat litter, but I worried it might be too rough on Lucy's paws."

She was quickly finding that when Steve was sweet to her cat, her insides turned to goo. "This is perfect."

Giving one of his short nods, he glanced at the grilled cheese sandwiches. "Smells good. Want some soup with that?"

"Sure." She flipped one of the sandwiches, pleased that it was a perfect golden brown. Her cooking skills were limited, but she could make a mean grilled cheese. "I was going to heat some up but didn't see any in the pantry."

He grinned proudly as he opened the freezer. "Micah's our chef. He's even better than Nate, and that's saying something. Micah went on a soup-making binge a few weeks ago when we had that cold snap. We ate so much soup that we finally said enough and froze all that was left." Pulling out a plastic container, he held it up so she could see. "Tomato basil."

"He made soup? From scratch?" It had never occurred to her to even try. "I'd never thought about soup coming from anywhere except a can."

As he popped the frozen soup in the microwave, Steve gave her a conspiratorial smile. "Me either, until Micah started putting soup bones and cooking wine on the grocery list."

With a laugh, she pulled two bowls and two plates out of the cupboard. "Your kids are sort of amazing."

"Yeah." He sounded proud but baffled. The microwave dinged, and he poured the soup into a saucepan, placing it on the stove to finish heating. "Growing up, I was so average, kind of doofy, even. Don't really know what I did to deserve such incredible kids."

Camille gave a little snort as she flipped the sandwiches onto the plates. "Please. I was there. You were *not* average, and you were definitely not doofy."

"That's because you were, what…four years younger than me? You were too young to notice the doofiness." He leaned a hip against the counter as he stirred the soup, one corner of his mouth creeping up into a teasing half smile. Once again, she was struck by the homey intimacy of the moment, cooking together as they talked about his kids. It was wonderful and surreal at the same time.

"Three years younger," she corrected him. "I was a freshman when you were a senior, and I was well aware of any doofy qualities in everyone else. Jeremy Dill, for example."

Steve groaned even as he laughed. "Dilly! I'd forgotten about him. Yeah, he was doofier than I was."

"By far, and he still is. He sells insurance in Ebba, but he still lives in Borne, and I run into him far too often." Putting the plated sandwiches on the table, she got two bowls from the cupboard and then filled a couple of glasses with water. "I'm still not convinced you have any doofy qualities." As she put spoons next to their plates, she realized that she hadn't taken into account whether his brothers would be there for lunch. "I forgot to ask if anyone else would be eating with us."

"Just us. Nate and Ryan are working the store and lot today. Weekdays tend to be quieter, so they'll swing by one at a time when they can grab something to eat." The soup started bubbling, and Steve hurried to lift it off the burner. "I'd be in trouble with Micah if he saw that. I'm not supposed to let it boil." As he divided the soup between the two bowls, Camille hid a smile. It was so obvious how much he not only loved his kids, but also liked them like crazy. "What?" he asked.

Guess she hadn't hidden her smile well enough. "You're such a good dad," she answered honestly.

His cheeks darkened, and he concentrated on getting the soup into the bowls. "Thank you. That means a lot. Now that they're older, it's gotten harder. I worry that I'm doing it wrong, that I'm going to mess them up somehow." He sounded so sincere that she felt a tight squeeze in her chest. If she wasn't careful, Steve Springfield could very easily put a serious dent in her heart.

CHAPTER 11

IT DIDN'T MATTER HOW MANY TIMES STEVE HAD SEEN A similar scene; it never got any easier. Today was especially hard, since it was Camille's house, and she was the one standing by him trying to keep it together as she took in the ruined mess that used to be her home. He thought about saying one of the usual platitudes about how good it was that no one got hurt but decided to stay silent. It was true, of course, but it was also true that losing a home and belongings to a fire was a terrible, traumatic experience. Camille didn't need to hear once again that she was lucky to have survived. It would most likely just make her feel guilty for grieving about things, and that was nothing she should have to feel bad about.

It was killing him not to be able to do anything to make her feel better, though. She looked so pale and small and sad, huddled in the oversized coat he'd loaned her. Underneath that, he knew her hoodie and shirt had small, burned holes and smelled faintly of smoke, an odor that washing hadn't completely removed.

He wished they were at a different point, that he could hug her and tell her how glad he was that she was okay, that he could've held her as she slept in his bed, wearing his clothes… He shifted his weight, uncomfortable with where his mind had gone. Once the image popped into his head, however, it was difficult to dislodge.

"I can't believe this is what's left," Camille said quietly, immediately snapping his attention back to where it should be. The wind caught a pale strand of her hair, blowing it across her cheek, and she absently tucked it into her hood. "It was so fast. One minute I was safe in my home, and the next it's like this." She swept a hand out, indicating the charred skeleton of the house looming above the broken and blackened pieces of what remained. "Can I go in there to see if I can find anything?"

At the crack in her voice, Steve couldn't take it anymore. He couldn't let her stand there, looking so alone and devastated. Wrapping his arms around her shoulders, he tucked her against him. Her body went stiff at the contact, but then she relaxed into him, leaning her slight weight into his side. She felt even smaller than she looked.

"Soon," he said, answering her question. "We need to make sure that what's remaining won't fall on you first."

"I don't mind waiting, actually." He felt her reach behind him and grab a handful of his jacket, as if to help hold herself up. "I'm honestly a little relieved. Digging through that and finding pieces of my life—well, what *used* to be my life—is going to be tough."

"You're tougher, so you'll be okay." He tightened his grip on her shoulder, pulling her in closer against him. The worst part of being a firefighter was when he couldn't protect people from things like this. "I mean, look at everything you did today."

She pushed far enough away to be able to look

up at him, wearing the tiniest of smiles. "I made a list and shopped—with your help. It wasn't exactly award-worthy."

He beamed at her, disproportionately elated by her small attempt at a joke. "You braved the DMV, Christmas-shopping-time Target, Borne Bank, *and* your first visit to your house, all while talking to your insurance agent and canceling utilities. If that isn't award-worthy, then I don't know what is."

Her smile grew, making him warm with pride. He'd actually done it—he'd made her feel a little better. Turning, she gave him a quick hug and a kiss on the cheek. By the time he'd unfrozen from his initial shock at the unexpected gesture and how very, very good it felt, she was already releasing him. Stepping back, she turned and headed to his truck. As warmth spread through his chest, he followed.

"Were you serious about…?" Trailing off, she looked around, as if checking for eavesdroppers. As he got closer, she finished in a loud whisper. "About the Zoe thing? With my car?"

He laughed. Something about Camille's exaggerated attempt at keeping Zoe's not-quite-age-appropriate skill a secret struck him as extraordinarily funny. "Yeah," he said. "The closest dealership is southeast of Denver, so that'd be an expensive tow."

"I know I've said it about a thousand times today, but thank you, Steve. I don't know what I would've done without you." She grimaced, her gaze faraway, as if she was thinking about terrible things. "I do know, actually. I would've run back into my house and probably died."

"No. Mackenzie would've stopped you. She was right

behind me. I just got to you first, so she ran back for the med kit and blanket." He opened the passenger door for her, using the movement to hide his discomfort. It'd always been tough for him to listen to people's heartfelt gratitude. He didn't know how to let them know that he understood how much they appreciated his help. A part of him didn't feel like he deserved the thanks when he was just doing his job. If it wasn't him, another firefighter or cop or EMT would've stepped in to do the same thing. He did his job, and he wasn't comfortable being called a hero.

"Hmm." The sound was noncommittal, but Steve had a feeling what he'd said hadn't made a difference. She was still going to thank him over and over for saving her and Lucy's lives. If it meant he could continue spending time with her—even if it was at the DMV—he was surprisingly okay with that.

She climbed into the truck, and he closed the door carefully before moving around to get into the driver's seat. As he buckled his seat belt, he caught another glimpse of the remains of the house, a stark, black silhouette against the gold of the late-afternoon sun. He paused, disturbed by the menacing grimness of the scene.

"Drive!" Camille whispered harshly, making him start. "Go! Now!"

"What is it?" Tense and alert, he scanned the area for real danger. His hand automatically reached for his truck radio mic, so he'd be ready to call for backup. There was nothing that he could see, though. The neighborhood was quiet as always.

She groaned dramatically. "It's too late now. She knows we've spotted her."

"Her? Who?" Steve leaned forward so he could see out Camille's window. He caught a glimpse of Mrs. Lin hurrying toward the car, and he suddenly understood Camille's rush to leave so she didn't get caught in a conversation. The realization was so anticlimactic that he snorted a laugh as his hand dropped off the mic. It was obvious that Camille was trying to glare at him, but she couldn't hold it.

"It's not funny," she wailed quietly. Despite her words, laughter bubbled in her voice. "We're trapped now. Next time I say 'drive,' you put your foot on the gas and floor it, got it?"

"Got it." He struggled to regain a straight face as he lowered Camille's window. Mrs. Lin was only a few steps away, carrying stuffed shopping bags.

"Good. I caught you." Mrs. Lin was puffing a little from exertion. "I thought you were going to drive off like mannerless heathens, leaving me coughing on your exhaust."

Steve fought the urge to chuckle again. It was Camille's fault. Normally, he knew people thought he was serious, even stern. He'd rather stay quiet and listen than talk. When he was around Camille, though, he became as happy and chatty as Maya on a sugar high. Camille made him feel lighter somehow, even when dealing with something as serious as a fire.

"No mannerless heathens here," she lied through her teeth, as if she hadn't been demanding that Steve do just that. He swallowed another laugh. "We're just in a hurry, since we're headed to the fire marshal's office, hoping to catch her before she leaves for the day."

Glancing at the dashboard clock, he saw it was four

forty. Even though Camille was using their rush as an excuse, it was actually true. They needed to move if they wanted to talk to Jackie.

"The fire marshal?" Mrs. Lin's voice was full of prurient interest, and Steve felt all of his good humor drain away. Camille didn't need nosy townspeople questioning her about her loss for their own gossipy amusement.

"Something we can do for you, Mrs. Lin?" he asked, knowing his tone came out short but not caring. Camille's feelings came first, and he was willing to be rude if necessary. In fact, he was willing to do a lot more than that to protect her.

"No. I have something for you, Camille." She lifted the two stuffed shopping bags she was holding. "This isn't much, just a few things from me and Gladys, but everyone in town heard what happened and wants to help, so you should be getting much more in a few days. What's in here isn't like your usual sloppy getups, but at least this way you'll have something to wear until you can manage to go shopping."

Suddenly realizing what Mrs. Lin was doing, Steve hopped out and circled the truck. "Here," he said, feeling much more kindly toward her than he'd been a minute ago. "Let me help."

"Thank you, Mrs. Lin. That was so kind of you and Mrs. Murphy." Camille got out of the truck as well. She moved as if to hug the older woman but awkwardly came to a halt when Mrs. Lin raised her hand and shook her finger in Camille's face.

"No getting up to any of your usual tricks with any of those Springfield boys, understand? It's bad enough when I was the only one watching, but now there are easily corruptible children to think of. Don't be leading them into any trouble, missy."

Steve stiffened. He didn't care what Mrs. Lin thought about him, but he was furious that she'd accused Camille of doing anything that might hurt the kids. This was Camille's neighbor and her grandma's friend, someone who'd known Camille her whole life. Mrs. Lin had to know her better than that, which made what she said so much worse, since her only reason was to be cruel.

"You—*oof*!" Camille's elbow caught him in the ribs, cutting him off. The nudge surprised him more than it hurt, and he got the message and closed his mouth, keeping his rant inside.

"I have no tricks to get up to," Camille said, somehow keeping a smile on her face as she held Mrs. Lin's narrowed gaze. "And I think Steve's children are more likely to lead me into trouble than to follow me there, so I think they're safe." She paused, looking thoughtful. "Safe from *me*, at least. If they manage to blow up the ranch, that's on them."

Mrs. Lin gaped at her, startled into silence. Steve couldn't hold back a grin. It was the first time he'd seen June Lin speechless, and he loved that Camille had won the argument—for now, at least.

"Camille, we should go," he said, putting the bags in the back seat with the box of sculptures they'd retrieved from her Buick, as well as all of Camille's purchases. Rose Varez, the manager at the bank, had known about the fire even before their visit earlier, and she'd helped Camille withdraw cash from her account and given her some temporary checks to hold her over until her new bank card arrived. It was a good thing, too, because

Camille had refused every offer Steve had made to pay for anything. He knew it would've crushed her pride if she'd had to accept money from him because she couldn't access her account.

"Right. Can't miss the fire marshal." Her smile brightened, becoming more authentic—likely because escape was imminent. "Thank you again, Mrs. Lin. And thank you for watching for looters for me, too."

Mrs. Lin glanced around, as if checking the area. "Well, no problems yet, but I imagine they'll be trying tonight."

"Make sure to get some sleep." Climbing into the passenger seat again, Camille waved as Steve closed her door and hurried around the truck. "Bye, Mrs. Lin."

Steve could only manage a short nod in farewell as he eased the truck away from the curb. Camille rolled the window up, and they traveled the short distance to Jackie's office in silence. As Mrs. Lin's words replayed in his mind, he grew more and more annoyed.

"I don't like how she talks to you," Steve finally said as he parked in the lot next to the county building.

"Me either." Despite her words, Camille didn't sound too concerned, and his irritation on her behalf rose even more. "Whenever she implies I'm a harlot—or just calls me that outright—I remind myself of how she was after Grandma died, so depressed and remote, and I try to be grateful that she's gotten her feistiness back. Besides, for her to successfully slut-shame me, I need to feel shame, and I try not to fall into that trap." She shoved open her door and hopped out. As they headed for the building entrance, she added, "Plus, I was so shocked that she and Mrs. Murphy got together to actually do something good that I wasn't paying much attention to what she was saying."

Steve chewed over Camille's answers in his head as he held the door and then followed her inside. "I still don't like that she implied you'd hurt the kids," he grumbled.

She gave him a smile over her shoulder, looking surprised and pleased. "Thank you."

His brows drew together. "For what?"

"For both knowing that and for being willing to take on Mrs. Lin for me," she said as he caught up to walk next to her. "Now, which way?"

"Straight ahead. It's the last office on the right."

As they walked into the fire marshal's office, Steve glanced at Camille and saw that her smile of just a few seconds ago was gone, and the grim set of her mouth was back. He knew the thought of the upcoming meeting was forcing her to mentally relive the fire, and it bothered him that he couldn't save her from the horrible memories, or from having to recount the entire experience to Jackie. He resisted the urge to put an arm around Camille again, knowing that it was one thing when they were alone at what remained of her house, and another in front of Len Gershowitz, Jackie's assistant and probably an even more prolific gossip than Deanna Lin. Steve didn't care what was being spread around Borne about the two of them, but he worried that Camille might be bothered by it.

Already, Len was looking back and forth between the two of them, his eyes bright with interest as he gave Camille a sympathetic grimace. "I'm so sorry about your house."

"Thank you," she said quietly, looking even more miserable.

"Hey, Len. Is Jackie still here?" Steve wanted to get this done so that he could take Camille home. There the kids could cheer her up and get her mind off of what had happened. He knew from personal experience that they were good at that.

"Sure is. Jackie!" Len hollered without leaving his chair. "Camille and Steve are here to talk to you!"

"Send them in!" Jackie yelled from inside her office.

Len waved them toward the door, and Steve followed Camille inside. "Camille." Jackie, looking a little more harried than usual, stood up behind her desk and offered her hand. "Sorry about the house, but I'm glad you didn't burn with it. Hey, Steve." After shaking both of their hands, Jackie gestured for them to take the two chairs facing her desk before retaking her own seat.

"Steve said you needed to get my statement?" Camille said, and Jackie reached back to grab a few sheets of paper out of a printer.

"Yeah, I do. Here." She handed Camille the paper and then shuffled some things around, hunting for a pen. She picked up a yellow highlighter, appeared to consider it, and then dropped it again and resumed her search. "Aha! Knew there was one around here." She seized the pen she'd discovered under a mound of papers and offered it to Camille. "Just write what happened last night. I find it best to wait to ask you any questions until you've given me your statement."

"Okay." Camille scooted forward, as if to use Jackie's desk as a writing surface, but stopped, blocked by the messy piles of papers and folders. "Um…?"

"Right. Sorry about that. Len!" She bellowed the last word, making Camille visibly jump.

"What?"

"Is there a clipboard up there?"

There was a pause, and then Len called back, "Yes!"

Jackie started to stand, but Camille rose, putting out a hand to stop her. "I'll go get it." She slipped out of the office before Jackie or Steve could argue. Through the open door, Steve heard Len start to pepper her with questions, and he grimaced. Retrieving the clipboard was going to take a few minutes.

"Still looking like the old wiring was the cause?" Steve asked.

Jackie settled back in her chair, her mouth pulling down on one side as it always did when she was thinking. "Seems likely, but I'm keeping an open mind. Her neighbor sure had a boatload of possible suspects."

At the word *suspects*, Steve tensed and leaned forward. "You're thinking it could've been intentional?" He kept his voice low, not wanting to add one more stressor onto Camille's already full plate.

"It's always a possibility." Jackie gave a slight shrug, her alert gaze fixed on Steve. "You're closer to Camille than I am. What're your thoughts?"

He immediately bristled at the implication that Camille could have had anything to do with her house fire. The image of her face when he told her it hadn't been her fault flashed in his mind. She'd been so relieved and grateful, and he didn't want anything to ruin that and return the heavy load of guilt he knew she'd been carrying. He tried not to let his feelings show as he asked, "My thoughts about what?"

"You were one of the first ones on scene last night. What were your impressions?"

"My impressions?" He sat back, mirroring Jackie's position, well aware that the fire marshal was intentionally keeping her questions vague. It was the same reason she was having Camille write her statement before asking any questions: to prevent influencing her report. Steve had been around cops enough to know that someone's first answer was usually the most truthful one. He spent a few seconds organizing his thoughts before speaking, focusing on what he knew and discarding any nebulous gut feelings. "The point of origin looked to be in the north wall of the workshop, which had originally been an attached garage. My first assumption was that the cause was most likely electrical…that mice had chewed and nested in the old wiring, to be specific."

"Hmm…" Jackie played with a paper clip, unbending and re-bending it until it came apart in her hands. Looking down at the two bits of metal in surprise, she tossed them toward a trash can. "Camille was in the workshop when it started?"

"I believe so. I know she exited through the front workshop door and tried to go back into the house to get her cat."

Jackie shuffled through the papers in a manila folder. "The neighbor called nine-one-one at…" She paused, skimming one of the reports. "Two seventeen, after hearing the fire alarm. Was that Mrs. Lin?" She read a little further and then shook her head. "A Mr. Walter Franklin, looks like. So, the first responders arrive on scene at two thirty-four." She looked up at Steve from under narrow brows. "You came from the ranch? Pretty quick response on your part."

Resisting the urge to shift his weight, Steve kept his body still and his gaze even. Somehow, what was supposed to be a chance for Camille to give her statement had turned into more of an interrogation—of both her and Steve. "In the past fifteen years as a firefighter—most of those in more remote places than this—I've learned that getting there fast is critical. I have it down to a science now."

Although Jackie kept her head down, Steve had the impression that the fire marshal was doing more listening and thinking than reading. "You seem to be pretty good friends with Camille."

When Steve stayed silent, Jackie finally raised her eyes from the papers.

"No answer to that?" she finally asked.

"It wasn't a question." Although he kept his tone polite, he felt annoyance built in his chest, as well as that same instinct to protect Camille that he'd felt earlier with Mrs. Lin. He could still hear Len chattering in the other room, and it made him antsy to go rescue her from the separate—less formal—interrogation that was happening out there.

"Okay, how about this." This time, Jackie picked up the highlighter and started popping the cap on and off again with sharp clicks. It made Steve glad that he didn't share an office—or even a fire department building—with the marshal. Her constant fidgeting would drive Steve crazy. "Any reason Camille would light her own house on fire?"

"No." Anger burned low in his gut, but Steve kept

it contained. Jackie was pushing to get a reaction, and Steve wasn't going to give her one. He understood why the fire marshal was doing this. It was all part of her investigation. "She's devastated at losing her home. Also, if she'd planned it, she would've made sure her cat was safe first."

After considering that, Jackie gave a slight nod. "How about anyone else? Is there an ex, someone with a grudge, a neighbor who doesn't like how she trims her hedges?"

"Not that I know of, but you'd know the answer better than I would, since she's lived in Borne most of her life."

That pinched his pride, but it was true. While Jackie had been Borne's fire marshal for almost twenty years, Steve had only been back a few weeks. As far as the town politics and gossip went, Jackie would be more likely to have heard about any local drama, even if it involved Camille. Steve had barely known her when she was young, and he had a lot to learn about her now. He wanted to, though. He wanted to know everything, and for her to really know him as well.

"True, but Camille Brandt is a mystery." Clicking the cap on the highlighter, Jackie pointed the pen at Steve. "You're the closest thing she has to a friend, which isn't too surprising, considering she never leaves that house of hers." She grimaced. "She never used to, at least. Anyway, except for your brother Joe, she's the closest thing Borne has to a local hermit. I figured if anyone knew what was going on in her life, it'd be you."

"Well, as the official Camille expert," Steve said flatly, "I can tell you that she had no part in that house fire, and I don't know anyone who'd want to hurt her."

"Good to know." Apparently, Jackie chose to ignore the thick sarcasm. "Just so you know, I'm with you on this. All signs are pointing to this being caused by the faulty wiring, but I need to do a thorough investigation, just on the off chance this was intentionally set."

"What?" Camille said, standing in the doorway clutching the clipboard that she must've finally wrestled from Len. Her face was starkly pale. "Intentional? You think someone set fire to my house on purpose?"

"No, she doesn't," Steve said, glaring at Jackie for her horrible timing. "There's no sign that it was intentional. Jackie was just saying that she has to investigate this fire as thoroughly as she does all fires, in order to get rid of all doubt."

Camille looked back and forth between them, her grip still tight on the clipboard. "Who would want to burn my house down?" she asked, sounding bewildered, and Steve couldn't stand seeing her lost expression for another second. Standing, he moved over to her and gently extracted the clipboard from her white-knuckled hands before tugging her against his chest. She went willingly, leaning against him.

Holding her with one arm, he handed the clipboard to Jackie with the other. "No one wanted to burn your house down," Steve said, trying to put as much confidence as he could into his voice so that Camille would have no choice but to believe him.

"He's most likely right," Jackie said, which wasn't all that helpful. Steve gave her a look that she ignored, focusing on the pages clipped to the board instead. "You finished your statement already? I thought you were talking to Len this whole time."

"He talked." Camille's voice was a little muffled by Steve's coat, but she didn't attempt to move away. "I wrote."

"Efficient," Jackie said approvingly, her eyes skimming over the pages. "This looks good." Her cell phone chimed, and she glanced at it before turning back to Camille and Steve. "I have to head home now. The grandkids just got dropped off for the weekend, and Margie's going to lose her mind if I leave her alone with them for much longer. If I have any questions, I'll call you. What's your number?"

Camille took a step back, and Steve reluctantly released her. It felt right to have her in his arms, just as he'd expected. After rattling off her number, she paused, looking stricken, as if she'd just remembered that her cell had burned along with everything else. "I don't have a new phone yet."

"You staying with Steve out at the ranch?" Jackie asked, a gleam of the usual Borne love of gossip in her eyes. When Camille nodded, Jackie made a note and attached it to the statement. "I'll call you there. I have the house number and Steve's cell."

"You'll let me know if you find out anything else about the fire?" Camille asked.

"That I will," Jackie said, pulling a business card out of a wire holder balanced on a teetering pile of folders. She held it out to Camille. "Call me if you think of anything you missed."

"Okay." Camille turned to leave but then paused. "There's one other thing. It's not related—I mean, I can't imagine how it would be—but you might know the reason for it."

Jackie blinked at her, obviously not following Camille's rambling comment. "The reason for what?"

"There was someone—a firefighter—on my porch one night a few weeks ago, but he didn't knock or ring the doorbell. At least I'm pretty sure he didn't. Mrs. Lin took a picture of him, but you can't see his face. Do you know if there was a fire call nearby or any other reason there'd be a firefighter at my house?"

A prickle went up Steve's spine. It was most likely innocent, but the fire made everything seem suspicious.

"What date was this?" Jackie asked, bringing up the call log history on her computer. Camille told her, and the fire marshal quickly found the right day and time. "There was a gas leak at the house a few doors down from you that night. I bet they were asking people to evacuate."

"Why didn't they knock, then?" Camille asked.

With a shrug, Jackie closed out of the call log. "Maybe they did, and you didn't hear. Could've been right as they cleared the house, too, so the evacuation order ended."

Although Steve hadn't been at the call, the chief had mentioned it to him the next day. His tension eased at the information that there had been a good reason for a firefighter to be at Camille's house. He almost laughed at the way he'd immediately become suspicious.

"Okay." Camille sounded as though she was relieved by the explanation as well. "Thank you."

She turned again to leave and Steve followed, placing a hand on her lower back and sweeping her quickly through the outer office, so Len didn't have a chance to ask any more questions. Even with her bulky borrowed coat, Camille felt fragile under his touch. It bothered him that he'd been the one to encourage her to come here. It almost would've been worth it to talk to Mrs. Lin an extra fifteen minutes so that they missed their chance to see Jackie and could wait until Monday, after Camille had the weekend to recover from her traumatic experience.

They were both silent until they were in the truck. "You okay?" Steve asked, knowing it was a stupid question even as he said it. Of course she wasn't okay. Her house had just burned down.

"Yeah," she said, to his surprise. "I will be, at least. It was just that I hadn't even considered... Even when I was worried that I might have accidentally started the fire, I never thought about someone else..." She broke off again, the sheer incredulity in her voice making his heart hurt. He hated that she had to think about someone being capable of doing such a horrible thing to her.

"You know it's very unlikely, right?" he said. Since he couldn't erase the idea from her mind, he hoped he could at least set her a little more at ease. "Jackie has to consider the possibility for every fire, since that's part of investigating, but there's no evidence to support arson. In fact, everything she's found so far points to mice making a nest in your ancient wiring."

"Okay." The word came out in a long gust of breath. "That makes sense. Someone wanting to set fire to my house *doesn't* make sense, since no one could possibly hate me that much." Glancing at Steve, she must've noticed his lips quirk up at the corners, because she gave an amused huff and quickly added, "Not because I'm especially un-hate-able or anything."

That got a chuckle out of him. "Un-hate-able?"

She poked him in the ribs, right in a ticklish spot,

and he flinched away, really laughing now. "You know what I mean. I hardly ever go anywhere. No one knows me well enough to build up that kind of hatred—except for Mrs. Lin, maybe, and she releases her aggression in other nearly as painful ways." Her joking words had an undercurrent of true bewilderment, and his amusement fading, Steve again wished with everything in him that she'd never had to even consider the possibility of arson.

"You are, you know," he said, reaching over and taking her hand. He felt her flinch in surprise before gripping him firmly, almost desperately.

"I'm what?"

"Un-hate-able." He glanced at her quickly before refocusing on the road, and she stared at him, a smile starting as if she thought he was joking and was waiting for the punch line. When he didn't laugh, her grip on his hand tightened. "Completely un-hate-able."

CHAPTER 12

STEVE WAS WRONG, CAMILLE DECIDED AS SHE USED A manure fork to sift through the shavings. He was the un-hate-able one—he and his four abnormally sweet children.

"Are you still working on Buttercup's stall?" Maya asked from the aisle.

"Yes. Sorry! For one horse, she makes a huge amount of poop."

"She may be only one horse," Maya said, "but she's a big one."

"True. Okay, I think I've finally picked out the last of it." Camille gave the shavings a final rake with the manure fork, making sure to bank them up around the sides of the stall, and then hoisted the muck bucket, carrying it out with her.

Maya leaned on the wheelbarrow handles, making the wheel pop off the ground a few inches. "Go ahead and dump it in, and I'll take it out to the compost pile."

"Thanks." Camille emptied the muck bucket into the already half-full wheelbarrow. "What other stalls need to be cleaned?"

"None. I did the rest."

Frowning, Camille said, "Now I feel really slow."

"You kind of are, but it's okay. You'll get faster."

After giving Camille a commiserating pat on the arm, Maya grabbed the wheelbarrow handles again and pushed it down the aisle, leaving Camille unsure of whether to be amused or offended by the critique. She snorted a laugh and went to switch out her manure fork for a broom.

By the time Maya returned and put the now-empty wheelbarrow away, Camille had finished sweeping the aisle clear of dust and bits of hay.

"Thanks!" Maya grinned at her. "Sweeping is my least favorite."

"Really? You'd rather clean stalls?" They walked through the quiet barn. All the stalls were empty, the horses either turned out in one of the pastures or, in Buttercup and Harry's cases, at work towing trees and giving rides to excited kids. Camille loved the quiet peace of the barn, the cold, late-morning sunshine streaming through windows and the open top of the Dutch door, and everything smelling of pine shavings and hay. She'd willingly spend the whole day in the barn, rather than join the busy crowd at the store or in the lot, but she reminded herself of her pledge to help out however possible, even if that meant putting her scant customer-service skills to work.

Maya considered the question carefully before answering. "Yes. I don't mind cleaning stalls that much, and I *hate* sweeping the aisle. All the dust, and I just get it done when someone walks through the barn with muddy boots or carrying a bale of hay—or worse, Tollie drags a pine branch in here, so there are pine needles *everywhere…*" She swung her arms out in huge circles.

Camille giggled at Maya's dramatic gestures, and

Maya joined in, and by the time they left the barn and walked down the path toward the store, they were laughing their heads off for no reason except that the other person's snorts kept setting them off again.

"Hey, beautiful ladies," Ryan said, and Camille quickly sobered. It was the first time she'd seen him since he'd dropped her off at Steve's after the fire, and he was a visceral reminder of why she hadn't been laughing much over the past day and a half. "What are you two up to?"

"We just finished cleaning the barn," Maya said, and Camille gave an agreeing bob of her head, thinking about how handy it was to have Maya around. If she planned it right, she might never have to speak to anyone she didn't want to ever again. At the thought, she mentally scolded herself. As pushy as Ryan had been before the fire, he'd been concerned and helpful that night, even offering to let her stay with him in his cabin—not that she would've taken him up on his offer. Holding on to that thought, she gave him a smile, which he quickly returned.

"Where are you headed?" Camille asked, doing her best to make an effort to be friendly.

"Harry pulled a shoe." He grimaced. "It's lost somewhere between the lot and the trees, so I doubt we're going to find it before spring. I'm going to grab Harry and meet the farrier by the barn. Just what we needed on one of our busiest days of the year."

See, Camille lectured herself. *He's perfectly nice when he's not trying to get you to go out with him.* "Can we help with anything?"

"Check with Steve. He's in the store," Ryan said

over his shoulder as he headed toward the lot, where Harry was tied to the hitching post. A crowd of people swarmed around the horse, making Camille cringe. It had been a long time since she'd had to interact with so many people at once. "He'll give you a list, I'm sure."

Maya jogged ahead of her toward the store, and Camille pretended that she wasn't moving at a turtle's pace to try to delay the inevitable. The gift shop wasn't that far away, though, and she reached the entrance far too quickly. Even getting inside was tough, with families and couples crowding the doorway as they walked in and out.

By the time she reached the register where Will and Steve were working, Maya was already busy refilling the coffee maker and cider warmer, and Camille was doubting her decision to stay at the ranch. *How bad could staying with Mrs. Lin really be?* Immediately, her inner voice assured her that it could've been very, very bad.

A man examining the wreath display stepped back, almost running into Camille. Although she managed to dodge, the closeness of all the people pressing in on her made her breathing speed up and her skin prickle with discomfort. Just as she decided to bolt, Steve looked up from the register and saw her. He lit up, a smile stretching across his face, making the corners of his eyes crinkle and erasing all of his habitual sternness. His welcoming look woke the butterflies in her stomach, and they swooped and darted around as she looked back at him, unable to hold back her own broad smile. Suddenly, being in the crowded, noisy store seemed a little less awful.

"Hey, Camille!" Will greeted her as he wrapped a

glass star-shaped tree topper in tissue. "We've sold two of your sculptures already this morning. I'm so glad they didn't burn."

"Will," Steve scolded, giving her a worried look, but she just choked on a laugh.

"I agree." She shifted behind the counter to stay out of the customers' way. Her new position had the secondary benefit of putting her very close to Steve. "I'm also glad that your dad knows how to break into a 1979 Buick Electra so we could get to those pieces." Peeking up at him through her lashes, she saw that he was giving her one of his stern-but-trying-not-to-laugh looks. It was quickly becoming one of her favorites.

Unlike his dad, Will just laughed outright as he slid the wrapped star into a bag and handed it to the waiting customer.

"Camille, if you're not too busy telling my son about my less-admirable skills, would you mind taking over packaging?"

As she watched Will bag up a box of bulbs, she gave an internal sigh of relief. Packaging didn't look so bad. She had plenty of experience from shipping her artwork, and the only customer contact was taking the items and handing them back when they were wrapped and bagged. "I can do that."

"Great. Thank you." Steve sounded almost as relieved as she felt. "Will, did you want to work the tree lot or the register?"

"Tree lot." Judging by the lack of hesitation, it seemed that Will needed a break from the store. Camille could fully empathize with that. "C'mon, Camille. I'll show you were you can hang up your coat."

He led her into the small office at the back of the store. "Just throw it on any of these hooks."

She slipped off the coat she'd borrowed the day before. Even though she had bought a new one at Target, she kept wearing Steve's, telling herself that she didn't want to get her new one dirty doing barn chores. The truth was that she loved his. When she was feeling sad or overwhelmed or shaky, she'd bury her nose in the collar and inhale the faint traces of his scent. It calmed her down and made her feel safe, just like his unexpected, comforting hug in the fire marshal's office the day before. She'd turned his coat into a warm security blanket, and she didn't want to give it up.

Stuffing her new stocking hat and mittens into one of the coat pockets, she tried to smooth her hair, but she knew it was hopeless. Glancing at Will, she saw he was smirking as he pulled on his coat.

"I know." She flattened her hands on either side of her head, trying to hide as much of her hair as possible. "I broke the cardinal rule: once the hat goes on, it has to stay on for the rest of the day."

"Nah, it's fine. Take out your ponytail." A little warily, she tugged off the hair band, not sure where he was going with this. "Bend over so your head's upside down, and shake it out."

Now she really thought he had to be messing with her.

"Hurry up," he urged. "Dad's having to ring things up and wrap, and he's horrible at wrapping. If he had his way, he'd roll everything up in newspaper, slap some duct tape on it, and throw it into a plastic garbage bag."

She did what Will said, amused despite herself by the silliness of it all.

"Okay, stand up and flip your hair back."

Her hair flip was only semisuccessful, so curly strands hung in her face. She shoved them out of her eyes and looked at Will expectantly.

"Nice, just..." He reached toward her head and then paused. "If it's okay?"

"Go ahead."

After he quickly adjusted a few strands, he stepped back and eyed the end result before giving a satisfied nod. "Check it out."

Glancing at her reflection in the small window, she frowned. It was hard to see much, since the sun was shining outside, but from what she could tell, it looked a little...wild. "It's not too...?" She blew out her cheeks and flicked her fingers in an explosive gesture.

"Nope." He grinned at her before dashing out of the office. "It's perfect."

She hesitated for a few seconds before deciding to trust Will. Leaving the office, she slipped behind the counter, taking the spot next to Steve, who was in the middle of wrapping a fat candle, his face screwed up in a mixture of frustration, concentration, and panic.

A laugh bubbled out of her. "Will wasn't kidding," she said, taking the candle and fifty sheets of tissue paper he seemed to think he needed to wrap it in. "You're really bad at this."

"I am," Steve readily agreed. With his attention no longer fixed on the candle, he looked at her, smiling. His expression froze, his eyes widening.

"What?" she whispered. Now she was the panicked

one. With her hands busy wrapping up the candle, she couldn't even pat her hair to see what was wrong. Had Will been messing with her after all?

"Oh. Uh…nothing. Just your hair. It…uh, looks nice." He finally yanked his attention off her and turned back to the register, but Camille was not convinced, especially since his face was brick red, and he seemed to be having issues hitting the right button on the register screen.

"It's horrible, isn't it?" She tucked the candle into the gift bag, forcing a smile for the woman who'd just purchased it. *She*, at least, didn't seem horrified by the mess on Camille's head. "Will talked me into it, and the window in the office is a terrible mirror. You're going to have to help me think of a good way to get him back. No! I'll ask Maya and Zoe. They'll know what to do, and they'll help me pull it off. They're awesome like that. Where'd Maya go?" She spotted the girl on the other side of the store, helping a mom with young children pick out a tree stand. "As soon as she makes her way back over here, I'm going to ask her to brainstorm revenge strategies."

By the time she finished rambling, Steve's face had almost returned to its normal color, and he looked like he was holding back a laugh. "First of all, please don't ask Maya or Zoe to help plan your revenge, since they'll come up with something much more creative and excessive than necessary, like an ejector seat in his new car or a trapdoor in front of the toilet or something that explodes."

Camille thought that two out of three of those ideas sounded genius, but she stayed silent as Steve handed her a small wreath to bag.

"That'll be thirty-one forty-four. Thank you. Second, Will didn't do anything wrong. I've just, uh, never seen your hair down before." He was flushing again, ears going red at the tips. "I like it."

"Thanks. I… Thanks." She flushed too, keeping her head down so he wouldn't see how red her own cheeks had gotten. Emotions churned in her chest—excitement and gratitude and nervousness, the usual combination she felt when she was around Steve. Her thanks seemed to hang in the air, feeling incomplete, so she blurted out, "I like yours, too." When he gave her a sideways look and offered a dry thanks, she became even more flustered. "Your face, too. It's nice." She waved a hand, indicating his whole form. "There aren't any not-nice parts of you, in fact. You're pretty much nice all over." She had to stop saying *nice*. In fact, she had to stop talking, period, but there seemed to be a delay between her thoughts and her mouth, because words were still pouring out of her. "So, basically, I like all of you. A lot. A whole lot. A whole, whole—"

Stop. Talking. Now.

She closed her mouth and pressed her lips together.

He cleared his throat. "Thank you?"

Camille instinctively opened her mouth to say "You're welcome," then decided not to risk speaking again, just in case. Instead, she gave a wordless grunt and focused on wrapping.

Thrilled and still embarrassed by the exchange, she concentrated on work, and they soon fell into an easy rhythm. It was a surprisingly enjoyable time, especially when she wrapped three of her own pieces after they sold.

"That reminds me," Steve said as she tucked a metal donkey into its cloth bag. "If you need to finish some orders, feel free to work in our workshop. There's welding equipment and tools you can use, and Joe has a collection of junk cars he keeps for parts. He already offered to let you have whatever you need." Steve concentrated on the order he was ringing up as he made the offer, and Camille was relieved for that, since he couldn't see the thankful tears that had welled up in her eyes at their generosity. Even Joe, cranky Joe, was letting her raid his junker stash. As a metalworker, she knew what a precious gift that was.

Blinking hard, she forced the tears back, but she couldn't resist giving Steve's arm a grateful squeeze. She felt him glance at her profile, but she kept her own gaze on the bag she was handing over to the customer. If she met his eyes and saw the sympathy and kindness she knew they held, she'd break down and cry all over everyone's purchases, and tears would completely ruin the tissue paper.

It felt wrong to stay silent, though, so she cleared her throat. "Thank you. My Christmas orders are all done, but there are others lined up. It'll help a lot to be able to work again." She remembered the piece she'd planned out the night of the fire. The sketches were ash now, but the details were still clear in her mind. She was suddenly antsy to check out Joe's old cars. "That's so kind of Joe. I love old vehicles. They have so many parts and pieces, and I can cut shapes out of the hoods, and..."

Steve's laugh cut her off. "I was going to say that Zoe feels the same way, until you started talking about chopping up the body." A customer approaching the register stopped in his tracks. Camille eyed him curiously, not sure what the problem was until Steve chuckled again. "Chopping up the *car* body," he clarified loudly.

Camille snorted a laugh, trying to hide it in a cough.

"You two are having too much fun," Nate said as he slipped between customers to join them behind the counter. "Especially for people who haven't had a lunch break. It's almost two. Go. Eat."

"Go ahead," Steve said to Camille. "I'll help Nate until you get back."

"I already have a helper lined up," Nate said, giving Steve a light push away from the register. As if that was his cue, Micah approached, his best scowl in place.

"Micah?" Steve moved around the counter, wrapping his arm around his son's shoulders and giving him a side hug. "Thank you for helping out. I know this isn't your idea of fun."

After a few seconds of letting his dad squeeze him, Micah wiggled out from under his arm and took Camille's place behind the counter, giving her a lift of his chin in greeting.

"Hey, Micah," she said, relinquishing her position happily. Now that she knew how long they'd been working, she could feel the tiredness in her legs and back... and in her brain. She'd interacted with more than her share of people and could use some alone time—or at least some alone-with-Steve time.

"Wrapping wasn't so bad." She kept her voice low so only Micah could hear her over the chatter of customers. The crowd had grown since she'd walked in, and people of all ages filled the space. Everyone seemed happy and excited to be there, filled to bursting with Christmas spirit. "I only scared a dozen or so customers. See if you can beat that record."

His expression lightened to an almost smile as he snorted. "Piece of cake."

After grabbing their coats, she and Steve headed toward the door. She looked around, not seeing a ten-year-old shop assistant anywhere. "Where'd Maya go?"

"She left an hour or so ago. From her hand signals, I think she was going to get some food and then either help with the tree sales or go ride her pony."

"Oh, I missed that." She had a feeling that she'd been so preoccupied with Steve for the past few hours that Maya could've ridden her pony *in* the store and she probably wouldn't have noticed. As they reached the door, Camille slipped through it, dodging a large group of people crowding in.

Outside, the air was cold and bracing, and she sucked in a deep breath. It wasn't until she'd stepped outside that she'd realized how warm she'd gotten, thanks to a combination of the crowds and Steve's proximity.

He caught up to her after holding the door for a few more customers. "After lunch, we'll help with the trees. Ryan can do gift-shop duty this afternoon." His voice was grumbly, and she glanced at him in surprise.

"Don't you like working in the store?" she asked. He'd been so patient and unrelentingly polite that she'd assumed he hadn't minded the endless waves of Christmas shoppers.

His face scrunched into a look of distaste that was so un-Steve-like that Camille had to laugh. "No. I'd rather clean five hundred feet of mildewed fire hose than be inside all day. On tree duty, at least, I get to work outside with the horses, and it's just one customer—or family, which is fine. I get along with most kids."

"Really?" They passed the lot, where Maya was holding Buttercup's lead rope while Zoe took a picture of her with a family. At just the right moment, the mare turned her head toward the camera and pricked her ears forward. Camille smiled, impressed at the horse's modeling skills.

"Really what?" Steve asked, drawing her attention back to him. "You're surprised that I get along with kids? Why? I do have four of them to practice on, after all."

"That's why." They followed the path toward the house. "I'm not an expert, but I've met enough kids to know that yours are not the norm." When he whipped his head around, eyes narrowed, looking for all the world like a papa bear ready to defend his cubs, she raised her hands in a soothing gesture and swallowed a laugh. She was beginning to really love his protective side. "No, it's not a bad thing. I meant that they're abnormally interesting and nice to be around. When you're with other people's kids, aren't you a little, well, horrified?"

It obviously took him a second to switch gears and absorb what she'd said. Once it had sunk it, his expression softened and he barked out a laugh. "Just between us," he said quietly, leaning in close enough to send a line of shivers down her back, "yes."

Despite the flush of heat running through her at the touch of his warm breath against her cheek, Camille let out an amused snort. Immediately, she was appalled at herself. He was leaning close, very possibly flirting, and she'd *snorted*? She had to have the least game of anyone who'd ever existed, and that included Steve's brother Joe.

Crazily enough, Steve didn't seem to mind. Instead of moving away, he just chuckled and stayed close enough for their arms to brush as they climbed the porch steps. She reached toward the doorknob, opening the door as he ushered her through with a light touch on her lower back. She'd noticed he tended to do that—put a hand at the low curve of her spine—and she was surprised by how much she liked that little bit of contact. It was comforting, that tangible sign that he was there, quite literally at her back. The past few days had been hard, but his constant presence and support had helped her get through them without breaking down. That was yet another thing she was grateful for.

As she stripped off her coat, she caught a whiff of something spicy and delicious. "Micah's been cooking again," she said.

Steve sniffed the air before shaking his head. "That's Joe's chili. Usually, Nate and Micah are the cooks around here, but I imagine Joe made it since he's feeling guilty for hiding from the customers when we're so busy."

Although Camille could empathize with Joe's distaste for nonfamily human interaction, she felt a little superior since she'd survived a long shift in the gift shop, of all places. She remembered sitting in her car, afraid to even walk into the store when she was delivering the first batch of her sculptures. Now, she'd not only managed to walk into the crowded shop, but she'd stayed for *hours*. Pride flushed through her, and her chest warmed with affection for Steve. He'd been so accepting, so matter-of-fact, as if he'd had no doubt that she could handle herself. It felt good to have someone who didn't dismiss her—who, perhaps, had more faith in her than she had in herself.

Her stomach gave a hollow pang at the mouthwatering smell, pulling her out of her thoughts, and she hurried to pull off her boots so she could go eat something. "I didn't realize how hungry I was."

"Me either." He followed her into the kitchen. Lucy eyed them from the top of the fridge, making Camille smile. The cat hadn't lost any time making herself at home. Camille couldn't really blame her—it was easy to do with the Springfields.

She moved toward the big slow cooker on the counter, but Steve stopped her with a hand on her arm. "Thank you for your help today, Camille. Working in the store isn't my favorite thing, but you made it bearable."

"Of course." She met his eyes and couldn't look away. His gaze had an intensity that turned his gratitude into something more. Her pulse jumped and stuttered as she tried to keep her words casual. "It's the least I could do, since you're letting me live here. Besides, it wasn't as bad as I thought it'd be."

"I'm glad you're here." The fingers on her arm were gentle, but his touch burned like a brand. She wouldn't be surprised if his fingerprints were etched into her skin. "Even with my brothers helping out, I still feel like I'm floundering. Having you around makes it easier, somehow, like I have an ally. Not that my kids and I aren't on the same side." He grimaced slightly. "I'm explaining this wrong."

Camille looked at him, her head tilted as she tried to understand what he was saying. It was almost nice to see the stoic and perfect Steve Springfield scramble for

words like she always did. He seemed more human...
and attainable. "Well...good. I like being here," she said
a little uncertainly, her face warming at the thought of
"attaining" Steve. "I like your kids, too."

His expression turned devilish. "And you said earlier
that you like *all* of me."

Instantly, her face went hot, and she was tempted to
duck her head, but it was impossible to look away from
his warmly teasing gaze. "Well, yeah. I do. I mean..."
She waved a hand at him. "Look at you. Of course I like
all of that. Not that you're just your body or anything, of
course. Your brain is pretty good, too." *Stop, Camille,*
she ordered herself. *Just stop now.*

"Thanks for noticing my brain." He chuckled, but she
knew he wasn't laughing at her. Instead, the sound was
filled with a kind affection and something else, something rough and hot that made her shiver. "Just for the
record, I like *all* of you, too."

He stepped toward her, and Camille stared at him,
knowing something was happening between them,
something both wonderful and scary. The urge to start
babbling again, to fill the charged silence, pushed at her,
but she swallowed the unsaid words, not wanting to stop
him—not when he was getting so close.

His hand on her arm slid down to her wrist and
back up, his fingers blazing hot even through her long-
sleeved shirt. She glanced down at where he touched
her and then back up. Their gazes caught, and she swallowed hard as he leaned closer. Even when their lips
were just an inch apart and she could feel his breath
warm against her lips, she still couldn't believe that this
was happening.

Steve Springfield is going to kiss me.

The front door banged open. "Steve? Camille? You in here?"

Startled, Camille jerked away from Steve and took a few backward steps on shaky legs until she felt the counter behind her. She leaned on it, using it for support as Ryan walked into the kitchen, still in his coat and boots.

He looked back and forth between her and Steve with an odd expression. "You *are* in here. Why didn't you answer when I yelled?"

Steve glanced at the floor by Ryan's feet, where chunks of snow had fallen from his boots and were now melting into dirty, icy-cold puddles. "You didn't really give us a chance. What's the emergency?" Since she was still dazed and breathless, Camille was glad that Steve had the wherewithal to answer. He even sounded fairly composed, although his face looked flushed and the heat in his eyes hadn't faded completely. There was an unusual snap to his voice that wasn't normally there, either.

"No emergency." Ryan looked at Camille, and she dropped her gaze to study her socked feet. It wasn't that she was embarrassed about almost getting caught making out with his brother. The heat between her and Steve felt new and fragile and wasn't anyone else's business—especially not Ryan's. "Just need to know where you put the extra bags for the shop. Micah's running low."

"They're not in the store supply closet where we usually put them?" Steve asked.

"Let me text Nate and ask if they've checked there." Ryan fiddled with his phone for a few minutes, while

Camille did her best not to catch Steve's gaze. If she did, she was sure she'd stare at him like a lovesick idiot.

"Huh," Ryan grunted, finally breaking the stiff silence. "They were in there. Micah must've just missed them the first time he checked."

"Right." Steve sounded irritated. "Now that that mystery's solved, are you headed back out, then?"

Pulling off his hat, Ryan eyed the slow cooker—and then Camille—with a tiny smile. "As long as I'm in here, I might as well get something to eat." He turned his oddly satisfied grin on Steve, who muttered something under his breath. Although Camille couldn't make out the exact words, she had a feeling the comment was something derogatory about his brother's timing—and lack of tact.

"Clean up your mess first," Steve snapped, gesturing at the wet, dirty boot prints and growing puddle around Ryan's feet.

With an affirmative shrug, Ryan headed back into the entryway. Steve glared at his retreating back before turning to Camille. His expression softened even as his eyes flared with renewed heat. "We'll finish that later."

She stared at him, nerves and anticipation and desire fighting for dominance. "Okay," she finally said, cringing a little at how breathless she sounded. Steve seemed satisfied, though, as he headed for the bathroom to wash up. As she watched him go, her eyes ran over him. She was fascinated by the way his muscles moved. Her gaze drifted lower, and she felt her cheeks flush with heat. *Later*, her mind echoed, and a small smile bloomed on her face.

I can't wait.

CHAPTER 13

CAMILLE DISCOVERED THAT WORKING OUTSIDE WAS MUCH more fun than in the store, especially since she was teamed up with Steve. He was very good at getting the customers talking, which filled any potentially awkward silences. For the entire afternoon, she helped take families out to cut their own trees, leading Buttercup or walking next to her, making sure the smallest riders didn't fall off her broad back. To her surprise, Camille's favorite job was working the tree shaker. There was something viscerally satisfying about knocking loose any dead bugs or loose needles or anything else that might be in the small evergreens.

The motor on the machine was loud, too, removing any opportunity for small talk. Bonus.

As the afternoon waned, and the parking lot gradually cleared of cars, the sun sat low on the sharp edge of the mountain peaks. Reddish-orange rays lit the mostly empty lot, illuminating Steve's strong form as he unharnessed Buttercup. There was a peacefulness to the moment, a feeling of satisfaction that a day's work was done. Camille didn't usually have that sensation. For her, there were always more orders to fill, more ideas that wanted to be given shape. Steve lifted the heavy collar off Buttercup's neck, his movements careful and smooth with the ease of long practice. Camille was unable to drag her gaze off him until Maya leaned against her, giving a full-body shiver.

"Why don't you head up to the house?" Camille suggested, wrapping an arm around the girl's shoulders to give her some extra warmth. The lights in the store windows went dark. "I overheard Nate and Micah talk about making Swedish meatballs for dinner tonight."

"I usually help Dad with the night feed," Maya said, although her gaze shifted to the house, its windows warm and gold, tempting after an afternoon working in the snow.

"I'll help him." Camille bumped the girl lightly with her hip. "You've been outside longer than we have. You must be freezing."

Maya nodded, her teeth chattering together in an exaggerated way that made Camille laugh. "Okay. Thanks!" She ran toward the house and its beckoning warmth. Camille's side felt chilly in her absence.

Ryan emerged from the store, locking the door behind him. "Here to the bitter end, huh?" he asked as he walked over.

Camille shrugged, not wanting to admit that she didn't want to go inside until Steve did. Her time at the ranch would be short, and she wanted to take advantage of all the moments—especially peaceful, golden ones like this—that she could get. "It's not bitter. The longer I'm out here, the better it'll feel when I go into the house."

"Guess that's true." He tugged his hat down over his ears. "I'm about to go bring the horses in. Want to help?"

"Sorry. She's going to give me a hand out in the

trees," Steve said from right behind her, making Camille jump. She looked over her shoulder and then tilted her head back to see him. He'd climbed onto Buttercup's bare back and was holding the lead rope attached to her halter. "We'll give you a hand when we get back."

Ryan gave a snort, but Camille couldn't tell if he was amused or annoyed. She was grateful for Steve's save. Although she'd told Maya that she'd help with feeding, Camille hated the thought of doing anything alone with Ryan. Although she wasn't really *afraid* of him, his constant come-ons made her uncomfortable.

"Ready?" Offering a hand, Steve smiled in a way that set her pulse to thrumming. Hoping that the fading light hid her blush, she locked wrists with him, placed her boot on top of his, and swung onto Buttercup behind him. She wiggled into a better position and then hesitated, not sure how she should hang on. Steve reached back and pulled her hands around him, latching them about his waist. Despite all the layers of clothes between them, Camille still felt heat suffuse her entire body. She didn't want to think too hard about the cause of that warmth, so she concentrated on staying on the horse. If she lost her hold on Steve and slipped off, it'd be a long way down to the ground.

As Buttercup ambled toward the trees, Camille remembered Ryan. Glancing over her shoulder, she saw him watching them, and she gave him a small smile in farewell. The dimming light made it hard to see his expression, but he lifted one hand in response before turning toward the barn.

Refocusing on Steve's back, she tried not to shift too much. She was already hyperaware of the feel of him.

Her thighs lined up with his, and her pelvis was tucked right against his butt. In fact, her entire front was plastered against his back. Despite his coat, she could feel the movement of his chest as he inhaled, and she found herself matching him breath for breath.

Except for the faint thuds of Buttercup's hooves hitting the ground, all was quiet. Usually, silence was her friend, but everything seemed so…intimate at the moment that she couldn't take one more second of it.

"What are we doing?" she asked, and then immediately thought of all the ways that simple question could be misinterpreted. "I mean, out in the trees. What do we need to check on, since it's not like the trees need to be fed or tucked in for the night?"

Steve's soft chuckle vibrated through her, and Camille swallowed hard. "We're just going to do a sweep, make sure all the saws are put away and we don't have any lost mittens or anything like that." He paused. "It's just something I like to do, like taking a final walk through the house right before I go to bed. It's reassuring to know that everything is where it's supposed to be. It helps me sleep."

"I get that." Camille kept her voice low as they entered the first row of trees. The sun had almost dropped all the way behind the mountains, and the shadows stretched far across the snow. It was different being in the trees without the noisy clusters of customers, without the barking of Joe's dog, Tollie, or the excited shrieks of kids sitting atop Buttercup. It would've been lonely, almost eerie, if she hadn't been plastered against Steve's strong back with steady Buttercup plodding underneath them.

Now, here with them, it was almost…magical.

They moved through the rows of trees in a pattern that Camille could tell was familiar to both the horse and the man. Steve's warmth and the easy rhythm of Buttercup's walk relaxed Camille, and she felt the stresses of the past day—past *weeks*—slip away. She knew the nightmares would return, as would all the hassles and sadness of losing her childhood home, but for now, she was content to lean against Steve and let Buttercup carry them both.

For the moment, she'd let herself be at peace.

―――――――――――

Satisfaction rolled through her as she looked at the fillet weld she'd just finished. It had turned out surprisingly well, considering she was using borrowed equipment. The miniature metal ladder she was working on was only a small part of the piece, but it was just so square and gratifyingly even.

"Whoa." Maya's voice was much too close for safety, and Camille turned to see the girl leaning over her shoulder, eyeing the incomplete sculpture. "I wasn't sure what it was going to be before, but now I'm starting to see it. Dad's going to *love* that!" She paused. "It is for Dad, right? I won't tell him about it if it is, I promise."

Shoving her borrowed welding goggles to the top of her head, Camille gave Maya her best chiding frown. It was hard to hold it, though, since the girl was so happy and bubbly. "If you keep leaning so close, you're going to get a spark in your eyeball or light your hair on fire, and both of those things would be extremely unpleasant."

"Sorry." Despite the apology, Maya didn't retreat.

"You're done using the torch right now, though, right? I'm okay here?"

"You're fine for now." Camille stretched, feeling the usual resistance from muscles that had been held in place for hours. She smiled. It'd only been five days since she'd last worked with metal, but it felt like longer. She was happy to be back at it.

"Is it Dad's present?" Maya repeated the question, and Camille dropped her arms to study her carefully.

"You'll keep it a secret?" She had the impression that most kids were terrible at keeping secrets, but Maya seemed trustworthy.

"She's good," Will said from his spot on the other side of the workshop, sprawled in an old office chair with a tablet on his lap. "Best secret keeper out of all of us...well, except for me."

"Hey," Micah grumbled. He'd set up his sketch pad at a workbench a safe distance from Camille and any flying sparks. Apparently, he was more safety-conscious than Maya. "I don't blab."

Will leaned back in his chair, looking thoughtful. "Yeah, usually, unless you think it's wrong not to tell. Remember when Zoe and I rigged up that homemade hang glider? You couldn't tell Dad fast enough."

"Yeah, 'cause I knew you were both going to *die*, otherwise."

Waving a hand, Will said, "We would've been fine. Probably. Anyway, my point is that Maya keeps her mouth shut, no matter what."

Privately, Camille wondered if that was a good thing, but it did mean that her secret was safe. "What about Zoe? Can't she keep a secret?"

"She's good, except if you catch her when she's in the middle of working on something," Will said. Micah and Maya agreed loudly.

"Dad knows that, too, so he waits until she's putting an engine back together before he'll ask her something. That's how we got caught when we were planning to sneak onto this militia guy's property when we lived in Monroe." Will looked disappointed and impressed by his father's ingenuity at the same time. "He knew we were up to something, but he didn't know exactly what, so he told her the truck was losing power when he pushed on the gas. As soon as she had the hood up, he started with the questions, and she totally spilled."

"We got in so much trouble," Maya said. "I've never seen Dad that mad."

Camille's respect for Steve's patience and fortitude had doubled since the start of the conversation. "Can't really blame him. I mean, sneaking into a militia compound? No offense, but that sounds really dangerous, and not in the fun way that homemade hang gliders are dangerous."

"It was a dumb idea," Micah agreed without looking up from his drawing. "If Zoe hadn't told, I would've."

Tossing a balled-up piece of paper at his brother's head, Will stretched his arms out in an exaggerated gesture of exasperation. "See? That's why Maya gets the award of best secret keeper."

"Nice." Maya grinned and then turned to Camille. "So, that sculpture you're working on is Dad's Christmas present, isn't it?"

"Yes," she said without hesitation. After what she'd just heard, she'd trust Maya with the secrets of the universe. "It's going to be an old horse-drawn fire wagon."

Micah's face lit with interest. Putting down his pencil, he walked over to Camille's other side to look at the unfinished piece.

"Let me see." Will stood behind Maya, since he was tall enough to see over her head. All three of them studied it for a few minutes before Will admitted, "I don't get it."

"Here." Camille reached for the sketchbook that she'd begged off of Micah. Pulling out the sketches she'd redrawn after the fire, she laid them out on the table around the sculpture in progress.

"See?" She pointed to a drawing of the side of the fire wagon and then picked up the metalwork she'd completed so far. "This will be this part here." Shifting to another sketch, she added, "The horses will be harnessed to the wagon like this, so—"

"Oh!" Comprehension lit Will's eyes. "I get it now. That's going to be really great."

Maya was almost dancing with excitement. "Isn't it? I told you, Dad's going to love it."

More focused on the sketches than the sculpture they detailed, Micah traced over a line on one of the horses. His finger hovered over the paper, close but never touching. "Why did you draw it this way?"

"What way?"

His brow knit as he considered the picture. "It's like it's just the... I don't know. Like, you drew the *idea* of horses, rather than what they actually look like."

"I always sketch out my ideas for sculptures like that," Camille said, speaking slowly so she could figure out how to put her process into words. Normally, she didn't talk about her art; she just *did* it. "I think it's to make it easier to find or cut the right part for each area. See, like this is going to be the middle horse's cheek." She dug through the box of smaller metal scraps that she'd salvaged from Joe's heavenly field of junk cars. If it hadn't been so cold, she could've spent all day harvesting parts behind Joe's cabin.

Pulling out an old washer, she held it up. "If I stick to general shapes and impressions in my drawings, I don't get stuck trying to find something to exactly match, which I'll never find." She looked around her small audience, trying to check if she was making sense to them. She'd never had to explain her process before. It was both intimidating and exhilarating.

Micah looked from the drawing to the washer and back to the sketch again. "So you draw the idea of a horse because your sculpture is just the idea of a horse?"

"Yeah." She smiled at the rightness of what he'd just said. "That's exactly it."

He didn't say anything else, but she could tell by his expression that his mind was still working things through.

"Why three horses?" Maya asked, taking Camille's attention off Micah. "Aren't there usually two or four in a team?"

"Or eight, like in those beer company ads?"

Pulling out more sketches, these more preliminary than the others, Camille put two sheets next to each other. On the first, she'd drawn two horses pulling the wagon, while on the second piece of paper, she'd drawn her current plan of three abreast. "I went back and forth between a pair and three horses for a while. When I did an internet search for old photos of fire wagons, most had one to three horses pulling it. I decided on three, since I like the wild, urgent look to it. There's a sense of barely controlled chaos."

"Chaos?" Steve's voice had them spinning around to see him in the workshop doorway. Camille rushed to flip the drawings upside down, and the kids, clearly experts in hiding the evidence, moved to block Steve's view of her section of the workbench. "Should I be worried that you're talking about chaos?"

"No," Maya said a little too quickly, and Will jumped in.

"What Maya means is that if we're talking about chaos, we can't be *creating* chaos."

Staying quiet, Micah just nodded.

"Hey, Steve." Now that Camille had all the pictures facedown and the completed portion of her sculpture tucked out of sight under the bench, she slid off her stool. Her welding goggles slipped down onto her forehead, and she yanked them off, mentally cringing at the messy state her hair had to be in. He always seemed to see her at her most disheveled.

After their mostly silent ride through the trees, they hadn't had a second alone. Between dealing with her insurance company and helping around the ranch and trying to squeeze in some metalworking, Camille felt like she was constantly running at full speed. There were always people around, too. As wonderful as spending time with Steve's kids was, she wished that the two of them could have just a few minutes—or, better yet, a few hours—to finish what they'd started. She felt like she was walking around with a low-grade fever, and her temperature spiked every time she caught a glimpse of Steve or their eyes met across the breakfast table for a charged moment or she remembered how his breath had felt as it warmed her lips. Things were getting desperate, and she was a little worried about the lengths she'd be willing to go to in order to get Steve alone.

"Hmm…" Despite his clear suspicion, he seemed to let their odd behavior go for now. Turning to Camille, he asked, "Can I talk to you for a minute?"

Or maybe he wasn't letting it go. Maybe he thought she was the worst secret keeper of all of them, and he was going to interrogate her. She was worried, since she knew she'd be helpless to resist if he touched her or hugged her or even whispered in her ear and warmed her skin with his words. There was a very high likelihood that Steve was right—she was the weakest link. "Uh…sure."

The kids must've been thinking the same thing. As she passed them, Maya whispered, "Don't tell," as Will muttered, "Be strong." Camille bugged her eyes out at them in a *not helping!* expression, which made Micah snort and Maya dissolve into muffled giggles. Camille made her way to where Steve stood in the doorway, feeling his gaze on her the whole time. It made her feel both hot and weirdly guilty, even though the only secret she was planning to keep was his Christmas gift.

He stepped back, giving her room to pass by him into the office before closing the door behind them. Once they were alone, she expected him to say something, but he stayed silent. He looked unhappy, and as soon as his hand came up to rub the back of his neck, she knew for certain that something was bothering him—and it was more than a silly Christmas secret.

"What's wrong?" She moved toward him automatically. By the time she realized what she was doing and came to an abrupt halt, they were only a half step apart. She looked up at him, so aware of how close he was that it was hard to think of anything except how it would feel if he pulled her against his broad chest and kissed her breathless.

"It's Zoe."

Her thoughts about kissing and touching came to a screeching halt. "Zoe? Is she okay?" His worried expression fueled her concern.

"I don't know." He grimaced, pivoting to pace away from her a few strides before returning. "I think I screwed up. When I picked her up after her robotics club meeting, I could tell she was upset. I asked her what was wrong, and she burst out crying. She's been sobbing like her heart's breaking or her leg has been ripped off or something even worse, and I'm getting more and more worried. I finally got her to admit that her friend's moving away, and I was so relieved that it wasn't something more serious that I just blurted out the first thing that came to mind."

When he paused, Camille made a *keep going* motion with her hand. "What'd you say?"

He strode away again, pacing back and forth between her and the conference table. "Something like 'Is that all?'"

Camille winced.

"*I know*. And when she stared at me like I was a monster, I just made it worse." His hand rubbed the back of his neck again. "I said, 'Haven't you only known each other for six weeks? You can't be *that* good of friends yet.'"

This time, Camille actually groaned out loud.

"She wouldn't talk to me after that, and she ran to her room when we got home." He stared at Camille. "How can I fix it?"

He was looking at her as if he wanted—needed—her help, and instinctive panic began to well up inside her. She didn't have kids. Even when she was a kid, she wasn't particularly normal. How was she supposed to figure out how to fix Zoe? Steve was the dad. If he didn't know what to do, what chance was there that Camille would?

But the thought of sweet Zoe being so sad broke her heart. "After you got home and she ran into her bedroom, did you try to talk to her?"

"Yeah. I knocked, but she yelled at me to go away."

Camille frowned. "Do you think she'd talk to Maya or one of her brothers?"

His mouth tightened into a grimace. "Probably not. When Zoe's upset, she tends to want to be by herself. Not that I blame her. As much as I love them, none of her siblings are especially...tactful."

"Should we let her have her space, then? Let her stay in her room until she decides to come out and talk to us?" The last word popped out so naturally, with no hesitation. It was true. Sometime over the last few weeks, it had happened. She and Steve had started to become an *us*.

Steve looked startled for a moment before giving her a slight smile. "I like having you on my team." Before his words had a chance to sink in, his frown returned. "Could you talk to her?"

"Me?" The panic that had mostly retreated rushed back to the forefront of her brain. "I've never… I mean, that's not something I'm going to be good at. What if I just make things worse?"

"You won't. You *get* Zoe." As if Camille had actually agreed to something, he grabbed her hand and tugged her to the door that led outside. Still rattled by his suggestion, she allowed him to tow her through the door and halfway to the house before the cold air brought her out of her head.

"Wait!" She put on the brakes, and he stopped when she pulled back. He turned to face her, although he didn't release her hand. "Hang on. Let's think about this first. I don't want to just burst in there and do something wrong and completely break your child."

"You won't," he said with complete assurance—something she did not share. "Where's your coat?"

Already off-balance, she answered automatically. "Your coat."

"Fine. Where's my coat, then?"

"Um…it's still in the workshop."

Steve shucked his jacket and dropped it over her shoulders. This one was even better than her other borrowed coat, since it was warm from his body heat and smelled even more like him. Catching her hand again, he led her toward the house. "I'll text Will to grab it when he comes inside."

She just nodded. Now that she was warm again, her abandoned coat was the last thing on her mind. "I really think this will go badly," she warned as they reached the porch.

"She might not even want to talk," he said, sounding like he was back to his confident, even bossy self now that there was a plan in place. Steve, she was finding, hated to be helpless. "If she *is* willing, then you'll do fine. Just listen to her. You're good at that. You always know what's wrong, even when they don't come right out and say it. Besides, Zoe—and all the kids—already love you."

"I don't know…" Despite feeling that it was very likely she'd make a bad situation worse and quite possibly feature in future Zoe's therapy sessions, she followed him into the house. At this point, refusing to even try to talk to Zoe seemed churlish. Still, her stomach churned with nerves as she stripped off her boots and second borrowed coat. "Do you really think—?"

"Yes." Steve didn't even let her finish. "You'll do great. Go up there and knock."

"Have you always been this bossy?" She gave him an annoyed glare that hopefully hid her apprehension. It was silly to be so nervous about talking to an almost-twelve-year-old, but that thought didn't help settle her stomach. Deep down in the most insecure corner of her brain, she acknowledged that she really liked Steve's kids, and it was important to her for them to like her. She was just worried that saying the completely wrong thing would make Zoe—as well as Steve and the rest of his children—realize what a socially backward outcast Camille actually was. If they dismissed her from their lives now, it would hurt—a lot. It would be all the pain of a breakup times five, because she'd lose the kids, too.

But Steve needed her. The bossiness was fueled by worry for his daughter. How could she turn away from that? Especially now that there was an *us*.

Pretending that she wasn't trembling in her socks, she marched up the stairs with as much confidence as she could muster. The sight of the closed bedroom door was a bit intimidating, and she glanced behind her to see that Steve had followed. He gave an encouraging nod, and she frowned at him. She didn't want Zoe to refuse to talk to her because Steve was there. "Stay downstairs," she mouthed.

He gave another short nod and headed back down the stairs. Raising a hand, Camille knocked.

"Dad, I told you that I don't want to talk to you right now." Although Zoe's voice was a little shaky and watery, she sounded a lot more coherent and less hysterical than Camille had feared.

"It's me," Camille said. Silence fell on Zoe's side of the door, and Camille held her breath.

Finally, there was a heavy sigh that was clearly meant to be heard outside the room. "You can come in."

Turning the knob, Camille cautiously opened the door just far enough to stick her head in. "Hi."

"Hi." Zoe was a pitiful sight sitting slumped on the edge of the bottom bunk bed, her eyes and nose red and the rest of her face pale. She was stroking Lucy, who was curled up on her lap. When Camille didn't move any farther into the room, Zoe asked, "Why aren't you coming in?"

"Just checking to see if you were building a revenge bomb or something before I put myself in the blast zone." When Zoe didn't laugh, instead just stared at her with sad eyes lined with wet, spiky lashes, Camille suppressed a wince and slipped inside, closing the door behind her. "Sorry. I know that you'd be a lot more creative about getting revenge if you needed to. In fact, your dad was just telling me last weekend how ingenious you can be when it comes to getting your siblings back, and how I shouldn't ask you to help me prank Will, since things would get out of hand."

Zoe blinked at her, looking confused. At least she'd distracted the girl from the thought of her friend leaving—for a moment, anyway. "Why do you need to get revenge on Will?"

"I thought he'd pranked me. Want to hear the story?"

"Sure." Zoe's breath hiccupped, and Camille felt her heart squeeze in sympathy. Instead of sitting in the desk chair, as she'd originally planned, she moved to take the spot on the bed next to Zoe.

"This okay?" she asked, perching on the edge of the mattress when Zoe nodded.

There were a few seconds of silence, broken only by Lucy's rumbling purr and another residual sob-hiccup from Zoe, before she asked, "What'd Will do?"

"It was on Saturday, after I cleaned stalls with Maya. I went right from the barn to help at the gift shop, and I'd been wearing my hat all morning, so I had a pretty sad case of hat hair."

"Yeah." Another hiccup caught the last part of the word. "I hate that about winter."

"Usually, only Lucy sees me without my hat, so I haven't had to worry about it."

"Until you worked in the shop." Zoe was starting to sound a little less shattered, and a knot in Camille's chest started to release.

"Exactly. So, Will showed me where to put my coat, and he was there when I took my hat off. He told me to take out my ponytail and bend so my head was upside down." Standing, she demonstrated each step as she recounted it. "Then, he had me flip my hair back as I stood up." She did a better flip this time, not having any strands hanging in her face. "I couldn't see my reflection in the window very well, so I had to trust him that it looked okay. He promised me it was fine and then left. I walk out of the office, and Steve sees me…" She trailed off, suddenly unsure how to tell the next part to Steve's young daughter.

"Then what?" Zoe looked at her with interest. Some color had returned to her checks, and some of the redness had faded from her eyes.

Camille knew she had to finish the story, so she cleared her throat, mentally trying to edit out the flirty parts. "He saw me, and made this face." She bugged out her eyes and let her mouth drop open a little. It was exaggerated, but not by that much, and it made Zoe giggle.

"Why? Was it that bad?"

"I don't know!" Camille flung out her hands dramatically before plopping down next to Zoe again. "I started talking about getting revenge on Will, and Steve said it didn't look bad, and he was just surprised, since he'd never seen it down." There was no way she was going to mention that Steve had admitted he'd liked it.

"Really?" Zoe looked skeptical, which was understandable since Camille was leaving out large chunks of the story. "That seems like a weird thing to be *that* surprised about. What'd you say to Dad after he said that?"

"Well…nothing for a while." When Zoe gave her a sideways glance, she added, "It was busy on Saturday! Later, I told him that I liked…" Too late, she realized that it could be a potentially awkward thing to say. Knowing Zoe would never let her leave that unfinished, Camille cleared her throat and then said the whole thing in a rush, wanting to just get it out and over with. "I told him that I liked his hair too. And that I liked his face… and pretty much all of him."

"What?" Zoe's eyes widened as she started to giggle. The giggles multiplied until she was laughing uncontrollably. "I can't believe you told my dad you liked his face."

"I know!" Camille flopped back on the bed, part embarrassed, part happy that she'd gotten Zoe to laugh. "I can't believe I said that. I'm such a dork."

"Do you really like his *hair*?" Her giggles finally fading, Zoe lay back next to Camille. Lucy snuggled in between them. "He's not Rapunzel or anything. His hair is really short and brown. It's kinda boring, actually."

"I do like it." In a burst of honesty, she admitted, "There's really nothing about him I don't like. I mean, I even like how hopelessly bad he is at wrapping things in the gift shop."

Zoe snorted. "He's horrible. Just wait until Christmas. He's even worse at wrapping our presents."

"I believe it." They were both quiet for a moment before Camille spoke again, turning to look at Zoe's profile. "He's worried about you. He feels really bad about saying the wrong thing."

"I know he does." Zoe's voice got that watery tone to it again, and Camille cringed, hating that she'd made her sad. "He just doesn't get it. He and Will and Maya all make friends really easily. I don't…not usually. When I met Wyatt on my first day here, it was like…

instant. I felt like we'd been friends forever." She let out a quavering sigh. "Now Wyatt's moving to Texas, and school is going to suck so bad. I won't have anyone to eat lunch with, and no one will pick me as a biology partner, and it's going to be like the first day all over again, but worse."

"Oh." Camille didn't know what to say that would make Zoe feel better. It wasn't really something she or Steve could fix, no matter how much they wanted to. "I'm sorry, Zoe."

"I didn't have a chance to finish his rocket pack *or* his robotic legs." A fresh tear slid down the cheek closer to Camille. Still not knowing how to console Zoe, she reached out and gently wiped the moisture off her cheek. With a choked sob, Zoe rolled over and buried her face in Camille's shoulder.

For a while, Camille let her cry, rubbing her back lightly and staring at the ceiling, racking her brain for something helpful to say that would somehow lighten the hurt Zoe was feeling. When her sobs started to taper off, Camille said, "You know, just because he'll be in Texas doesn't mean you should stop working on your projects. He could still come visit and try out the jet pack or the robotic legs."

Zoe turned her head so her cheek was resting on Camille's shoulder. "I guess."

"It'd be like a movie." Camille stared at the ceiling as the possibilities played in her head. "You'll design these amazing robotic legs and change a bunch of people's lives. Then, when you go away to college to…MIT?"

"Colorado School of Mines," Zoe corrected. "It has one of the top twenty robotics engineering programs.

Besides, it's closer to the ranch, so I can come home to visit a lot."

"Okay. When you go to your first class at Mines, Wyatt walks through the door using his robotic legs... the design you invented. He sits down next to you, and you start talking, and it's like you never were apart. The two of you build a jet pack together. When Will, Micah, and Maya come to visit, all five of you test out the jet pack, but you don't tell your dad, because he'd huff and puff and pace until you were all safely on the ground again, because that's what good dads do."

With a small giggle, Zoe wiggled closer. Lucy made a small sound of complaint before moving to another section of the bed to groom herself. "I like your stories. Tell me more about me and Wyatt in college."

Camille complied. In just a few minutes, she heard Zoe's breathing deepen to a soft snore. Raising her head slightly, she saw that the girl was asleep. Carefully lowering her head back to the mattress, Camille stared at the ceiling. She was stuck. If she moved, Zoe might wake up, but what if she slept until morning?

She heard a light tap on the door and turned to see Steve stick his head in. When he saw the two of them, he smiled. "When it got quiet, I figured one or both of you had fallen asleep."

"What do I do?" she whispered. There was an itch behind her right knee, and she couldn't scratch it without disturbing Zoe. "Am I trapped here for the night?"

He muffled a laugh behind his hand as he walked over to the bed. "No," he said softly. "Once Zoe's out, she's dead to the world." He gently lifted her, and Camille scooted out from underneath, immediately scratching the itch on her leg with utter relief. Steve turned Zoe so she was lying the long way, her head on the pillow. Stroking her hair back from her still-damp cheek, he gave her a kiss on the temple and then ushered Camille out of the room.

As he closed the door softly behind them, Camille started to move toward the stairs, but he caught her hand. Surprised, she allowed him to gently tug her toward him, not stopping until they were almost touching.

"Thank you," he said, raising their clasped hands and brushing his lips against her knuckles. "You're such a kind person."

"Oh…" The kiss and unexpected compliment—as well as Steve's proximity—threw her off-center, and it took a second for her to recover her ability to speak coherently. "Zoe's easy to be kind to. Did you hear any of that?"

"Yeah." He grimaced in sympathy. "I didn't realize how close she was with Wyatt, but I should've guessed. She's always had a tough time making new friends. The moves have been hard for her."

The guilt that flashed in his eyes made Camille bold enough to reach up and cup his jaw with her free hand, running her thumb over the slightly bristly skin next to his mouth. "From what you and the kids have told me, you had good reasons for moving. They'll always have three built-in friends in each other, too."

His smile stretched wide enough to reach her thumb. "Yeah, I heard. They have friends who will help Zoe test her rocket pack while I huff and puff."

"And pace." With the corner of his mouth right there, she couldn't resist the urge to run her thumb over the fullness of his bottom lip. "Don't forget that part. Oh, and you rub the back of your neck when you're upset or worried."

He sucked in a breath at her touch, his lips parting slightly. She moved her fascinated gaze from his mouth to his eyes, and she was instantly caught by the smoldering heat she saw there.

"Camille…" His voice was so low and guttural that it was almost a growl. The sound of it vibrated through her, melting her, turning her insides into molten heat. Her hand slipped from his face to his chest, and she knotted the flannel fabric of his shirt in her fist, needing to hold on to something and feeling not quite brave enough to grab a handful of *him*.

He released her fingers and cupped her face in both hands, his burning gaze flicking back and forth between her eyes and her mouth. Camille went still, unable to believe that this was actually happening. If she hadn't felt his gentle, calloused hands or the warmth of his breath against her lips, she would've thought it was yet another daydream.

This close, she could see the heavy sweep of his lashes and the light laugh lines at the corners of his eyes. She inhaled deeply, taking in his peppermint and evergreen scent, tucking it firmly into her memory so that she'd never forget this moment with Steve.

He shifted closer, and her breath caught, her heart pounding like a jackhammer in her chest. Finally, *finally*, he closed the last inch between them. With a low groan, his lips pressed against hers.

CHAPTER 14

SHE'D BEEN WAITING FOR IT, WANTING IT, NEEDING IT, BUT SHE went still, startled, when his mouth finally met hers. He was usually so polite, so considerate, often even reserved, but the way he took over her mouth was something totally different. It was hungry and desperate and intense, and it made everything else in the world disappear.

He was kissing her. Steve-*freaking*-Springfield was kissing her. Despite all her unspoken hopes, Camille had never imagined it would ever happen…or that it would be so incredibly, unbelievably *good*.

He tilted her face up, and her paralysis broke. Pressing closer to him, she made a sound so filled with need that it startled her. *Did that come from me?* Desire roared through her body, heating her skin from the inside out, and she returned his kiss with a hunger that matched his.

His teeth closed lightly on her bottom lip, and she groaned at the unexpected pleasure bubbling up inside her. Taking advantage of her parted lips, he deepened the kiss. The touch of his tongue and the firm pressure of his lips made her shiver and burn at the same time. It was so much more than she'd ever expected, ever imagined in one of her frequent daydreams. The real-life version took her breath away and set her on fire.

She needed more. Clutching his shirt with both

hands, she dragged him closer. He came willingly, his
chest meeting hers, and he walked her back until her
shoulder blades touched the wall behind her. Kissing
her even harder, he pressed into her, his hands slipping
from her face and finding her sides, tracing the curve of
her waist before landing on her hips.

His body holding her against the wall shouldn't have
been as arousing as it was, but she loved it, loved the
heavy weight of him as he kissed her deeply. It made
her feel both utterly safe and incredibly aroused at the
same time. Releasing his shirt, she reached up to slide
her fingers around to the back of his head and pull his
mouth even more tightly against her own, needing him
as close as they could get.

"How's the Zoe situation? Will you be wrapping
things up pretty soon?" Will's voice got gradually
louder, and Steve broke the kiss, lurching back several
steps until he bumped into the opposite side of the hallway. Camille panted for breath, and she could see that
Steve's chest was heaving just as much as hers. Her
muscles felt so watery that she didn't trust them to hold
her up, so Camille leaned against the wall behind her,
letting it take her weight. It was a poor substitute for
being plastered against Steve, but Will's voice was getting closer, and she knew they couldn't continue making
out in front of one of the kids.

"Not to make it all about me, but I'm starv—oh!"
Will came into view and stopped abruptly, looking back
and forth between the two of them. Even though she
and Steve were several feet apart, Will's slow smirk
showed that he knew exactly what they'd been doing
before he'd interrupted.

"We'll be down in a minute." Steve's voice was rough, but Camille was impressed by his ability to form an intelligible sentence. Not trusting herself not to babble endlessly if she opened her mouth, she just gave Will an awkward smile that he returned with a wide grin.

"Sorry," Will said, doing an about-face. "Never mind. We'll just go ahead and eat. Carry on." His words faded as he hurried back down the stairs, but his yell to Micah and Maya carried clearly up the stairs to them. "Dad and Camille are making out, so they'll probably be a while. Let's eat."

Steve leaned his head back against the wall, and she let hers fall forward, taking a second to catch her breath before she allowed herself to be mortified that a fourteen-year-old—Steve's *son*, no less—had almost caught them kissing. Just calling it kissing made it seem too mild, too tame for what had just occurred. Complete-body kissing? Full-contact kissing? Whatever it was, it'd been mind-blowing, and Camille had to admit to herself that she couldn't wait to do it again.

With a quiet groan, Steve pushed himself away from the wall behind him. Suddenly, Camille felt unsure and resisted the urge to wrap her arms around her middle. Oddly shy, she kept her eyes on his chin, since she figured it was the safest place for her to focus on. Too high, and she saw his full, slightly swollen mouth, and she'd remember exactly what wonderful things he'd just done with it. Too low, and she'd be looking at his hard chest, and she'd remember just how it felt pressed tightly against her.

"So...?" He drew the word out, and the hint of amusement in his voice made her eyes dart to meet his, suddenly worried that the kiss had just been a joke. The still-burning heat in his gaze and his dark, aroused flush quickly destroyed that fear.

"So...?" she echoed. Now that they weren't tangled together, she felt her awkwardness quickly flood back in, and she started hunting for something to say. What *was* the etiquette for getting caught by your co-kisser's teenage son? Her gaze darted around, and she shifted her weight, her brain spinning from what had just happened. Part of her wanted to escape the uncomfortable aftermath, while another part of her was tempted to hurl herself against him again. *Kids are waiting*, she reminded herself firmly, clasping her hands together as if she could physically hold herself back.

As the seconds ticked past, she couldn't stand in silence one more second. She had to say *something*. "That was nice." She resisted the urge to close her eyes in humiliation and bang her head against the wall behind her, and instead managed to keep holding his gaze.

His eyes widened in surprise before a huge smile took over his face, and Camille was suddenly glad that she was looking at him—and even that she'd said such a silly thing in the first place. "It *was* nice," he said, his voice low with that growly undertone she was starting to really like. "More than nice. I wasn't really planning to do that right here and now, but I—" He broke off when Zoe's bedroom door opened.

"Hey," she said, blinking a little sleepily. "Sorry I fell asleep on you, Camille."

"No problem." She smiled at Zoe, wishing Steve had finished what he'd started to say, but also a little relieved that the charged conversation was over, and she could have some time to work through how she felt about it in her head before having to discuss it any more. "Are you hungry?"

"Yeah." She glanced at Steve before dropping her gaze to her feet. "Sorry about earlier, Dad."

He quickly moved toward his daughter and wrapped her in a hug. "Nothing for you to be sorry about, sweet girl. *I'm* sorry about Wyatt leaving, though. I know he's a good friend, and I shouldn't have said what I did."

"Thanks, Dad." Her voice got tight, but she didn't start crying again. "Can he maybe come visit, if his mom says it's okay?"

"Sure." Steve held her for a long moment before kissing her head and releasing her as Camille watched quietly, smiling a little. Seeing him be sweet to his kids always made her stomach warm in a completely different way than his kisses. Both were nice, though—really nice.

As Zoe hurried down the stairs in front of them, Steve caught Camille's hand and gave it a squeeze. She held on tightly, her stomach doing a happy backflip. Whatever was happening between them, it was a good thing, and it wasn't over. Knowing that was enough for now.

The nightmare was different this time.

The flames were the same, and the choking smoke, and she was still trapped in a dream version of her workshop—one without any doors—but this didn't have the same feel. She knew it was a dream this time, but she couldn't force her brain to wake up. Instead, she lay in the inferno, unable to move or even blink.

The figure in bunker gear drew closer, leaning over her in a way that should have been comforting. She should've felt relief that help was there, that she'd be carried to safety, but somehow she knew that this firefighter wasn't there to help her. The dark form was backlit by red flames, shadowing the features hiding under the helmet.

The firefighter loomed over her, closer and closer until she should've been able to see hazy features, but there was nothing but emptiness behind the face shield. A single blackened hand reached for her and—

With a gasp, Camille jerked awake, her eyes searching the moonlit room before she convinced herself it had been just another nightmare. She could almost smell a hint of bitter smoke, and that rattled her enough to send her fumbling for the bedside lamp. The softly glowing clock next to it told her that it was almost five.

She flicked on the light and then sucked back a scream, inhaling so hard that it ripped at her throat. On the bedside table was the blackened shape of her failed sculpture. The demon horse seemed to stare straight through her as she reached out, wondering if it was real or if she'd stumbled from one nightmare to the next.

Her hand trembled as she touched the sharp edge of the horse's ear and then jerked her fingers back at the feel of cold, sooty metal. It was real, and she was awake.

Her brain flipped through rational explanations— one of the firefighters must've recovered this from the wreckage of her workshop. Had Steve placed it in her room while she was sleeping? It didn't seem like something he'd do. He'd been very considerate about not intruding, even though it was his bedroom. Maybe he'd put it in there yesterday, and she hadn't noticed before falling asleep.

That seemed unlikely, but she clung to that theory, not wanting to let more imaginative and scarier ideas sneak in. There was no way an inanimate object had somehow found its way from her burned house to her bedside table. That was something that would happen in a horror movie, not in real life.

Despite her firmly logical thoughts, she slid out of bed, deciding to start her day early. She wouldn't be sleeping any more that night.

At breakfast, Camille couldn't stop sneaking glances at Steve as the kiss ran through her mind over and over again. She was grateful for the kids' chatter but at the same time wished she could be alone with him so that they could do a real-life replay of that kiss instead.

"Any problems when you were feeding the horses this morning?" Steve asked Micah, who shook his head as he carried his cereal bowl to the sink. The other three kids followed, clearing the table and rinsing their dishes.

The mention of horses reminded Camille of her unpleasant surprise that morning. "Did you find that...?" She paused, wanting to say *hell beast* but then remembering there were children around, even though they were busy prepping for school and didn't look as if they were listening to the conversation. "The horse sculpture. Did you find that in the remains of my house?"

Steve's eyebrows drew together in confusion. "What horse sculpture?"

"The one on my bedside table." She flushed at claiming his bedroom as her own, the memory of the kiss popping back into her brain. "I mean, *your* bedside table."

His expression stayed blank. "I haven't seen it. Was it one that was in your workshop during the fire?"

"Yeah. It was a reject. An ugly thing—hideous, actually." She frowned. "If you didn't find it, who put it in your room?"

His expression smoothed. "Most likely, one of the other firefighters found the sculpture and dropped it off. One of the kids probably put it in your room to surprise you." He smiled as he rose, collecting her dishes along with his. The kids had scattered, and she was alone in the kitchen with him. "I'm sure they didn't realize it wasn't one you wanted to keep."

That made sense, although Camille couldn't seem to shake the discomfort she'd felt at seeing it so soon after waking from her nightmare. The kids wouldn't know about her bad dreams, though, and she decided not to grill them about the sudden appearance of the demon horse. She didn't want to make them feel bad for doing what they believed was a nice thing. Pushing her chair back, she stood, just now realizing that he'd cleaned up for her. "Oh, you didn't need to do that. Thank you, though."

"You're welcome." He stepped closer, his voice dropping to a low tone that vibrated through her. "I like doing things for you."

It was such a simple statement, but it set off a whole army of wild butterflies in her stomach. "Thank you." She watched, her cheeks warming as he took another step closer, tipping his head down. His gaze dropped to her lips, and her body heated, thrilled at the prospect of another kiss.

"Dad! Have you seen my green leggings?" Steve and Camille took a synchronized step back as Maya charged through the kitchen toward the laundry room.

"They're in the dryer," Camille said, her voice sounding a little rough, even to her own ears. Steve's gaze never left hers. "I washed them this morning, since you said you wanted to wear them today."

"Thank you, thank you, thank you!" Leggings in hand, Maya rushed out of the laundry room, oblivious to the thick tension between the two adults.

Steve cupped Camille's cheek, his thumb brushing against her heated skin. "Thank you for doing that."

She shifted closer and then stepped back again quickly as Will entered the kitchen. Steve dropped his hand to his side.

"What's up?" Will asked with a growing grin, his gaze flicking back and forth between Camille and Steve.

Clearing his throat, Steve turned to his son. "Do you have your history paper?"

"It's in the printer." Doing an about-face, Will headed out of the kitchen.

Camille wasn't about to risk getting caught by the kids a third time, so she kept her distance from Steve. He gave her a secret smile that warmed everything inside her, only breaking their intimate gaze when Micah walked into the kitchen.

As she moved to help distribute the kids' lunches, she found that she was grinning. Thanks to Steve, her morning had vastly improved after a nightmarish start.

Camille hesitated at the entrance of the elementary school auditorium.

"You okay?" Steve asked from his spot behind her. Will, Micah, and Zoe had already gone inside to find seats, but Camille could hear the voices of everyone inside, and it sounded like an awful lot of people. She'd known it would be. Borne didn't have many social events, so even a school's holiday concert drew almost everyone in town.

"Sure," she said, even though she wasn't sure at all. Maybe she should just go hide in the truck until the concert was over. She'd take the frigid boredom of two hours in the parking lot over the waiting crowd.

"Would it help or make it worse to hold hands?" Steve asked, his voice low, his mouth close to her ear— something that always made her shiver in a delighted way. They hadn't touched since their first kiss the previous evening, and the idea of holding Steve's warm, rough-skinned hand was so appealing that it would be worth braving the stares of the townspeople.

"It'd help," she said, pulling off one of her new mittens and holding her hand out. If they were going to deal with all the stares and whispers, then she was going to get the full effect of holding Steve's hand—skin to skin. His grin was huge as he wrapped his big hand around her smaller one. That instant feeling of safety enveloped her at his touch, and she felt her shoulders relax a little. She was right; holding his hand did indeed help. Now she just had to brave the townspeople's stares.

The idea made her tense up again.

"Ready?" Steve asked. She couldn't force out an affirmative answer. He seemed to realize that she'd frozen up at the thought of facing the crowd, since he gave her hand a warm squeeze before heading inside, towing her along with him. The auditorium was already packed, but it was too early for the majority of the people to have taken their seats. Instead, the adults and older children stood in pairs and groups, chattering, while the younger kids ran up and down the aisles.

Just as she'd expected, there was a ripple of interest as people noticed them, and then a louder wave of gleeful whispers as they saw Steve and Camille's linked hands. A few people started to move their way, and Camille braced herself, knowing they'd soon be surrounded.

"Camille!" Zoe's voice was a relief. Camille turned to see the girl approaching, a boy about her age in a wheelchair next to her. "This is Wyatt. Wyatt, you already know my dad, and this is *Camille*."

Zoe put a heavy emphasis on her name as she and her friend exchanged glances, and Camille looked back and forth between them, wondering what the subtext was. She made a mental note to pry it out of Zoe later and gave the boy a nod. "Hi, Wyatt."

"Wyatt," Steve greeted. "Heard you and your mom are heading to Texas."

Camille immediately looked at Zoe and saw her eyes start to shine with unshed tears, so she gave Steve's hand a hard warning squeeze and stepped on his toes for good measure. He looked at her, confused, and she gave a slight tilt of her head toward Zoe. She felt him tense as he got the message.

"Yeah," Wyatt said, not sounding excited about the move, although nowhere near tears. Camille was grateful for that, since two crying preteens was a little more than she felt she could handle. "Austin. We're moving the day after Christmas."

"Well, you're welcome at the ranch anytime you want to visit," Steve said, and Camille gave him a more gentle squeeze to let him know that was a pretty good save. She interpreted his return squeeze as a thank-you.

"Camille!" Swallowing the groan that wanted to escape, Camille turned toward an approaching Jodi Lin. She clung to Steve's hand, suddenly so grateful for his presence that she ignored the fact that it was his fault— well, his daughter's fault—that she was at the concert in the first place. "Good! I was hoping you'd come," Jodi puffed, out of breath from her sprint across the auditorium. Camille figured she'd wanted to be the first one to get the latest gossip. "I am so sorry about your house burning down. When I heard what happened, I just..." She put her hand on her chest, as if trying to think of a way to express her sense of horror.

"Thank you, Jodi," Camille said when Jodi's sentence hung unfinished for a beat too long.

With the condolences over, Jodi gave Camille and Steve's joined hands a lightning-quick glance. "I bet you're here for Maya. She's such a sweet girl. It's so good that she has a mother figure around now, rather than just a ranch full of men."

Camille was squeezing SOS in Morse code when the lights dimmed and brightened again for the five-minute warning. "Better find our seats I bet the kids are waiting for us thank you again Jodi we'll talk later bye!"

She basically sprinted away, with Steve close behind her. She could hear him chuckling softly, but she didn't care. She was taking full advantage of the opportunity to escape the inquisition.

"This way." Steve took the lead again, weaving among people with enough speed and dexterity that no one had a chance to engage them in conversation. Camille approved.

"Camille!"

"Nooo," she groaned under her breath, making Steve laugh again. Mrs. Lin—the older version—was waving at her from the opposite aisle. Camille waved back, grateful for the seats blocking Mrs. Lin from getting close enough to talk, and took the seats that the kids had picked out. They were on the aisle so that Zoe could sit next to Wyatt, and Camille appreciated the location for the quick getaway it offered. She wouldn't have to shuffle past half a row of seats in order to escape.

Nate and Ryan were already there, sitting next to Will and Micah.

"Hey," Ryan greeted, his smile growing stiff as his gaze fell on Camille and Steve's joined hands.

"Hi." She gave them a little wave and then settled into her seat between Steve and Micah, who sat hunched forward, gripping his program a little too tightly. Leaning toward him, she murmured, "How much do you want to run out of here right now?"

He sent her a sideways look before refocusing on his crumpled program. "A lot."

"I thought about sitting out in the truck for the whole thing, but I figured I'd get pretty cold out there for an hour."

He snorted and tilted the program so she could see the list of performances...the *long* list. "Two."

"Two...hours?" Why couldn't she be in the shop, alone, working on Steve's Christmas present right now?

"Yep. Sometimes longer." He looked slightly less hunched, and one corner of his mouth had turned up. Camille was glad that her misery had made him feel a little better. "I've been to lots of these."

"Do they at least have cookies at intermission?"

"What intermission?"

Turning to Steve, she said very quietly, "If this goes for more than two hours straight, it's just cruel that they don't have people going up and down the aisles selling alcohol to the adults." The lights began to dim, and she settled into her seat, leaving him muffling his amused snort with his free hand. By the time he'd cleared his throat and settled again, it was full dark, and the curtain opened to show a group of children arranged on risers. They were too small to be Maya's age, so Camille quickly lost interest as they started singing about Rudolph the Red-Nosed Reindeer.

"Here," Steve whispered, sliding something into her hand.

When she realized it was a flask, she couldn't stop herself from lifting up to kiss him on the cheek. It might've been the promise of alcohol, or the fact that she'd almost made Micah smile, or just sitting in the midst of all the Springfields, feeling like a true part of their family, but the next two hours weren't looming as horribly as they'd been before.

"You," she whispered, unscrewing the lid, "are a wonderful, wonderful man."

There was just enough light to see his broad, pleased smile.

━━━━━━━━━━

It was close to ten before they filed into the house, and Maya was weaving with exhaustion.

"Bed," Steve said, eyeing his kids' tired faces. "Tomorrow's a school day."

Will let out a little huff. "Barely. It's the last day before vacation, so no one's going to be doing anything."

"I have two tests," Zoe grumbled, not much more awake than Maya. "Why does Will have it so easy? He's older than me. Isn't school supposed to get harder?"

"It does. Will, you have that algebra test and two papers due," Steve scolded lightly. "So bed, now. Good night. Maya, you did a great job tonight."

Maya gave him a sleepy smile as the rest of them called their good nights, and they headed upstairs without any more complaining. That, Steve knew, was a true testament to how tired they really were. When Camille started to follow them, he caught her hand, and she turned toward him in surprise.

"Hang on a minute," he said quietly, and she gave him an agreeable smile and relaxed against him. Closing his eyes, he fought the temptation he'd been struggling with all evening. Camille, he'd discovered, became sweetly affectionate after just a couple sips of whiskey. During the concert, she'd leaned in to him, whispering occasional comments into his ear, and afterward she'd tucked her hand into his arm when they'd walked out to the parking lot. It hadn't been anything extreme, nothing for the other Borne residents to exclaim over, but it had battered his defenses against her.

Living with Camille for the past week had already tested his self-control, and now, with her sleepy, relaxed body pressed against him, her back against his front, he felt his weakened willpower eroding even more. He opened his eyes. The darkness just made him concentrate more on the feel of her curves and how good she always smelled, like burnt sugar and vanilla.

"That," Camille murmured, reaching back to catch his hand, "was both torturous and more fun than I expected it'd be."

"You've pretty much described parenthood," Steve said dryly. "Thank you for going. The kids really enjoyed having you there, especially Micah. I don't think I've ever seen him so relaxed at one of those events before."

"I understand why. We both have the same hatred of crowds." She played with Steve's fingers and ran her thumb over his palm. He shivered at her touch, somehow feeling hot and cold at the same time. Unable to resist, he moved his free hand to her waist, telling himself he'd just leave it there. Only seconds passed before he was sliding it across her middle, pulling her even more firmly against him.

Stop, he told himself. *She's been drinking.* Even though she'd only taken a couple of small slugs of whiskey from the flask hours ago, and she never showed signs of being tipsy, he didn't want to take advantage. He was already too aware of the fact that she was staying with him because her home had burned and she had nowhere else to go...well, nowhere that wasn't Mrs. Lin's or Ryan's. He never wanted her to feel pressured by him or for her to do anything she didn't want as much as he wanted it—and he really wanted it…urgently.

Clearing his throat, he dragged his mind off of his desperation. "You're so good with him…with all of them."

Tipping her head back, she smiled at him once more, giving him those hot and cold chills again. "It's more like they're good with me."

As he stared down at her, fighting the urge to kiss those full, tempting lips, he remembered how good she'd tasted the previous evening. Camille had been so willing, so eager—almost as frantic as he'd been—and he'd been overwhelmed by the need to lose himself in her. If Will hadn't accidentally interrupted them, Steve wasn't sure he would've been able to stop.

"Did you need something from me?" she asked as if reading his mind, and he jerked in surprise, his arm tightening around her waist for a moment.

"I…" He paused, unsure how to answer that in a way that was truthful but didn't reveal his desperate hunger. Clearing his throat to give himself a moment to think, he finally answered, "I just wanted to thank you for going tonight, even though I know it was hard for you." He found he couldn't leave it at that. The previous day's kiss hadn't been one-sided. In fact, she'd told him it'd been nice. The memory made him snort, and that amusement centered him enough to continue. "I also wanted to have some time alone with you. We haven't had much of that this week."

Her hand went still on his for a moment before she started her rhythmic stroking of her thumb across his palm again, sending pleasure streaking straight from his hand to his groin. He swallowed a pained laugh at that.

She affected him so strongly that just the touch drove him wild.

"Not much, no," she said, and he dragged his mind away from the sensations her fingers were creating and back to their conversation. "I want that, too. It isn't that I've been trying to avoid you."

Shifting his hand so that it cradled the back of hers, he lifted it to his mouth and pressed his lips to her palm. "I know. The ranch has been busy, and you've had to deal with the aftermath of the fire, too. You've been a huge help around here. Thank you for that. I know the gift shop isn't your ideal place to be, but you've really come through for us."

"If Micah can manage to work among all those customers, then so can I," she said, setting her chin. Her resolute expression made him smile, even as it inspired another rush of heat. "I've heard he's a better packager than I am, though, which is a little upsetting."

He laughed softly, marveling once again at how happy she made him. "He's a better packager than *anyone*," he reassured her. "It's the artist in him."

"There's artist in me, too, so I have no excuse." Tugging her hand free of his hold, she turned to face him. "I'm determined to up my wrapping game."

He'd thought having her backside up against him made it tough to control himself, but that was nothing compared to having their *fronts* pressed together. Struggling to drag his mind off the feel of her breasts against his chest, he responded hoarsely, "At least you'll always be better at it than me."

Her lower lip protruded in a pretend pout. "That's no comfort. You're terrible."

His laugh was a little choked as he focused on her lips. The only thing stopping him from kissing her was knowing that his control was holding on by a thread. If he put his lips on hers, it would be incredibly hard to stop with a kiss. He opened his mouth to make a joke, but what came out was, "How sober are you right now?"

Instant comprehension lit her face, and her lips parted. She licked the bottom one, and Steve could barely hold back a groan. "I'm very sober." The way she said it made it clear she knew why he was asking. "I only had a few sips, and that was hours ago."

"That's what I thought." His voice was rough, and he couldn't seem to stop his hands from traveling up and down her sides. With her right in front of him, leaning against him, it was impossible to pass up the opportunity to touch. "I wasn't sure, though, since you seemed a little more...cuddly than usual." *Cuddly?* He made a face at his choice of words, but she seemed amused by it rather than offended.

"I'm not normally cuddly?" Her quiet laugh was breathless, and he had a feeling that the flush on her face was caused by arousal rather than embarrassment.

"Yeah, you are." His fingers traced up her ribs. He loved the feel of her, so soft and warm and alive. "I'm thinking about cuddling you pretty much all the time."

Her flush deepened, and she rested her forehead against his chest. Under his hands, he could feel her ribs expanding and contracting with rapid breaths, and he loved that he was the cause, that he could excite her so much.

"Steve?" She raised her head and looked up at him.

"Yeah?"

"Can I stay down here with you tonight?"

CHAPTER 15

Steve went still, and Camille felt a horrible, sinking dread. Had she misread him? Did he not want her as desperately as she wanted him? The evening had been endless and painful—at least the singing part—but Steve had made it so much better. He'd held her hand and snickered at her whispered comments and squeezed her fingers against his side when she'd taken his arm, and every little contact had added fuel to the fire burning inside her until it'd felt like one more touch would either make her combust or melt into a drippy puddle at his feet.

When he'd stopped her from going upstairs with the kids, when he'd wrapped an arm around her and kissed her hand and run his fingers along her sides, leaving trails of sparking heat in their wake, she'd been sure that he felt the same aching need that had been building in her since she first saw him back in Borne Market.

Now, however, as she waited for him to move or speak, to somehow respond to her question, she doubted her interpretation of every moment from that point on. She'd thought he'd been flirting, that he'd been as intrigued as she was, but what did she know? She was a socially inept, homeless sort-of-hermit who'd barely left Borne, and he was Steve-*freaking*-Springfield, with his perfect hair and strong body and calm competency and his habit of saving lives and putting out fires and rearing wonderfully interesting children and looking insanely hot in bunker gear and—

Steve kissed her, hard.

It was her turn to be taken off guard. She'd been so caught up in her chaotic thoughts that it took a moment to realize that his mouth was on hers, and he was kissing her with a ferocious intensity that laid every one of her worries to rest.

He did want her—badly. She could feel it in the tightness of his muscles and the almost frantic pressure of his kiss. When he slid his hands down her sides to grip her hips, yanking her against him, she could tell in another, more obvious way as well.

Then he lifted her, picking her off the ground with ease, his lips never leaving hers. She wrapped her legs around him and pulled him closer. With his hands free, he roved over her back and down her thighs, exploring and possessing her at the same time.

Tangling her arms around his neck, she tightened her legs, once again overcome with the need to get as close as possible. She made a sound of protest when he pulled his mouth away, but the line of nibbling kisses down her throat more than made up for the loss of his lips on hers. Tilting her head back to give him better access, she moaned as heat built in her, fueled by his mouth on her neck and the press of their bodies.

As the sound reached her ears, a small, still-functioning corner of her brain couldn't believe that needy, almost feral noise had come from her. She'd never thought that she'd feel the fiery, mind-stealing, overwhelming passion that she'd read about in books. She'd bounced between figuring that it was a made-up thing, something no real person ever experienced, and thinking it was reserved for a lucky few—a group that definitely would never include her.

She'd been so wrong. This was hers. The so-good-that-it-almost-hurt sensation of Steve lightly scoring her neck with his teeth before he soothed the spot with his tongue belonged to her—and so did he. A ferocious wave of hungry possession crashed over her, and she tightened her grip on him, needing to keep him there with her. She'd never been able to keep anyone she loved, but she was determined that she wouldn't lose Steve. He was hers now, and she was never going to let go.

He tumbled her back onto a soft surface, and she realized that he'd been walking them into the moonlight-filled den as they kissed. She'd been so caught up in the feel of his lips and teeth and tongue on her skin that she hadn't even noticed them moving. When Steve tried to pull back, she clung to him, and he gave a throaty chuckle that dialed her desire up even more.

"I'll be right back," he whispered, giving her a hard, needy kiss on the mouth. Reluctantly, she released him, watching through lust-dazed eyes from the sofa bed as he closed and locked the study door before turning on the light.

The kids, she remembered, glad that one of them had the presence of mind to not get down and dirty on the kitchen floor when his four children were sleeping upstairs. Instead of returning to her immediately, he moved to the heavy wood desk and rummaged in the very back of the bottom drawer.

Her mind was clearing of the fog his kisses had left her in, and she pushed herself up to get a better view. "What are you looking for?" she asked, trying to see around him to the contents of the drawer. It looked like it was filled with hanging file folders, and she couldn't imagine what records or documents would help them at this particular moment.

In answer, Steve pulled out a small box and held it up triumphantly. "I knew I had some in there," he said with satisfaction, tossing the container to her as he shut the drawer with his foot. She fumbled the unexpected catch, and the box landed in her lap. When she saw what it was, she gave a laughing snort, which she immediately regretted. Snorting wasn't going to fuel Steve's lust for her. But still, who kept condoms in with their files?

"Is this for when you get randy with your accountant?" she teased, and another unfortunate snort slipped out before she could stop it. She mentally scolded herself, both for the pig noises and for mentioning his accountant—and the word *randy*. If he became completely turned off and left her hanging, she'd have no one to blame but herself.

He laughed, but it had a rough edge to it. Lifting her up, he tossed her farther back on the bed, and she bit back a surprised squeal. She found it shockingly arousing how easily he picked her up, her weight barely straining the muscles of his solid arms and chest. It wasn't just his physical strength that made him so attractive, but also his ability to deal with the crises and day-to-day drama of the ranch and his kids and the fire department with a steady, unruffled calm.

"No. Richard isn't my type. I just figured it's the one spot where the kids wouldn't stumble over them."

"You don't want them to know that their dad has sex?" she asked, honestly curious. She'd never considered the issues of dating as a single parent until she'd gotten to know Steve and his family.

He gave a wry grimace. "More that I'd come home to find a bunch of condoms blown up like balloons."

The mental image made her laugh, although it didn't seem quite accurate. "Balloons? No. With your kids, you'd be more likely to come home to find they'd been incorporated into an art project or used to fix a fan belt or something."

He chuckled even as he cringed. "That's unnervingly accurate." When he picked up the box and looked at the side, Camille snickered.

"Reading the directions?" she asked innocently.

With a mock-snarl, he dropped the box on the bed and pounced. Straddling her hips with his knees, he began tickling her, making her giggle and squirm beneath him. "No, smarty-pants." He paused, looking a little sheepish. "I'm checking the expiration date. It's…" He cleared his throat. "It's been a while. Not to, ah, bring down the mood, but after Karen died, I was focused on the kids. Even after some time passed, I didn't want to bring anyone into their lives who'd leave them. They'd had enough loss. Keeping things separate doesn't really work that well, so it became easier just to…do without." He gave her a quick, almost bashful glance. "Until you. I don't want to do without you."

Her amusement slipped away as she looked up at him. "I'm so glad."

"Me, too."

They exchanged a smile as heat started building in Steve's gaze again. Camille's breath caught in her chest as he slowly lowered his upper body toward hers, his biceps bulging with the effort of holding his weight. She wasn't sure where to look; every part of him was so entrancing. Her gaze moved from his arms to his chest to his parted lips—lingering there for an extra beat—to his square, stubbled jaw to his eyes. Although she enjoyed looking at each part of him, his heavy-lidded eyes were her favorite, since they expressed so clearly how irresistible he found her to be.

Then his lips were on hers again, and she was lost, reveling in the feel of him—his exploring mouth and his weight pressing her down into the mattress and his hands finding all the spots that she didn't even know were sensitive until now. They kissed for what felt like hours, until her arousal had built to the point that she felt like she'd go up in flames if she couldn't feel his skin against hers.

She yanked up his shirt, wanting it gone and not willing to wait until he'd unfastened all the buttons. He jerked it over his head, oblivious to the pop of buttons flying off and even the rip of a seam giving way. His T-shirt came off even faster, and then Camille was faced with the most beautiful chest she'd ever seen. She could hardly believe it was hers to explore.

She ran her hands over him, feeling the wiry layer of hair and the silk of his skin over hard muscle, clenching and releasing under her touch. His audible inhales and groans as she found a sensitive spot made her feel powerful, and she especially liked the way he reacted when she kissed his breastbone. As she ran her tongue over a flat nipple, he hissed, his back arching at the sensation.

It was as if he couldn't take any more of her explorations. His mouth found hers again with an extra edge of frantic desperation, kissing and licking and nipping at her equally needy lips. They yanked and pulled and sometimes even tore until they were both completely free of their clothes.

The first time Steve's naked body pressed full-length against hers was branded into her head, and she knew she'd remember even the most minor details of that moment for the rest of her life. From the way his breath caught and he went rigid against her, she knew that he felt the same way.

After a perfect, frozen moment, they both snapped back into action. Camille needed more—more of his mouth on hers and more of his hands on her skin. Their kisses grew wilder and their touches bolder, their explorations of each other gaining more and more of a desperately needy edge.

She tasted the salt on his throat as he groaned against her ear, and she felt the sound of his pleasure all the way to her toes. He left her for a moment, kneeling above her and grabbing for the abandoned box at the foot of the bed. It was only seconds before he was stretched over her again, not even enough time for her hot, sweaty skin to cool, but it was still too long for her liking.

Wrapping her arms and legs around him, she held him tightly as he entered her. He felt just as she'd expected—as if he belonged inside her, the two of them connected intimately, fitting together in every way possible. He kissed her as they started to move, quickly finding a rhythm that made them both gasp and groan.

As pleasure built inside her, an incredible tension taking hold of her muscles, she felt that same sense of unreality from before. How could she be so lucky to be feeling this much, to be experiencing such a flood of wonderful emotions and sensations, to have found such a connection with this ridiculously perfect man? How had she gone from her solitary, ordinary life to being so intertwined with Steve? It seemed too good, too incredible, to be true.

Her arms and legs tightened, pulling him in more deeply. Even if it was a fantasy, some realistic daydream that had gotten out of hand, it didn't matter. She was going to savor every second she had with Steve, wallow in every touch and kiss, every bit of pleasure he offered her.

Her thoughts started to blur around the edges as he moved faster, driving her closer to her climax with every stroke. Clinging to him, she broke their kiss and buried her face into his neck, breathing in his scent of peppermint and pine and sweaty, sexy man.

As she came, her orgasm rocketing through her, pleasure filling every place inside her, she cried out, calling his name against his skin. His muffled shout followed hers as he held himself deep inside her, his body rock hard against her own. She lifted her head to watch him as his eyes closed and his face grew tight, and she felt like she'd never grow tired of this—of him.

Gradually, her tension started to seep away, her tight muscles releasing their hold as pleasure continued to ripple through her. For a heady, bliss-filled moment, Steve let his weight press her into the mattress, and she felt safe and secure under the cover of his heavy form. Too soon, he rolled to the side. His groan turned to a chuckle as she moved with him, reluctant to lose the connection she'd just found.

Turning over again, he tucked her beneath him and pushed up to his elbows so his full weight wasn't flattening her. "It'll be just for a second. I'll be right back," he said, affection clear in his voice. Pressing a quick kiss to her lips, he started to move off of her—only to return for another kiss.

His second groan was deeper and dramatic enough to make her laugh. He kissed her nose, her cheek, under her jaw, and then her ear when she scrunched her shoulder up and turned her head to hide a ticklish spot. Leaving her giggling breathlessly, he got up to toss the condom in the trash and turn off the light before jumping back into bed. Grabbing hold of her, he tugged her across the bed into his arms. She tickled him where she'd just discovered he was very, very sensitive, and he jerked in response.

"Really?" His pretend annoyance was ruined by the amusement in his voice. "You think you can beat me in a tickle war?" He retaliated, finding her weak spots with precise accuracy. She obviously wasn't the only one who'd learned from their mutual exploration earlier. When she couldn't breathe from laughing so hard, she begged for mercy.

"Say it," he prodded her, ceasing his attacks and gathering her against him, spooning her so her back was against his front.

"Fine." Her huff was broken by a hiccup of laughter. "You're the king of Tickle Town."

"Your Majesty," he prompted, and she snorted. She liked tussling with playful Steve. It was a side of him that she hadn't really seen before. Normally, he was too mature for his own good.

"Your Majesty," she parroted, squirming around to get comfortable and nudging her hips back against him to get a reaction. She succeeded.

"Camille…" His growl made parts of her melt and other parts tighten in anticipation.

"Yes, Your Majesty?" She wiggled again, and he caught her hip, pressing more tightly against her for a breathless moment before he released the pressure and wrapped his arm around her waist.

"Little devil," he grumbled, sounding completely and utterly satisfied. She couldn't stop her proud grin at knowing she'd done that to him. They felt silent, and sleepiness gradually crept over Camille, but all her parts not pressed against Steve's warmth were starting to get chilly, and the pullout bed's support bar was digging into the side of her thigh.

She heard Steve's breathing deepen, and she started shifting toward the edge of the bed. The arms around her tightened immediately.

"Stay with me," he said in a sleepy grumble.

"On one condition," she said. Tension tightened her belly, and she almost hesitated to say the words. It seemed like a big step, one that would shift their relationship to a whole new level. "We go upstairs to your real bed."

He froze, and she knew he was aware of just what she was asking. "You're sure you want this?"

She wanted to keep Steve more than anything else in her life. "Yes."

He was off the bed and standing before she even finished answering. "I'm all for that." Grabbing his pants, he tugged them on.

Shaking off the distracting knowledge that Steve was going commando, even if it was just for the short trip upstairs, Camille narrowed her eyes at him. "I thought you said this sofa bed was comfortable, you liar."

"I didn't want you to feel bad about stealing my bed." He grinned, the satisfaction in it clear despite the dim room. "I'm really glad we're going to be sharing it now."

Leaning over, he gave Camille a lingering kiss. When he pulled away, she stared at him, heated and dazed, marveling at how quickly he could get her desperate and wanting.

"Yeah," she said, her gaze on his mouth. "I'm glad, too."

For the first time in almost a week, something besides nightmares about the fire woke her. She opened her eyes to see Steve's muscular and naked backside sliding out of bed, and she smiled. This was so much better than being startled awake by images of flames and choking smoke.

"Hey," she said softly, her voice husky with sleep. Stretching, she rolled until she could see the clock on the nightstand. "You're up early."

The moonlight made interesting shadows on her face, but she could tell he was smiling as he leaned in for a gentle kiss. It was so nice that she didn't even think about the possibility of morning breath until his lips left hers.

Straightening, he moved to his dresser and began

to pull out some clothes. "I go snowshoeing with Will every morning before school. You're right, though. It is early. Try to get some more sleep." After pulling on long underwear that molded to his muscular form, he glanced over his shoulder at her. Even though his expression was hidden by the dim light, she just knew he was giving her a wonderfully satisfied smirk. "I kept you up pretty late."

"Nuh-uh," she said through a yawn that more than proved his point. "I kept *you* up late."

This time, she didn't need to guess at his expression, because he laughed out loud, albeit softly. "Yeah, you did. It was worth it, although it was hard getting out of bed this morning. I think that was your fault, too."

She really loved this flirty, playful side of Steve. Flipping off the covers, she offered her best seductive-beast pose. "I *am* a temptress."

With a fleece top pulled halfway over his head, he froze for a second, and she had a sudden worry that the comment had been too dorky. Yanking his shirt down, he strode over to the bed and kissed her hard again, more intensely this time. By the time he pulled back, they were both panting for breath.

"Yeah, you are. I've never been so tempted by anyone. If Will wasn't waiting for me..." Making a sound low in his throat, he turned away. Giving her frequent, hungry glances, he finished getting dressed and disappeared into the bathroom. As soon as he was gone, Camille felt a bit let down and lonely...as well as wide awake. She stretched again, pulling up the covers and closing her eyes in an attempt to regain the peaceful sleep she'd had before Steve, but his kisses and flirtatious banter had gotten her heart beating too fast to doze off again. Besides, she didn't want to fall asleep just to have one of her terrifying dreams.

Even though she'd escaped physically unscathed from her burning workshop, the experience played through her mind over and over when she tried to rest. It was usually the same, but somehow even worse than reality. She was lost in the flames and thick, choking smoke, searching fruitlessly for Lucy—except when she was searching the fiery room for Lucy and Steve and the kids. No matter how many times she'd had the dreams, they always made her feel as helpless and terrified as the very first one.

The bathroom door opened, and Camille looked toward it, eager to be distracted from her dark thoughts. Steve did exactly that by coming over for a final not-so-quick kiss.

"Be careful," she said once they'd managed to separate. "Don't run into any moose or serial killers."

"Both of those are pretty rare here on the ranch, but I'll keep an eye out." With a final short but still steamy kiss, he slipped out into the hall, closing the door silently behind him.

With thoughts of nightmares clashing with the warm comfort Steve's kisses inspired, Camille was more awake than ever. Throwing off the covers, she quickly dressed, shivering in the chill of the room. No sense in lying in bed, awake and restless. Shoving aside her lingering memories of the fire, she headed downstairs to start making breakfast for everyone.

CHAPTER 16

BY THE TIME STEVE AND WILL RETURNED, BRIGHT-EYED AND flushed from the cold, the other kids had made it downstairs, looking much sleepier than the snowshoers. The younger three had, however, perked up at the smell of bacon and were filling their plates with it, as well as pancakes, eggs, and fruit.

"You made breakfast?" Steve said, moving over to stand next to her by the stove, where she was monitoring the last round of pancakes. It was hard to be that close to him and not kiss him, but Camille didn't want to shove their new relationship in the kids' faces, especially at this ungodly hour. Besides, she was a little nervous about what their reactions would be.

"There's bacon?" Will broke in before she could answer, sliding into his seat at the table. "Can Camille live here forever?"

"I'd be okay with that," Steve said under his breath, making her stomach do a funny little flip and squeeze that only seemed to happen when Steve was around. He leaned in to her briefly, pressing their shoulders together for a fraction of a second before stepping back to a more discreet distance. "Can I help?"

Flustered by even that small touch, she focused a little too intently on flipping the pancakes onto a plate.

"Here." She shoved the plate at him, desperate to have some kind of barrier between them so she wasn't tempted to start climbing him in front of the kids. "That's the last of them. Can you put them on the table with the rest?" She gave him an apologetic look, knowing she was behaving oddly. Seeing that the corners of his mouth were tucked in that way they did when he was holding back a smile, she knew that he was well aware of why she was so discombobulated—and he was amused by it.

The sound of the front door opening caught her attention. Lucy, who'd been eyeing the platter of bacon with a scheming look in her eyes, darted into the other room. Although she got along well with everyone in the family—especially Micah, who let her share his pillow at night—new arrivals always made her wary.

"'Morning," Nate called out. By the amount of stomping and rustling as outerwear was being taken off, he wasn't the only one who'd arrived. She raised her eyebrows at Steve, who gave her a slight shrug. As soon as their uncles had arrived, all four kids grabbed for the bacon, piling extra on their plates.

"Manners," Steve said, although he sounded more resigned than upset. He pulled out Camille's chair and waited for her to sit before taking his own seat next to her. "The kids are right, though. You'd better get some bacon now before my brothers get a crack at it."

Nate, Ryan, and Joe came into the kitchen, all three looking like they'd just rolled out of bed. Their eyes fixed on the food, even as Nate and Ryan greeted everyone, and they hurried to take their chairs at the end of the table.

"Since when do you three come for breakfast?" Steve asked mildly, piling some bacon on Camille's plate before taking his own and passing the platter to Joe. As she watched in amazement, the rest of the bacon disappeared from the serving plate.

"Zoe texted us," Ryan said, reaching for the scrambled eggs as Joe forked a huge stack of pancakes onto his plate. "Said that Camille cooked and"—he popped a piece into his mouth, winking at her—"that there was bacon."

Everyone's eyes turned to Zoe, and she held her hands out in a shrug. "I thought I was just texting Uncle Joe, but I guess it was a group text. Sorry."

"Hey," Nate grumbled, and Ryan raised an eyebrow at her.

Zoe didn't look at all ashamed she'd played favorites. "What? Uncle Joe gets me all the parts I need, even when they're really hard to find."

"There's plenty," Steve said calmly, prying the pancake platter out of Nate's hands before he could take any and offering it to Camille. She took two, giving him a small smile of thanks, and he returned the platter to Nate. Steve offered her eggs the same way, and she had to hold back a snicker at the indignant look on his brothers' faces when he pulled the food right out of their hands. "It does mean that you're going to be here for a family discussion."

Ryan seemed unbothered, while Joe looked up, his fork halfway to his mouth. He stared at his food, as if debating if it was worth staying, and then gave a soundless sigh and resumed eating.

Nate looked back and forth between Steve and

Camille. "What's the discussion about? Are the two of you finally admitting that you're dating?"

At Nate's direct question, Camille stopped breathing for a second. Her gaze darted around the table, looking from face to face, trying to judge their reactions. The kids didn't seem obviously upset, but she wondered if they were hiding their true feelings.

"Now that you've just blurted it out..." Steve gave Nate an exasperated look. "Yes, Camille and I are in a relationship."

For some reason, Steve's bald confirmation of Nate's guess made Camille even more uneasy. The kids seemed to like her, but there was a world of difference between liking a temporary guest and liking their dad's girlfriend. Also, she and Steve hadn't discussed the whole relationship thing or even touched on what they were going to say to the kids—or his brothers.

"We are?" she blurted, drawing everyone's attention. She focused on Steve's brothers first, since a negative reaction from the kids would hurt a lot more than one coming from Ryan or Nate or Joe. Nate shook his head, Joe concentrated on eating, and Ryan stared at her, his lips in a tight, straight line. Uncomfortable, she glanced away and ended up meeting Steve's gaze, which wasn't much better.

"Yes," he said firmly, although she thought he looked hurt. Instantly, she felt guilty. "At least, I thought we were. Don't you want to be?"

"Yes, I just..." Everyone was staring at her, and she felt the urge to babble pushing at her, but she resisted. "I wish the two of us had talked about it first."

"Talk about what?" Steve sounded honestly confused,

and she tried to think of the best way to express her feelings, which was hard enough to do when they were alone, without seven pairs of eyes on them.

"Whether you're actually in a relationship, for starters, sounds like," Ryan muttered, and Camille shot him a *shut up* look. He must've interpreted it correctly, because he imitated Joe and focused on his food.

"Do you not want to date me?" Now the hurt was evident in Steve's voice, even though his tone was calm and steady, as usual. All four kids turned accusing eyes toward Camille, and she put her hands up defensively.

"It's not that!" She scrambled to put her thoughts into phrases that made sense, even as her brain spun with everything that was happening. "I do want to, and I'm happy we…" She quickly edited what she was about to say to make it suitable for the kids' ears. "I'm glad we're in a relationship, and I like you…a lot." Mentally wincing at the understatement, she plowed on, willing to humiliate herself if that would make the hurt in his eyes go away.

"I'm just not good at this, at talking…about this feelings thing, especially, and it's hard enough when it's just the two of us, so it's even harder when I'm in front of everyone, because I like the kids, too—so much— and it's so important to me that I'm worthy of all of you liking me back, so having to do something that I'm brutally bad at in front of everyone, knowing I'm going to crash and burn and babble and not make any sense…" She trailed off as she got turned around in her thoughts and lost her nerve, pretty much at the same time.

Silence settled heavily over the kitchen as Camille poked at her pancakes with her fork, wishing that Nate had started this discussion after they'd eaten — or, better yet, never started it at all. She sighed silently, knowing they would've had to talk about it with the kids at some point. She just wished she could've had a little more of the floaty, happy feeling before she destroyed everything.

"I like you." Maya was the first one to speak, and Camille felt a huge rush of gratitude. If she'd been a hugger, she would've given Maya a squeeze. Since she wasn't, especially with the awkward tension hanging over the kitchen at the moment, she gave what she could — a piece of bacon from her plate. Maya accepted it with a grin and promptly ate it.

"I like you," Will said. Camille had to wonder if the bacon had been part of his motivation to speak next. Even so, she appreciated the sentiment, so she reached across the table and dropped a piece on his plate. Picking it up, he saluted her with it. "I'm fine with you two dating or whatever. I'm just glad you and Dad have stopped doing that weird, awkward flirting thing you've been doing."

"I second that," Nate added. "I've never seen two people so *bad* at flirting. It was painful to watch. And here I thought Steve was good at everything." Camille winced a little, and Nate hurried to continue. "I like you, too, Camille. You're a really likable person."

She suddenly worried that they thought she'd been fishing for compliments with her mess of a monologue, and she started to say something to that effect, but Zoe interrupted before she could.

"Uncle Nate and Maya and Will are right," she said, "and not just about you being likable and nice to all of us. I'm glad you're with Dad and that you're going be staying here."

Staying here? The words rang through Camille's head, making her realize that there was another aspect of her and Steve's relationship she hadn't thought out. She'd planned to get a new place once the insurance company payment came through, but she hadn't considered whether she'd be leaving now that they were together. Of course, maybe the reason she hadn't thought about it yet was because they'd been together for *one night*. Shoving that whole minefield out of her head, she gave Zoe a piece of bacon.

"Where's mine?" Nate asked. "I said nice things about you."

He'd also said that she was painfully bad at flirting—and started this whole mess to begin with—but she really couldn't blame him for that, since it was true. She handed over the bacon.

Steve had been quiet next to her, and she'd avoided looking at him so far, even though she could feel the heavy weight of his gaze on the side of her face. Was he angry, still hurt, confused? Or, even worse, amused? She wished he'd say something before her imagination made her start panicking.

"You're fine." Micah's scratchy voice surprised her, as did his obvious irritation. When she glanced at him, he wasn't looking at her. Instead, his scowl was focused on his father. "We all like you, including Dad. He's being a dick."

"Language, Micah." Despite the correction, Steve didn't sound angry.

"Fine, a jerk, then. She's like me. She needs to have

time to think about things. You and Uncle Nate dumped this on her with all of us here, and then you acted like it was her fault for freaking out. It's kind of a big deal. I mean, she's not getting just you. She has to take all of us. That's a lot for someone who doesn't really like people. Give her a minute to think about it."

Camille wanted to stand up and applaud, but she knew Micah wouldn't appreciate it. Instead, she blinked back tears and reached for a piece of bacon. Hers was gone, so she took one off Steve's plate and handed it to Micah. He gave her a small lift of his chin as he accepted the slice.

She heard Steve let out a heavy breath, and she braced herself for whatever he was going to say. She had access to her money now, and she'd gotten new keys made for her car, thanks to Zoe's hot-wiring skills, so she could go stay at the hotel in Ebba if he kicked her out. The thought of it made her sick to her stomach, though.

"You're right, Micah." Steve turned toward Camille, leaning his head closer to hers. "I shouldn't have announced it like that without talking with you. I seem to be screwing up all sorts of conversations lately. I'm sorry." His voice was so quiet that she felt the words against her ear as much as she heard them. "I knew I said the wrong thing, but I wasn't sure how to fix it." He moved his hand so it brushed against hers. Even with the whole disastrous family meeting happening, she couldn't stop the shiver that zipped down her spine at that small touch. "Forgive me?"

Her whole body relaxed as his words penetrated, and she felt as though her bones had transformed into jelly. She hadn't been sure what he was going to say, but she hadn't expected an apology. Unable to speak without her voice shaking, she gave him a small, stiff nod and interlaced her fingers with his.

He squeezed her hand, his forehead resting against her temple for a moment as he let out a long breath. Camille wondered if he was as relieved as she was that they were back on less-shaky footing. They stayed like that until Joe cleared his throat.

"Camille," he muttered, and she looked at him in surprise. He never spoke much unless he had to, especially to her. "You're okay."

For some reason, that struck her as almost as touching as the kids' statements—until she saw him eyeing Steve's pile of bacon and then turning his expectant gaze to her. The lump in her throat turned into a choked laugh, and she shrugged. Grabbing a piece of bacon, she handed it over to Joe, who gave her a slight, Micah-like nod and the bacon a tiny, triumphant grin.

Maya started giggling, which set Camille off, and then everyone at the table—except for Joe and Ryan—started laughing. Camille knew it was the tension relief that everyone needed, rather than a reaction to something actually funny, but it did its job. Everyone relaxed, the conversation turning to other less emotional topics as they finished their breakfast and started cleaning up.

"Okay," Steve said, loudly enough to get everyone's attention. "Will, Micah, and Zoe, your bus will be here in fifteen minutes. Maya, you have twenty-five, so you're on lunches since the others will be rushing. Micah, after school, plan on helping me and Buttercup move that downed tree in the north pasture and then fixing the fence it took out."

The three older kids scattered to get ready, and Maya started a packed-lunch assembly line with Joe and Nate's help. Mumbling something about an appointment, Ryan rushed off. He'd been unusually quiet all through breakfast, and Camille hoped things wouldn't be weirder than normal between them.

Steve helped her finish loading the dishwasher, standing a little closer than absolutely necessary, but Camille didn't mind at all. After accepting his apology, her mood had bounced back up to pre-family-meeting levels, and she couldn't wait for the next time they were alone together.

Micah was ready a minute or so before his siblings, so he was double-checking the contents of his backpack at the table when Camille approached him.

"Is what you said earlier the reason you have tree-and-fence duty this afternoon?"

He glanced up, looking surprised. "It's not a bad thing. Dad knows I like working with Buttercup."

"Good." She shifted as he lowered his gaze to his books and folders. Giving in to impulse, she wrapped an arm around his shoulders and squeezed him in a side hug. "Thank you for having my back earlier. I promise I'll do the same for you if you ever need it." She started to pull away, worried that the quick embrace might have made him uncomfortable, but he leaned into her side, surprising her into holding the hug longer. Emotion tightened her chest, and she blinked rapidly, batting away any potential tears. She had a moment of enormous gratitude that she had a chance to be in this sweet kid's life—in all of their lives. It wasn't until he started to shift away that she withdrew her arm, schooling her expression so she didn't reveal how deeply touched she'd been by his simple acceptance of her hug.

Zipping up his backpack, he gave her a sideways look. "You're willing to call Dad the d-word for me?"

"Yes. The d-word, the s-word, the a-word, the c-word if he's being really rude, and even the m-word," she promised.

He paused, his gaze distant with thought.

"Let's go, Micah!" Will said, blasting by him into the entryway, Zoe close behind.

Micah picked up his backpack and headed after them, but he stopped in the doorway and looked at Camille over his shoulder. "Oh! *That* m-word." He actually grinned, and the smile lit up his face. "I can't wait to see that."

"See what?" Steve asked as Micah left, looping an arm around her waist. Her first instinct was to stiffen, but then she realized that they were now alone in the kitchen, since Maya was upstairs getting ready and the remaining two uncles had taken off once the packed lunches were completed. She melted back into him, enjoying their brief moment of privacy.

"Oh, it might not happen." The thought of Micah's happy expression made her smile.

"Camille," he said after a slight pause, and she looked up at him, instantly wary at the hesitation in his voice.

"Yes?" She almost didn't want to hear whatever he was going to say, since she was pretty much maxed out as far as dramatic moments went.

"I'd like us to be together." He cleared his throat, sounding so nervous that, if he hadn't had both arms around her, she was pretty sure he'd have been rubbing the back of his neck. "If that's what you want, too."

She relaxed, the words running through her like liquid sunshine, warming her everywhere. "Yes. I do want that. And I want to be with your kids, too. I'm not so sure about your brothers, but they don't live with us, so I should be fine with limited contact."

His laugh sounded relieved and so, so happy. "That is exactly the way I feel about them, so this should work out beautifully."

She hugged his arms against her middle, smiling. Maybe it wasn't just a daydream. Maybe real life actually could be this wonderful.

CHAPTER 17

THE FARMHOUSE WAS DARK, EXCEPT FOR THE LIGHT IN THE room where Camille was staying. He stayed in the shadows along the back of the store, watching as she looked out the window, her cat cradled in her arms. The night was clear and cold, the moon bright, making him feel exposed.

Headlights panned over the pasture as a truck turned into the driveway. He stepped back, his coat brushing the siding, wanting to disappear even more in the darkness. The truck rumbled past, heading for the pole barn. Although the vehicle didn't slow, he still felt exposed as the headlights lit up the cluster of buildings.

Once the truck disappeared inside the pole barn, he glanced up at Camille's window again, but she was gone. The kitchen window was illuminated with a buttery-yellow light, and then the porch lamp turned on. Camille stepped outside, wrapping her long sweater around her, her arms crossed over her stomach in an attempt to stay warm.

She bounced on her toes as Steve crossed the yard, his gaze focused on her as his lips turned up in a smile. He was still wearing his bunker coat, and the reflective strips lit as he bounded up the porch steps.

Their kiss was brief, their lips meeting for only a few

seconds before they pulled apart and looked into each other's eyes. Steve opened the front door, standing back so Camille could enter first, and then they were inside the house. The kitchen light went off and then, a few minutes later, so did the one in Camille's room.

The house was dark and still, but he kept watching from the shadows, hands curling into fists at his sides.

Camille was tromping through the snow toward the workshop when fat, soft snowflakes started to fall. At first it was just one or two, but soon they were floating down in great numbers, landing on her eyelashes and the tip of her nose.

"Of course," she said, looking up at the sky.

"Of course what?" Ryan asked, coming up behind her. He'd seemed to have gotten past his snit over the past few days, although he wasn't quite as talkative as before he'd found out about her and Steve. *Me and Steve.* Even their names linked together made her shiver happily. She mentally rolled her eyes at her silly smitten self, but that didn't stop her smile.

"Of course it's snowing on Christmas Eve. This place is like every holiday cliché rolled into one ranch."

"Just wait until tomorrow," he said. "We open presents at Steve's place and then hitch Buttercup to the cutter for a sleigh ride. It's like a Christmas card come to life." He winked at her, and she felt a moment of gratitude that he seemed to have come around and that he'd pretty much stopped hitting on her, so that Christmas at the ranch wouldn't be a mess of awkwardness.

"That definitely sounds"—*wonderful*—"like the ultimate Christmas cliché." She couldn't wait. The mention of presents reminded her that the bag of wrapping paper she was carrying was getting more and more snow-covered the longer she stood there. Besides, just because he'd been behaving himself recently didn't mean that she felt immediately comfortable with Ryan. "Better go." She held up the bag. "My wrapping's going to be soggy."

Giving him a wave, she hurried the rest of the way to the shop. All four kids were there, waiting for her so they could wrap presents. They sat in a circle on the heated floor with their backs to each other so that they couldn't see the others' presents and possibly get a peek at their own gift.

After knocking the snow off the top of the bag, she dumped out all the wrapping paper and gift bags and scissors and tape and Sharpies for writing names. "This is everything from your house and what we ordered online."

The kids picked through the options, scrambling to grab their favorite colors and patterns. Once everyone had the supplies they needed, they returned to their spots in their outward-facing circle. Gathering the remaining items, Camille plopped down in the spot they'd left for her between Maya and Will, resisting the urge to sneak a glance at the others' unwrapped gifts. The kids all seemed very disciplined about not peeking at other people's presents. It made Camille feel extra guilty about the temptation she'd felt to try to see what they'd gotten or made for her. Sometimes she felt like they were more mature than she was. Focusing on unrolling some silver wrapping paper, she shifted into a more comfortable position. A peaceful quiet settled over them, broken only by the rustle of paper or the sound of tape being pulled from a dispenser.

"You never finished your story, Camille," Will said, breaking the silence.

"What story?" She started with Steve's sculpture. It had turned out really well, she thought, but she was still anxious about his reaction. She was finding that giving a piece as a gift was more nerve-racking than selling it. After all, if someone was willing to pay money for it, then they obviously liked it. When she gave it to Steve, he'd have to keep it to be polite, even if he hated it. It made her antsy, and she wished Christmas would just arrive already.

"That first day I met you in the store, you said that you liked Dad the best, but Uncle Ryan interrupted before you told me why."

Camille's face heated as she groaned, and she was suddenly glad that they were facing away from each other so they couldn't see her blush. "Really? You want to hear about that? How about some other story, one that doesn't make me sound like such a sad little dorkus."

"No, tell that one!" Maya sounded gleeful, and they all took up the chorus, as Camille should've expected.

"Fine," she grumbled. "So, your dad was three years older than I was. When I was in school, they didn't have the new, bigger middle school yet, so the high school was ninth-graders through twelfth-graders. This meant that we went to the same school for a year when I was a lowly freshman and he was a senior."

"Quit stalling," Micah grumbled, and the others laughed.

"I'm not stalling." *Not exactly*. "Just setting the

scene. The Springfield brothers were like royalty when I was growing up—the four handsome princes. Just like you four, they were just a year or two apart, so the high school was filled with them for a while. Everyone had their favorites, although most people thought that Ryan was the most handsome and Nate was the most charming. The Joe fans thought he was a bad boy rather than just crabby."

The kids laughed.

"Not me, though. Even though Nate and Ryan were closer to my age, I was a diehard Steve groupie from the time I was twelve. I thought he was the most attractive of the four, but I was most drawn to him because he seemed so kind and steady."

She turned over Steve's wrapped gift and popped a premade bow on the top before adding it to her "done" pile. Next, she grabbed the box holding Maya's present and chose another color of wrapping paper.

"So, on one side of the school social spectrum, there was handsome prince Steve, and on the other side, there was ninth-grade me, incredibly shy with clothes my grandma picked out and braces and a habit of dropping things when I was nervous…which was most of the time. I was a mess, and you know how other kids can just sense that? Like wolves that can pick out the deer with the broken leg, only there's more mental torture involved in high-school packs."

She paused, staring at the ribbon in her hand, suddenly back there with her fourteen-year-old self.

"What happened?" Maya prompted, bringing Camille out of her head.

"For my art class, our final project was putting

together a portfolio of our best paintings from the year. I worked hours and hours outside school on the pieces for that portfolio. I was really into watercolors at the time, and I tended to overwork things. Once they lose their light—the white paper showing through—and get muddy, it's really hard to salvage them."

Micah gave a grunt that she took as agreement, but she sensed the others' growing impatience.

"Sorry to go all art geek on you," she said, "but that's just so you see how much time went into this thing. I think I destroyed about ten paintings to every one that worked out. Anyway, the day came to turn in our portfolios, so I carefully put mine in this oversized folder and held it on my lap on the bus and carried it to every class I had before art. I didn't want to put it in my backpack or locker in case the edges got bent."

"I don't want anything to happen to your paintings," Maya wailed, "but I know something's going to happen! I don't think I like this story."

"There's a happy ending," Camille assured her. "I'm walking down the hall, clutching my portfolio to my chest, and I've made it through half the day. Art class is next, and I'm really excited for my teacher to see it. Someone walks by and bumps into me. I don't think it was on purpose, but it was hard enough to knock me off-balance, and I fell. The pictures mostly stayed in the folder, but when I started to get up, this nasty kid named Justin grabbed my portfolio out of my hands.

"He started throwing each painting up in the air, laughing as I ran after each one, begging him to stop. The hall was crowded, and I knew people would walk right over them if I didn't get there first, leaving shoe prints and rips. Everyone saw what Justin was doing, but they just laughed or ignored it and kept walking."

She heard Maya suck in a horrified breath and hurried to get to the happy ending.

"Pretty quickly, Justin got tired of doing it one at a time, so he decided to throw the whole thing in the air. I knew it was over. There'd be no way I could get to all of them in time to pick them up before they were stomped on and ruined. He started to toss the portfolio, this huge, stupid grin on his face, and then Steve was there. He grabbed the portfolio right out of Justin's hands, midthrow."

"Go, Dad!" Maya yelled, and the rest of them laughed.

"He handed me the portfolio and just loomed over Justin, staring him down until that dumb grin of his disappeared and he ran off, his tail between his legs. Steve didn't have to threaten him or hit him or anything. He just looked at him with that stern expression he gets."

"I know that one," Will said ominously, and the others made sounds of agreement. "It's why his 'serious talks' are worse than his punishments."

"I hate when he does the 'I'm disappointed in you' face, too," Zoe said.

"Well, he must've been born with the ability, because he was doing it before you guys even existed," Camille said.

"What'd Dad say after he chased away Justin?" Maya asked.

"He asked if I was okay and then helped me put the paintings I'd just picked up back in the portfolio. Only one had a shoe print on it, and it was on the back, but Steve still did his best to wipe it away. Then he said, 'You're a really talented artist,' and walked me to my classroom."

"What grade did you get?" Micah asked.

"An A, and two of my paintings went into the school showcase."

His grunt sounded approving.

"So Dad's always been really nice," Zoe said.

"Yes. He's the kindest man I've ever met." Camille concentrated on lining up her piece of tape exactly square so she didn't start getting all mushy and teary-eyed over Steve. "All those kids just walked by, but Steve didn't. He stopped and helped, and that one moment made a huge difference in my life."

The kids were quiet, as if processing, and Camille decided she needed a distraction.

"How can we be wrapping presents without Christmas music playing?" she asked, keeping her voice intentionally light as she found a station on her phone.

Will groaned dramatically. "I'm so sick of Christmas songs from working in the store."

"Too bad." Camille unrolled the gift wrap and centered Micah's present on it. "We're going to be filled with Christmas spirit while we wrap, and you're going to like it!"

They chatted about other things as they finished wrapping and only ended up having one crumpled-paper fight. As they stacked up their presents on the "gift-transport sled" that Zoe had made just for this purpose, Maya gave Camille a quick, unexpected hug.

"I'm glad he's with you now," she said quietly enough that just the two of them could hear. "It's like it's supposed to be. You love him for what's on the inside, not just because he's handsome."

"Thanks." A little overwhelmed, especially by the mention of love, Camille gave her a shaky smile. "You have to admit he is really handsome, too, though."

"Gross." Maya made a face. "He's my dad."

Camille laughed and hugged her back.

After they stacked the gifts under the tree, Camille stepped back and eyed them. "That's a lot of presents." Lucy sauntered over to investigate the presents but was sidetracked by a dangling ornament, which she started to bat. Camille moved the temptation higher on the tree, even though she knew that Lucy would just climb up to get it.

"I know, and Dad and the uncles haven't added theirs yet," Maya said, sounding delighted.

"Maya," Steve called from the entryway. "Come here." At his serious tone, she and Camille glanced at each other and headed into the kitchen, the other kids following.

"Are you in trouble?" Zoe asked in a whisper.

"I don't think so, unless he knows about the hay thing."

Camille blinked, but she didn't get a chance to ask about the "hay thing" before they reached the entryway where a grim-looking Steve was standing. He didn't have the exasperated-but-loving expression that he usually wore when the kids had gotten into some mischief. Instead, he looked serious...and concerned. Camille's chest tightened with worry as she wondered if someone was hurt—maybe one of his brothers?

"What's wrong?" Camille asked, bracing herself for bad news.

"Q is showing signs of colic," he told them, his voice serious but calm. Maya sucked in an audible breath, her face paling as he continued. "I've already called the vet, but I could use your help."

She hurried to jam her feet into her boots, and Camille and the other kids followed suit. In worried silence, they yanked on their coats and hats. Everyone looked upset, reminding Camille that Q wasn't just Maya's pony. All of the kids had learned to ride on him, and they were all obviously torn up with concern.

In a solemn group, they trooped down to the barn. As they got close, Maya hurried ahead, sliding open the barn door and rushing down the aisle to Q's stall. Camille followed, her stomach tightening with concern when she got a glimpse of him. The pony looked miserable, his coat dark with sweat and his head low. Steve and Maya went into his stall with him, while the rest of them stayed in the aisle, looking in.

"Poor Q." Maya's voice was shaky, but she wasn't crying. Camille was impressed, knowing she wouldn't be nearly as calm if it'd been her horse. After Maya slid a halter on Q, Steve took the pony's temperature. Q nipped at his side before hanging his head again.

"No fever," Steve said. "Maya, what else should we check before the vet gets here?" He asked the question in a patient, teaching tone.

"Um…temperature, pulse, gut sounds, the gum thing—"

"Capillary refill," Will offered, and Maya nodded. As she listed and then checked her pony's vital signs, she grew steadier, and Camille began to understand why

Steve had asked for her help. If she'd stayed inside, she would've worried, but now she had something to focus on and a feeling that she was doing something, rather than being powerless.

"How serious is this?" Camille asked Micah in a quiet voice.

"Hard to tell," he said, raising one shoulder in a shrug.

"Isn't colic just gas pain?" She felt a little silly for the question, especially when Steve answered.

"It can be, but it can also be impaction colic—kind of like constipation—or even a twist in the intestine causing the block."

She winced. That sounded so painful. "What happens if he has that?"

"He'd need surgery." Maya had gotten pale during their discussion, and Steve gave her a glance before saying, "I doubt it's that serious, though."

Camille didn't want to see what a serious colic situation looked like, if this wasn't one, since poor Q was obviously in a miserable condition.

"Should we walk him?" Maya asked.

"Can't hurt. Let's cover him up first so he doesn't get a chill. He's still sweating a lot from the pain." Steve moved out of the stall so Maya could lead her pony into the aisle, and Micah hurried to grab the fleece blanket and buckle it on the pony. Their small group huddled together, watching as Maya and Q made their slow way down to the other end of the barn.

"Were you just saying that so Maya wouldn't be scared?" Zoe said quietly. "About it not being serious?"

Steve wrapped his arm around her and pulled her against his side. "No. I wouldn't lie to her. Once the vet gets here and gets some pain meds and mineral oil into him, he'll feel a lot better really fast."

After twenty stress-filled minutes, the vet arrived. "They always seem to decide to get sick on a holiday, don't they?" she said as she headed down the aisle toward them, bundled up in insulated coveralls and a stocking cap. As she examined Q under Maya's anxious supervision, Camille ran inside to make some coffee for Steve and the vet. While it was brewing, she filled two travel mugs with warm cider for the kids.

Being in the warm house made her realize how cold she'd gotten, and she worried about the kids getting chilled. She grabbed a couple of fleece blankets and carried them and the hot beverages back to the barn.

"If it doesn't pass in a few hours, you might try taking him on a short trailer ride. The motion sometimes is the best thing for an impaction." The vet peeled off her gloves and tossed them in a nearby trash can. "I need to go to Ebba for a mare having some trouble foaling, but call me if anything changes."

"Coffee for the road?" Camille offered the vet one of the travel mugs.

"You're a goddess," she said, accepting the coffee before hurrying out of the barn to her truck.

"I just gave away one of your mugs," Camille said as she handed the second coffee to Steve, who took it with a grateful smile. "Sorry about that."

He waved away her concern. "Don't worry about it. I accidentally steal my share of travel mugs when I'm on calls, so it all works out."

"What's the verdict?" she asked, handing one of the ciders to Zoe after noticing that she was looking pinched with cold. Micah and Will both looked more comfortable, so she wrapped one of the blankets around Zoe's shoulders, getting a grateful smile in return.

"The vet agreed with Dad." Maya was the one who answered from her spot by the open stall door where she was watching her pony. "He does look a lot better now."

"Drugs are amazing things," Camille said absently, handing the other cider to Maya before wrapping the second blanket around her. When Steve cleared his throat, she realized what she'd said. "Oh. Um...just prescription drugs are amazing, and only when used legally and responsibly." Glancing at Steve, who looked amused, she asked, "Okay?"

"Good save." A smile snuck out that he hid behind his coffee mug.

"You guys are going to have to share the cider," she said, taking up a spot next to Steve where she could see into Q's stall. "I ran out of carrying hands."

"That's fine. We'll share." Will snuck the travel mug from Zoe before she knew what he was doing.

"Hey," she complained, although she didn't try to take it back. "Sometimes I think it'd be nice to be an only child."

"Eh." Camille gave in to the urge to lean against Steve, needing the reassurance of his strength and steadiness. It'd already been a long day, and she had a feeling it'd be a while before it was over. He rested a hand on her back, making her wonder if he needed some tactile comfort, too. "Being an only child isn't all that it's cracked up to be. Besides, who'd test your inventions if your siblings weren't around?"

"Good point," Zoe said, drawing the blanket more tightly around herself.

Steve frowned. "You three should go inside and warm up. Maya, you too. I'll watch Q for a while."

"No." Maya didn't take her eyes off of her pony. "I'm fine. Camille brought me cider and a blanket. I want to stay with Q."

"I want to stay, too," Will said, and Micah gave his trademark short nod.

"Me, too." Zoe stole her cider back and took a drink.

Steve's frown deepened, but he didn't argue with them. He turned his head to eye Camille.

"Don't look at me," she said, leaning more heavily against him. "You're keeping me warm, and I just had some house time getting the drinks."

With a small huff that Camille thought was meant to sound more irritated than it actually did, Steve pulled her closer against his side. "Fine. Now we all wait."

"Um…" Camille knew she was going to sound like the ignorant one again. "What are we waiting for?"

Maya gave a little giggle, her first one since she'd learned her pony was sick. "Q needs to poop."

Camille blinked. "We're waiting for poop?"

There was a chorus of snickers from the other three kids as a slow smile curved Steve's lips. "Better settle in. Looks like no one's leaving until the pony poops."

Settling in as she'd been told, Camille nestled closer to Steve and rested her head against his shoulder, thinking of how sideways her life had gone. Even a month ago, she'd never have expected to be sitting in a cold barn with Steve Springfield and his kids on Christmas Eve, waiting for a pony to poop.

Honestly, she wouldn't want to be anywhere else.

CHAPTER 18

HE MOVED THROUGH THE FIRE STATION WITH CONFIDENT steps. It was empty, with everyone either home or out on the latest call, but he still acted like he was supposed to be there, just in case. He slipped into the storage room and quickly gathered what he needed. This should be the last time he'd have to play the part. The plan was in place.

After tonight, he'd finally get what he was owed.

Camille never thought she would cheer when a pony pooped, but that was exactly what she did. All of them cheered, and the mood in the barn grew much lighter. This time, when Steve insisted they all head to the house, they listened, leaving him to watch Q a little longer, just to make sure the colic had resolved.

As the kids took turns taking hot showers, Camille heated up some of Micah's crab bisque for a late dinner. While the others ate, she took some soup out for Steve but ran into him halfway to the barn.

Taking one look at his scowl, she asked, "What's wrong? Did Q get worse?"

"No." He took her hand as she fell in next to him. "I got called in."

"Again? What is that, the fourth fire in three days?"

His shoulders lowered in a silent sigh. "Yeah, although this time it's already out. I'm just needed to help mop up. Tucker, one of the other firefighters, caught his hand in the truck door, so the chief's driving him to the ER in Ebba. They're down two people, so they asked if I could come in to help finish up. All these fires are typical of the season, though. There are candles and dried-out, unwatered trees in people's homes, plus the extra electrical use means packed outlets. Oh, and fireplaces and heaters, although those are more winter-related than Christmas..." He trailed off when he saw she was trying to hide a smile. "What?"

"You're babbling. You never babble." Secretly, she kind of liked it. Whenever she noticed some quirk or flaw of his, it reassured her that he wasn't perfect—just really close to it.

"Sorry." He rubbed the back of his neck with his free hand. "I'm just tired. All the recent calls, and then being out all evening with Q, plus we're just finishing up our busy time here. I feel like everything's been full speed ahead since moving back to the ranch."

Camille squeezed his hand, wishing she could do more. "Just get through tonight, and then things will quiet down. Q's going to be fine, and the kids have some time off school, so there won't be so much running around. People will toss their dried-out trees and put away their candles, and you'll be able to get some rest."

"Yeah." Steve glanced at her, his tired frown lightening. "Not sure I really want to rest once I get some free time, though."

"Oh?" Her heart gave a happy little skip. "What would you be interested in doing instead?"

"I don't know... Something like this?" Bending down, he pressed his cold face into the curve of her neck. She gave a laughing shriek at the chill of his skin. His lips quickly warmed her as he kissed her neck, however. Tipping her head to the side to give him better access, she closed her eyes as he worked his way up to the sensitive spot under her jaw.

When he pulled away, she made a disappointed sound as she turned toward him. "I wish I could." The heat in his gaze proved his words were true. "I have to go on this call. Will you check on Q in a couple of hours if I'm not back? I tried calling my brothers, but none of them are answering their phones."

"Of course I will, but none? Are you worried?"

"No. They're at this Christmas Eve party they go to every year. It's probably too loud to hear their phones."

That didn't seem right. "Joe went to a party?"

He laughed. "No. Ryan and Nate are there. Joe probably turned his phone off, like he always does. Thanks for watching the kids and looking in on Q." Pressing a quick—too quick—kiss on her mouth, he turned to go.

"Wait! Take some soup." She handed him the travel mug. Giving her another kiss, he jogged toward the machine shed where his truck was parked.

She headed back to the house, glad that he at least had gotten some food before he left. The kitchen was clean and quiet. She found the kids in the living room, reading or playing on their tablets, with the Christmas tree all lit up. It rustled, and she winced, knowing that

Lucy was climbing it again. Hopefully, the cat wouldn't knock over the entire tree.

"Hey," Camille said, and the kids looked up. "Your dad had to go on a call."

"Another one?" Will echoed her words from earlier.

"He said this is a busy time of year for fires."

Zoe nodded. "That's true. I remember that from other Christmases."

"How's Q?" Maya asked.

"Good. Your dad asked if I'd check him in a few hours if he's not back." When she saw Maya's uncertain look, she added, "If Q looks at all uncomfortable, I'll come get you, if that's okay? You can tell me if something's wrong or not. If he relapses, we'll call the vet again."

This seemed to soothe Maya's worries, and she nodded before turning back to her book. Camille lingered for a moment, taking in the quiet peace of the room. She'd always considered her solitary existence peaceful, but this farmhouse, Steve and his kids and brothers, made her realize how lonely and isolated she'd been. Standing there watching the kids filled her with a contentment so deep it was hard to leave the room. The lure of a hot shower finally was enough to tear her away from the cozy scene, and she made her way upstairs.

Once she was clean and finally warm all the way through, Camille returned to the living room. The kids had turned off all the lights except the multicolored ones on the tree. They spent an hour telling stories about other Christmases, although Camille listened more than she contributed. She and her grandma had celebrated quietly, which didn't lead to many interesting tales. It was yet another Christmas-card moment, and she carefully added the memory to the others she held close to her heart.

The kids, tired by the hours in the barn and the stressful evening, went to bed early, despite their muted excitement about the next day. Zoe gave her a sleepy smile, and Maya hugged her hard around the waist before they climbed the stairs, and Camille had to blink back tears once again. She still couldn't believe that she'd been welcomed into this amazing family. Micah gave her one of his side hugs—quick but almost unbearably sweet—as Will watched with an unreadable expression. Once Micah was upstairs, Will turned to Camille, his face serious.

"I'm glad you're here."

Without waiting for her to respond, he headed upstairs, taking the stairs three at a time. Camille stood in the now-vacated living room, staring at the tree with a smile. Even despite the pony's colic, she couldn't remember ever having a better Christmas Eve.

Camille checked on Q—who was happily munching on hay with no sign of pain and, best of all, had several new piles of manure in his stall—before heading to bed. When she stuck her head in to give Maya a pony report, she saw both girls were already sleeping, so she slipped back to Steve's room—*their* room. She felt a warm glow at the thought.

She set her phone alarm to go off in two hours so she could do another pony check. She wished she'd asked Steve where the kids' presents were hidden, so she could make sure they were under the tree by morning if he was stuck on a long call.

Resting her cheek on her pillow, she looked at the empty half of the bed. The horrible horse sculpture still sat on the bedside table, even though she'd threatened to toss it in the scrap pile. Steve said he was fond of it, because it showed that she wasn't always perfect. Remembering that moment, Camille snorted, even as her chest warmed. It was nice to have someone think she was so amazing that he needed proof of her flaws— really nice. She started to frown as she stared at the horse. Even if one of the kids had placed it in her room with good intentions, the presence of the sculpture bothered her.

Feeling a little silly, she slid out of bed and grabbed the horse, placing it on a shelf in the closet. "Don't kill me while I sleep," she warned the little demon riders, who looked even more menacing with fire damage discoloring their little bodies. Closing the closet door, she snuggled back into bed, her gaze on Steve's empty pillow again.

Even though she hadn't been sharing a bed with Steve for very long, it felt empty when he wasn't there with her. She slid a hand over the fuzzy flannel pillow-case, picturing him asleep. It was rare that she woke up before he did, but she loved seeing him relaxed and soft, the worry lines on his face invisible in the dim light. Smiling at the thought of him, she fell asleep quickly. When her alarm went off at midnight, she felt like she'd just closed her eyes a second ago.

Dragging herself out of bed, she dressed and headed downstairs with her eyes still mostly closed.

"Checking the pony?"

Nate's voice startled her, bringing her fully awake.

She saw him standing by the stove, pouring something from a pan into a travel mug. "Yes. Sorry, I didn't see you. I'm mostly sleepwalking."

His soft chuckle sounded a little fuzzy around the edges, and she smiled. He must've had a few drinks at the Christmas Eve party he and Ryan had attended. "Do you want me to check him for you?"

"That's okay." She felt a little awkward refusing his help, but she'd promised Maya she'd personally make sure that Q was still recovering. "I'm awake now, and I won't be able to sleep unless I see him with my own eyes."

"Here," he said, holding out the mug. "Take this, at least. Hot chocolate with peppermint. It'll help keep you warm."

"Thanks." She accepted the mug. "How was the party?"

"The party?" One of his shoulders lifted in a small shrug. "It was fine. Same as every year. You know how it is, living in the town you grew up in. Everyone thinks they know you." There was a melancholy sound to his voice that Camille was feeling too sleepy to interpret. Even on her best days, she wasn't very good at counseling people.

She made a *hmm* sound that could be taken as agreement. "Where's Ryan?"

"Not sure. He left the party early, said he had to take care of something." He gave a slight eye roll. "You know Ryan."

She didn't, really, but she let that go. "Thanks for coming over. I'm always a little nervous when Steve has to go on a call at night."

He paused. "You don't ever have to worry, Camille. I'll always be here to protect you."

"Well," she said, inching toward the door, the mug gripped in her hand, and feeling a little awkward at the intense turn of their conversation. "Thank you for the hot chocolate." Raising it in an awkward salute, she slipped out of the kitchen.

The cold air erased the last of her sleepiness when she stepped outside, and she took a second to appreciate the beautiful night. The stars were so bright and close, and light from the three-quarter moon made the snow covering the pastures glow a bluish-white. Micah's snow horse was still there, and it made her smile every time she looked at it.

"Merry Christmas," she said quietly, speaking to the snow horse and the ranch and all its residents, even those not there at the moment. She hoped that Steve was safe, that mopping up the last bits of the fire had been as simple as he'd expected, and that the injured fire-fighter's hand wasn't damaged too badly. She silently gave thanks, loving that she was a part of this ranch and connected to all the people who lived there. As she walked to the barn, the only sound was the crunch of snow under her boots.

There was a gap between the sliding door and the wall. It was just a few inches, but she frowned at it, the dark space sending a ripple of unease through her. She distinctly remembered closing and latching the door when she'd checked on the pony earlier. Had someone else been in the barn? Who?

Shaking off her nerves, she scolded herself for letting such a small thing unnerve her. It was just the late night and the quiet of the barn that were making her overthink things. Opening the door a little more so she could slip inside, she moved to turn on the lights and then hesitated, looking around. The open door had spooked her, and the strange moonlight shadows didn't help. She listened, trying to hear anything out of the ordinary, but the only sound was the rustling of the horses moving in their stalls.

Letting out a long breath, she shook her head at her jumpiness. She was getting spooked over nothing. She reached for the light switch again. Before she could turn it on, there was a loud thud. She froze, not even breathing as she waited for the noise to come again. When it was quiet, she moved cautiously forward, starting to feel like it had been a figment of her imagination.

She moved down the row of stalls, peering into each one, her heart beating so loudly in her ears that she worried she'd miss hearing other more menacing sounds. Was someone in the barn? She tried to dismiss her fears, telling herself that her nightmares had her on edge, but her body stayed tense, her eyes seeing menacing intruders in every shadow. Slowing her breathing, she passed the dark shapes sleeping in the stalls, the shadows turning regular horses into nightmare forms. Each rustle and exhale made her jump. All the noises that would've been innocent and innocuous during the cheerful light of day became ominous in the dim light of the barn.

As she passed Buttercup's stall, the mare snaked out her head, and Camille sucked in a breath at the sudden movement. She spun toward the stall, peering through the gloom to see the mare catch the lip of her hanging grain bucket in her teeth and then let it go. The pail swung back and thumped against the side of her stall. Her heart still pounding out of control, Camille let out the breath she'd been holding, her legs wobbly with leftover adrenaline and relief.

"Buttercup," she said, whispering for some strange reason. "You scared me to death."

Determined to quit jumping at shadows, she moved to the pony's stall. He whickered at her, sticking his head over the stall door, and she smiled. If he was feeling well enough to beg for treats, then he'd be just fine.

It wasn't until she got right up next to his stall that she saw the dark shape in the far corner. Her heart jolted for a moment until she recognized what—who—it was. Maya was curled up, asleep, wrapped in the fleece blanket Camille had brought from the house earlier.

"Maya," she said softly, nudging Q back so she could slip into the stall with them. Crouching down, she put a hand on the girl's slight shoulder, and Maya awoke with a start. Remembering her earlier moment of panic, Camille quickly said, "It's me. I came to check Q and found you."

Pushing up to a sitting position, Maya shoved her hair out of her face. "Sorry. I woke up, and I was worried."

"It's okay." Suddenly chilly, Camille sat down in the shavings next to her, wrapping an arm around Maya's shoulders and tugging the edge of the blanket over her. "Give me some of that, and you can have some of this hot chocolate. I'm freezing."

With a small laugh, Maya rearranged the blanket so it covered both of them and then took the travel mug out of Camille's hand. They sat quietly for a moment, Maya taking sips of hot chocolate. After a few minutes, she passed back the mug and laid her head on Camille's shoulder. Wrapped up together like that, Camille actually felt warm.

"Merry Christmas," Camille said.

"It's Christmas?"

"Very, very early on Christmas."

"Merry Christmas." There was a smile in Maya's voice. "I've already gotten what I wanted, though."

"Q being okay?" Camille guessed.

"Yeah." She paused. "Plus you're here for Christmas. That's a pretty great gift, too."

"I'm glad I'm here." Unable to stop the beaming smile that took over her face, Camille looked at the pony as he lipped at some stray bits of hay. "He's so much better. When I walked up to the stall just now, he was nickering for treats."

"Good." Maya paused and then asked tentatively, "Do you mind if we watch him, just for a few minutes? It's hard to believe he's okay when I can't see him."

"Sure."

Silence fell over them, and Camille thought about how, oddly enough, sitting in the pony's stall with Maya was really very peaceful. As Maya's head grew heavy on her shoulder and her breathing deepened with sleep, Camille watched Q doing contented pony things and enjoyed the small sounds of a horse barn at night.

A loud bang woke her, but the smell of smoke brought her back into her nightmare. She opened her eyes to a gray haze. The faint, flickering red light fighting to cut through the layer of smoke was uncomfortably familiar, but it took her too many seconds to realize why.

Fire!

Sucking in a terrified breath, she immediately choked as her lungs filled with smoke. It felt like a clamp was pressing down on her chest, making it impossible to inhale. The horribly familiar claustrophobic feeling overwhelmed her. Everything—the smoke and flames and bitter rasp of the smoke in her throat—was too horribly familiar.

The pony gave a sharp squeal and struck the stall door with a front hoof again. He nervously paced the far wall, adding to her growing panic. It felt like she was reliving the workshop fire, only this time there was a pony and she was in a stall and Maya was sleeping on her shoulder.

Maya!

Camille jolted. This wasn't a nightmare. It was real. The barn was on fire, and she needed to get Maya out. The thought filled her with resolution, clearing her head of the panic that clouded it, leaving only a steady, anxious thrum of urgency.

"Maya." Her voice came out too soft to hear, and she realized that the nightmarish roar of the flames was getting louder. Horses whinnied and paced in fear, and Q struck out at the door again. The resulting *bang* made Camille flinch in startled reaction, but she forced the terror down. "Maya! Maya, wake up!"

She shook the girl with the arm still wrapped around her, panic gripping her again when Maya didn't open her eyes, her head still a heavy weight on Camille's shoulder. With shaking fingers, she pressed the side of

Maya's throat. When she felt the steady pulse of a heart-beat, she sagged in relief.

"Wh-wha?" Maya slurred, and Camille's heart squeezed in panicked relief.

"Maya! Are you with me?"

Maya's lids cracked open, but her face remained slack, her eyes blurry and confused. Fear choked Camille. Had Maya inhaled too much smoke? The dangers of carbon dioxide poisoning flashed in her mind, and a wave of dizziness rolled through her. *Stop it,* she commanded her brain. She couldn't psych herself out now. She was their only hope at getting out alive.

"Can you walk?" Camille demanded as Maya's eyes slid shut again. "Wake up, Maya!"

This time, Maya's eyes stayed closed. Camille tried to force her thoughts into a logical order, rather than just spinning around uselessly in her head. Maya was alive, but she wasn't coherent or mobile. They needed to get out immediately. That meant Camille had to carry her out.

The relief of having a plan was instantaneous, and she scrambled to her feet. Crouching down next to Maya, she gathered the girl against her chest and started to lift her. Her arms and back strained at the weight, but she managed to stand with Maya cradled in her arms. She was suddenly grateful for all the heavy lifting she did while sorting through scrap.

She rushed to the stall door, shouldering Q out of the way. With both of her arms cradling Maya, she didn't have a hand free to reach over the door and unlatch it. A frustrated sob escaped, and she started to cough.

Stop it, she mentally snapped at her rising panic.

Think! Crouching down again, she tried to ignore the way the pony was crowding her, as anxious as she was to get out of the stall and the blazing barn. Placing Maya down on the shavings, praying that Q didn't strike at the door again and hit her instead, Camille shifted her to a sitting position and hauled the girl over her shoulders.

"Wha's going on?" Maya's words were barely comprehensible, but Camille was thankful that the girl was at least semiconscious.

"The barn's on fire." She tried to channel Steve, to keep her voice calm, but it was hard not to let her words quaver. "I'm getting you out of here."

They both wobbled as Camille tried to balance Maya's limp weight. Clamping an arm over the back of the girl's thighs, she struggled to stand, grabbing the top of the stall door with her free hand to keep them from both toppling over into Q. Images of them being stomped under the pony's nervous feet played through her mind, and she quickly cut off that train of thought.

Plan, she ordered her mind. *Follow the plan. It's simple. Get Maya out of the barn.*

This time, she managed to unlatch the stall door. As it swung open, the pony rushed to get out, pushing Camille forward. She stumbled out into the aisle and twisted out of the way, letting Q thunder past her. As he galloped down the aisle, the other horses' panic ramped up dramatically. They snorted and whinnied their distress while several kicked at their stall walls.

Camille rushed toward the closest sliding door at the end of the aisle, staggering under Maya's weight. She saw the flames now, eating away at the tack room wall, and she felt a flash of relief that the fire hadn't reached any of the stalls...not yet, at least.

The thought pushed her faster, and she moved through the choking, smoky dimness, fumbling to unlatch each stall as she made too-slow progress down the aisle. She heard hooves on the rubber mats, but she didn't look behind her, knowing she wasn't able to concentrate on the horses right now, no matter how scared they were.

First, she had to get Maya out, and then she'd return for the horses.

The tall sliding door was suddenly there in front of her, and she gasped with relief—and immediately regretted that when the smoke made her lungs seize. Fighting back her coughs, she reached for the handhold and pulled. All she had to do was slide open the door, and she and Maya and the horses she'd managed to free would be safe.

The door didn't move.

She pulled harder, unable to understand why it wasn't opening. Usually, it slid smoothly along its tracks. She yanked again, but it didn't budge, not even shifting a fraction of an inch.

Could it have swelled from the heat, making it stick? She kicked it, frustrated, and felt a dull pain in her booted foot, but the door stayed stubbornly shut. Dropping her hand, she forced herself to think again. As she fought with the door, Maya was breathing in more smoke, and it wasn't getting them any closer to escaping the barn.

Turning, she moved to the other door on the opposite end of the aisle. Her head spun, and she knew that she shouldn't be breathing so much smoke, but there was no way to crawl while carrying Maya—besides, that would be too slow. As it was, her shuffling steps felt nightmarishly difficult and snaillike, their escape slowed even more by having to open each stall to free the trapped horses.

She moved closer and closer to the blazing tack room, and the smoke thickened, creating an opaque wall between them and the door. Holding her breath, she plowed through the choking blackness, keeping her gaze focused forward, trying to ignore the flames flickering in her peripheral vision. Her mind kept wanting to take her back to that night in her workshop and to each subsequent nightmare—the ones where she never got out of the fiery room.

Stop it. She slammed a mental door on those thoughts. Her lungs were squeezing with a lack of air, and she was forced to drag in a bitter, painful inhale. Her breathing was wheezy now, threatening to send her into a coughing fit at any moment. She forced one foot to move and then the other, clinging to Maya desperately. She refused to think about the little girl breathing the same harmful smoky air.

When she reached the door, Camille was too lightheaded and terrified to rejoice. Grimly, she yanked at the handle. This time, she wasn't shocked when it didn't move. She'd almost been expecting that, and she didn't waste time with futile struggling. She and Maya didn't have any time to lose.

Get Maya out. Get Maya out. The mantra repeated in her head as she tried to think, despite the fear and smoke clouding her brain. The doors were useless, so what was next? A window? All the windows were set so high up that they were essentially vertical skylights. Swallowing the terrified sob that wanted to escape, Camille mentally scanned the barn in her mind.

The Dutch door! In her panic, she'd forgotten it. Stumbling back toward the center of the barn, she saw that flames had climbed the wall and were spreading to the feed room. A small pile of a half-dozen hay bales stacked in the aisle next to Maybelle's stall had caught fire, and Camille knew they didn't have much time before the barn was completely alight.

She coughed, her lungs burning, and realized they didn't have much time...period.

Reaching the door, she unlatched the top and bottom portions and pushed, half expecting it not to open, like the other two. When it swung open, bringing a wave of fresh, cold air, she gasped with relief. A horse shrieked with fear behind her, and she turned her head to see that they were hunched against the door she'd first tried to open, crowded in a terrified mass in the only place they knew to go—the door they went through every morning to get out to the pasture. Q was the only one not milling frantically in their huddle. Instead, he was trotting back and forth behind Camille, snorting in fear.

"What...What's happening? Camille?" Maya's hoarse voice, more coherent than before, almost brought Camille to her knees with relief. As she'd carried the girl through the flaming barn, a part of Camille had been dreadfully sure that Maya wasn't going to make it. At the sound of her voice, cracked but coherent, a new, desperate plan formed.

"Maya?" Rushing outside, Camille crouched and carefully slid her off her shoulder, catching her when Maya started crumpling to the ground. "Are you with me?"

"What's going on?" With Camille's support, Maya caught her balance, although she swayed as she stared frantically into the barn.

"The barn's on fire. I need to get the horses out." She caught Maya's face in her hands, holding her gaze. "You need to ride Q away from the barn. Go to the house and get help. Understand?"

"You want me to ride Q?" Maya started coughing, and Camille released her. When Q made his next pass down the aisle, she looped her arm under his neck, grabbing a hank of mane. The pony slid to a stop. After a couple of half-hearted attempts at trying to free himself from her hold, he stilled, and Camille led him through the door to where Maya was waiting.

"Get on," she said, and Maya automatically moved to the pony's side. Camille gave her a leg up, tossing her onto Q's back. Maya gripped the pony's mane, sliding off-center as he sidestepped nervously, still anxious about the burning barn so close behind them. Camille gave Maya's leg a tug, centering her again. "Now ride carefully. Don't go too fast. I don't want you hurting yourself trying to get help."

Maya's face was starkly pale in the moonlight, her gaze terrified but finally clear. "You'll get the other horses?"

"Yes."

Maya nodded, and Q leapt forward into a fast canter. Camille's heart squeezed as Maya was jostled sideways before she regained her balance. The wind whipped Camille's hair around her as the pony and his rider disappeared into the night. *Maya's out.* Camille's knees went soft, but she forced them to stiffen, turning back to the barn. The black and red interior, so ominous and frightening, made her want to run to safety, but a horse's shrill scream sent her rushing back into the inferno.

The horses were in full panic, bumping and shoving each other in a frantic rush to escape. They didn't see the open Dutch door, too focused on the closed one at the end of the aisle. Camille stared at the churning mass as flames roared higher, creeping too quickly down the row of stalls toward the terrified horses.

She didn't know what to do.

A flash of gray caught her eye through the smoky haze, and she saw Buttercup standing slightly apart from the others. Although her head was high and her tail clamped down in fear, she didn't seem as panicked as the others, and the vague outline of a plan formed in Camille's mind.

Grabbing a rope off one of the stalls, she hurried toward the mare, wanting to run but knowing that it would just spook Buttercup and the others even more.

"Hey, Buttercup," she said, her voice rough and shaky. The mare snorted nervously as she approached but didn't move away as Camille reached her side. "You need to be the boss mare for me now. Show the others what they need to do."

Looping the rope around Buttercup's neck right behind her ears, Camille moved toward the open door. The mare didn't move at first, and Camille had a moment of fear that she wouldn't cooperate. The horse was huge, taller than Camille at the shoulder, and she knew she couldn't force Buttercup do anything she didn't want to.

"Come on," she begged, her eyes stinging from tears as much as the smoke, and tugged at the rope circling Buttercup's neck. The mare stepped forward, one huge hoof after another, and Camille felt dizzy with relief. "Good girl." Raising her voice, she called to the other horses. "Let's go, guys!" She had no idea if it would help, but she just hoped they would see the big mare leaving through the Dutch door and figure out that was the way to escape.

A small shape darted out of the group toward Buttercup, and Camille recognized Maybelle. As soon as the goat glimpsed the open door, she shot ahead of them out into the night. Two more—Harry the draft horse and a pony she didn't recognize—broke off from the milling herd to follow.

Camille started to think that her plan would work. As they reached the open doorway, she pulled the rope away from Buttercup's neck and stepped back, afraid that both she and the horse wouldn't fit through the opening. The big mare charged outside, followed by the other two—and then five more in quick succession.

Tears flowed freely down her face now as one horse after another escaped the burning barn. Wiping her eyes with the heel of her hand, she peered into the gloom. The smoke had thickened, and the barn was getting darker even as the flames grew, casting light that created demonic shadows.

Only one horse remained against the closed sliding door, pacing back and forth across the aisle, his head up and eyes wild, completely panicked now that he was alone. The flames reflected off his sweaty coat, turning the horse a devilish red. With the rolling smoke surrounding them and the roar of the fire, the cozy, comfortable barn had transformed into a frightening hellscape. Everything inside Camille wanted to run, to flee the inferno, but she couldn't leave the panicked horse to die.

"It's okay," she crooned, her voice cracking from fear and the smoke as she walked toward the last terrified horse. Adrenaline made her shake as she struggled to hold back a cough. Her words were buried in the crackle and thunder of the flames, and she forced her aching throat to speak louder. "Just follow them outside. You'll be okay then. Simply go through that door like the others did." She moved toward his side as he snorted in terror, and she saw his entire body was trembling. "You're okay." She reached up to loop the rope around his neck.

As the braided cotton brushed against his wet coat, he exploded into action, charging forward toward the open door. She froze, unable to move. Instead, she watched as the horse ran right at her, his wide, frightened eyes and flared nostrils filling her vision as he thundered past. His powerful shoulder knocked into her, sending her flying back into the wall. She felt weightless for a long moment before she collided headfirst, white stars dotting her vision over the growing wall of flames.

The impact stunned her, and she lay sprawled on the ground, watching with blurry eyes as that final horse galloped through the opening and into the night.

Get up, that commanding voice in her head ordered. She tried to move, but pain overwhelmed her, making her head spin so badly that she didn't know which direction was up. The roar of the fire filled her ears, but the urgency that had driven her seemed remote now.

She made another attempt to rise and pushed up to her hands and knees, but the pain in her head and the dizziness were too much. The world turned black as she collapsed to the ground.

Seconds or minutes later, consciousness returned, and she felt the heat of the fire and heard the roar as it ate its way through the barn. She managed to peel her eyes partway open, but her limbs wouldn't obey her commands. She was back in her nightmare again, surrounded by flames and smoke but unable to move, to escape.

A figure moved through the fire toward her, and she watched, fear jolting through her limbs as she recognized the bunker gear, the face shield and mask. He was here. Oh God, he was *real*. Her fingers twitched as she tried to force her unresponsive body to move, to push to her feet and run...but it was too late.

The faceless man was bending over her, flames throwing grotesque shadows behind him. He reached for her, sliding his arms beneath her back and legs.

All she could do was scream silently in her mind.

CHAPTER 19

STEVE YAWNED AS HE DROVE ON THE EMPTY COUNTY ROAD toward home. Glancing at the clock in the dash, he smiled. It was Christmas. The stars looked close enough to pluck out of the sky, and the snow lay in a thick, white blanket on the surrounding fields.

He couldn't wait to get home, to shower off the smell of smoke from the last call and crawl into bed with Camille. In the morning, the kids would open presents and pretend that they weren't as excited as when they were five. His life had seemed off-balance for so long, with the problems in their former towns and the moves and the years of sleeping next to that empty pillow. Then he'd run into Camille again, and everything had seemed to right itself after that.

He tilted his head to the side, stretching his neck. The previous call had been frustrating. Even though he'd just been mopping up a garbage fire in the alley behind the gas station, it'd still been a bear. Just when they thought they'd put it out completely, they'd find another hot spot. Having to pick through garbage looking for embers was not his idea of a fun Christmas Eve activity. He'd much rather have been with Camille and the kids in their warm house, the lights from the tree decorating the room as they talked and told stories and hung stockings.

At least he'd have tomorrow with them. He couldn't wait to see Camille's reaction to her gift. His smile of anticipation faded as he spotted a red glow in the distance. *Fire*. His gut clenched as soon as he recognized it, adrenaline rushing through him, making his hands grip the wheel tightly. It had to be very close to the ranch, and all he could picture were Camille and his kids, asleep in their beds. Grabbing his phone, he started to call dispatch when the cell rang in his hand.

It was the house number. His muscles tight with tension, he answered. "What's wrong?"

"Daddy," Maya sobbed, and his heart squeezed with dread. "The barn's on fire!"

As soon as he'd seen the call come in, he'd known that the fire he'd spotted had to be on their property, but her words still hit him like a closed fist. "I'm five minutes away, honey. Have you called dispatch?"

"Will did."

"Good. Are the horses out?"

"Camille…" She sucked in a quavering breath as her voice broke. "Camille's getting them out."

His mind blanked with terror. Camille was inside the burning barn, trying to lead panicked horses to safety? He wasn't sure what else he said to Maya, how he ended the call. All his focus was on getting home and saving Camille. His foot pressed down on the gas, and the truck flew, juddering around tight turns and fishtailing as he hit the driveway.

Passing the house, he drove right up to the barn, his eyes locked on the horror in front of him. The structure was fully engaged, flames licking the red walls all the way up to the shake roof. The wind blew flaming debris off the roof and sent it dancing toward the trees. In the rows of cultivated evergreens, light flickered, and he knew that the fire had spread. Shoving the pickup door open, he jumped out, charging toward the front of the barn.

"Dad!" Will was suddenly in front of him, blocking the way.

"I need to get her out!" He had to raise his voice to be heard over the roar of the fire. "Camille's in there!"

"Dad, you can't! Not that way!" Will's eyes were huge in his pale face, and he suddenly looked much younger than he was. "The door's locked."

"Locked?" That didn't make sense. There wasn't a lock on the outside of the sliding door.

"Padlocked. There's one on the other door, too."

Padlocked. The realization that someone had locked Camille inside a burning barn sent cold rage tearing through him.

"Will, the fire's spreading. Bring the others to the main road. Keep them safe."

Will gave him a tight-lipped nod. Steve stalked back to the toolbox built into the bed of his truck. He pulled out his heavy-duty bolt cutters and strode to the barn door. Someone was yelling something, but Steve couldn't make out the words, his head buzzing with the anger that had temporarily masked his terror.

The padlock on the door sent a fresh surge of fury through his veins, and he snipped the thick metal as if it were baling wire. Yanking the remains of the lock off the door and throwing them violently to the side, he reached for the handle and jerked the door open.

The flames roared at the influx of oxygen, and Steve

was glad he was still wearing his bunker gear. He'd been so anxious to get home to Camille and the kids that he hadn't wanted to delay by changing at the station. Without his SCBA gear, the heat and smoke felt alien, the air harsh and deadly as he pulled it into his lungs.

Pushing away all of his thoughts, all of the alarms screaming at him to wait for the other firefighters, the ones who'd have the gear for this, he stepped into the burning barn. The heat was overwhelming, and the smoke scratched at his throat, reminding him of his unprotected, vulnerable lungs. It didn't matter. Camille wasn't safe, either, and she'd been in there too long already.

He jogged down the aisle, trying to see through watering eyes and the thick smoke. The entire barn was ablaze, and a small part of him mourned for the building, one he'd been in thousands of times since his childhood. To his dawning surprise, he saw the stalls were empty. Buttercup, Freddy, Q, Maybelle…none of them were trapped and burning.

As he grew closer to the end of the aisle, his hope rose. Maybe Camille had gotten out when she'd freed the horses. Doubt tugged at him, though, making him move faster. If she'd gotten out, she would've been with the others. She never would've watched as he'd run into the barn without trying to stop him, especially when there wasn't anyone left to save.

He reached the end of the aisle, but Camille wasn't there. His stomach dropped as his frantic gaze darted around the barn, trying to peer through the thick smoke and darkness to see where she might be trapped. Where could she be? He'd checked all the stalls and the full length of the aisle. The feed room? The tack room? Had she gotten turned around and was passed out in a corner somewhere, hidden in the shadows?

Terror choked him worse than the smoke. Coughing, he crouched lower and rushed back toward the other side of the barn. He tried to cling to his usual calm logic, but it slipped out of his grasp, panic fighting its way into his thoughts as the fire grew wilder and Camille was still nowhere to be found.

A movement in his peripheral vision caught his eye. Turning, he squinted, peering through the haze of smoke and the disorienting shadows caused by the leaping flames. A figure was outlined by the darkness outside the gaping Dutch door, and Steve lunged in that direction. His heart squeezed with hope, even as his brain told him that the form was too big to be Camille.

The light from the fire bounced off the person's jacket as he turned sideways and stepped through the opening. Steve recognized the reflective stripes as bunker gear, just as he noticed the firefighter was cradling a smaller figure against his chest. His heart leapt again, jolting almost painfully. Backup had arrived, and one of the firefighters was saving Camille.

"Camille!" he shouted, and the firefighter jerked his head around. The face shield and SCBA gear hid his features, so Steve couldn't recognize him. As Steve rushed toward them, the firefighter ducked through the door out into the night. Stumbling over the remains of a fallen board, Steve caught his balance and surged toward the opening, overwhelming relief whipping through him. Camille was out of the barn. The firefighter, whoever he was, had gotten her out, and an EMT would be there to help her.

She'd been so still, though. He ruthlessly shoved the thought out of his head, refusing to consider how limply she'd lain in the firefighter's arms. Coughing, he ran through the opening and looked around, blinking his watering, stinging eyes as he tried to see where the firefighter had carried Camille.

Something was wrong, though. There was no rescue truck, no flashing lights, no crew of firefighters swarming the area. Except for the roaring flames behind him, everything was quiet...too quiet.

Just as the realization that backup *hadn't* arrived was starting to take root in his mind, he saw the firefighter from the barn. He was jogging toward the flaming trees, Camille still in his arms, his gait rough and uneven. Steve wasn't sure if the firefighter had an injury or was thrown off-balance by the person cradled in his arms. All he knew was that he needed to get Camille to safety, *now*.

"Get back here!" Steve bellowed, but the wind and his ravaged lungs conspired against him, and his words were barely audible over the background noise. He started running after them, his brain fogged with fear for Camille. Why was the firefighter carrying her toward the burning evergreens? It didn't make any sense.

Steve chased after them, but the unshoveled snow was too deep, slowing him down to a frustrating slog. His body protested every movement, wanting to stop and cough, but he pressed on. Despite his ragged breathing, he was gaining on the fleeing figure. As they got closer to the tree line, Steve sucked in a hard breath. The fire was spreading quickly, the wind sending sparks and flames from tree to tree before whipping the inferno into a fury. Snowflakes and embers bit at his face, the contrast between hot and cold strange and terrible.

The destruction hit him low in the gut, but he pushed it away. He needed to get to Camille. That was the priority right now.

The firefighter paused at the edge of the fiery trees, looking over his shoulder. For a split second, Steve thought that he'd stop and wait, that he'd end this chase that made no sense. Just as he started to hope, the firefighter ran into the trees.

"No!" Steve yelled, agony filling him as he watched the two dive into the rows of trees. He couldn't lose Camille, not now that he'd just found her. He ran after them, heading straight toward the smoke-clogged forest. His agonized lungs and the deep snow slowed him down to a nightmarishly slow speed, but he plowed on. He had to save her.

Without hesitating, he plunged into the inferno after them.

Camille woke in yet another fire-ravaged nightmare.

The Christmas trees all around them were blackened skeletons dressed in flames, the evergreen scent she loved so much tainted and bitter from smoke. Hard arms held her against a chest covered in rough fabric. Looking up, she bit back a scream. It was the faceless man from her nightmare.

This time, though, he was all too real—and she wouldn't let him take her.

Reaching up, she shoved at the shield covering his

face. He let out a shout as his head snapped back, and she swung her elbow at his chest. His arms loosened, just slightly, and she threw herself forward, needing to get away from this nightmare come to life. She rolled out of his hold, falling weightlessly for the longest moment before she hit the ground hard.

He reached for her, looking so much like the menacing figure from her nightmares that she almost froze again. *No!* she shouted in her head, managing to roll away and scramble to her feet. Her legs didn't work well, her muscles shaky and stiff, but panic gave her strength to run.

Stumbling and fuzzy-headed, she sprinted forward, trying to find a way through what looked like an impenetrable wall of flame. She ducked between the trees and ran, two blazing rows of trees hemming her in. Flames billowed out, tossed by the wind, and heat seared her skin. She skittered to the side, away from the fire, but there was nowhere to go. A second wall of flame blocked her on the other side. Just as in her nightmares, there were no doors, no escape. It was just her and the hungry fire and the dark figure chasing her down.

With a crack, a burning tree fell to the side, blocking her way. She stumbled to a stop, barely managing to halt before she tumbled right on top of the flaming evergreen. She whirled in a circle, searching for a hole, some opening clear of flame that she could squeeze through, but there was nothing but fire.

"Camille!" Steve's voice made her freeze, and she sucked in a breath to respond. A hand gripped her arm, yanking her around, and her shout emerged as a hoarse shriek of fear.

The nightmare firefighter dragged her close, and terror seized her mind, making it impossible to think. She could only stare at the flames reflecting off his face shield, her own horrified reflection caught in the burning depths.

"Camille!" Steve's shout jolted her out of her panicked paralysis, and she jerked back against the firefighter's hold. This wasn't one of her nightmares. This was just a person, and she could fight—she *would* fight. She'd just found contentment and love and family. She wasn't about to give up her life easily.

She swung her arm, wishing she knew how to fight, but he easily blocked her with his free hand. With a sound of rage, she struck out again, this time catching the edge of his face shield. Locking her fingers around it, she shoved it upward as hard as she could, taking a grim satisfaction in his grunt of pain. The helmet and shield tumbled to the ground, revealing his all-too-human face.

Shock turned her rigid as recognition hit her.

"*Nate?*"

"Don't be scared, Camille," he said, and it was somehow so much more horrible to hear the familiar voice coming from this threatening figure. His attempt at a smile sent a shiver of horror through her. "I'm rescuing you. I got you out of the barn."

"I don't understand. Why'd you drag me in here?" A flare of doubt, telling her that she might've been wrong to run from him, tickled her stomach, but she squashed it. "This isn't safe!" She waved an arm at the burning trees surrounding them.

"I know." He took a step and staggered slightly, reminding Camille of his slurred words in the kitchen. "I was going to take you to safety—I *wanted* to take you to safety—but Steve was following us. He would've taken over, and everyone would've called him the hero. *Again*. All of this would've been for nothing."

"You're not making sense!" Her voice went high with panic as the wind blasted, sending a shower of sparks swirling around them. She jumped away, frantically looking around, searching for an escape.

"Camille!" Steve's shout came again, closer this time. It was the best thing she'd ever heard.

"Steve!" she shouted back. "We're here!"

"No!" Nate lunged for her, grabbing her arm and pulling her back against him. "He doesn't get to be the hero. Not this time!"

"Camille!" Steve burst into their small clearing, and Camille had never seen anything so beautiful as his sooty, terrified face. He lunged toward them but then froze, his gaze locked on her attacker's face, his soot-streaked face blank with shock and horror.

"*Nate?*" Steve's voice, filled with utter disbelief, cracked as he said his brother's name.

Nate's arm looped around Camille's neck as he yanked her closer, pressing against her throat when she tried to fight back and making it even harder to breathe. "Why are you here? You were supposed to be at the fire! Why do you make everything so hard?"

"What?" Grief and anger replaced the shock in Steve's expression as he took a step toward them, and Nate's arm tightened. Struggling, her vision slowly fuzzing, Camille began to choke. "Let her go! What are you doing?"

"It's my turn to save the day," Nate shouted as Camille fought to pull air into her lungs. "I planned everything so carefully. *I* get to be the hero this time!"

With a roar, Steve lunged forward, swinging a fist at Nate's face. When the arm around her neck loosened, Camille dropped to the ground, banging her chin on Nate's forearm hard enough to leave her stunned. Her head spun as the flames shot higher around them, embers and sparks hissing as they hit the snowy ground. A burning branch broke from one of the trees and fell next to her arm, and the flare of heat brought her out of her daze.

Shaking off her dizziness, she crawled away as Steve let out a pained grunt. Fear for him clutched her when she saw Nate's fist swing toward his center, hitting with a thud that bent Steve in half. Looking around frantically, she spotted a wooden box of the handsaws they used to cut down the trees. Stumbling toward the box, she grabbed one of the saws and turned back toward the pair, unsure how she was going to use her newfound weapon, but unwilling to let Steve battle it out alone.

With a primal wordless cry, Nate plowed forward, driving his shoulder into Steve's middle. The two brothers tumbled to the ground, hitting the snowy ground as a shower of sparks cascaded over them. They rolled over and then over again, each struggling for control of the other, locked in a tight battle.

Camille took a step toward them, breathing hard, fear and smoke squeezing her lungs, unable to tell who was who in the uneven light of the flames. Steve rolled them once more, flipping his brother over so that Nate was on the ground, knocking slush and blackened branches to the side. Rearing up, Steve swung, his fist striking Nate in the face: once, twice, three times.

Finally, Nate went limp, his head and limbs falling

into the melting snow beneath them. Panting, Steve stared down at his brother for a long moment before slowly pushing himself to his feet. Swaying, he looked at Camille. Dropping the saw, Camille launched herself at Steve.

He gathered her into his arms, holding her tightly but carefully, as if she was something precious. It was over too soon, though, and he set her away from him, his eyes raking over her as if checking for injuries.

"Can you walk?" he asked, his voice a husky rasp as he stripped off his bunker coat and wrapped it around her.

She nodded, although she wasn't sure how long she could stay on her feet. Steve propped his unconscious brother up and pulled him over his shoulders. Camille stared at Nate, unable to accept that Steve's sweet brother was the figure from her nightmares...and the person who'd almost led her to her death. She dragged her eyes away from him and met Steve's gaze instead.

"Let's get out of here." She grabbed onto the back of his belt with a shaking hand, willing to follow wherever he'd lead, knowing that he'd get her to safety.

That was what Steve did. He kept her safe. Always.

CHAPTER 20

"This is not," Camille told Maya, who was cuddled up next to her in the hospital bed, "a Christmas-card moment."

"No." Maya's voice was still hoarse. Both of them had been brought to the hospital for smoke inhalation and, in Camille's case, a concussion. The drug that Nate had dosed the hot chocolate with had passed through Maya's system with no aftereffects except a lingering headache. "I'd rather be opening presents right now."

"I'd rather be on the sleigh ride." *Preferably snuggled under a warm blanket with Steve.*

"Me, too. I'd rather be riding my pony."

"I'd rather be riding your pony, too, and I heard he can be extremely naughty."

Maya gave a rough-sounding chuckle. "Not last night, though. He was a hero, just as brave as a cavalry horse."

"Yeah, he was. You were, too."

"Not really." Dropping her gaze, Maya pinched a fold of the blanket between her fingers. "I was pretty scared."

"You can be scared and brave. In fact, I don't think you can be brave *without* being scared. It's part of the definition."

"I cried a lot, and Will had to tell me what to do before I remembered to call Dad."

Camille shrugged and then regretted it when a sharp throb of pain shot through her skull. "You did it, though, and that's what matters. Just think, right after regaining consciousness, you rode a horse bareback out of a burning building and went for help. That's like a braver, more bada—...ah, tougher version of Paul Revere."

"Nice save," Steve said dryly as he came into the room. He'd been there most of the day, but he'd left an hour earlier to, as he vaguely put it, "take care of some things."

"It *was* a nice save, Maya," Camille said, pretending she didn't know he was talking about her almost-swear. "You and your dad saved my life and most of the ranch. If you hadn't called for help, more than just the barn and that acre of trees would've burned. The whole place could've been lost. Thank you." Her voice became serious as she hugged Maya against her, looking at Steve over the girl's head.

Their gazes met, and she could see all the pain and exhaustion and relief in his eyes. It exactly echoed her feelings, and she felt a little lighter to be able to share them with him.

"Dad?" Maya's voice was small as he pulled a chair closer to the bed and settled on it. "What's going to happen to Uncle Nate?"

Steve's eyes closed for a moment, the lines of his face heavy with anger and grief. Reaching out, Camille took his hand, and he clutched hers so tightly that the pressure was just short of painful. "Uncle Ryan and Uncle Joe took him to a place where people will help him figure out why he did such a terrible thing."

"So, he's in rehab?" Maya asked, and Camille bit her lip to stop a completely inappropriate laugh from escaping. Sometimes Maya seemed very young, and other times she seemed to be old and wise.

"Not really. It's more like a hospital."

"Can't he just leave if he wants?"

"No." Steve's jaw tightened as he squeezed Camille's hand tightly, revealing how conflicted he'd been about the decision. "He knows that if he doesn't spend at least ninety days at this place and work hard with the therapists there, we'll be talking to the sheriff, and he'll be arrested."

"Why wasn't he arrested now?"

Steve scrubbed a hand over his face. "Joe and Ryan cut off the other lock and got rid of the evidence before the fire marshal got there. As far as she knows, Nate got drunk and accidentally lit the barn on fire. He went for help, but tripped and hit his head and passed out. He didn't know Maya was inside."

His eyes took on a gloss that made Camille's insides twist with sympathy.

"Is this okay with the two of you? I would've thrown him in the sheriff's car myself if Joe and Ryan hadn't convinced me to give therapy a try. You were the ones hurt by his actions, though. If you want him to go to jail, I'll change my report." Steve looked back and forth between Maya and Camille, looking so torn apart inside that she hurt for him.

"I don't want Uncle Nate to go to jail," Maya said, shooting Camille an anxious glance, as if she was worried about Camille's reaction. "He didn't mean for anyone to get hurt, not really. He was really, really dumb, but I'm glad he's going to therapy instead."

"I agree," Camille said and felt Maya relax against

her. "I'm still really angry at him, but I think therapy is a better solution than jail." She didn't mention it to Maya, but she knew that Steve was already aware how very, very angry she was at Nate.

"Okay." Giving a tight nod, he sat back in his chair, although he didn't relinquish her hand. "This isn't a very Christmassy place, is it?"

"No," Maya said mournfully. "Camille and I were just talking about what we'd rather be doing than sitting here on Christmas, like opening presents or going on a sleigh ride or riding Q." Her eyes widened. "Where are Q and the rest of the horses staying?"

"We moved them to the pasture next to Joe's cabin. There's a run-in shed there, so they'll have somewhere to go out of the weather. You two did a great job getting all of them out. They're still a little spooked, but none of them have even a scratch."

"Good." Camille leaned back as the knot at the back of her head pounded with the beat of her heart. "Except for the barn and the acre of trees closest to the barn, it turned out to be a happy ending, after all."

"Thanks to the two of you." Leaning forward, he gently kissed Maya and Camille on the forehead. His phone chimed, and he pulled it out with his free hand. Whatever he saw made a smile tug on one corner of his mouth. "Well, we can't bring the sleigh in here, but…"

Zoe, Micah, and Will piled into the room in front of a wheeled cart filled with gifts. Camille smiled, happier to see the other kids than she was about the gifts.

"You brought the presents!" Maya cried happily, climbing off Camille's bed.

"Is that remote-controlled?" Camille asked, eyeing

the wagon-like cart when she noticed none of the kids seemed to be pulling it.

Zoe's face lit up. "It follows my legs and stops when I stop." She did a short tour around the room to demonstrate, and the cart did indeed trail after her like a puppy. "I designed it based on a robotic mail cart I saw on the internet."

"Ingenious," Camille said, sitting cross-legged on the bed as she ignored the pain in her head. Having Steve and the kids there helped distract her. She'd discovered that it felt worse when she just lay quietly with nothing to focus on except her headache.

Steve gave his daughter an approving nod. "Very."

Dancing with excitement, Maya started passing out the presents, and everyone settled on Camille's bed or in the chairs. Zoe sat cross-legged in the now-empty cart.

"Do we take turns or just all rip into our gifts?" Camille asked, turning over something from Will. When it'd been just her and her grandma, that hadn't really been an issue.

"Let's just rip," Maya said with a wicked grin, and the other kids chorused their agreement. Pressing back a smile, Steve gave a nod, and wrapping paper started flying.

Despite her headache, Camille couldn't stop laughing as everyone raced to open their gifts, stopping only to exclaim over them and yell thanks and toss a bow at someone else's head. When the last gift was revealed, Camille looked around at her haul, fully impressed by the Springfields' gift-giving skills. Somehow, they'd managed to find and replace some of her favorite tools that had been lost in the fire. Maya had even made a stuffed catnip mouse for Lucy. Zoe's gift was a new torch that she'd promised would "blow Camille's socks off."

Camille reached for her new welding helmet and the gloves Micah had given her, intending to take the torch into the bathroom and quickly see what special features Zoe had added, but Steve plucked the super-torch out of her hands before she could get more than a couple of steps. "Don't set the hospital on fire. It's an hour to the next closest one."

Wrapping an arm around her waist, he tugged her down to sit on his lap. She stiffened, checking the kids for their reaction, but they were too busy investigating their presents to notice. Micah glanced up, but he just grinned, looking sweet and shy, and held up the box of oil pastels she'd gotten for him. "Thank you."

"You're welcome. Thank *you* for the gloves. Those are the best kind, since they're protective, but you can actually pick things up while wearing them, rather than feeling like you have bear paws."

"Did I get you the right kind of clamps?" Will asked. He didn't look at all bothered by Camille's position on his dad's lap, either, so she finally relaxed against him. It was warm and safe and so much nicer than the hospital bed.

She nodded. "They're perfect. How'd you know I hated the one in the workshop?"

"You only complained about it a hundred times," Will said, rolling his eyes in an exaggerated way that made her join in the others' laughter. "I love my present. Thank you." He held up the gift card for a set of new tires for his yet-to-be-purchased car.

"Me, too! Thank you!" Maya started pulling her new winter riding breeches on over her leggings.

"You're all welcome." Camille looked at Zoe a little anxiously, since she was staring down at her gift—a pair of tickets to a Denver robotics expo in January—without saying anything. "Is that an okay gift, Zoe?"

When she looked up, her eyes were shiny with unshed tears, and Camille felt her heart sink.

"You don't have to go," she said quickly, scrambling to fix whatever she'd just messed up. "We can scalp the tickets and use that money to buy you more parts or tools or whatever you'd like."

Climbing off the cart, Zoe threw herself at Camille, grabbing her in a hug, fully sobbing. Steve grunted at the impact, and Camille patted the girl's back, looking frantically at the others, wishing desperately that someone would tell her how to fix this. They just stared back at her, as startled as she was.

"I'm so glad you're not dead!" Zoe wailed between sobs, and Camille blew out a breath of relief as she hugged Zoe back.

"I'm glad I'm not dead, too." When Steve turned a chuckle into a cough, Camille widened her eyes at him, but he just smiled at her and held both of them closer until Zoe finished crying and pulled away, snuffling. Grabbing a tissue from the box on the bedside table, Camille handed it to her.

"Thanks," she mumbled, wiping her face and blowing her nose. "Sorry. I love my present. Will you…go with me?"

Camille blinked, not expecting the invitation, and Zoe started to duck her head. "Of course!" When she'd ordered the tickets, she'd gone over the robotics expo website multiple times, more than a little jealous of Zoe.

"I'd love to. We are going to come back with so many great ideas."

"Uh-oh," Will said under his breath, and everyone laughed, relieved. Zoe returned to her perch on the cart, and the rest of the kids turned back to their presents, chattering happily.

Steve tipped his head down to speak softly into Camille's ear. "Their gifts are good, but my present is the best." He'd put the horse-drawn fire wagon sculpture on the table next to them and ran a thumb lightly across one of the wheels. "I love this."

A little envious of that wheel, she shifted in his lap. "Really?"

"Really." He paused, his hand stilling. "Not as much as I love you, though."

Her heart stuttered. "I... You... I'm sorry. What?"

His hand came up to rub his neck—a neck that was rapidly turning red.

"Hey, Dad?"

Camille turned to look at Will, grateful for the interruption so she could have a moment to try to sort out her spinning emotions.

"We're going to go find something to eat, if that's okay?" At Steve's nod, Will ushered out the other three kids.

Maya's voice carried back into the room. "Why are we getting food? I'm not hungry."

"They're having a *talk*." Will's voice was lower but still clear enough to understand, to Camille's chagrin. "Remember what happened at breakfast the last time they *talked*? Do you really want to watch that train wreck again?"

"Oh. No. That was uncomfortable. Let's be gone a while."

Their voices finally faded, and Camille still didn't have any idea of the right way to respond.

"You don't have to say it back." Even though they were alone in the room, Steve kept his voice low and his mouth close to her ear. "You don't have to say anything right now. I just wanted you to know."

Suddenly, she knew exactly what she felt and what she wanted—needed—to do. Turning her head, she pressed her mouth against his. After a startled second, Steve kissed her back, and she could feel how much he really did love her. It was obvious in the way he held her, as if she was something precious, something that deserved to be protected and cherished…and loved.

She deepened the kiss, and he groaned against her mouth, his hand coming up to cup the back of her head. When he pressed on the swollen knot, she yelped, pulling back.

"I'm sorry," he said, remorse quickly replacing the heat in his eyes. "Did I hurt your head?"

"It's fine." She wanted to say the words now that she'd actually figured out how she felt. "*I'm* fine. I'm good. I love you, too."

By the way his eyes widened in surprise, he hadn't expected her to say it back. She took advantage of his startled moment of silence to keep talking.

"And I love your kids. They're really interesting people. If everyone was as awesome as your kids, I wouldn't mind talking to people. I might even go to the grocery store during the busiest time of the day."

His mouth started to curve up at the corners, and

his smile stretched until it was a full-faced beam. She just looked at him, basking in the beauty of him and the knowledge that she was the one who'd made him so happy.

When he moved to kiss her again, though, she held him off. "Can I ask you one thing before you make me forget everything except for how great it feels when you kiss me?"

"Of course." His grin widened even more at her question, and she almost chickened out, not wanting to bring back his grim look. She needed to know, though.

"Did Nate burn down my house?"

As she'd feared, his smile fell away, and she dreaded what his answer would be. "No. Jackie has officially declared it an accidental fire caused by compromised wiring."

Her body sagged in relief. "Thank you. It wouldn't have changed how I feel about you, but it would've made it hard to forgive him, and he's your brother, so... It's just good to know."

"I understand." His mouth quirked wryly. "Jackie told me she actually suspected I'd set it."

"What?" The idea was so preposterous that Camille could only stare at him, her mouth open.

"Mrs. Lin showed her that picture of the person on your porch in bunker gear, and she knew I was interested in you, so she thought I might have done it so I could be a hero."

Camille scoffed at that. "As if you need any help with that. You're constantly being heroic."

His smile was slowly returning. "Not constantly."

"Well, no, but usually. You're really intimidatingly

close to perfect." He snorted, and she knew she wouldn't be able to convince him of it. That didn't change the truth, though. She brought the subject back to Nate, unable to let it go without asking one more question. "Was he the one in that picture?"

"I think so. He admitted having borrowed my bunker gear—or breaking in to take it from the station when he couldn't get his hands on mine—and he liked to go to your house and…" He paused, the anger building in his eyes again. "He would watch you through the windows. We'd always been too competitive, growing up. Ryan, Nate, and I…" He shook his head. "With Ryan, it was always about girls. With Nate, it was sports, grades, attention…everything. I thought we'd outgrown all that, but I guess in his head, he was still competing for who got to be the center of attention. He wanted to be the *hero*. After I helped you at the scrapyard and we started to reconnect, Nate got a little…obsessed with the idea of being the one to save you. Even if he had to put you in danger first to do it."

"Oh." She absorbed that, feeling her stomach cringe away from the idea. "I guess I can kind of understand that."

"You can?"

"Not really. I mean that I can eventually forgive him for it." Giving in to temptation, she stroked the line of Steve's jaw, trying to smooth away the tightness there. "It's not your fault, you know. He may have felt competitive, but all you've ever done is try your best to help people. You're the *real* hero."

He cupped her face gently, careful to avoid the back of her head. "Thank you."

"You're welcome. And thank you for the welding helmet. I've coveted that kind for years." She loved how he supported what she did without trying to dismiss or diminish it. Even her grandma hadn't understood how much a part of her that her artwork was.

"You're welcome, but that's not your whole present."

"It's not?" Anticipation sparked in her. "What's the rest?"

"I'm going to remodel the workshop, and half of it will be done however you like."

She stared at him, feeling a warm happiness spreading through her until it filled her completely. "I can't believe I get to stay at the Christmas-card ranch."

"I can't believe I have you." His face softened. "And that you love me."

"I do." Leaning closer, she closed the distance between them. Just before their lips were about to touch, she gave a soft laugh. "Steve-*freaking*-Springfield. I still can't believe I get to kiss you whenever I want."

"Believe it."

His lips met hers, and she finally did believe it. Her daydreams of this wonderful man and his amazing kids and the beautiful Christmas-card ranch...

They were real.

READ ON FOR A SNEAK PEEK AT THE
FIRST BOOK IN A THRILLING NEW SERIES
FROM BELOVED AUTHOR KATIE RUGGLE,
FEATURING A FAMILY OF BOUNTY
HUNTER SISTERS...AND THE MEN WHO
GET AWAY WITH THEIR HEARTS.

IN HER SIGHTS

CHAPTER 1

"I'M HEADED TO THE PARK," MOLLY CALLED AS SHE LET the screen door slam shut behind her. It slapped against the edge of the frame, too warped to close properly. She absently made a mental note to fix it later...along with the hundred other things that needed doing around the house.

"You need backup?" Charlie yelled back, and Molly resisted the urge to roll her eyes. Her sister would do anything to get out of paperwork, but Molly wasn't about to enable her, even if it would be nice to have someone along to counter some of the boredom.

"Nope, this should be easy-peasy."

"You're taking Warrant?" Cara, Charlie's twin and the worrywart of the family, peered at them through the screen door.

The enormous, hairy Great Pyrenees mix dog in front of her cocked his head when he heard his name. "Yes." Leash in hand, Molly allowed Warrant to tow her down the porch steps as she gave Cara a wave over her shoulder, wanting to get out of earshot before her sisters thought of any more questions. If Molly was delayed long enough, then Charlie would somehow finagle her way into coming along, and that meant Molly would be stuck sorting her sister's expense reports. That prospect

wouldn't be so bad, except that Charlie was terrible
about taking care of her receipts. They were always
sticky or stained or wrapped around chewed gum. *Nope*.
Charlie could do her own expense report. It was a beautiful night for a walk to the park, and Molly was going
to enjoy it.

Warrant trotted along beside her as she walked past
her neighbor's scarily perfect yard. Mr. Petra silently
watched her from his wide, immaculate porch, his
narrow-eyed glare boring into her.

Baring her teeth in a wide smile, Molly waved. "Hey,
Mr. P! Beautiful day, isn't it?"

As he continued to glower, Molly felt her forced smile
shift to a real grin. Being passive-aggressively friendly
to her sourpuss of a neighbor was oddly satisfying. She
felt his disapproving glare follow her until she reached
the end of their street and turned the corner. Warrant
happily bumbled along next to her, although his broad,
pink tongue was already hanging out of his mouth.

"We've gone a *block*," she said. "You can't be getting tired already."

Warrant just blinked his oblivious dark eyes at her,
and she sighed.

"You're the laziest dog in the world. It's a good
thing you're cute, or we wouldn't put up with your shenanigans." The last part was a lie. Molly and her sisters
would have put up with Warrant even if all of his fur
fell out and he sprouted leathery, bat-like wings. They'd
probably even get him specially made sweaters with
appropriately placed holes for his new appendages. She
smiled at the mental image as she ran a hand over his
silky-soft head.

The sun beamed down warmly on them as they walked, light filtering through the leaves of the trees that lined the residential street. Langston was close enough to Denver—just an hour's drive from downtown to downtown if traffic was light—that commuters were snapping up new cookie-cutter homes on the northern edge of the small city as fast as they could be built. Set tucked against the foothills of the Rocky Mountains, the new part of Langston had wide stretches of fresh sod and spindly saplings that cast barely any shade, but Molly's house was in the older, richer, southern part of town. That meant neighbors eyeing her family's worn and raggedy property from their own perfectly restored Victorians with lush, Mr. P-approved lawns, but it also meant that the trees were old enough to spread their sheltering branches over the yards and quiet streets, protecting Molly and Warrant from the strong Colorado sun.

Although it was mid-September, it still looked—and felt—like summer. The only hint that fall had begun was the absence of kids running around at two thirty on a Tuesday afternoon. Despite Warrant's slowing pace, the mile-long walk went quickly, the peace of the quiet, warm day soothing her too-busy brain.

After much coaxing and a minimal amount of dragging her increasingly lazy dog, Molly made it to the park. Only a handful of people were there, mostly parents watching their preschool-age kids play on the equipment. Warrant perked up once the dog run came into view, but Molly towed him in the opposite direction toward an empty bench next to the swings, doing her best to pretend that she couldn't see his sad look.

"I know, Warrant." She sat and tried to ignore the guilt swamping her. "We need to make some money, though. You eat a lot, and it's not the cheap stuff either. Your food is the equivalent of dog caviar, so I don't think it's too much to ask for you to help out occasionally."

With a soul-deep sigh, he lay down next to the bench and rested his chin on his front paws. Molly turned her attention away from the dog and eyed the shops across the street. Her spot on the bench was the perfect vantage point.

She pulled her phone from her pocket and pretended that she wasn't watching the door next to the cute ice cream parlor. The apartment above the shop was leased by Maryann Cooper, who seemed to be a law-abiding, responsible citizen. The same couldn't be said about her younger brother, Donnie. He had a habit of taking things that didn't belong to him—like wallets and cell phones and the occasional car—and he hadn't shown up for his most recent court date.

Molly had a strong suspicion that Maryann knew where Donnie was hiding, and she would leave for her shift at the turkey-processing plant in an hour or so. Molly started playing a game on her phone while keeping one eye on the apartment across the street, just in case Maryann decided to leave early. Warrant stretched out on his side and dozed, snoring softly.

After a peaceful half hour drifted by, Molly stood and stretched, knowing it was time to move closer to the ice cream shop. Warrant provided an excuse to hang out at the park without her looking like a lurker—and he'd also proven to be an excellent conversation starter with people who wouldn't have given her the time of day if she'd tried approaching them alone—but having the dog along did require some additional planning. Warrant's top speed was a slow amble, so she had to allow enough time to get him through the park and across the street. Before she could make her move, an all-too-familiar voice made her groan and plop back down in her seat.

"Molly Pax. Just the person I wanted to see." John Carmondy started rounding the bench but paused to rub Warrant behind the ears. The dog—traitor that he was— thumped his heavy tail against the ground and rolled over in a plea for belly scratches. To Warrant's obvious delight, John complied.

"John Carmondy. Just the person I *didn't* want to see." If she'd known that he was going to be at the park, she would've stopped and talked at Mr. P for a while longer. Molly sent a quick text and then slid her phone into her pocket. "Why are you here?"

Still crouched to pet Warrant, John grinned up at her, his teeth white in contrast to his tan skin. Her dog's back foot pedaled in the air as John found just the right spot. Molly wasn't surprised. She was well aware that the man knew exactly how to hit everyone's buttons. Too bad he seemed to take as much pleasure in pestering her as he did playing with her dog. "Why am I at the park?" he asked. "Why does anyone go to the park on such a beautiful day?"

Across the street, Maryann slipped out of the door next to the ice cream shop and hurried toward her ancient Honda parked on the street. She was leaving early today. Molly watched her go, holding back a growl when she saw Maryann get in her car and pull away from the curb. There went her chance to talk to the bail jumper's sister.

"You're such a happy dog, aren't you?" John cooed. "Not all crabby like your owner."

Molly rolled her eyes hard enough that she was surprised they didn't spin right out of her skull. "I'm not crabby." She hesitated, honesty pushing her to add, "Well, not to most people."

With a snort, John gave Warrant a final belly scratch before straightening to his full—and significant—height. Crossing over, he took the spot next to her on the bench, and Molly fought the urge to shift to give him more room. He was just so darn *huge*, with biceps as big as her head and thighs like muscled tree trunks. His ridiculously enormous body took up almost the entire bench. "I'm special, then?"

"Special's one word for it," she muttered, sneaking another quick glance across the street. Even though Maryann had left, Molly still kept a furtive eye on the shops even as she pretended to watch the kids playing on the jungle gym. She hoped that her unwelcome companion would wander away if she ignored him.

"So…who are we staking out today?"

Of course he didn't wander away. She should've known better. John Carmondy was as hard to get rid of as head lice—and twice as irksome. Shooting an irritated glance his way, she saw he was gazing across the street at the ice cream shop, the corner of his mouth tucked in the way it did when he was trying to hold back a grin. He wasn't fooling anyone, though. The deep crease of his dimple gave him away.

Her sigh sounded more like a groan. "Did you want something or do you have some kind of daily annoyance quota you need to fill?"

When he laughed, she couldn't help but dart another quick look his direction. The harsh lines of his face — the square jaw and dark, intense eyes and bumpy nose that had obviously been the target of a fist or two in the past — were softened by his full lips, the lush sweep of his long eyelashes, and that stupidly appealing dimple. Someone that attractive shouldn't be so incredibly irritating, but that was John Carmondy in a nutshell: ridiculously pretty and just as ridiculously obnoxious.

"Oh, Pax… Such a jokester." He continued before she could protest that she was completely serious. "What's happening in your life? It's been a while since we last got together, and I want to know everything. That's what good friends do. They share thoughts and ideas and feelings with each other. So share, my good friend. Whatcha up to?" He turned toward her, slinging his arm over the back of the bench so that his enormous hand rested behind her. Although she tried to ignore it, she couldn't help but shiver. She tried to tell herself it was her imagination, but it felt like the heat from his arm was burning the skin of her back like a brand.

"First of all," she started, even as the adult in her brain told her not to encourage him, to just ignore him until he gave up and left, "I saw you only three days ago, when I grabbed that bail jumper from the hardware store."

"The one *I* tracked down? The one you stole while I was in the bathroom? *That* bail jumper?"

Ignoring his — accurate — comment, she continued. "Secondly, we're not friends, so there will be no sharing of any kind. Thirdly, please go away." Tearing her gaze away from his obnoxiously distracting face, she focused on the playground. A toddler who'd been playing on the base of the slide was swept up by her mom, and the two walked toward the ice cream shop. Even though it was the middle of the day, the place seemed to be doing a brisk business. An older couple entered the shop as a young woman in running clothes peered through the front window, as if tempted by the thought of a cone.

John chuckled and seemed to settle in even more comfortably on the bench. "Has it only been three days? It *felt* longer, probably because I missed this." In her peripheral vision, she saw him gesture back and forth between the two of them, and she had to swallow an amused snort. He was persistent; she'd give him that. When she didn't respond, he turned to follow her gaze, although his arm remained stretched behind her. "So…? Who are you hunting these days?"

And there it was…his true motivation. "Who says I'm working? Why couldn't I just be walking my dog on a beautiful day?" Even as she spoke, she scolded herself for encouraging him. John Carmondy was the human manifestation of *give an inch, take a mile*.

He laughed in a low, husky way that she refused to think of as sexy. "Because you have that look you get when you're on the trail of a skip. You're a bloodhound, Miss Molly Pax, and you don't lift your nose from the ground until you find your target."

Sighing in a deeply exaggerated way, she stood, and he immediately followed suit. Of course it was too much to ask that she could lose him that easily. She was going to have to get creative. "As much as I would love to stay and listen to you compare me to a smelly, drooly dog, Warrant and I have things to do."

Although Warrant got to his feet reluctantly, he

perked up as she headed toward the dog park and walked willingly at her side.

"When are you going to come work for me, Pax?" John asked, catching up easily.

"Never ever." She paused and then added for good measure, "Ever."

"I offer a really good health insurance plan," he said in the tone of someone dangling candy in front of a toddler. The sad thing was that Molly would've been tempted by that...if this were anyone but John. She enjoyed being a bail recovery agent more than she'd ever expected, but the paperwork of owning a business was much less fun. There was no way she'd ever accept a job from John, though. She'd murder him before she completed her first day.

"Good for you." As they drew closer to the dog run's gate, Warrant trotted in front of her, eager to get inside with the other dogs. Molly's phone buzzed in her pocket, and she pulled it out to glance at the text. Showtime. Get over here. She held back a smile at the perfect timing. Sometimes things really did work out beautifully, even when John was sticking his nose where it didn't belong. "Here. Hold him a second."

She tossed the end of the leash to John, and he caught the lead automatically. Turning, she jogged toward the road. In front of the ice cream shop, the runner who'd been peering wistfully through the window now looked to be flirting with a scruffy-looking white guy in his mid-thirties.

As Molly paused by the side of the road to let a car pass, she typed Donald Cooper, ice cream shop on Walnut St NOW and sent the text before glancing behind her. She couldn't hold back a smirk. John was trying to follow her, but Warrant had put on the brakes. He'd plopped his fluffy hundred-pound butt down in front of the dog park entrance and braced his front legs, refusing to move. *That's right, baby*, she thought gleefully. *Earn your expensive dog food.*

"Don't you want to go with your mama?" The distance between them made his voice faint, but Molly could still hear his cajoling words. "I bet there's some bacon over there. Wouldn't you like some bacon? Mmm…salty and meaty?"

A laugh escaped Molly as she glanced at the text that had popped up on her phone.

On our way from Clayton and 5th. ETA four minutes.

Four minutes is doable, she thought as she jogged across the road. "Felicity!" she said, the last syllable raising in a well-practiced squeal as she trotted over to the runner to give her a hug. "I thought that was you." Keeping an arm around Felicity's back, she turned toward the man who was not even trying to hide the way he was checking her out. She gave him a small smile that he returned with a leer.

"Are you two twins?" he asked.

"Just sisters," they chorused, before bursting into giggles.

Molly kept her expression as dumb and happy as possible. "Who's this?"

"This," Felicity said, "is Donnie. I dropped my apartment key without realizing it, and he picked it up for me.

The stupid tiny pocket in these shorts is useless." She flipped the waistband of her shorts over, revealing the small inside pocket and a smooth, bronze patch of her hip. Donnie's gaze locked onto the exposed skin, and his eyes bugged out a little.

"That's so sweet of you, Donnie," Molly cooed, resisting the urge to glance over to see if John had gotten Warrant to move and was headed her way.

"It's *so* sweet." Felicity tossed her glossy, dark hair over her shoulder, and Donnie's eyes followed the movement as he swallowed visibly.

"You should buy him some ice cream as a thank you." Molly gave him an approving smile, carefully not looking over his shoulder. Surely four minutes had passed by now.

Pouting a little, Felicity said, "I'd love to, but I left all my money at home."

"I have money." Molly patted her pocket. "You can pay me back later, Fifi."

Felicity gave her a quick, covert glare at the hated nickname, but the expression disappeared as quickly as it arrived, replaced by a beaming smile. "Thanks, Moo!"

Hiding her grimace, Molly accepted that as well-deserved payback.

"I should…" Donnie trailed off as he glanced over his shoulder, his whole body going stiff as he saw the approaching sheriff's deputies. "Shit! Gotta go!"

He bolted.

"Wait!" Molly tried to grab his arm, but he dodged her outstretched hand.

"Sorry, ladies!" he shouted over his shoulder. "You can buy me that ice cream some other time!"

Sharing an exasperated glance with her sister, Molly took off after him, Felicity close behind. "Way to be stealthy, Deputies!" she called back over her shoulder before focusing on the chase.

"Why do they always run?" Felicity grumbled as they sprinted past a Mexican restaurant and a bank.

"Because they know they're going to jail?" Unlike her sister, Molly was already sucking air, and she cursed her love of pastries and hatred of exercise for the hundredth time. "At least *you're* wearing appropriate clothes."

"Could be worse," Felicity said as they chased Donnie across an empty lot. "You could be in a dress and heels, like when we crashed that wedding to bring in the maid of honor."

"True."

Donnie darted sideways, heading for a six-foot wooden fence enclosing the backyard of a large Victorian house, and Molly and Felicity groaned in unison.

"Not it," Molly said quickly, just before Felicity said it.

"But I'm in shorts and a sports bra!"

She sighed. "Fine. I'll do it." Although Molly would much rather be the one who gave her sister a leg up rather than the person dropping into a stranger's backyard, Felicity had a point. Molly's T-shirt and capris were slightly more suited to hurdling a fence.

Donnie didn't slow down as he approached the wooden barricade, using his momentum to haul himself up the side of the fence. Driven by the intense desire to avoid doing the same, Molly surged forward, leaping up to latch her arms around his waist. Her weight unbalanced him, and his grip on the top of the boards slipped, sending them both tumbling to the ground.

Molly hit the sunbaked earth first, grunting as the air was driven out of her lungs from the force of the fall. Although she managed to twist slightly so that his entire weight didn't land on her, he still pinned her right arm and shoulder to the weedy ground. Then Felicity was flipping him over, and Molly was free of his weight.

Rolling over and pushing to her knees, Molly blinked a couple of times to orient herself. "You good?" she asked, and Felicity gave her a fierce grin. Her knee was pressing firmly into Donnie's spine, and she had a strong grip on his hand, using it to twist his arm behind his back. Donnie was swearing and muttering, his words muffled by the thick thatch of weeds his face was shoved into.

"Never better."

"I'm not," Donnie whined. "Who the hell *are* you?"

With a breathless chuckle, Molly stood up and did a quick inventory, checking for any injuries of her own. Although her shoulder was throbbing where Donnie had landed on it, she knew there was no major damage done. She'd just be bruised and sore for a few days.

The two deputies ran toward them, barely winded, and she raised her eyebrows. "You were slow on purpose, weren't you?"

"I'm admitting nothing." Maria winked at her as she and her partner, Darren, took Felicity's place on top of Donnie. "Just think of it as a measure of trust in you. We knew you'd run him down. You always get your guy."

"Besides," Darren said as he cuffed a protesting Donnie's hands behind his back, "this way you really feel like you earned the payout."

"I'm fine with not earning it," Felicity said, and

Molly nodded in agreement. "If we'd ended up having to go over that fence, I would've been *annoyed*."

"I'll leave the acrobatics to you youngsters," Maria said, helping Donnie to his feet.

"Youngsters?" Molly exchanged a skeptical look with her sister. "What are you? Thirty?"

"Thirty-*two*."

Rolling her eyes, Molly fell in behind the trio as they headed back in the direction of the park. "Okay, Grandma."

"I can't believe you played me like that," Donnie whined from his spot between the two deputies. "That's why I don't trust chicks."

Darren gave him a look. "How were you not suspicious when they started paying attention to you? Those two are *way* out of your league."

As Donnie sputtered indignantly, Molly tuned him out and turned to her sister. "Thanks for getting here so fast after I texted. How'd you sneak away without Charlie tagging along?"

Felicity grinned. "I asked her to help me clean the garage. That's the one thing she hates more than paperwork. There's no way she'll come out to the garage to check if I'm there. She'll be too worried that I'll make her help."

"Genius."

"Yep."

As they reached the ice cream shop, a shout across the street caught Molly's attention. When she turned her head and saw John and Warrant, both looking equally stubbornly annoyed, she pressed her lips together to hold back a laugh.

"Talk about genius." Felicity sounded just as amused

as Molly felt. "You finally figured out a way to ditch Carmondy. Nice one, Molls."

"Thanks. I just wish he'd give up on following me around and chase his own skips."

Her sister's eyebrows bobbed up and down comically. "I told you why he's really always trailing after you."

"Not that again." Molly groaned. This was a regular joke that Felicity—all of her sisters, actually—teased her with, but it was as far from reality as it could possibly be. "He wants me to work for him. Since I keep refusing, he wants to steal my skips out from under me. That's all there is to it."

"He's in *loooove*," Felicity cooed, and Molly jabbed her sister in the side with her elbow.

"Hush."

Although Felicity smirked at her, she did fall silent, to Molly's relief.

"Would you mind finishing up with Maria and Darren?" Molly asked. "I need to retrieve our dog."

"Sure." Felicity jogged to catch up with the deputies, who were ushering Donnie around the corner where they must've parked their squad cars.

"You're my favorite sister!" Molly called after Felicity before crossing the street. Her pace slowed as she neared John and Warrant, their twin accusing stares making her feel a bit guilty.

"Thank you for holding him," she said, taking the leash. "I just had to take care of something."

Instead of yelling about getting ditched, however, John's attention ran over her grass-and-dirt-stained clothes and settled on the scrape on her forearm. His eyes narrowed. "What happened?"

She flapped her hand to dismiss his concern. "I just didn't feel like climbing over a fence today."

"That makes no sense." He eyed her carefully, as if searching for other injuries. "You okay?"

"Of course. All in a day's work." She couldn't help smiling at him. No matter how aggravating John Carmondy was, it was kind of nice having someone worry about her.

She quickly nipped that thought in the bud. If she allowed herself to get mushy where John was concerned, he'd start stealing jobs from her left and right. Even worse, if she didn't stay on her guard around him, she'd end up agreeing to work for him, and one of them would end up dead in short order. It was important for their safety that she resist any urge to soften toward her biggest rival.

"You *are* hurt, aren't you?" His voice was full of concern as he took a half step closer, as though ready to administer first aid. Molly didn't find the idea of John's big hands on her as repugnant as she should have.

That thought brought her back to reality, and she turned sharply away, tossing him a muttered "bye." That was why it was important to not let Felicity's insinuations take root in her brain. Molly had to be careful, since she had a habit of playing the sucker for a pair of puppy dog eyes and a sob story. Although she'd been forced to develop a hard shell when she and her sisters had started their bail recovery business, there was nothing she could do about her soft, marshmallow-y center. She was pretty much stuck with that.

"Remember," she muttered as she strode toward the dog park, Warrant happily trundling along at her side now that he was finally, *finally* getting his way, "that way leads to death or prison time."

"What?"

She turned her head to see that John had tagged along. His scowl had softened, and a corner of his mouth was even threatening to twitch upward again. "I was talking to Warrant."

"About death and prison?"

"He's a good listener."

"I'm sure he is." John caught up with her and strolled alongside them, as if they were a couple taking their dog for a walk. Molly tried to speed up, but his long legs easily kept pace, and she was the one who was starting to get sweaty and breathless.

Slowing down again, she gave him an exasperated look. Since she had four younger sisters—and a mom who acted more like a kid than any of her offspring ever had—Molly knew her glare was on-point. "Why are you still here?"

For some strange reason, that question banished the last of his scowl, and he grinned at her. There was no sign he'd ever been annoyed *or* concerned. "It's a beautiful day. Why wouldn't I want to spend it in the park?"

"The park is pretty big." She didn't believe for a second that he was following her around for the fun of it. John Carmondy wanted something from her. "Can't you spend this beautiful day in another part of it? One that's *away*?" She gestured in a broad circle, encompassing the entire area around them.

He chuckled. It was like he was incapable of being offended. "But it's nicest right here."

"It smells like dog poop right here." They reached the gate of the exercise area again, and she paused, wanting to run John off before they entered the fence. It was one thing for him to follow her around the park, but standing together, watching Warrant play, laughing together over the dogs' antics…it all felt too dangerously intimate for her comfort. John wasn't her boyfriend. He wasn't even a friend. He was a rival and a competitor, and Molly knew it was ill-advised to let John into the dog park with her. There was no way to watch some big hulk of a guy play with adorable animals and not soften toward him.

"All I smell is flowers." His grin widened, and Molly let her head fall back as she mentally swore at the sky.

"Fine." She opened the gate and followed Warrant through it. "But there will be no laughing. And no playing with puppies."

"O…kay?" He sounded like he was about to disobey that rule already.

"No cute behavior, either. Understand?" Unclipping Warrant's leash, she let him into the main part of the run. He immediately galumphed over to make friends with an overweight black Lab.

"Not really?"

She glanced at his confused but still amused face and quickly turned away. She could already tell that this wasn't going to end well. There was going to be cuteness, and she was going to get mushy, and it was all going to end with someone's death.

He smiled at her dog, flashing that aggravatingly adorable dimple, and she had to admit…it wouldn't be the worst way to go.

CHAPTER 2

MOLLY YAWNED AND BLINKED, TRYING TO CLEAR HER FUZZY eyesight. It didn't help. The numbers in the spreadsheet still looked like someone had smeared Vaseline over the laptop screen. Letting out a huff of frustration that morphed into another yawn halfway through, she sat back in her chair and squinted at the clock on the microwave display.

"Almost one. No wonder I'm tired," she muttered, rolling her head to stretch out her tense neck muscles. Her right leg felt stiff, and she was dying to move it, but a snoozing Warrant had his huge head resting on her foot, and she didn't want to disturb the dog. She knew she should just go to bed and finish work in the morning, but it was almost impossible to get anything done while everyone else was awake. There were always distractions and crises to manage, as well as research to be done. It was good to be busy, to be offered almost too many jobs, but it was also tiring. The business was only two years old, though, and Molly hated to turn away work. Even though it wasn't exactly logical, she worried that everything would collapse underneath them if she paused to take a breath.

Glancing back at the screen, she grimaced. The numbers weren't any clearer than they'd been a minute ago. Saving the file, she shut down the laptop. If she tried to finish it tonight, she'd just have to fix the mistakes tomorrow.

The kitchen was dimly lit by the gentle glow from the light over the stove. It was just large enough to fit the small table that Molly used as a desk. No matter how much she would've loved to have an office with a door she could use to shut out the hubbub, space was at a premium when six women shared one house. There were officially three bedrooms, although solitude-loving Norah had tucked a twin bed into what was supposed to be an upstairs sitting room and had appropriated the hall closet for her own use. Molly and Felicity shared, and the twins—Cara and Charlie—took another. It irked Molly that their mother, who contributed the least to the household expenses, had her own room.

Tapping her finger absently on the closed laptop, she frowned, knowing that she was going to have to have a conversation with her mom soon about paying her way or finding another place to live.

With a groan, she let her head tip forward to rest on the cool laptop lid. She dreaded the drama that conversation would cause. Molly'd had similar talks with her mom over the years—the first was when she was twelve—and Jane had always somehow wiggled out of her promises or negotiated more time or had such a fit that Molly had backed off. Lifting her head, she drew her shoulders back. Not this time. She was determined to stand strong.

The overhead light flickered on, making her blink from the glare. Warrant's snuffled snores cut off abruptly. He raised his head off of her foot when Jane swept into the kitchen, as if Molly's thoughts had summoned her. Her tall, angular form was dressed in black skinny jeans and a dark, form-fitted top, with her red hair pulled back in a severe bun.

"Molly!" Bending, Jane pressed a kiss to the crown of her head.

"Hey, Mom." Molly turned in her chair so she could examine Jane's outfit as her mother pulled a water bottle out of the fridge. "What's with the...look?"

"What?" Keeping the refrigerator door propped open with her hip, Jane took a long drink of water, screwed the cap back on, and returned it to the shelf before letting the fridge close again. Molly resisted the urge to ask her mom if she planned to air-condition the entire house via refrigerator. Even though Molly was only twenty-seven, being around Jane somehow made her feel like a cranky parent. "You don't like it?" Jane asked as she did a turn, as if modeling.

"It's very...cat-burglar chic, I guess." When Jane jerked around with a reproving look—presumably for her skeptical tone—Molly just shrugged. She was used to having her mom's disapproval. Molly was much too responsible to ever be the favorite. Usually, that was Felicity or Charlie, depending on Jane's whim, but they'd all learned not to allow their mom to play them off one another. They were sisters first—sisters who shared the misfortune of having an often irresponsible mother. "Where are you off to at one on a Wednesday morning?"

Jane flipped her hand as if the words smelled bad. The familiarity of the gesture caused Molly to blink when she realized that she did exactly the same thing when she wanted to change the subject. She immediately made a firm resolution to stop. "I have to ask my daughter for permission to go out?" Jane scoffed. "Don't forget who the mother is around here."

Unfortunately, Jane made it all too easy to do exactly that. Her words reminded Molly of her earlier thoughts. "Will you be back by tomorrow—this afternoon, I mean? I need to talk to you."

Smoothing her hair even though the strands were perfectly flat, Jane lifted her shoulders and let them drop. "Possibly. If the perfect opportunity to be spontaneous presents itself, I'm not going to pass it up. You're an adult now. You need to learn that you don't need your mom around all the time anymore."

Molly had to clench her jaw shut and count to fourteen before she trusted herself to speak semi-civilly. "Text me if you're going to be gone more than a day so I don't have to start searching hospitals and jails."

With a light laugh—as if the suggestion was ridiculous and not a regular thing her kids had to do since they'd been much too young to be dealing with that nonsense—Jane headed for the door to the garage.

"Why are you going that way?" Molly asked, standing up, prepared to tackle her mom if necessary. There were hard lines, and her beloved Prius was one of them. "Your car is parked in the driveway."

"Oh!" Jane paused, her hand on the doorknob. "I thought we could swap for a few days. Yours gets better gas mileage, and mine's making this strange rattling sound every time I go over eighty."

There were so many things wrong with what her mother said that Molly couldn't decide where to start. She ended up going with a flat "No."

"Molly…" It was her stern mother voice, which had lost all of its power by the time Molly was a teenager.

"If you take my car, I'm going to report it stolen." She grabbed her backpack off the hook next to the door and rummaged through it, searching for the key fob that she always kept tucked in the front pocket. It wasn't there. Setting her backpack down with a solid thump, she held out her hand, maneuvering her body to block the garage door. "Keys."

"My car isn't safe right now." Jane tucked her fingers into her back pockets, but Molly knew that she was protecting her access to the keys rather than moving to pull them out and hand them over. "Do you really want your mother driving around Denver in a dangerous vehicle?"

Molly kept her hand outstretched, palm up expectantly. "Do you want your *daughter* driving around in a dangerous vehicle?"

Jane did that familiar sweep of her hand again, doubling Molly's resolution to remove the motion from her own repertoire. "You're in Langston. You don't need a car. Where would you need to go that you couldn't just walk to?"

"Work." Her tone was heavy with sarcasm, but her position in front of the door didn't waiver. "I need to work, so that we can eat and have nice things like heat in the winter. The same work that often requires me to go to Denver to chase after skips or meet with bail-bond agents. Why don't you stay home tonight and take your car to the shop tomorrow morning?"

Dropping her chin, Jane peered at Molly through her lashes. "I can't afford to have it fixed. Can I borrow some money from you?"

"No." The response was immediate and unhesitating. "You know the rules. We let you live here, but you have to support yourself otherwise." Even though she didn't want to get into another drama-filled conversation so late at night, the words just popped out. "That's one of the things we need to talk about. You're supposed to be helping with utilities and groceries, but you haven't contributed in months." *More like years*, Molly thought, but she was trying to be a little tactful, at least. "I know you scammed some money from Cara last week. If you're not going to give that back to her, at least use it to fix your car."

Annoyance flickered over Jane's face, disappearing so quickly that Molly would've thought she'd imagined it if she hadn't known her mom so well. Jane's expression morphed into something that somehow radiated sad guilt and martyrdom in equal measures. "I didn't *scam* my own daughter. Just because you're hard and suspicious doesn't mean you should bully your sister into being that way, as well. Cara's sweet and caring, and there's nothing wrong with that."

It was difficult for Molly to resist the urge to roll her eyes. *Apparently, Cara's the favorite tonight.* "You're right. There's nothing wrong with being caring and sweet. There *is* something wrong with taking money that your daughter needs for school."

Shifting her weight, Jane jutted out one hip, her hands still tucked into her right back pocket—guarding the keys, Molly assumed. "If Cara doesn't have enough money for school, that's not on me. Maybe you should be paying her more for the work she does. You know she doesn't like this bounty-hunter nonsense. The least you can do is offer her a fair wage."

"Stop." The word came out with a snap that showed just how close Molly was to losing her temper. "We're not talking about this now…or ever, really. What we *are* talking about is how you're going to hand over my car keys right now."

Still Jane hesitated, and Molly knew her mom's mind was clicking away, trying to come up with a new plan to get what she wanted. Jane always had a plan B, and she consistently figured out a dozen ways out of any trap. That was how she'd survived for almost fifty years when she'd been conning people out of money since she was old enough to bat her lashes and talk her way into getting an extra piece of candy—or, if that failed, just stealing it.

"Mom." Molly used the firm tone that Jane had tried on her. "Keys. Now. You know I won't hesitate to tackle you."

Her mom's mouth drew down in an unhappy frown. Molly tightened her jaw and didn't lower her arm or her gaze. After a tense few seconds, Jane dug out the keys and slapped them against Molly's extended palm.

"Thank you." Fighting not to let her relief show, Molly fisted her fingers around the key fob and dropped her arm to her side. She didn't move away from the door, holding her ground as her mom gave a dramatic huff and flounced into the living room—at least as much as someone wearing skintight cat-burglar gear could flounce. "Be safe," Molly called softly from her spot in the kitchen.

Jane's only response was to slam the front door behind her. Grimacing at the loud noise and the acrid taste the scene had left in her mouth, Molly leaned back against the garage door and waited for the inevitable sound of footsteps from the upper floor. Nails clicked against the ancient linoleum as Warrant crossed the kitchen to press against her legs. Grateful for the support, she rubbed behind his ears.

"Everything okay?" Norah was the first to pop her sleep-mussed head into the kitchen.

"Yeah." Holding up the key fob, Molly gave it a little shake. "Just preemptively stopping some grand theft auto."

"Mom?" Norah moved the rest of the way into the kitchen, tugging the hem of her oversized sleep shirt over her shorts. Cara and Charlie came into the kitchen just in time to hear Norah's question and immediately turned to head back to bed, Warrant following the twins. He knew Cara was a sucker and would let him sleep on her bed, even though he was notorious for taking over the entire thing.

Charlie's voice filtered back into the kitchen. "It was just Mom, Fifi. Go back to bed."

The sound of three sets of footsteps and one set of paws thumping up the stairs along with Felicity's grumbles—although Molly couldn't hear whether she was complaining about Jane's lack of courtesy or the hated nickname—gradually quieted, and Molly turned her attention back to Norah, who still seemed to be waiting for an answer, even though it was obvious.

"Yeah, Mom tried to *trade* cars with me." Molly forced a smile for her sister. Although Norah was almost twenty-four, she looked younger, thanks to her usual anxious expression and the way her baggy pajamas overwhelmed her slight frame.

"Why did she need your car?" Norah asked.

Molly made a face as she moved over to her abandoned seat and plopped down in it. "Apparently, I'm not the mom, so I don't get to ask that."

The tension in Norah's face faded slightly as she settled on the other chair. "Did she sell her car again for cash?"

"No. It's just making an odd noise—or that's what she said, at least." Propping her elbow on the table and setting her chin in her hand, Molly arched her eyebrows at Norah. Her sister knew just as well as Molly did that their mom played fast and loose with the truth. "I'm guessing it's something else, like she dropped part of her burrito under the seat and it's starting to really stink."

Norah gave a small huff of a laugh, and Molly grinned, triumphant that she'd gotten her sister's anxiety to ease—at least temporarily. Not wanting her to dwell on where Jane was going or why she'd wanted Molly's car, since Norah always assumed the worst possible scenarios were true, Molly quickly changed the subject.

"I hate having conversations like that with Mom," she said, slumping forward even more to rest her cheek on her crossed arms. "I turn into this strict, mean, no-fun, *rules, rules, rules* nun-teacher person who I kind of hate."

"You have to." Norah mirrored her position so they both had their heads down, facing each other. "If you don't set rules, then there will be no rules. *Mom* certainly isn't going to set any. And I don't hate your nun-teacher person. I find her reassuring."

"Not very fun, though."

"Fun has its place," Norah said seriously. "Without rules, fun can be really scary."

As she chewed over her sister's words, Molly started to smile. "How did such an incredible person like you come from Mom and a guy nicknamed *POS*? That's a genetic miracle right there."

"Hey!" Norah sat up straight. Even though she was obviously trying to sound indignant, a grin tugged at her lips. "She's your mom, too. Fifty percent of your genetic material came from her." She paused for a moment. "Though I have to admit that being half Lono is better than being half POS."

Stifling a sudden yawn, Molly stood and reached to pull Norah to her feet. "Well, POS must've had some good dormant material, because you turned out pretty perfect."

Although Norah rolled her eyes, she fought a smile, too. "Thanks, strict nun-teacher person."

Molly poked her sister in the side, just where she knew Norah was ticklish. "Maybe not completely perfect."

With a giggle, Norah bumped her with her painfully pointy elbow before heading up the stairs. As Molly followed, her thoughts turned back to her mom, and her smile faded. After the scene earlier, it was even more evident that they needed to have a serious conversation…one that might very well end with Molly having to kick her mother out of their house. Firming her jaw, she straightened her spine. It was past time Jane learned to stand on her own two feet and quit mooching off her kids. As much as Molly dreaded the dramatic scene it would cause, she was going to evict her mom…for all of their sakes.

ABOUT THE AUTHOR

A graduate of the police academy, Katie Ruggle is a self-proclaimed forensics nerd. A fan of anything that makes her feel like a badass, she has trained in Krav Maga, boxing, and gymnastics, has lived in an off-grid, solar- and wind-powered house in the Rocky Mountains, rides horses, shoots guns, trains her three dogs, and travels to warm places to scuba dive.

MISTLETOE IN TEXAS

Bestselling author Kari Lynn Dell invites us to a Texas Rodeo Christmas like no other!

Hank Brookman had all the makings of a top rodeo bullfighter until one accident left him badly injured. Now, after years of self-imposed exile, Hank's back and ready to make amends... starting with the girl his heart can't live without.

Grace McKenna fell for Hank the day they met, but they never saw eye to eye. That's part of why she never told him that their night together resulted in one heck of a surprise. Now that Hank's back, it's time for them to face what's ahead and celebrate the Christmas season rodeo style—together despite the odds.

SEARCH AND RESCUE

In the Rockies, lives depend on the
Search & Rescue brotherhood. But this far
off the map, secrets can be murder.

By Katie Ruggle

Hold Your Breath

Louise "Lou" Sparks is a hurricane—a
walking disaster. And with her, ice
diving captain Callum Cook has never
felt more alive...even if keeping her
safe may just kill him.

Fan the Flames

Firefighter and Motorcycle Club
member Ian Walsh rides the line
between the good guys and the bad.
But if a killer has his way, Ian will
take the fall for a murder he didn't
commit...and lose the woman he's
always loved.

Gone Too Deep

George Halloway is a mystery. Tall. Dark. Intense. But city girl Ellie Price will need him by her side if she wants to find her father…and live to tell the tale.

In Safe Hands

Deputy Sheriff Chris Jennings has always been a hero to agoraphobe Daisy Little, but one wrong move ended their future before it could begin. Now he'll do whatever it takes to keep her safe—even if that means turning against one of his own.

For more Katie Ruggle, visit:
sourcebooks.com

ROCKY MOUNTAIN K9 UNIT

These K9 officers and their trusty dogs will do anything to protect the women in their lives

By Katie Ruggle

Run to Ground

K9 officer Theo Bosco lost his mentor, his K9 partner, and almost lost his will to live. But when a ruthless killer targets a woman on the run, Theo and his new K9 companion will do whatever it takes to save the woman neither can live without.

On the Chase

Injured in the line of duty, K9 officer Hugh Murdoch's orders are simple: stay alive. But when a frightened woman bursts into his life, Hugh and his K9 companion have no choice but to risk everything to keep her safe.

Survive the Night

K9 officer Otto Gunnersen has always been a haven: for the lost, the sick, the injured. But when a hunted woman takes shelter in his arms, this gentle giant swears he'll do more than heal her battered spirit—he'll defend her with his life.

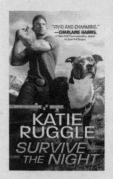

Through the Fire

When a killer strikes, new K9 officer Kit Jernigan knows she can't catch the culprit on her own. She needs a partner: local fire spotter Wesley March. But the more time they spend together, the hotter the fire smolders… and the more danger they're in.

For more Katie Ruggle, visit:
sourcebooks.com

ALSO BY KATIE RUGGLE

ROCKY MOUNTAIN SEARCH & RESCUE
On His Watch (free novella)
Hold Your Breath
Fan the Flames
Gone Too Deep
In Safe Hands
After the End (free novella)

ROCKY MOUNTAIN K9 UNIT
Run to Ground
On the Chase
Survive the Night
Through the Fire